WALKING ALONE

WALKING ALONE

|||||||||||||||||| SHORT STORIES ||||||||||||||||||

Bentley Little

CEMETERY DANCE PUBLICATIONS

Baltimore

❖ 2018 ❖

Copyright © 2018 by Bentley Little

All rights reserved. No part of this book may be reproduced in any form or by any electronic or mechanical means, including information storage and retrieval systems, without permission in writing from the publisher, except by a reviewer who may quote brief passages in a review.

Cemetery Dance Publications
132-B Industry Lane, Unit #7
Forest Hill, MD 21050
http://www.cemeterydance.com

The characters and events in this book are fictitious. Any similarity to real persons, living or dead, is coincidental and not intended by the author.

First Limited Edition Printing

ISBN: 978-1-58767-617-8

Printed in the United States of America

Cover Artwork © 2018 by Elderlemon Design
Interior Design © 2018 by Desert Isle Design, LLC

TABLE OF CONTENTS

9	——	Milk Ranch Point
17	——	Snow
27	——	Children's Hospital
37	——	Palm Reader
43	——	Slam Dance
55	——	Last Rodeo on the Circuit
65	——	The Car Wash
75	——	The Feeb
83	——	The Mall
95	——	Hunting
109	——	The Piano Player has no Fingers
127	——	The Man Who Watched Cartoons
141	——	Apt Punishment
143	——	Black Friday
157	——	MoNA Retrospective, Los Angeles
165	——	Jorgensen's Fence
179	——	The Silence of Trees
197	——	Sticky Note
205	——	The Smell of Overripe Loquats
227	——	The Maid
241	——	Schoolgirls
245	——	Under Midwest Skies
259	——	Pictures of Huxley
267	——	My College Admission Essay
273	——	Pool, Air Conditioning, Free HBO
287	——	The Train
299	——	A Random Thought from God's Day

MILK RANCH POINT ||||||||||||||||||||

(1984)

He rode in around sunset, coming over the Rim from the direction of Prescott. He rode straight in his saddle, unmoving, and his horse, a great gray stallion, made its way surefootedly down the steep cliff, following the remnants of the old mule trail.

Townspeople came out of their homes to see the stranger. It was not often that they had visitors in the fall, particularly this close to snow season, and they were curious. They could see, even from this far away, that the man carried with him some sort of light, and they watched that light zigzag across the face of the Rim in the darkening dusk. The light was hidden for a few moments by the pines as he reached the bottom of the Rim, and they stood still, waiting, until it reappeared at the edge of the meadow in front of the forest.

The man rode slowly toward the gathered crowd, stopping just beyond the stables at the edge of town. He nodded slightly, his hat dipping. "Hello," he said.

The sheriff stepped forward. "Hello, stranger."

A thin smile flickered across the man's features, barely visible in the half-light. "I'm not a stranger," he said. "Name's Clay."

The sheriff nodded. "All right." He stepped up to the horse's side and offered his hand. "I'm Chilton. And this," he said, gesturing toward the assembled crowd and the smattering of buildings beyond, "is Randall." He stared up at the man. "You looking to stay the night?"

He shook his head. "Just passing through."

"That's just as well." Chilton smiled. "We got no hotel."

"I'd appreciate a meal, though, if someone'd be willing to stake me."

The sheriff looked around. "I think we can find sump'n for you."

The man dismounted, and the crowd dispersed as Chilton led him into town, most of the people heading back to their homes for the night. A few of the men accompanied the sheriff, talking low amongst themselves and eyeing the stranger as they walked toward the mercantile. Clay ignored them, as did the sheriff.

"We don't get many visitors this time of year. What brings you out our way?"

"Heading north," Clay said simply. "Got family there."

"North?" The sheriff looked suddenly toward his fellow townsmen, a few of whom muttered in surprise. One man conferred with his friend then took off down the street as if rushing to tell someone the news. The sheriff tried to laugh and only partially succeeded. "Maybe you'd *better* stay here for the night. You look like you've been travelling quite a while. You could probably use a soft bed."

Clay stopped his horse, looking from the sheriff to the men accompanying him. "What'd I say?" he asked. One man turned away, another stared at the ground. "What's up north?"

"Nothing," Chilton said, again trying to laugh.

"Why don't you want me to go there?"

The directness of the question seemed to take them by surprise. "You came in from the west," one man said non-sequiturially. "We thought you was going east."

"Why don't you want me to go there?"

The man stepped closer. Clay could see his long beard and longer hair beneath the fur cap and the bundles of pelts. "None of your damn business," he said. "Just stay away."

"What's out there?"

{ MILK RANCH POINT }

"Nothing," Chilton said.

"What are you afraid of? Apache? You been having Indian trouble?"

The sheriff grabbed the reins to Clay's horse. He looked for a moment as if he were about to say something, then his features collapsed into resignation. "Come on. We have to get you something to eat." He started walking.

Clay let the matter drop.

———◆———

They fed him beef—real beef—and some type of grain mush. After, someone brought out a bottle and they passed it around. The talk was harmless—town business mostly—but he saw several of the men exchanging surreptitious glances as they spoke.

And he noticed that he was the only one making any kind of dent in the bottle.

He put the whisky down and looked directly at each of the men, glancing from one face to another. There were six here now, all gathered around the lone table at the back of the mercantile, and each of them looked away as he met their eyes.

He took the lantern from the post behind him and placed it in the middle of the table. "All right," he said. "I know what you're trying to do here. I want you to tell me what this is all about. Why don't you want me to go out tonight?"

"We're not—" the sheriff began.

"Cut the bullshit. What's going on?"

One of the men at the far end moved forward in his seat and leaned over the table. "You can go tonight," he said. "Just don't follow the trail north. Go east awhile, *then* head north."

"Why?"

A cold wind blew from between the cracked boards. The lamp flickered, casting strange shadows on the unshaven faces of the townsmen.

"Stay away from Milk Ranch Point," the sheriff said softly.

Clay looked again at each of the men. The fear showed clearly in their faces now, drawing skin tight over cheekbones, causing little rivulets of sweat to drip from under hats onto bearded faces. He adjusted his own hat. "What's at Milk Ranch Point?"

The men were silent for a moment. "People have heard things there at night," the sheriff said finally. "People have...seen things."

"What kind of things?"

"Don't you have no respect?" said the man who had spoken earlier. "Can't you leave well enough alone?"

The sheriff nodded toward the other men at the table. "Look at them," he said, and Clay saw the terror in their eyes. "We're not making this up. We wouldn't tell you if it wasn't so."

"What's out at Milk Ranch Point?"

Chilton sighed. "Things happen," he said slowly. "Sometimes a calf is born lame or born with two heads or...something is wrong with it."

Clay nodded. "Yeah."

"And you have to put them out of their misery."

"Yeah."

The sheriff's hands fidgeted nervously on the table. "Well, sometimes that happens to babies, too." He reached for the bottle, took a swig. "Sometimes a baby is born...wrong. It don't have a hand or one leg's shorter than the other or..."

"So, you put them out of their misery," Clay said. "And you bury them at Milk Ranch Point."

The sheriff shook his head. "No," he said. "We're a God-fearing town. We don't believe in killing. But..." He paused. "Sometimes there's a young'un born that...well, you just know he's not gonna make it. He's some kinda mistake."

"What do you do with someone born like that?"

"Food here's kind of scarce," the sheriff said. "Sometimes we don't have enough for—"

"What do you do with them?"

The sheriff took another drink. Some of the other men looked away.

Clay nodded. "You leave them there. You leave them up at Milk Ranch Point."

"We don't kill them," one man said defensively.

MILK RANCH POINT

Clay looked at him. "They just die. Of natural causes."

Sheriff Chilton nodded.

Clay stood. "Thanks for the food," he said. "But I gotta get going. It's getting late."

The sheriff pounded his fist on the table. "Damn it! Didn't you hear what we said?"

"Yeah."

"You going east, then?"

"No."

"What the hell do you think—"

"Look," Clay said. "What you do in your own town's none of my business. I don't care what you do with your unfit babies."

"That's not the point!"

"I also don't care about your ghost stories. I don't care if some old woman heard noises up on Milk Ranch Point."

"It weren't no old woman."

"I don't care." Clay picked up his saddle from the floor next to his chair. "I have to go. Thanks for the grub."

The sheriff grabbed his arm. "Now hold on—"

"Let go of me," Clay said. His voice was low, threatening. His coat swung open, revealing a holstered gun that glinted in the lantern light.

The sheriff let go. He watched Clay walk out of the mercantile and saddle up his horse, still feeding out of the trough out front. "Go east," he said. "Then go north."

Clay nodded absently. He pulled a candle from his pack, shoved a long stick into it and lit the candle. He hopped onto his horse and stuck the stick in a special hole drilled into his stirrup. "Goodbye," he said. "Thanks for everything."

He headed past the sheriff's office, past the blacksmith shop.

And turned north.

WALKING ALONE — Bentley Little

The trail started to climb around a half hour out of town. The forest was thicker here than it had been to the west, aspens and oaks mingling with the ever-present pines. The trail wound slowly up a long ridge, switch-backing gradually up the slope, and Clay wondered if this was Milk Ranch Point. He should have asked someone to point it out to him so he'd know when he was there.

The stallion stopped suddenly, halfway up the ridge, its head cocked and its ears pricked. He patted the animal's neck. "Hey, boy, what's wrong?"

From somewhere above came the cry of an infant.

Against his will, Clay felt a wave of cold pass through his body. He shivered, giving the horse a quick kick in the side. "Come on, boy. Let's get a move on." The horse bucked and balked, but he held firm on the reins and the animal continued its ascent up the trail.

The moon was well across the sky by the time he reached the top. Clay stopped to give the stallion a rest as the trail leveled off, dismounting. He knew this had to be Milk Ranch Point, but it was not the flat brushless mesa he had expected. He was still in the same heavily wooded forest he'd been travelling through since leaving Randall.

There was a rustle in the bushes off to the right.

He reached for the reins as his eyes followed the sound. "Come on, boy," he said softly. He mounted the horse.

There was another noise directly below the animal.

A soft squishing sound.

He clicked his teeth, and started the stallion slowly forward along the trail. The sounds were everywhere now, all around: low cries, plaintive yelps, quiet rustlings. Suddenly there was a high-pitched screech, and the horse bucked up onto its hind legs, throwing Clay to the ground. He could see even in the dim moonlight that the stallion had stepped on something soft and round—

—and alive.

The horse took off the way it had come, galloping as fast as it could back down the winding trail toward Randall. Clay stood, holding his throbbing head, and promptly fell back down.

⟅ MILK RANCH POINT ⟆

The noises were close now and getting closer, low sounds in the underbrush growing louder as *things* crawled toward him. He groped around on the partially wet ground for his candle. He found it and pulled a match from his shirt pocket, lighting it.

There were hundreds of them, all moving toward him on disfigured limbs, making strange noises as they emerged from the bushes next to the tall trees. He could see them in the flickering candlelight: blank stares on their idiot faces, malevolent grins on their deformed mouths.

He felt a wet tickling on his right hand and pulled it back, crying out. A hideously disfigured baby was trying to suckle on the skin of his hand. He attempted to stand up but couldn't, his equilibrium still off balance, and he grimaced with repulsion as more of the infants attached themselves to his skin, their grotesque lips puckering.

Clay crawled to his knees and picked up the nearest baby. It had no eyes and a little pig's snout. He held it next to the candle so he could see, then threw it down. It wiggled back into the bushes.

He picked up another baby, this one with no legs, and promptly dropped it away from him.

He began going through them faster, holding them up to the candlelight then tossing them.

After several minutes, he closed his eyes, breathing deeply. This was harder than he'd thought it would be. He grimaced as he looked at another deformed infant and pulled away in disgust as a different one attached itself to his arm.

"Your mama's sorry, Jimmy!" he called. He knew the little things could not understand him, but he kept talking anyway as he continued searching through the infants. It made him feel better. "Don't worry, son! We'll find you!"

And he sat there through the night and the following day.

SNOW

(1985)

Hal Katz awoke early despite the cold, and after showering, shaving and putting on warm clothes, he woke up his wife, shaking her gently and whispering in her ear: "Come on, honey. It's time to go." He paid the bill and turned in the room key at the front desk while she got ready, and they were on the road out of Flagstaff by eight.

It had continued snowing throughout the night, and while the highway was clear, large drifts of snow were piled up along the side of the road. The leafless trees, silhouetted against the morning sun, stood out in sharp contrast to the white blanketed ground. They drove in silence, eating donuts and sipping coffee, looking out at the passing scenery. Suddenly April pointed out the front windshield. "Hey," she said. "Look at that!"

He followed her finger but could see nothing. "What?"

"A snowman."

He saw it now. Small, not more than three feet high, it stood on the side of the road, facing their car, one white arm stretched outward in a classic hitchhiking position.

"That's cute," he said.

They zoomed past.

She turned to him. "Did you ever make snowmen when you were young?"

"In Los Angeles?" He laughed.

"We did." She stared out the side window, talking softly. "We always tried to make one like Frosty; you know, one that was alive. We tried spells and prayers and magic hats and magic wands, everything we could think of."

He smiled at her. "Did it work?"

"Not that I know of."

They drove past Lake Mary and through the one-gas-station-one-restaurant town of Mormon Lake. It was a beautiful day, clear and cold, the sky a brilliant dark baby blue punctuated by billowy white clouds. Ahead, on the Rim, they could see a mirrored flash between the trees as sunlight reflected off the tin roof of Baker Point lookout.

"Hey," April said. "Another one."

Sure enough, a small snowman sat by the side of the road, facing them. This one was set a little further back than the first and had two arms, both stretched out. As they drove past, they could see two irregularly shaped pieces of plastic set in its face for eyes.

"Looks like the same person made it," Hal said. "Same height, same style."

"Yeah."

They drove for a while in silence, then Hal reached over to put on a CD. Cool jazz. Dave Brubeck. He was soon lightly tapping the edges of the steering wheel in time to the music, and April smiled. "Some people never grow up," she said.

He made a face at her. "Die."

She shook her head, still smiling. "Like I said…"

The road curved through a series of low hills covered by an especially thick stand of ponderosas before levelling off and cutting across a wide snow-covered meadow. Hal leaned forward, looking through the windshield, as they emerged from the trees. He let out a long low whistle. "Would you look at that?"

The meadow was covered with hundreds of snowmen.

Like the two they had seen previously, all of these snowmen were small, under four feet high. Some had faces and some did not, but all had arms. And all of the arms were pointing in different directions. Hal laughed

{ SNOW }

delightedly. "Jesus! Do you know how long it must have taken someone to make all these?"

"We did that once," April said quietly. "Made a whole bunch of them. We worked for a week on them. Didn't make any difference, though."

He looked over at her. "What are you mumbling about?"

"Nothing." She smiled at him.

"I want to get a picture of this. Do we have any film left in the camera?"

April shook her head. "You used it all up at Meteor Crater, remember?"

"Damn." He slowed down until they were barely moving and looked out the window at the nearest snowmen. He laughed. "That's really amazing."

He saw something move out of the corner of his eye.

"What...?"

A small white shape scurried across the road.

"Jesus!" He slammed on the brakes. "Did you see that?"

"What?"

"One of those snowmen just ran in front of the car!"

"Don't be stupid," she said. "It was probably just a rabbit." But she was not laughing at his claim. There was fear in her eyes.

She saw it, he thought. *She saw it, too, but she won't admit it.*

He put the car into Park, looking around. The only movement on the flat white meadow was the spastic skip-hopping of several small birds far off to their right. His gaze moved along the front of the car, following the path taken by whatever it was he had seen.

"Come on," April said. "Let's go." Her voice was calm, but he could sense the panic just below the surface. "We need to check into the hotel by one."

"Just a minute. I want to see something."

He looked around, but there was nothing moving on either side of the road. He rolled down his window to check the spot right next to his door, and stuck his head out.

A large blob of snow flew up and hit him square in the face.

April screamed. More snow flew upward from the road, attaching itself instantly to Hal's head. Still screaming, April reached over and yanked him toward her as she rolled up the window. Clawing the freezing substance from her husband's head, she threw handful after handful of it onto the floor of the car.

"…couldn't…breathe…" Hal gulped in air, wheezing and coughing as he tried to speak. His red face slowly paled into normalcy as the cold dissipated. He threw the last bits of snow off his forehead, wiped the melted water from his cheeks and looked at April. "How the hell could that happen?"

She shook her head silently, her eyes still wide with shock.

"There was a snowman down there, crouched right next to the door. And he…jumped up at me."

"Hal!" She suddenly grabbed his arm and pulled him to her, pointing at the floor of the car, where individual hand-sized scoops of snow were gently quivering. Three of the small mounds moved closer together.

Hal smashed his shoe down on the frozen white substance, crushing it, grinding it into the floor mat, where it melted, metamorphosing into a small puddle of water that trickled out from under his foot. He continued grinding his shoe until all of the snow was liquid.

"Let's get out of here," April said. "Let's go."

Hal nodded, put the car into Drive. He had half-feared that the engine would stall, as in some B-movie, stranding them in the field of snowmen. But the car took off, tires sliding for a second on the icy asphalt before gaining traction. They drove out of the meadow and into the comparative safety of the forest.

Moments later, they passed a farmhouse. "We could've gone *there* if we had to," Hal said. "If worst came to worst."

April said nothing. She stared out the passenger window, periodically glancing back out the rear windshield to make sure…what? That they weren't being followed?

Hal sped up.

They passed another hitchhiking snowman by the side of the road, this one without a face. Hal was tempted to run into it with the car, to swerve and smash the little bastard all to hell, but he was afraid that the car might get stuck in the high drift and passed by without doing a thing.

{ SNOW }

Ten minutes later, they saw the truck.

Hal slowed to a stop. The truck had jackknifed on the slippery road and was lying cattycorner across the highway on its side. It was a semi—a Kenworth—and had apparently been carrying some sort of livestock. Warm blood, steaming in the cold winter air, was draining out from under the side of the downed vehicle in multiple rivulets.

"Jesus," Hal breathed.

"Don't stop!" April cried, latching onto his arm. "Keep going! Don't stop!"

He pointed at the overturned truck. "I can't. The road's blocked."

"Then go around it!"

"I can't. We'd get stopped in the snow." He inched the car forward, looking all the while for signs of life near the truck. Suddenly, he braked, cutting the engine. "Look."

A hand was frantically waving from around the side of the semi.

Hal unbuckled his seatbelt.

"No!" April cried. "Don't!"

"He's in trouble. I have to help."

"He's not signaling for help," April said. "He's waving us away. It's too late for him, and he knows it. He's warning us to leave."

The driver staggered out from behind the truck. The upper half of his body was covered in white, but the snow seemed to have retained some semblance of a shape. The top tapered to a modified point, and two red plastic eyes glared downward.

The man was being devoured by the snow.

Hal stared in shock. The truck driver *was* waving them away, he realized, and he continued waving even as his body fell to the ground.

Hal put the car into Reverse.

The pile of snow atop the driver looked up, red eyes jerking instantly toward them.

"Go!" April yelled. "Go!"

He floored the gas pedal, but although the engine was racing, the car would not move. Their tires spun impotently on the ice. Hal hit the gear shift and rammed the transmission into Low. They started to move forward, and he shifted immediately into Reverse. The car began moving backward, gaining speed.

A large glob of snow smacked into the rear windshield, covering the glass and blocking Hal's view. He snapped his gaze forward and saw the red-eyed snowman moving quickly toward the car, scuttling low over the icy asphalt.

"Ram it!" April screamed.

He shifted the car into First and sped forward, tires squealing. The front bumper cut the snowman in half. Red plastic eyes popped out of the frozen head.

Hal backed up. The top half of the snowman was on the car's hood, and the eyeless form seemed to be wiggling toward the windshield. He slammed on the brakes, spinning the car around, and the pile of snow flew off. Putting the car into Low once again, he floored the pedal and the tires caught. They took off the way they had come.

◆

The snowmen were blocking the road.
All of them.

◆

Hal stopped the car. The meadow, on both sides, was clear, because all of the snowmen, hundreds of them, were lined up in solid formation across a section of the road, facing them.

"Go!" April cried. "Ram them!"

Hal shook his head. The snowmen were packed too closely together. If the car rammed into them, it would be like hitting a wall of ice. The front rows of snowmen might be taken out, but the front of the car would be smashed and the vehicle permanently damaged. They'd never make it through.

April closed her eyes. "We'll wait here, then. In the car. Someone's bound to come eventually. We can't be the *only* people on this road."

{ SNOW }

Hal said nothing. Beneath April's panicked panting and his own labored breath, he could hear low slurping noises coming from the bottom of the car. He turned toward his side window. Outside, snow started creeping up the glass.

"Oh, God," April moaned, "they're going to bury us in here."

The army of snowmen began shuffling up the road toward them.

Hal hit the window glass with his palm, trying to shake the snow loose. It did no good. The icy substance continued its measured growth over the car. For the first time, fear—*real* fear—sounded in his voice. "I can't believe this is happening."

"I can," April said.

Her voice was low, even, determined, and he turned to look at her. "What does that mean?"

"It happened before," she said, and she seemed to be talking more to herself than to him. "They turned on us. We didn't understand what was going on."

"What?"

Her eyes focused on him. "We *did* make a snowman that was alive. Several of them. And we taught them to walk, and we..." Her voice trailed off.

"And you what?"

"They turned on us. They turned on us for some reason. They surrounded us and started closing in." Her eyes shifted quickly from Hal to the snowmen and then back again. "We had to give them something to keep them away from us. A sacrifice."

He couldn't believe what he was hearing.

"We gave them a kitten. And they let us go."

Hal didn't know why he believed her, but he did. "What are you saying? You're not suggesting...?"

She opened the door. A patch of snow fell on her, quivering, and she shoved it off. She leaned over and kissed him. "Get out of here."

"No!"

But she had already stepped out of the car and was slamming the door. "Goodbye," April said. "I love you." She started running across the meadow.

WALKING ALONE — Bentley Little

As one, the army of snowmen turned toward her and began moving. The snow slunk off the windows of the car and flowed over the road in an almost liquid stream.

She's too fast for them, Hal thought. *She'll get away.*

But other snowmen emerged from the trees at the far end of the meadow and began closing in on her. She was trapped, he realized. She could not escape them. But he did not drive away. Instead, he watched, leaning on the horn, hoping the noise would distract them or alert someone. He prayed out loud for God to save her.

The snowmen moved faster as they drew upon her, and he saw them fling themselves forward, knocking her down.

The last thing he saw, before they engulfed her entirely, was her long slender hand, reaching upward, heavenward, sunlight glinting for a second off her diamond wedding ring.

And then she was gone.

It felt as though the inside of his body had been suddenly scooped out, leaving him hollow. A barely mixed amalgam of rage, fear and uncontrollable grief rushed in to fill the emptiness. He had no time to sit and wallow in his feelings, however. April had wanted him to get the hell out of here, had given her life so he could do just that, and before they could return, he took off, his vision blurred with tears.

He did not even realize he was screaming until his throat started to hurt.

It was afternoon when he finally pulled into the outskirts of Flagstaff. Clouds had come up—a dark gray ceiling that uniformly covered the sky—and a light sprinkle of snow was falling. He pulled into a Shell station. "I need the police," he told the attendant.

"Anything the matter?"

Hal tried to remain calm. "My wife is missing. I just need to know how to get to the police station."

"Turn left at the third stoplight, just past the curve, then go on for a block or so. Can't miss it."

He followed the directions, pulled up in front of the police station and got out of the car. On the steps of the building, a young boy, no more than

❴ SNOW ❵

ten, was scooping up a handful of snow and attempting to fashion it into a snowball. Hal grabbed the boy's arm. "Drop it," he ordered. "Drop it and get out of here you little son of a bitch."

The boy, eyes wide with fear, let the snow fall from his hand. Hal released his arm and the kid took off.

He ground the lump of snow beneath his heel and walked into the police station.

CHILDREN'S HOSPITAL

(1985)

"So, what are you? A hemo, a homo or a Haitian?" Armstrong, leaning on one arm in the bed next to him, grinned hugely as he tapped a cigarette against the bed's metal side rail. His earring, a silver Maltese cross, dangled freely, catching the rays of the early morning sun streaming through the hospital window.

Toby looked at the older boy, and his heart started to pound. "What?" he said. His voice sounded high, thin, nervous.

"Howja get it?"

"Leukemia?"

"AIDS." Armstrong lit the cigarette and rolled onto his back. He tossed the match on the recently waxed tile floor. "Don't give me that leukemia crap."

"That's what I have!" He looked fearfully at Armstrong, expecting some sort of retaliation for his outburst, but the older boy simply blew cigarette smoke into the air, ignoring him.

"Jimmy Goldstein, little kid two beds down, he had AIDS, too," Armstrong said. "That was about a week or two before you got here. They took him off to a special ward or clinic or something. Looked like a goddamn skel when he left."

{ **WALKING ALONE** } Bentley Little

Toby looked instinctively down the ward where Armstrong had gestured. Jimmy Goldstein's old bed was empty, as were all the other beds in the room. He glanced back toward the smoking figure in the bed next to him. "Why did you stay here? Weren't you afraid of getting AIDS?"

Armstrong smiled. "I didn't give a shit. I figured I'd take my chances." He blew out smoke. "That's why I'm still here with you, fag boy."

"I'm not gay!" Toby said.

The nurse walked in, a short overweight black woman with thick muscular arms. She frowned as her eyes scanned the room, and she strode purposefully over to Armstrong's bed, grabbing the cigarette out of his hand. "How many times do I have to tell you?" she said harshly. "No smoking in here!" She dropped the cigarette into a white plastic sanitary bag. "I don't know how you get those cancer sticks in here anyway."

"Good fairy brings 'em to me," Armstrong said. "Same fairy that gave twinkle toes AIDS over there." He nodded toward Toby.

"I don't have AIDS!"

"That's right," the nurse said. "He has leukemia." She glared at Armstrong. "If you can't manage to get along with anyone else, we'll just have to put you in a room by yourself."

Armstrong grinned. "That's all I ever wanted."

The nurse shook her head. "You're impossible."

An orderly wheeled in another boy, this one about Toby's age. His skin was pale, and there was a white bandage wrapped around his head. His arms were rail-thin and anemic looking. Toby tried to smile at the boy, and the boy nodded tiredly back.

"This is Bill," the nurse said. "Bill Ives. He's going to be here for a couple of days under observation." She stared hard at Armstrong. "You try to be civil."

"I'll try."

The orderly lifted the new boy off the gurney and placed him carefully on the bed next to Toby's. Toby watched the boy's face as the nurse explained ward rules and regulations to him. His face was drawn, weak-looking, as though he had neither strength nor spirit left.

The nurse finished her memorized speech, then turned toward Toby.

"You be nice to Bill, you hear? He's only going to be here for a couple of days. You try to make him feel at home."

"I will," Toby promised.

"What's the matter with him?" Armstrong asked. He leaned over the railing of his bed, grinning. "We got another pansy in our midst?"

"The doctors aren't sure what's wrong," the nurse replied evenly. "He's here for observation."

Armstrong shook his head and sighed sympathetically, leaning back on his pillow. "Will this plague never end?"

"That's enough from you!" The nurse turned toward Toby. "If he bothers either of you, you tell me."

Toby nodded, glancing toward Armstrong, afraid to answer her verbally because of how the other boy might react. The orderly wheeled the now empty gurney out of the room, and the nurse followed, shooting one last harsh glance at Armstrong.

Armstrong sat up. He ran a hand through his spiked hair and pulled a cigarette from under his pillow, lighting it. "So, what *are* you here for?"

Bill smiled feebly. "I don't know. I think it really might be AIDS."

Armstrong looked interested. "You serious?"

The boy shrugged. "I had a burst appendix a few months ago, and they had to give me blood transfusions. That was before they were really testing for AIDS. Then I came down with this a few weeks ago. My doctor doesn't seem to know what it is. They've been giving me tests up the wazoo for the past two days..." His voice trailed off.

Armstrong puffed on his cigarette, letting the smoke out through his nose. "What makes you think it's AIDS?"

"That's what my dad thinks it is. The doctors don't want to admit it— they don't want a malpractice suit—but my dad says that's why they're giving me so many tests. They're afraid they screwed up."

Toby looked at the frail boy. "Aren't you scared?"

He smiled slightly and shook his head. "Not really."

"It's not catching is it?"

Armstrong laughed. "Not unless you—"

"No," Bill said quietly, cutting Armstrong off. "Don't worry. *You* won't get it." He looked toward Armstrong, and the older boy suddenly stopped laughing. He licked his lips nervously, puffing on his cigarette.

Bill smiled.

Curfew was at ten. The lights in the ward were shut off, as was the TV. "Hey!" Armstrong said loudly as the room was thrown into darkness. "I was watching a movie here!"

Standing in the doorway, the nurse looked at him. "Everything goes off at ten. Those are the rules. You should know that by now."

"But I was watching a movie! How the hell am I supposed to find out what happens?"

She glared, pointing her index finger at him. "You watch your mouth, young man."

"You can't tell me what to do."

The nurse smiled. "No, but I can turn the TV off at nine instead of ten."

Armstrong shut up.

The nurse left, closing the door behind her, and Toby stared up toward the ceiling, thinking. With the heavy shades shut and the lights off, the ward was completely dark. In the bed next to him, Bill slept silently. The boy had slept through most of the day, looking small and thin and pitiful, and Toby had felt sorry for him. Bill seemed really sick, and Toby wondered whether he would live or not.

"Kid!"

Toby stiffened and lay there completely unmoving, trying to keep silent, hardly daring to breathe. "Kid!" Armstrong whispered again. "Toby!"

Toby closed his eyes, pretending to sleep just in case Armstrong could see him in the dark.

"Shit." Armstrong rolled over on his bed and Toby heard the crinkle of hospital sheets.

"*I'm* here."

The voice came from the bed next to him, Bill's bed, and this time it was Armstrong who was silent. There was something strange in that whispered voice, something scary, and Toby kept his eyes closed. He forced his breathing to become regular, his chest rising and falling in an even sleep rhythm for the benefit of whomever might be watching.

"*I'm* here, Armstrong."

Armstrong remained silent, pretending to be asleep, and Toby knew that the older boy was afraid.

Afraid of what?

There was the soft sound of sheets slipping to the floor. Small feet, light feet, padded past the foot of Toby's bed. He shut his eyes tighter.

"No."

Armstrong's voice was muffled. There was the sound of fighting, thrashing around on silent sheets. Toby heard a finger punching the button to call the nurse.

Click click click click click.

"No."

It was the last word Armstrong said.

Then there was silence.

The ward was still silent when Toby really fell asleep.

In the morning, everything was normal. Armstrong was puffing on a cigarette, looking toward the window, sunlight glinting off his earring. Bill was sleeping in his bed, looking small and frail and sick.

But not quite as sick.

There was the beginning of a rosy glow in his cheeks. His skin looked healthier, less pale. His overall frame seemed…well, stronger. Not bigger—he hadn't gained weight during the night or suddenly sprouted weightlifter muscles—but stronger.

As though he could fight his illness, as though he could survive.

The nurse came in with an orderly, bringing three trays of food. "How'd you boys sleep last night?"

"Fine," Toby said.

Armstrong grunted.

The nurse placed a tray of hot cereal, toast and orange juice on the bed in front of Toby. Bill was still asleep, and she placed a tray on the table next to his bed, not wanting to wake him. "Poor boy. He needs all the sleep he can get." She walked around Toby's bed and handed the last tray to Armstrong.

"I need a Band-Aid," Armstrong said.

"What's the matter?" The nurse sounded concerned.

"I cut myself."

"Where?"

"On my neck."

Toby's heart started pounding. He glanced over at Bill, still sleeping in the bed next to his.

The nurse was bending close, examining Armstrong's neck. "You sure did," she said. "How did that happen?"

"Just get me a Band-Aid."

"I'm going to have to put some disinfectant on that."

"Fine," Armstrong said. "Do you think you can get me a Band-Aid at the same time? If it's not too much trouble. I mean, I don't want to put you out or anything."

The nurse walked out of the ward, shaking her head. "You have a mouth on you, boy."

"Most people do."

The nurse snorted. "I'll be back in a minute. Don't you pick at it or scratch it or anything. That'll just make it worse."

Toby looked at Armstrong. He thought he could see a red splotch on the other boy's neck, and a small scratch running through the redness. "What happened?" he asked.

Armstrong glared at him. "None of your business, *Prancer*."

Toby turned away. His gaze fell on the sleeping form of Bill Ives in the bed next to him. He sucked in his breath. Bill was still asleep, but he had shifted position. He was facing Toby and his mouth was hanging open.

His teeth and lips were both lightly coated with red.

◆

Bill was getting stronger.

And Armstrong was getting weaker.

It was nothing really noticeable; even the doctors and nurses did not seem to sense any appreciable change. But Toby lived with the two boys, lived with them day in and day out. All three of them were confined to their beds, and they spent all day every day in each other's company. Small changes were readily apparent when living in such close quarters.

Of course, Toby still did not know exactly what was happening. And after that first night, he forced himself to fall asleep well before curfew. Now he nodded off while the TV was still on, while the lights were still lit, while other people were still around. He did not know what occurred in the darkness, in the night, when the boys were all alone. He did not want to know.

But the bandage had been taken off Bill's head, and the boy's skin, if not ruddy, was at least normal. The doctors still hadn't determined what was wrong with Bill, but Toby thought that when they finally did decide on an illness, Bill would probably be ready to go home.

Armstrong, on the other hand, was paler and much more nervous than he had been. He seemed to have shrunk in spirit, if not actual size, and Toby found that he wasn't afraid of him anymore. Armstrong had the same silver earring, the same rough clothes, the same defiant hair, but he was no longer the fearsome dominating presence he had been those first few days. He seldom spoke now and had even stopped talking back to the nurse.

Strangely, Toby found himself empathizing with Armstrong. He still couldn't say he liked the older boy, but he felt closer to Armstrong than he did to Bill. He could understand what Armstrong was going through. The older boy had scared him at first, but it was a physical fear, the fear of the school bully.

WALKING ALONE — Bentley Little

The fear he had of Bill was not simple. Nor was it physical.

Toby wasn't sure why the smaller boy frightened him. But there was something not quite right about Bill Ives, something he couldn't comprehend, something that went beyond normal human fears, something connected with that whispering sound at night, with the furious quiet struggle in the darkness.

He glanced involuntarily at Bill and found the boy staring at him.

Toby looked quickly away and closed his eyes, pretending to sleep.

When Toby awoke, the TV was off and the ward was in darkness. He opened his eyes, though he could see nothing, and held his breath, listening, though there was nothing to hear.

He felt a light tap on his shoulder.

He jumped in shock, crying out, moving away from the unseen touch.

There was a quiet boyish laugh in the darkness. "It's all right. It's just me. Bill."

Toby's heart was pounding. His hand reached slowly out from under the covers and along the side of his bed, feeling for the button to call for the nurse. "Really?" he said, trying to keep his voice calm.

"Really." Bill's hand found his and held it. "There's no reason to call for anyone."

Toby pulled away. He slipped both hands under the covers and held the blankets tight. "What do you want?" he asked.

"Haven't you guessed?"

Toby remained silent, not responding.

"Haven't you noticed any changes around here?"

Toby swallowed hard. "You're a vampire," he said.

Bill laughed. His laugh was light, airy, musical. "No," he said. "Not quite."

"Leave me alone." Toby tried to make his voice sound assured, commanding, but it came out scared and small.

Bill reached over and grabbed the edge of Toby's blanket, pulling it down. "Come here," he said. "I have something to show you." His hand found Toby's, pulling on it.

"No!"

"Yes." And he was dragging Toby out of bed, making Toby's muscles move against their will as he was pushed across the room toward Armstrong. "Just open your mouth," Bill said softly. "And when I tell you, bite down."

"No!"

"Yes." There was light pressure of a hand on the back of Toby's head, pushing his face downward. He opened his mouth to object and felt his teeth touch the soft flesh of Armstrong's neck. "Don't worry," Bill said. "He won't wake up." He adjusted Toby's head slightly. "Now bite."

Toby bit. There was a warm flood of salty blood gushing into his mouth, healthy life-giving blood, and he began drinking it, lapping it up, feeling the strength flow into him, feeling the disease retreat within his body.

"No," Armstrong muttered in his sleep. His legs kicked out against his blanket, causing it to fall off the bed. "No."

Toby drank.

Toby awoke in the morning as usual. Sunlight was streaming into the ward and…he wasn't afraid of it. Slowly, carefully, tentatively, he moved his hand into a beam of sunlight. Nothing happened.

He wasn't a vampire.

Armstrong was still sleeping, one hand thrown over his face, but Bill was wide awake. Toby looked at him, confused. "Last night—" he began.

"It happened," the other boy said.

Toby found that he was no longer afraid of Bill. He was no longer afraid of either of them. He felt better and healthier than he had in weeks.

The nurse came in with an orderly, served them all breakfast and left. The smell of toast and oatmeal woke Armstrong. He grunted and stretched and rubbed his eyes. Toby watched him in silence for a while, suddenly realizing that the older boy hadn't smoked in two days.

"Why are you here?" he asked Armstrong finally. "What's wrong with you?"

Armstrong glared at him. "I don't have AIDS, gay boy."

"What do you have?"

Armstrong sighed tiredly, and for once his voice sounded serious, honest. "I don't know," he admitted. "They won't tell me."

"How long are you here for?"

The older boy looked at him, fingers worrying his silver earring. He looked uncertain, confused. "I don't know. They won't tell me."

"How long have you been here so far?"

Armstrong stared into his oatmeal for several seconds. He took a sip of his orange juice, then looked at Toby. Their eyes met. "Five years," he said. "I've been here five years." He picked up his toast and started eating, staring out the window, and Toby noticed that the sunlight glinting off his earring made it look almost like a crucifix.

PALM READER

(1985)

Madame Carol sat in the dingy reading room staring through a crack in the curtained windows at the street outside. Very few cars came by these days, and it was rare to see more than one or two pass at the same time. She stared across the street at the Ford factory. It was closed now, and several of the front windows were broken. The once carefully trimmed hedges and neat rows of gladiolas were now overgrown with weeds, and even the weeds were turning brown due to the lack of water.

Her gaze returned to the reading table in front of her, and she looked at her appointment book. A Mr. Paul Burroughs was supposed to be in for a reading at ten o'clock. According to her watch, it was already ten-fifteen. And she had another man coming in for a consultation at ten-thirty. She couldn't wait much longer.

A car pulled up out front. Peeking through the curtains, Madame Carol saw a thin, harried-looking, middle-aged man get out of a beat-up station wagon and walk across the small parking lot to the front door. She moved into the waiting room just as he rang the bell and opened the door. "Mr. Burroughs?"

The man nodded, trying to smile. "Yes."

"You're a little late, and I have another man coming in in fifteen minutes, so we'd better start right away."

WALKING ALONE — Bentley Little

She led him into the reading room and gestured for him to sit down in front of the table. She placed his right hand in the proper indentation, palm up, and walked around to the other side of the table.

"Get much business these days?" he asked.

She knew he was nervous, just trying to make conversation, like so many of her customers, so she nodded pleasantly. "Surprisingly, yes. Quite a few people have been coming in recently." She reached out and began stroking his palm, her long fingernails lightly tracing the lines, outlines and marks on his hand. His lifeline was short—very short—but she tried not to let it show on her face. She had long since given up telling people the truth about when they were going to die. The truth had been bad for business—it made people angry, it made people scared, it forced people to be skeptical. "You are going to live for a long time," she intoned. "Your lifeline is long. You will live to be eighty-eight."

The man smiled and relaxed somewhat, his features softening as the tension drained out of his muscles. "What about illness?" he asked.

Her fingernail traced the lines. There was illness looming up soon. Bad illness. "You will have a serious illness when you are sixty-five," she lied. "But you will get over it. It will recur in your last year, and there will be nothing you can do. You will die a painless death, however."

The man nodded. That was a long time away; he could afford not to worry about it.

Madame Carol decided to stick with what she really saw. "Someone close to you has died recently," she said. "A woman. You loved her very much."

"My aunt Helen," the man supplied.

Madame Carol nodded. "You were planning a trip to visit her."

The man's face brightened. "That's right." There was a look of awe, of respect on his face.

She knew she had him now. She had established her credibility. He would believe anything she told him. Her fingers continued gliding lightly over his palm. "Your children. You have two of them. Boys."

He nodded.

"The oldest will become some type of writer, working for a newspaper or a magazine. It is hard to tell which. The other will be a teacher. It is unclear now what grade he will teach. I see somewhere in high school or junior high."

The man leaned forward eagerly. "What about my wife?"

The bell in the waiting room rang, and Madame Carol's fingers stopped moving. Her other appointment must be here. She stood up, excusing herself, and went out to open the front door. A young friendly-looking man in his late twenties was standing there, taking off his coat. "It's hot," he explained. He walked in as she held the door for him. "Madame Carol? I'm Baker Collins." He smiled at her.

She motioned for him to sit down on one of the couches in the waiting room. "Have a seat. I'll be right with you. I'm just finishing up another reading."

The man nodded, still smiling. "No hurry." He bent down to pick out a magazine from the rack next to the couch, and she was suddenly conscious of the fact that all of the magazines were old. She felt embarrassed, aware that he would find nothing there to interest him, and she hurried back into the reading room to finish Mr. Burroughs' reading.

Sitting down again at the table, Madame Carol began stroking her client's hand, making ever-widening circular motions. "Your wife will be fine," she said. "Her life will not alter drastically. Next year will be a bad financial year for you, but you will snap out of it the following year." She was aware that she was lying, babbling, and she was sure that he knew it, but she just wanted to get the reading over with. She stopped touching his palm. "I'm sorry, but my next appointment is waiting for me." She started to make out a receipt. "Here. I'll only charge you half price. You can come in for the rest of your reading later."

The man stood up. "No. I heard what I came to learn. I'll pay the full price." He happily counted out the bills, leaving an extra five-dollar tip.

"Thank you," she said, genuinely impressed.

He smiled at her. "Thank *you*." He walked out, his step considerably lighter than when he'd come in.

Madame Carol stuck her head out the door into the waiting room. "Mr. Collins? I'm ready for you now."

WALKING ALONE — Bentley Little

The young man walked into the reading room and automatically sat in the chair. "Call me Baker," he said.

"Okay, Baker."

He looked her over, smiling, and she felt a trifle embarrassed, shy. She could feel herself reddening. "You're not at all what I was expecting," he said.

She smiled back. "Is that good or bad?"

"Oh, good. Definitely good." He put his hand in the indentation on the table. "You're a lot younger than I expected. And a lot prettier."

Now she *was* blushing. She didn't know what to say. Her hand reached out and began automatically stroking his palm. Consciously or unconsciously, her fingers went straight to his loveline. "You're not married," she said, both surprised and a little excited at the discovery.

"No," he admitted.

"You broke up with a girlfriend within the past year, and it was a very bitter break-up. You still harbor resentment toward her and you miss your life together, although you would never take her back."

He looked both pleased and surprised. "You're right."

Her fingers flicked to his lifeline.

It stopped almost immediately.

She felt a tinge of…what? sadness? dismay? frustration? She tried to let nothing show on her face. Her fingers moved instantly to other lines, touching, feeling. "You are unhappy with your job…"

"When will I die?" he asked bluntly.

Her fingers stopped moving, surprised by the question. She traced his lifeline again, to make sure she hadn't made a mistake. She hadn't. "You have awhile," she said vaguely. She felt a strange pull within. Half of her wanted to tell him the truth; the other half wanted to spare him the truth.

"How long?" he said, leaning forward.

"You will live until you are sixty-five," she lied. "Your death will not be painful. It will come as a surprise."

"What about my brother?" he asked, now intensely interested.

"It is unclear," she said. "It is too hard to tell."

He stood up. "Thank you. That is all I wanted to know."

Madame Carol stood up, too, aware that her heart was pounding. She looked at him. "Are you sure you don't want to hear more?"

He smiled and shook his head. "That's okay." He got out his wallet. "How much do I owe you?"

She decided to take a chance. "Nothing," she said. She smiled. "It's on the house."

He nodded, looking slowly around the dingy room at the faded carpet, at the cheap prints of the Old Masters on the walls, before letting his gaze settle back on her. He took the bait. "Maybe I can take you out some time to make up for it, to even it out?"

She could feel herself blushing again, but it was a pleased blush. "I'd like that."

"Here." He took a pen from the table and scribbled a phone number on a scrap of paper. "This is my number. You probably won't have to use it, but I'll give it to you to show my good faith." He handed the paper to her. "I'll call you tonight. Would that be all right?"

"That would be fine."

She walked out to his car with him. They said an awkward goodbye, and she went back into the waiting room. The next appointment—a woman—wasn't due to arrive for another twenty minutes. Locking the front door, she walked through the reading room to the makeshift kitchen in back. She turned on the radio and started to make some coffee. The coffee supply was getting low. She'd have to see if she could get some more.

If there was any left.

Music droned on the radio for a few minutes, then the newscast came on. There was only one story. That's all there ever was these days. That's all anyone cared about. She turned up the broadcast.

"…Some parts of the Valley have already reported massive doses of fallout, and the radiation levels in drinking water are unnaturally high. People are advised to drink only bottled water. Scientists say that while the blasts themselves did not do as much damage as expected, the after-effects have turned out to be far worse than could have been predicted…"

She turned off the radio. The newscasters had been repeating the same thing for the past week. There had not even been any changes in the wording of the story. That just showed what kind of talent they hired on these local stations.

As the coffee boiled, she fooled with the radio dial, trying to pick up another station, trying to get even the semblance of recognizable noise from another city.

Nothing.

The front bell rang, and she poured the coffee into the drip-pot and went out to the waiting room. The woman standing at the door tried to appear easy-going, nonchalant, but the worry showed in her face.

Madame Carol led her into the reading room and sat her down. She retreated to her side of the table, and her hand reached out to canvas the other woman's palm. Her fingers found the lifeline.

It stopped almost immediately.

"How long will I live?" the woman asked.

"You will live to be seventy-six," Madame Carol lied.

SLAM DANCE

(1985)

The portrait of St. Millard hung at the front of the classroom between the clock and the flag, a ragged horrific figure standing before a crowd of huddled peasants, an emaciated, nearly naked man with wild hair and piercing demonic eyes that glared out of the painting and down at the six rows of neatly ordered desks and the twenty-three students busily working on their math assignments. Anna, as usual, had finished her worksheet early. She had turned over the paper on her desk so no one else could copy her answers and was now staring at the portrait, curious.

The portrait stared back.

She could never seem to reconcile the hate in the eyes of this harsh and terrifying visage with the Christianity preached by Jesus, that meek and gentle martyr she learned about in chapel. They seemed like two opposing entities with absolutely nothing in common.

"Anna!" someone whispered.

Her eyes dropped from the ragged figure of St. Millard to the calm figure of sister Caroline, reading peacefully and obliviously at her desk, before searching out the source of the whisper.

"Anna!"

She turned to look behind her and felt the square hardness of a book being shoved into her left hand. Her fingers closed around the object, and she nodded to Jenny McDaniels, acknowledging receipt of the item. Jenny turned quickly back to her assignment.

Anna kept her eyes on Sister Caroline as she slowly and surreptitiously maneuvered the book from her lap to the top of her desk. *Slam Book*, it said in felt-pen letters on the cover, and Anna felt a thrill of forbidden excitement pass through her as she read the words. She glanced back at Jenny, but her friend was staring down at her worksheet, busily writing.

Anna's gaze returned to the bound volume before her. Slam books had been all the rage at St. Mary's for the past semester, and though she and Jenny had tried their hardest to lay their hands on one, neither of them had seen, much less held, one of the famous and dreaded items. Father Joseph had declared last October that slam books were not allowed at the school, promising that any student caught with one would be punished, but the ban had really had no effect. If anything, the books grew in popularity after Father Joseph's decree.

How in the heck had Jenny gotten ahold of one?

Anna carefully opened the book to the first page. "Gerard Starr," it said at the top in neatly printed script. Beneath that was a list of personal information: height, weight, age, favorite color, favorite musical performer, favorite movie, favorite food. Below the statistics were the comments. All unsigned, of course.

What a babe! I love his hair!!

Soooo cool! I want to marry him.

Dork.

Probably a fag. Gay haircut.

Fairy.

What a hunk!

Anna smiled. The comments were pretty much divided along male-female lines. Still, the good observations outweighed the bad. And even the slams were generic and not all that cutting.

She skipped over Sandra Cowan's page and all the pages of Sandra's cheerleader friends until she found Jenny's entry. Her eyes skimmed the stats and went straight to the comments.

Too shy. Too quiet.

SLAM DANCE

Not bad looking. Average.

Plain Jane.

Would be ok if she didn't hang around with Anna Douglas all the time.

Anna's heart raced, her pulse pounding. Her face grew hot as it reddened with embarrassment.

Not much to look at but seems alright.

Nice but doesn't talk much.

Fine except for her retarded friend Anna.

Afraid to look but needing to know, Anna turned to her own page. She noticed immediately that her name and statistics were sloppily written, as though whoever had created the book hadn't cared enough to make an effort. Most of the information was wrong. Holding her breath, she read the comments.

A scuz.

I hate her.

If I was its owner, I'd shave its ass and walk it backward.

Severe problems.

Major damage. Should be locked in her house until she dies so the rest of us don't have to suffer.

Snoopy come home!

She smells. I don't think she bathes or knows about deodorant.

Puke! Barf! Puuke!!! Baaaarrrfff!!!

She'll grow into a lonely old lady and die alone. Who wants her?

An arrow pointed to this last one, and a scrawled black arrow led to another connected comment: *She should do us all a favor and kill herself.*

Heart thumping, Anna turned the page, looking on the back for more comments. There was only one, in Jenny's small, neat handwriting.

My best friend. Very smart, very kind, very special. I'm lucky to know her.

Anna looked gratefully back at Jenny, but her friend was still working on the math assignment.

She turned her attention to the front page again, her gaze returning to the cruel comments below her name. The criticisms were harsh, unnecessarily so, and she knew without looking that no other people in the book would have such hostility directed toward them.

And this was only one slam book in one class. There were probably dozens more floating around the school.

She wondered what the other books had to say about her.

No.

She didn't wonder.

She knew.

She'd known what she would find even before opening *this* book.

Anna glanced up at St. Millard standing before the peasants, that look of twisted hate on his haggard face. He was undoubtedly preaching about Jesus in the depicted scene. But Jesus promoted peace and understanding. He exhorted everyone to love their neighbors.

Her neighbors didn't love her.

It was Jesus who taught that she should turn the other cheek, but even his disciples had not been able to live up to that standard. She had the feeling that the saint before her now, the one at the front of the classroom, would not stand for such softness, such…submission.

She stared at the ragged figure, meeting those demonic eyes.

The figure stared back.

◆

Molly Caulfield.

Anna finished writing the final name and closed the book. She put her pen down, flexing her fingers, which were starting to cramp. Picking up the volume, she examined its cover. It looked almost identical to the slam book she had read this morning. She smiled. This would show them. She would write her own comments, disguising her handwriting, then pass the book around. *They* would know what it felt like to be unpopular for once, to be the butt of jokes. *They* would know what it felt like to be hated.

She put the book down and opened it to the first page. *Sandra Cowan.* Anna stared at the blank page for a moment, then wrote: *An airhead.*

A strange tingle passed through her, a rush of forbidden pleasure. Always, when Sandra had made fun of her in the halls, Anna had lowered her head and hurried past, trying to ignore the laughter, trying not to let it hurt. She had never had either the strength or the guts to fight back and stand up for herself. Now, in one quick moment, she had passed judgment on Sandra Cowan. Writing from on high, a voice of anonymous omniscience, she had dismissed the girl and decreed her stupid.

Anna laughed, experiencing a sudden thrill of power. She picked up another pen and, changing her handwriting, wrote: *A bitch.*

She reread the word and giggled, glancing quickly around to make sure her mother or her sister hadn't sneaked into her room to peek over her shoulder. She was feeling brave now. She could say anything. She could be as cruel to Sandra as Sandra had been to her.

She's a whore, Anna wrote in red. *She'll do it for a dime.*

Moving on to the next name in the book, Sandra's friend Brittany, Anna wrote: *A godless witch.* The phone rang out in the living room, and Anna waited a moment to see if the call was for her. There was a seven-second lag, then her mother called, "Anna!"

Putting down her pen, she closed the book and ran out to the living room, wishing not for the first time that her parents would let her have a cell phone or, at the very least, get an extension of her own. She took the receiver from her mother's proffered hand. "Hello?"

"Guess what?" It was Jenny. Her voice was breathless, excited, something that came through even with the cheap mobile connection. "Sandra just got arrested! By the police!"

"What?"

"I saw it! Right here, right this second! In front of the mall!"

"Where are you?"

"By Nordstrom's. I can't talk much longer. My mom's on her way out."

"Well, what happened?"

"I'm not sure exactly. I came just at the very end. But it looked like she was trying to, you know…*sell* herself to some guy. Only the guy turned out to be a cop!" Jenny let out a loud, disbelieving breath. "I never liked Sandra, but I never thought she'd be doing this. Total shock."

Anna was no longer listening. She was thinking of her slam book in the other room. *She's a whore,* she had written. *She'll do it for a dime.*

Anna was suddenly certain that the cheerleader had offered her services for ten cents.

"Gotta go," Jenny said. "My mom's here. I'll call you when I get home."

There was the sound of a dial tone, and Anna hung up the phone.

"Who was it?" her mother asked.

"No one. Just Jenny." She walked back to her room in a daze. This was too bizarre to be just a coincidence. She *hated* Sandra Cowan, and even *she* didn't believe Sandra would do such a thing. She didn't even think that Sandra, despite all her talk, had had sex yet.

Anna looked at the slam book on her desk, feeling slightly afraid of it. She knew she should throw the thing away or, better yet, burn it, but it suddenly occurred to her that if she did so, all of the kids listed on its pages might…die.

She took a deep breath, filled with fear and weighted down with responsibility. What had she done? And how could she put a stop to it?

Did she want to put a stop to it?

That was the real question, but even as she asked it of herself, Anna knew the answer. She thought of that harsh, wild saint at the front of the classroom. *He* wouldn't back down, she knew. He would see this through to the end.

Slowly, carefully, she picked up the slam book and one of the pens lying next to it on the desk. First things first. She had to find out if this was really happening. She glanced up at the clock on her dresser. Four thirty-five. There was still time. She just needed to get Jenny to call her.

Anna made her way out to the living room, checking first to see where her mother and sister were. Her dad wouldn't be home for another hour, so she was safe there. Luckily, her mom was in the bathroom, and her sister was in her own bedroom doing homework. Anna quickly called Jenny's cell and, when her friend answered, told her to call her back immediately.

"I'm in the car with my mom!"

"It's an emergency," Anna said. "All you have to do is dial my number and hang up when I answer. I'll explain everything later. Please?"

"Okay."

⊢ SLAM DANCE ⊣

Jenny hung up, calling back moments later. Anna let it go two rings so everyone could hear, then shouted, "I'll get it!" She answered the phone, and then Jenny hung up. Anna mumbled into the mouthpiece as though she were talking, then hung up herself.

"Mom!" Anna called down the hall.

Her mother was just emerging from the bathroom. "Yes?"

"Jenny just called back. She forgot her math book at school. We're supposed to do twenty questions at the end of the chapter, and she needs—"

"She wants to come by, that's fine."

Anna felt a split second of panic. "No. She wants me to come over there. She's…grounded. She can't leave the house. I'll just speed over. I'll be back way before dinner." She spoke quickly, hoping her mother wouldn't notice her nervousness.

She didn't.

"You have forty-five minutes, young lady. I want you back here by five-thirty. And if you're late, *you'll* be grounded."

"Thanks, Mom." Anna ran back into her room, grabbed the math text, placed the slam book beneath it, and hurried out the front door.

Where to go?

Liz Waite, Sandra's chirpy little toady, lived closest, on the next block over, so it was to her house that Anna went. She had no concrete plan, assuming that she would think of something on the way over, but when she reached Liz's driveway and still had not come up with a viable test, she decided to throw caution to the wind and just go for it. Opening the slam book to Liz's entry and using the math text for support, she took out her pen and wrote: *Sandra would like her better if she wasn't so buddy-buddy with Anna.*

Books in hand, she walked up to Liz's door.

Knocked.

"Anna!" Liz threw open the screen and hugged her like a long-lost sister. It was all Anna could do not to cringe.

"Hey," she said.

"You should have called and told me you were coming! We're just getting ready to eat."

"That's okay. I was just on my way to Sandra's and thought I'd stop by."

"*Sandra's*? Oh my God! She wouldn't…you're not…you're joking, right?"

Anna shook her head. "She asked me to come over."

"Sandra?" Liz looked stunned. "I can't believe it."

Anna opened the slam book to the page being marked by her finger and clicked her pen.

"What's that? A slam book?"

"Uh huh." *Liz is a lez*, she wrote. *She's in love with Sandra.*

"What are you writing?"

Anna closed the book, clicked shut her pen. "I know about your crush on Sandra. I'm telling her."

Liz looked stricken. "Anna!"

"Everyone's going to know."

"No!"

Anna turned away, walking down Liz's driveway toward the sidewalk, ignoring the increasingly anguished pleas behind her.

She smiled to herself.

It worked.

◆

After dinner, Anna sat in her room, door shut, staring at the slam book on her desk. She'd told her parents she was going to be doing homework, though her real plan had been to write in the slam book. Now she just sat there, thinking.

Returning from Liz's house, she'd been elated. She had power. She could do whatever she wanted to whomever she wanted. She was queen of the world!

What had she actually learned, though? That Liz had a thing for Sandra and didn't want anyone to find out about it? That could have been true regardless. The fact that she'd written it in the slam book might very well be coincidence. Wasn't it logical that a girl as fanatically devoted to Sandra as Liz was might have a secret crush on her? And of course, she wouldn't want such information to get out to the other backbiting cheerleaders.

SLAM DANCE

Even Liz's friendliness to her was open to interpretation. After all, her parents had no doubt been home, probably standing right behind her, so of course she would be on her best behavior. And maybe Liz wasn't such a bad person away from Sandra's influence, maybe she just acted like a bitch because of peer pressure.

Then again, maybe not.

There was no way to know. What Anna needed was a more definitive answer, concrete proof that the slam book could do what she thought it could.

Another test.

It had to be something both serious and concrete, something that could not occur any other way, something that would happen instantly. It also had to be verifiable, something she could see with her own eyes. Tonight.

And it had to involve Sandra Cowan.

That was the most important part, wasn't it? That was what she really wanted—to see something happen to Sandra. It wasn't enough to just make it happen; she wanted to be there when it did.

Anna glanced up at the shelf above her desk, her gaze falling upon the spine of an E.B. White book, one of her favorites from childhood. An idea suddenly came to her. She looked down at the cover of the slam book.

And grinned.

◆

The street seemed scary at night.

It wasn't really that late. And it was a suburban street in her own quiet neighborhood. But Anna had never sneaked out of the house before. She was a good girl, and the fact that she was going behind her parents' backs, doing something she shouldn't, made her feel guilty and gave a darker, more malevolent tinge to everything.

Up the next block, on the opposite side of the street, a man was walking a dog. She could see only his silhouette, but he seemed to be moving much slower than he should be, almost as though he were casing houses. Or waiting for someone else to pass by, someone he could attack.

{ WALKING ALONE }   Bentley Little

She opened the slam book, prepared to use it.

The man and his dog turned the corner onto First Street.

Anna relaxed a little. Sandra's house was only another block away, and she quickened her step, praying that neither her parents nor her sister would get up to go to the bathroom, peek into her bedroom and discover that she was gone. If she would just be allowed to get away with this one transgression...

She could write an entry for her family in the slam book, make sure *they didn't find out.*

She pushed that thought immediately out of her mind.

The Cowans' house was two stories with a three-car garage. Anna stood on the sidewalk staring at the darkened windows, trying to determine which one was Sandra's. This was the part of her plan that was flawed. If she'd had a cell phone, she could have called the cheerleader and told her to come out. If it was earlier in the evening, she could have simply rung the doorbell. But as it was, the best idea she could come up with was to throw rocks at Sandra's window until she opened it.

She was about ready to sneak around the side of the house and check out the back when a car came up the street. Anna feigned casualness as she stood on the sidewalk, waiting for the vehicle to pass by.

But it didn't.

It pulled into the Cowans' driveway, triggering motion-sensitive lights that illuminated the entire front yard. Seconds after stopping, the car's doors flew open.

"Not another word out of you, young lady," her mom said angrily, getting out.

A beaten Sandra emerged from the backseat, saying nothing.

The prostitution arrest! Anna had forgotten all about it. She watched from the shadows as Sandra's briefcase-carrying dad and perfectly coiffed mom herded her toward the main door. It must have taken her parents this long to bail her out of jail.

Anna's plans were all screwed up. There was no way she'd be able to do what she had planned, so she quickly opened the slam book to Sandra's page and under the cheerleader's name and stats wrote: *She is a rat.*

{ SLAM DANCE }

It was something that had always been true metaphorically, but that was not how she meant the phrase this time. And that was not how the slam book took it.

The change happened instantaneously. Sandra's pretty face pushed forward, suddenly covered in fur, whiskers twitching above huge front teeth. Still in her cheerleader outfit, she dropped to all fours on arms and legs that were thin, hairy and clawed.

Mrs. Cowan screamed to wake the dead. Mr. Cowan tried to grab his madly scrambling rat daughter, crying, "Oh my God! Oh my God!"

Anna watched for a second from the sidewalk.

Then ran home as fast as she could.

It had been a long hard night. She had not slept at all but had written and crossed out, written and crossed out, until she heard her father's alarm clock ring at five. Natalie Tyron had been given the head of a cow, then the head of a dog, then her own head back. Bonnie Behar had been killed in a bathtub accident then brought back to life. Lynn Fitzgerald, perhaps the prettiest girl at St. Mary's, had been hideously deformed before her looks had been restored. Anna had liked punishing those who had punished her, and the feeling of revenge had been sweet. She had even, during one brief, crazy, power-mad moment, considered writing in Jenny's name. Jenny may have been her best friend and may have written nice comments about her in the slam book from Sister Caroline's class, but Jenny was also the one who had handed her the book. She had known what Anna would see; maybe she'd even *wanted* her to see it.

Anna had forcefully and immediately dismissed the idea of doing anything to Jenny, shocked and suddenly scared by the fact that her mind had even conceived of such a notion.

She thought of that ragged horrific saint in the portrait at the front of the classroom, then thought about the gentle, loving Jesus she learned about in chapel.

{ WALKING ALONE } Bentley Little

This morning, she had finished writing one comment for each person, and had then hidden the slam book in the bottom drawer of her dresser.

And that was where it would stay.

Before class, Anna went into the chapel and prayed, offering her thanks and love to that benign martyr above the altar, and when she reentered the school hallway, she was greeted with salutations of "Hi!" and "Hello, Anna!" from students who had never before spoken to her. She was given three slam books to write in, and when she looked at her own pages, they were filled with complimentary comments.

She was popular.

Jenny met her outside Sister Caroline's room just before the bell rang. "What is going on?" her friend said wonderingly. "Everyone's being so…nice."

Anna laughed. "It's like we died and went to heaven."

"I know. Everything seems so different today."

"Except us."

"Except us."

They walked into class, taking their seats. Sister Caroline began talking, but Anna didn't listen. Instead, she stared at the frightening visage of St. Millard at the front of the room. The twisted face was staring down at her with a mixture of hate and disgust, its demonic eyes boring into hers.

She met the gaze, held it.

Then triumphantly looked away.

LAST RODEO ON THE CIRCUIT

(1986)

The car began making noises just after Blythe.

Joni, always on the alert for engine trouble after the experience they'd had on their last trip, immediately turned down the radio. "What's that?" she asked.

"What?"

"That noise. Listen."

Ken shook his head. "I don't hear anything."

Joni did not move. She sat listening to the car. There was an unfamiliar bump from somewhere beneath their seat. "There," she said. "Did you hear that?"

Ken laughed. "It's nothing. Crummy Arizona roads. You know how bad the highways are in this state."

"It's something," she said.

Fifty miles later, it was obvious that it was something. The bumps from beneath their seat came at regular intervals now, and there was a hideous grinding noise each time Ken put on the brakes. They had turned the radio off several miles back, and the air conditioner, hoping that by listening attentively to the noise and not putting any unnecessary drain on the car's power they could somehow make it to Phoenix before the vehicle broke down entirely.

No such luck.

The car's speed fell to just above thirty miles an hour, and by the time they saw what looked like an old gas station down a dirt road far off to the right, the car was limping along at a jogger's pace, even though Ken had the gas pedal floored.

"I hope it's nothing bad," Joni said.

Ken snorted. "Are you serious? Out here? You know damn well that no matter what it is, they're going to gouge us for all we're worth."

"Well, maybe they have a phone. We can call to Phoenix and get the car towed."

"A hundred miles? It'll cost just as much, if not more." He shook his head. "We're screwed."

They pulled to a stop in front of the gas station, the braking tires kicking up a cloud of dust. There was a faded Enco sign above the old brick building and the gas pumps were boarded up, but the doorway of the garage was wide open. In back of the building, surrounded by a rickety chain-link fence, was a yard filled with dozens of dead cars. Many of the vehicles were rusting, but a surprising number of them were fairly new and still sported decent paint jobs. Ken looked at his wife. "Popular place to break down," he said drily.

A man emerged from the blackness of the garage. He was grossly overweight and was wearing ripped, faded Levi's and a greasy t-shirt which did not quite cover his huge gut. The hot desert sun glinted wetly off his bald sweating head. Behind the man, a skinny cowering dog moved tentatively out into the sunlight.

Ken got out of the car as the man approached. "Hey," he said. "How's it going?"

The man smiled, revealing rotted tobacco-stained teeth. "Whatc'n I do for you?"

Ken told him what had happened, trying to describe the sequence of noises in detail. He kept his tone light, as if by minimizing his concern he could somehow minimize the problem.

LAST RODEO ON THE CIRCUIT

The man nodded after he had finished. "Sounds like brakes and bearings to me," he said. "But I'd have to take a look to make sure."

"What would it cost if that was it?" Ken asked.

The man spit. "Depends on which way you want to go. If you wanted new parts, I'd have to order 'em. That'd take a day or so, cost you maybe a hundred parts, a hundred-and-fifty labor. Used parts, I have them out back. That'd cost you somewhere between twenty and forty bucks, a hundred-and-fifty labor. That's as cheap a price as you'll find anywhere."

Ken nodded. "All right, check it out."

The man drove the car into the garage. He put it up on ramps and told Joni and Ken to make themselves at home. "This'll take me about an hour or so," he said. "You two just look around, do what you want. There's a Coke machine in the office if you get thirsty."

Ken followed Joni slowly around the building. The place was out in the middle of nowhere. Although they had seen the gas station from the highway, the highway was not visible from where they stood. They appeared to be alone in the desert.

"How can anyone make a living out here?" Joni wondered.

Ken shrugged. "There's lots of cars out there."

They walked around the corner to the rear of the gas station and stopped. In front of them, adjacent to the lot of wrecked and broken automobiles, was an elaborate series of wire cages stretching back for perhaps a quarter of a mile. The cages were of all shapes and sizes, many of them stacked one upon the other. Next to the cages was a large garden, and on the other side of the garden a makeshift corral.

Joni walked up to the first cage and peeked in. Empty. She moved on to the next cage, this one quite a bit bigger. Inside, lying on the hard wire floor, was an emaciated calf.

"My God," Joni breathed, staring at the sickly animal. She looked up at Ken. "This is inhuman."

In the next cage was a midget horse with a broken leg. The leg had not been set, and the horse was laying down, obviously in agony.

"What's that man's name?" Joni asked, her mouth set in grim

determination. "I'm going to report him. He shouldn't be allowed to get away with this."

"Roscoe," Ken said. "Gil Roscoe." He put a hand on her shoulder. "But shut up about it until we're gone. We need our car fixed."

"Hey, you! Get away from there!"

Joni looked at Ken at the sound of the man's voice. They both moved away from the cages. "Sorry," Ken said. "We didn't know it was off limits."

The man wiped his bald head with a handkerchief. "Well, it is. Come on back here."

They followed him around to the front of the building. Joni noticed that an old red pickup truck was now parked next to the broken gas pumps. The truck had not been there before, and neither of them had heard anyone pull up.

"It's your brakes and bearings," the man said, walking into the garage. "Just like I thought. You wanna go for new or used parts?"

"Used," Ken said.

"All right, then. I'll see what I can find."

Ken cleared his throat. "You do take Visa, don't you?"

The man stared at him. "No." His eyes were hard. "Cash only."

Joni looked at her husband, signaling with her eyes that she had no money either.

"How about a personal check?" Ken asked.

The man shook his head. "Cash only." He smiled, and Joni shivered. "Looks like we'll have to figure out some other means of payment," he said.

It was then that she noticed the four dwarves getting out of the truck.

◆

"Maybe we should call the police," Teena said. "It's not like them to be late like this."

You know Joni always calls if something's wrong, if they're going to be late."

Rob took his receipt and credit card from the gas station attendant, smiling and nodding at the man. He turned to Teena. "Give it a rest. Jesus. They said they'd meet us either in Scottsdale or Las Vegas. Wait 'til we see if they're in Vegas first before you start panicking."

"But Joni would have left word."

"Obviously she didn't. Maybe they were too busy. Maybe they decided to skip Arizona altogether. God, can't you just enjoy your vacation without making everything into a big problem?"

They pulled out of the gas station and onto the highway, driving silently for over an hour, neither of them speaking. The forests of northern Arizona gave way to dry brush and high desert.

"Where do you want to stay tonight?" Rob asked. "Do you want to stop somewhere, or do you want to drive all the way through?" Teena did not answer.

"Fine. Then we'll stay in Sheep Springs."

They drove for several minutes in silence. "What's in Sheep Springs?" Teena asked finally.

Rob smiled. "The guy at the gas station said it's the last rodeo on the circuit. We happen to be going through at just the right time."

"I don't like rodeos," Teena said, frowning. "I don't like the way they treat those animals."

"You've never been to a rodeo."

"It doesn't matter."

"Well, this one's different," Rob said. "This is just for fun. It doesn't count for anything. They just let off a little steam, have a good time."

"Great," Teena muttered. "A bunch of drunk rednecks."

They pulled into Sheep Springs in the early afternoon and checked into a motel. It was the only room they had available. "You're lucky you found a room at all," the desk clerk told them. "This is rodeo weekend."

Indeed, the whole town was talking about the rodeo. In the stores they visited, it seemed to be the only topic of conversation. The gas stations were filled with pickup trucks and horse trailers. People were already starting to file into the rodeo arena, though the event wasn't set to start for several hours.

The excitement was catching, and by late afternoon, even Teena decided that she wanted to go. Rob bought them two advance tickets.

{ WALKING ALONE } Bentley Little

After dinner, they followed the crowd to the arena. The motel was only a block and a half away, so they walked. Around them, people were talking and laughing excitedly.

"Maybe we should try calling their hotel in Las Vegas," Teena suggested. "Just to see if they're there."

"We'll be there tomorrow," Rob told her. "Jesus. Try to enjoy yourself for once, okay?"

"They left over two weeks ago, and we haven't heard from them since."

"Shut up for a while."

They walked into the arena, not speaking, the only silent members of the excited crowd.

They held each others' hands not out of choice but out of necessity, not wanting to get lost in the rush.

The arena was big, much bigger than would have been expected from a town of this size.

The wooden grandstands were three stories high, and in back of the grandstands were snack and concession booths, selling beer, soft drinks, hot dogs, hamburgers and tacos.

Rob and Teena each bought a beer and climbed the wooden steps to their seats. Next to them, two cowboys were discussing a rodeo they'd competed in last week in Prescott.

A half-hour later, the lights in the arena snapped on and there was a loud hum from the PA system as microphones were connected.

"Well, we finally made it," said the announcer with a pronounced southwestern drawl. His voice echoed throughout the arena. "Last rodeo on the circuit!"

There was a huge cheer from the audience.

The announcer read off a list of names, people who had contributed time and money to the rodeo, people who needed to be thanked. "We'd also like to thank all the cowboys who rode this year," the announcer said, and there was a big cheer. "This is our way of paying you back for all the pleasure you've given us this season. So sit back, relax, and enjoy the fiftieth annual Sheep Springs rodeo!"

⊦ LAST RODEO ON THE CIRCUIT ⊦

A chute opened, a spotlight trained on the swinging gate, and Teena gasped.

A midget came out, riding on the back of a naked man.

Teena's hand found Rob's and held it tight. She stared as the naked man, his uncombed hair flying wildly, his body caked with dirt and mud, ran around the arena on all fours, trying to buck the midget off. The midget held onto the man's hair with one hand, his other hand raised to the sky. The spurs on his tiny boots dug into the sides of the bucking man's stomach, and twin trickles of blood fell onto the arena dirt.

The crowd was laughing uproariously. The two cowboys seated next to them were rocking back and forth, wiping tears of laughter from their eyes.

Teena stared at Rob. His face was white with shock. It looked as though he were about to be sick.

The midget jumped off, and two other small men, riding miniature horses, forced the dirty bucking man through a gate on the other side of the arena.

"A score of two-twelve!" the announcer said. "Not bad!"

The crowd was laughing and cheering wildly.

Teena felt someone tap her shoulder. She swiveled instantly around. An elderly woman smiled at her, holding forth a pair of binoculars. "Do you want to try these?" she asked kindly. "You can see better."

Numbly, Teena accepted the binoculars. She held them to her eyes. Another raggedy filthy man came bucking naked out of chute number two.

Ken.

The gorge rose in her throat, and she had to force herself to keep it down. Silently, she handed the binoculars to Rob, who took them and held them in front of his eyes. He dropped them almost immediately, and they fell into his lap.

Teena closed her eyes. Even above the roar of the crowd, she could hear the agonized screams of pain as the midget shoved his spurs into Ken's side. She opened her eyes. Ken was bucking near their section of the arena. His mouth was opened wide in a scream of tortured agony. Blood was dripping down his side. Large welts and bruises covered his body.

{ WALKING ALONE }   Bentley Little

The midget yanked hard on his hair, and both of them fell over. Ken tried to stand on his two feet, but the midget horseman pushed him down on all fours and herded him out the exit gate.

Teena felt a tap on her shoulder. "Can I have my binoculars back?" the old lady asked.

She handed them back unthinkingly.

Too shocked to move, too shocked to do anything, both of them watched as a succession of midgets and dwarves rode bareback on dirty wild men. After that, other men, these with large leather straps tied between their legs, were wrestled to the ground by teams of dwarves.

"Where's Joni?" Rob asked at one point, and neither said a word, though they both feared that they knew the answer.

"Time for the roping event," the announcer said. "We have sixteen contestants in this contest, let's not waste any more time."

A chute flew open, and out ran Joni. She was naked and on all fours, and there was a look of blind wildness on her face. Behind her, another chute opened, and a small man on a miniature horse came bounding into the ring, swinging a lasso in the air. The rope came down over Joni's head and chest, and the man pulled it tight, sending her flying onto her back.

He tied his end of the rope to the horn on his saddle and jumped off the horse, pulling two shorter lengths from his pocket. Moving swiftly, he tied Joni's hands together, then her feet, leaving her struggling on her back on the hard dirt of the arena floor.

"Two minutes and one second," the announcer said. "Tied with last year's best time!"

The dwarf pulled the ropes from Joni's hands and feet, untied the lasso and watched as she ran crazily toward the exit gate.

Teena felt Rob's strong hand grab her upper arm. "Come on," he said firmly. "We're getting the hell out of here."

Teena held tight to him as he led the way down the stairs of the grandstand. They walked past the concession booths, out the front gate and stopped. Rob looked toward the contestants' gate.

{ LAST RODEO ON THE CIRCUIT }

"No," Teena said, trying to pull him toward the car. "No, Rob. Come on. Let's get out of here and call the police."

He pointed at a uniformed officer patrolling the area outside the gates. "There's the police," he said.

The officer waved at them.

"I mean in another town. Back in L.A. or Las Vegas. Someplace real."

Rob looked at her. "Stay here, then. I'm going in." He started toward the contestants' gate.

Teena thought for a moment, then followed.

Surprisingly, the policeman standing outside the gate did not question them. They did not have to show passes or tickets or proof that they were contestants. They simply walked through the gate and followed the dirt path behind the announcer's booth.

Sitting in two cages, on a loaded truck ready to leave, were Ken and Joni.

Teena rushed over to Joni. She grabbed the door of the cage, trying to pull it open, but it was locked. "Joni," she sobbed, the tears rolling down her cheeks, "What happened?" Her friend looked at her in frightened incomprehension. Her eyes were wild.

"Joni," Teena repeated. She wiped the tears from her eyes.

Joni moved to the back of the cage, cowering in fear. She smelled of mud and blood and urine.

Teena looked over at Rob, who was trying to talk rationally to Ken and having no luck either.

"What the hell do you think you're doing?"

They both turned around at once. Coming toward them, from the direction of the chutes, was a fat bald man wearing faded Levi's and a blue work shirt. In his hand, he carried a bullwhip.

Four solidly built dwarves followed close behind him.

"Stay away from the stock," the man said, gesturing toward the cages. His voice was threatening.

Teena started to back away, trying to drag Rob with her, but he held his ground. "Who are you?" he demanded.

WALKING ALONE — Bentley Little

The man stared at him. "I'm Gil Roscoe, stock supplier. Who the hell are you?"

Rob blinked. "Stock supplier? You mean you're the one who does this? You're the one who—"

The fat man smiled. His teeth were brown and rotting. "I understand," he said. He looked at the cages containing Ken and Joni. "You know these people, huh?"

"We're going straight to the cops," Rob said. "They'll nab your ass so fast—"

"You know these people," the man repeated. He shook his head. "That's too bad. For you, I mean. We can always use new stock." He motioned toward them with his head, and the dwarves moved forward, running with graceful, practiced ease. Two of them jumped on Teena, tying her arms roughly behind her back. The other two attacked Rob, pushing him to the ground and trussing him up. The fat man opened two empty cages.

"You'll never get away with this!" Rob screamed.

One of the dwarves shoved a sock in his mouth, and the stock supplier laughed. "A feisty one."

"They're hard to break," one dwarf said.

"It's a year until the next rodeo. We did those two in a week. We'll have plenty of time to work on him." He held open the cage door as the dwarves threw Rob in.

The two dwarves who had tied up Teena tossed her into the other open cage. The fat man reached through the wire bars and grabbed her hair. She screamed. He felt her breasts.

"Healthy," he said. "Maybe we'll breed 'em. Or cross-breed 'em. It's been awhile since we've had this many at once. Hell, maybe we'll start a whole herd!"

Teena looked toward Rob, screaming his name. Both of them heard the roar of the crowd inside the arena as another event ended.

"Yeah," the fat man said. "I think we'll breed 'em."

He slammed a lock on each of their cages, wiped the sweat from his bald head and walked back toward the announcer's booth to watch the rest of the show.

THE CAR WASH

(1987)

Timmy picked up a rock and turned it over in his hands, examining it, before lobbing it over the low brick wall that surrounded the abandoned car wash. The rock clattered against a cluster of small pebbles on the faded blacktop.

"Hey!" his grandpa said. "Don't do that!"

Timmy turned to look behind him, then glanced away, an empty feeling in the pit of his stomach. It was a horrible thing to admit, but he did not like to look at his grandpa. The old man was really frail, much worse than he had been the last time they'd come to visit. His formerly healthy cheeks now sagged tiredly, as if his face had lost a lot of weight, and his too-large smile seemed almost skeletal. His entire frame looked stooped and brittle, and when he walked it was with the hesitant shuffling of a man in pain.

Timmy stared down at the ground. He neither knew nor liked this new grandpa, this tired old man who had taken the place of the alert and fun-loving person he had grown up with. He had succeeded for most of this visit in staying with his parents and his grandma, not wanting to be alone with his grandpa, but he had felt guilty about this emotional betrayal, and today he had agreed to walk with him to the store.

The walk was just as painful as he'd known it would be. He was ten now, too old to fall for his grandpa's simplistic attempts at conversation, and he could tell that the old man was really working hard to make him happy. He could see the mechanics behind the magic, and he didn't want to see. He had stepped outside the special bond that had existed between the two of them, and now, try as he might, he could not get back in. Though neither of them acknowledged this change in their relationship, both were aware of it, and that made Timmy feel even more depressed.

He looked toward the abandoned car wash. He had spent many happy hours in that long narrow building, sitting in the air-conditioned lobby with his grandpa, drinking a Coke and looking through the plate glass as a steady stream of cars passed through the cleaning assembly line. It had been fun. He had followed each car's progress from a dusty, dirty, old-looking vehicle, through the pre-rinse, through the wash, through the rinse, then back into the open air where it was dried until the chrome and paint shone.

Now the car wash was empty, its once busy interior dark, its windows broken, obscene graffiti on its brown brick walls. A victim of the times.

"It's haunted," his grandpa said, moving next to him. "You know that?"

Timmy looked up into the old man's face, and the excited gleam in his eye made Timmy's gloom abate somewhat. He found himself smiling, ready again to resume the comfortable role of adoring grandson. "Really?" he said.

His grandpa nodded. "That's what they say." He pointed toward the black open square where vehicles had once come out of the car wash. "A few months ago, a kid about your age was found dead in there. His hair and clothes were all gone, and his skin was rubbed raw and bloody. It looked like he'd been through the wash. They even found his lungs filled with soapy water, but the car wash floor was dry and all the machines were covered with dust." He cleared his throat. "Ever since then, the place has been haunted."

Timmy stared at the car wash and tried to imagine the body of a kid lying dead over the track, surrounded by dark and silent machines. He felt a pleasant shiver of fear pass through him.

His grandpa put a hand on his shoulder. "Come on," he said. "It's getting late. We'd better head back."

They walked to the house silent but in sync. His parents and grandma were sitting on the porch talking, and Timmy ran up the porch steps excitedly. "Remember that car wash?" he said. "The one around the corner?"

His father looked at him, puzzled.

"It's haunted!"

His parents laughed, and his grandma shook her head at her husband, just coming up the steps. "Don't listen to him, Timmy. He's been on about that for weeks now."

The old man stood leaning against the porch railing. "It's haunted." He was tired and almost out of breath, but the look on his face was defiant. "I've heard the noises myself."

Timmy's eyes widened. "You heard noises?"

"James," his grandma said warningly.

The old man nodded. "It was about a month ago, a few weeks after the boy was found. I couldn't sleep, and I was standing by the window, breathing the night air. All of a sudden, I heard it. There was a whirr of machinery, the sound of the car wash starting up—"

"You heard no such thing!" His wife glared at him.

"I was here when that car wash was built. I know what it sounds like."

Timmy's father stood up. "Dad," he began, "It could have been—"

"Don't patronize me. I'm not a child, and I'm not yet senile. I know what I heard."

Timmy stared at his grandpa, proud of the way the fire flared in his features, feeling a strange elation course through him. He had never seen this side of his grandfather before, this willful adult determination, but it was a side he liked.

"The car wash was working. In the middle of the night. But in the morning, everything was exactly the way it had been the day before." He looked at his wife. "And you know I'm not the only one who heard it."

She shook her head. "You're impossible."

He looked at Timmy. "It's haunted," he said.

WALKING ALONE — Bentley Little

Timmy stood at the open window, listening. Around him, the old house was silent, his parents and grandparents fast asleep. Outside, a half-moon shone down on the empty street, its bluish light comingling with the fluorescence of the streetlamps to create a surrealistic series of double shadows. It was warm out, a typical July night, but his arms were covered with goosebumps.

He thought of the car wash and shivered.

Was it really haunted? he wondered. Or was his grandpa just pulling his leg? It would not be the first time his grandpa had not told him the truth. When he was smaller, the old man had told him that rain was God's pee, that steak sauce was made from squished bugs, that the flu was caused by lying. And he had believed it all.

But his grandpa had been serious about the car wash. He had even argued with his grandma over it, and Timmy could not remember the two of them arguing over anything before.

He tried to imagine the car wash in the moonlight. He could see in his mind the shadowed indentations of the long low building, the crumbling bricks and the scraps of twisted metal. He could see the square black holes that had once been windows and the gaping mouthlike entryway.

And then he heard it.

He held his breath, not identifying the sounds his ears were registering, yet knowing those sounds could be caused by only one thing. There was a clacking of metal on metal, the voice of an old machine coming to life. Electrical engines whined and keened, gears grinding. Through the still night air came the unmistakable sound of the car wash's big brush spinning quickly.

It was true!

Timmy stood there listening, unmoving, staring at nothing, his mind drifting with the white noise of the working car wash. The cadences were rhythmic, almost soothing, and he did not know how long the sounds continued.

As suddenly as they had started, they stopped. And it was a minute or so before his brain registered the fact that the car wash had quit for the night. He was about to go back to bed, when a quick movement down the

{ THE CAR WASH }

street caught the corner of his eye. He turned to look again out the window and saw his grandpa coming toward the house from the direction of the car wash.

He was running.

◆

Timmy awoke late, long after everyone else was already up. The events in his mind were jumbled, unclear, and he could not remember if he had dreamed them or if they had actually happened. He slipped on a bathrobe, tied it shut and walked down the hall to the kitchen.

His grandpa shuffled slowly from the sink to the counter, where he turned up the radio.

"—has not yet been identified," the announcer said.

His grandpa looked at his grandma with an expression of triumph. "See?"

She reached over and turned down the radio. "See what? It was probably an accident. Knock off this foolishness."

Timmy sat next to his father at the breakfast table and poured himself a glass of orange juice. He watched his grandpa move painfully across the kitchen, his slippers making loud scratching sounds on the tile, and he remembered the dream he'd had of the old man running down the street. He grabbed the last two pieces of bacon from the plate in the center of the table and turned toward his mother. "What happened?"

She shook her head, "Nothing, dear."

He looked at his father. "What happened?"

"They said on the news that a little girl was found dead inside the car wash this morning."

"It's haunted," his grandpa said, and Timmy glanced away from him.

He no longer liked the look of the old man's face.

◆

After breakfast, Timmy followed his father and his grandpa down the street to the car wash. A crowd had gathered around the abandoned structure, and bright yellow police tape cordoned off the area. Two police cars and several unmarked vehicles were parked in front of the open entryway.

Timmy's father lifted him onto the low brick fence, and he scanned the crowd of investigators, policemen, photographers and reporters, looking for a body covered with a sheet. Then he realized that if the death had already been on the news, the girl had long since been taken away.

His grandpa walked down the sidewalk and tapped the shoulder of a bystander who had obviously been here for some time. "Do you know what happened?" he asked.

Timmy hopped off the fence and, grabbing his father's hand, moved closer.

"Little girl," the bystander said shortly. "I didn't see her, but apparently her face had been scraped off. They're cleaning it off the brushes now."

"I always said it was haunted," a woman in back of them said.

Timmy recalled sitting in the lobby, watching the spinning brushes taking the dirt off a car's roof, hood and windshield. He imagined the brushes spinning over a person's face, the stiff bristles running through hair, cutting into skin, ripping off clothes. He felt cold, chilled, and he glanced toward his grandpa.

The old man was smiling.

He looked happy.

Timmy turned back toward where the policemen were clustered around a window of the building. It wasn't possible. He was imagining things. He was overreacting.

But he had seen his grandpa running—*running!*—down the street, away from the car wash, in the middle of the night, immediately after the noises had stopped.

Just after the girl had been killed.

"Why do you think she was there in the first place?" he heard his father ask. "Don't you think it's kind of strange for a young girl to be exploring an empty car wash in the middle of the night?"

"I don't think it was an accident," someone said. "I think someone killed her and left her body there."

His grandpa shook his head. "It wasn't an accident. The car wash killed her."

⟨ THE CAR WASH ⟩

"But why would she even be out that late at night?" his father said.

Timmy focused on the policemen dusting for fingerprints around the edges of the splintered doorjamb, afraid to look at his grandpa's face, afraid of what he might see.

He lay in bed, the thin sheet pulled up to his chin for protection, listening to the night noises of the house. From his grandparents' room, he could hear the sound of the bed creaking as someone turned over sleeplessly.

His grandpa.

Timmy listened, unmoving, waiting for the moment when his grandpa would get out of bed and walk outside.

To the car wash.

His mouth was suddenly dry, and he tried to will saliva back into his mouth so he could lick his lips. He felt almost like gagging. In his chest, his heart was pounding and the sound reverberated in his ears.

His grandpa got out of bed, and in the silence of the house Timmy heard him put on his pants, shoes and a shirt. Though the old man tried to tiptoe, the sound of his shoes on the wooden floor of the hallway were clear to Timmy's ears. He heard the front door open, then close, and he hopped out of bed, rushing to the window to see.

His grandma, her white blouse flapping eerily in the moonlight, ran down the street toward the car wash.

The next morning, everything was normal. His parents and grandparents were sitting around the breakfast table, trying to decide if they would go on a picnic today or go out to eat at one of the local restaurants. No mention was made of the car wash.

Timmy stared at his grandma, cheerfully pouring coffee for everyone and talking excitedly about the plans for the day. Her happy exterior, her surface friendliness, once so comfortable and reassuring, now seemed hopelessly false to him. Though he saw no outward indication of it, beneath that front he saw a cold, hard woman.

She had not come back home until well after three o'clock.

Soon after the noises had stopped.

They decided to go to the beach for the day and eat at an outside seafood restaurant near the pier. After cleaning up and getting ready, they all piled into the station wagon, Timmy in the back behind his grandparents, and headed toward the beach.

Later in the afternoon, he got his father alone and told him he didn't want to stay for the entire two weeks. He wanted to go back home.

But his father didn't understand, and Timmy couldn't bring himself to tell his dad the truth.

After dinner, Timmy went immediately to bed. He didn't want to stay up tonight. He didn't want to know what went on after everyone was asleep. He wanted to be deep in slumber before his parents even turned off the TV in their room. It was tough at first. He wasn't tired at all, and he tossed and turned fitfully in the bed, panic welling within him as he realized that the hour was growing late. He even heard his parents and grandparents retire to their respective rooms.

But then he was asleep, drifting, dreaming of a world where he was six and his grandparents loved him and the sun always shone.

He was shocked awake into blackness, feeling the sock stuffed in his mouth, feeling the blindfold pressed against his eyes and tied roughly at the back of his head. He struggled and kicked, and he was gratified to feel his bare heel connect with something soft.

He heard his grandpa's muffled grunt of pain.

Leathery old hands grabbed him around the waist, forcing all of the air out through his nose, and he was lifted off the bed and carried down the hall, through the family room, out the front door. He kicked and punched, his

THE CAR WASH

arms and legs flailing wildly, and once his hand connected with a wall. But neither of his parents heard the noise, and neither of them came to save him.

He was crying as the old man carried him down the street.

The night was warm, but there was a breeze, and the slight wind tickled its way through his sleep-mussed hair, caressed his bare toes. He tried to pull the bony old fingers off of him, using his hands to pry them loose, but the old bastard was strong. He felt neither hurt nor sadness as he thought of his grandpa. Their former relationship, their former lives, meant nothing now and he did not even think of them. He was filled only with a black rage of hate, and he hoped with all his heart that a huge semi would suddenly come barreling down the street and kill his grandpa, ramming into his body and smashing his fragile bones, turning his face to pulp, his brains to mush. He would be killed too, but it would be worth it. The semi would put a painful end to the old bastard's miserable life.

But no semi came.

He felt his grandpa turn a corner, and he knew they were approaching the car wash. As they drew closer, he heard voices, as though a large crowd had gathered. Snatches of conversation reached his ears.

"—I don't even feel the arthritis anymore. I can hardly believe—"

"—when it scraped off her little dress, I thought I was going to—"

"—sorry to see Julie go, but now I feel—"

Several pairs of hands grabbed him and threw him to the ground. He heard his shoulder smack against the concrete, and he felt a sharp flash of pain sear through the right side of his body. His arms and legs were tied with coarse twine, and he felt the bottom half of his body being wrapped in some type of cloth, like a mummy.

The blindfold was pulled from his eyes.

He was on the ground in front of the car wash, directly before the open entryway where cars were once ushered in to be cleaned. Around him, around the entire car wash in fact, were hundreds of old people, seemingly all of the grandparents in the city. They were standing, sitting on folding lawn chairs, leaning up against the low brick fence where just yesterday he had sat watching the police.

⦃ WALKING ALONE ⦄ Bentley Little

Maybe the police will come, he thought wildly. *Maybe the police will come, maybe the police will come, maybe—*

His grandma and grandpa were standing next to him, and beside them were two men wearing purple robes. The sheet wrapped around the bottom half of his body was purple as well, he noticed.

His grandma looked at him kindly, and there were tears in her eyes. "I'm sorry," she said. "We didn't want it to be you. Really we didn't." She shot a look of poisonous hate at her husband. "It was his fault." She spat on the ground, and the hardness Timmy had imagined showed through. "Haunted!"

His grandpa smiled, and there was a look of rapture on his face.

Timmy scanned the crowd of old faces, looking for some sign of sympathy. His eyes alighted on a fat woman knitting in her folding chair. Their gaze met and she looked away. "I liked the old ways better," she said.

One of the purple-robed men lifted him up and placed him on the center of the track that went into the car wash. Timmy promptly pushed himself off, onto the cement. "A fighter," the man said. He brought a flat board, and Timmy was tied securely to it. The board was placed on the track.

As one, the crowd stood. Their faces were deadly serious, and they chanted a single alien word as the two men in purple raised their hands above their heads. The machines within the car wash roared into life, gears grinding, metal screeching, brushes whirring. No lights came on, but the track lurched once, and Timmy's board started forward. He struggled and squirmed, but it was no use. He could not push himself off the track.

All of the old people were singing now, something that sounded vaguely like a nursery rhyme he had heard as a child. Above the other voices, he could hear his grandma and grandpa singing loud and clear.

The singing was drowned out by the noise of the car wash.

He did not see the brushes come down.

THE FEEB

(1988)

Jimmy T was a crippled little feeb who lived alone in a house with no furniture. Although he was somewhere between ten and fifteen years old, no one really knew his exact age. No one really cared. Jimmy T was not the sort of kid you gave much thought to.

Not at first.

When Jimmy T's mama died, we all thought he'd end up in Riverview. We assumed someone from the County would have him committed. We sure as hell didn't think he'd be able to take care of himself. But as the weeks passed, and then the months, and we saw Jimmy T hobbling down the footpath into the woods, collecting berries and molds and fungus the way he always had, we realized that he was going to be able to get by. And when no one came to take him away, we realized that the authorities were going to let him live alone.

The crops began dying soon after that, stricken by a blight the likes of which the agriculture man had never seen. Henry said it was bugs, said he could see the places where the plants had been gnawed, but the agriculture man found traces of a fungus on the roots and branches, and he said it was some sort of disease. At night, fires could be seen on the various ranches as Henry and Lowell and their friends tried to smoke out the bugs.

I had my crops treated with an anti-fungoid spray.

All of our crops continued to die.

I began getting up even earlier than usual. Despite the fact that I'd seen the agriculture man's white fungus on my plants, I also saw tiny teeth marks. I wanted to know what the hell was going on.

On the fourth morning, I saw Jimmy T out in my pasture. "Hey!" I yelled at him. "You get away from there!" But either he didn't hear me or didn't understand. It was hard to tell. I saw him bend down, pick something up and put it in a bag.

I ran across the field toward him, and he turned slowly around. He hobbled toward me, then changed his mind and began limping away, toward his house. I caught up to him almost immediately. "What are you doing?" I asked.

He stared at me dully, his mouth open.

I held out my hand. "Let me see the bag, Jimmy T."

He handed me the canvas sack, and I opened it. Inside were handfuls of white fungus. He'd been collecting them off my plants. I put a finger into the bag and touched the stuff. It was slimy and felt like jelly. I knew the feeb probably ate the fungus, and my stomach churned.

He was lucky he hadn't poisoned himself yet. I handed the bag back to him. "Stay off my property," I ordered. I grabbed his shoulders and looked him in the eye. "Do you understand me, Jimmy T?"

He nodded stupidly, and I let him go. He started walking back toward his house.

Later that day Tim Hawthorne's cow was found dead in the barn, her udders completely sealed shut with fungus. One of Henry's chickens had it growing inside her mouth, and she died, too. I checked my livestock carefully, but they all seemed to be okay.

We felt like we were in some damn science fiction movie.

We stayed out all that night. We didn't want to split up—we knew we wouldn't find anything that way—so we just picked a ranch at random, and all of us went over there. We picked Booker's place, and we stationed ourselves all around the barn and pasture, but none of us saw a thing. I went home the next morning tired and dirty and discouraged, only to find that two of our cats were dead. There was no fungus on them, but they'd been gnawed ragged. I found some fungus by their cat dishes on the porch.

I called up Henry, and we went to see Mrs. Caffrey. We figured if anyone could solve this it was her. Neither of us liked going to the witch woman's, but sometimes there was no other choice.

She met us in her trailer, and it looked like she was expecting us. She nodded a greeting, told us to sit down and asked what we wanted. We told her about the blight on the crops, about the dying animals, and she nodded silently.

"Is there anything we can do?" Henry asked.

Her answer shocked us. "It's the feeb," she said. "Kill him."

I stared at her. "What?"

"The feeb," she said. "Kill him and the blight will be gone."

I looked over at Henry and shook my head, warning him not to say anything until we left. We both knew Mrs. Caffrey hated Jimmy T. Jimmy T's mama had always blamed Mrs. Caffrey for her son being born the way he was. She said it was because of the roots and herbs Mrs. Caffrey gave her and told her to take when she was pregnant. Mrs. Caffrey's business actually fell off a little after Jimmy T was born, and though she denied it, everyone knew she hated the boy. But I never would have thought she hated him this much.

We thanked Mrs. Caffrey for her help and left. Henry tried to press a few bills in her hand, but she refused, as always. Before we took off, she ran up to the window of the pickup. She must have known we weren't going to follow her advice. She reached out and held my hand for a moment, cocking her head as if she were listening for something. "Be in the north end of your field tonight," she said. "Then you will see."

I was shaking as I drove home, and I realized I was scared. "Should we?" I asked, looking over at Henry.

"What else do we have to go on?"

{ WALKING ALONE } Bentley Little

We met in the pasture after dinner. I brought a flashlight and an extra jacket in case it got cold. Henry brought a shotgun. "What's that for?" I asked.

"Just in case."

The orange at the edge of the horizon faded into purple and then into black. Henry and I shot the breeze a bit, but there wasn't a whole lot to say and the conversation just kind of died. I was tired, and I could tell Henry was, too. Neither of us had gotten any sleep lately. We decided to take turns on watch. Henry pulled the short straw, and I gratefully leaned up against the fence post and closed my eyes.

Henry shook me awake. He had my flashlight in his hand, and he was shining it on the ground. It was dark, but I could still see his face. He was frightened. I stood up. "What is it?"

"Come here," he said.

I followed him through a row of cotton to the edge of the irrigation ditch. He shone the flashlight down, but I couldn't see anything at first. Then something moved on the periphery of the beam. I took the light from him and pointed it myself.

A white fungoid creature was dancing along the bottom of the ditch.

It was joined by another. And another. And another.

They began to crawl up the side of the ditch toward us. I saw horrible jellyish skin, toothless mouths, webbed little fingers. I turned to run, but Henry was already shooting. I swung back around in time to see the first creature explode, blown into fungus fragments by Henry's shotgun. Screeching, the other two creatures ran the length of the ditch the way they'd come. I followed them from on top of the bank, but they were faster than I was. I saw one of them leap out of the ditch and dash across the open space.

To Jimmy T's house.

I stood in shock, watching as the other one followed, pushing its way through one of the holes in Jimmy T's screen door.

I hurried back to tell Henry. He was examining what was left of the creature he'd killed. He didn't touch the bits of white fungus but prodded them with his shotgun. They quivered like they were still alive, and Henry grimaced in disgust. I looked at him. "The other ones went to Jimmy T's," I said. "I saw them go inside."

He didn't say anything.

"Get the guys," I told him. "We're going in."

A half hour later, there were eight of us standing in the drive leading up to Jimmy T's. All of us were armed. Even old Randolph had brought a pitchfork.

Since I was the one who had seen the creatures, I led the way.

The feeb's house was dark, but it was always dark. He had no electricity. I shone my flashlight over the face of the house, into the glassless windows, but nothing moved. "He's just a kid," someone behind me said.

"You didn't see those things," Henry told him.

I thought of what Mrs. Caffrey had said, and I knew Henry was thinking the same thing. "Jimmy T!" I called. "Jimmy T!" I shone the flashlight on the screen door, letting the beam rest on the rips at the bottom where the creatures had gone in, but there was no movement and no sound. "Jimmy T!" I called again.

"What are we planning to do here?"

I turned around to see Charley staring at me. I realized he was the one I'd heard before. "He's just a kid. And a feeb, besides. He don't know what he's doing."

"Let's just go inside," Henry said.

I walked up the rickety porch steps, the others following.

Jimmy T was sitting on the bare floor in the middle of the empty front room, staring at the wall. His canvas bag, now empty, sat beside him. "Jimmy T," I said. He turned slowly around, and I expected some sort of reaction, but his eyes were as dull as ever. I walked forward, my footsteps loud in the empty house, and I could hear the other men moving in behind me. "Where are they?" I asked. "Where are those creatures?"

Jimmy T said nothing.

I picked him up and jerked him to his feet. He let out a high girlish squeal. I clamped my hand around his thin little arm and forced him in front of me. "We're going through every inch of this place until we find them," I said.

WALKING ALONE — Bentley Little

We moved from one empty room to another, seeing nothing but dust and occasional leaves. Upstairs it looked like it was going to be the same thing. The first room, nothing. The second room, nothing.

But in the third room, in the middle of the floor, was a naked woman, her legs spread wide.

No. Not a woman. As I moved into the room and looked closer, I saw that she was made from mold and fungus and lichen, shaped into female form.

Standing in the doorway, Jimmy T started quivering all over. His hands shook, his knees knocked, and his lips began twitching. Even his eyelids started to flutter. With one quick motion, he pulled off his pants. I saw the boy's erection for only a second, then he was on top of the fungoid form, pumping away between its legs. We watched in disgust as his bare buttocks moved up and down, as his torso squirmed, as his hands caressed the lichen hair. He was babbling something high and whiny and entirely unintelligible. Someone behind me muttered a sickened "Jesus."

"Pull him offa there," Henry said, grimacing. "Make him stop that."

But Jimmy T was already finishing. His body stiffened noticeably, he let out a loud screech, and then he lay slumped on top of the slimy white figure, spent. A moment later, he stood up and pulled on his pants. His face, as always, was blank, and I had no idea what he was thinking. I glanced toward the mound of fungus, surprised to see that it had kept its female shape, even after Jimmy T's exertions.

And I saw the first creature run out from between its spread legs.

Everyone else saw it at the same time, and Campbell, who was wearing gloves, reached out and grabbed it. Grimacing distastefully, he held it up. The creature was made out of fungus, but it looked like a miniature Jimmy T. Its eyes were closed, and its little legs were pumping, as though it were running across solid ground.

"Put it down," I said.

Campbell put it down, and the creature took off. I ran to the window, and a moment later I saw it dash out the screen and make a beeline for my pasture.

I turned back around. Others were coming now. Three other slimy creatures, all tiny copies of Jimmy T, rushed out from between the fungoid woman's legs and ran toward the door, heading out to my pasture.

Henry's eyes were focused on Jimmy T, and there was fear on his face. The feeb was staring at the wall, oblivious, his head rocking back and forth as if in time to slow music.

"What're we gonna do?" Henry asked.

"Let's wait," I said. "Let's wait until they come back. We saw them return here once. They'll probably come back again."

Jimmy T picked up his empty canvas bag, scooped out a small bit of fungus and applied it to the woman's breasts, molding it skillfully into nipples. He hummed as he worked, some strange little song I didn't know.

We stood around, not talking. Flashlights were turned off in order to save batteries, and the only light came from the moonbeams shining through the window. Jimmy T continued to put the finishing touches on his lover, sculpting her face.

Twenty minutes later, Henry saw the first creature come running up the drive. "They're here," he said, looking out the window.

Charley started down the stairs first, and the rest of us followed close behind. "There!" he shouted, pointing. Two of the slimy creatures ran through the kitchen door and darted down the basement stairs, carrying what looked like a half-eaten cat between them.

"I can't go down there," Charley apologized. He was holding his nose. "I'm sorry. I'll throw up."

I got a whiff of the smell through the door and almost gagged myself, but I kept on. Henry followed, and so did everyone else. Someone flipped on the light.

The creatures were sloughing off their skin, shedding it the way a snake would, and beneath the white fungus they looked human. Too human. Ten or fifteen other creatures, ones that had already shed their skin, were also in the basement. They were clustered together in a group, and when they split up, we could see behind them rows of tiny women made out of dirt.

The new creatures, each with an erection, fell on the closest dirt women, writhing lustily.

WALKING ALONE   Bentley Little

They pulled out moments later, and from between the legs of the dirt figures came brown creatures the size of spiders. They were too small to see clearly, but I had the sickening feeling that they all looked like Jimmy T.

Henry and two of the other men started shooting. Skin and fungus and dirt went flying every-which-way, and the basement was filled with baby screams.

I started shooting, too.

We killed the feeb like Mrs. Caffrey said we should. None of us could shoot him in cold blood, so we just tied up his hands and feet and pushed him down the stairs. He didn't say anything, didn't even scream, as his body jerked and flopped down the steps. He was dead before he reached bottom.

We torched the house afterward.

And the crops started getting better, and no more animals died.

And two months later, when Doug's wife gave birth to a feeb, we drowned it and buried it in the field in an unmarked grave.

THE MALL

(1991)

"I saw Daddy."

Marylynn stopped fastening Glen's bulletproof vest and looked into his face.

"Where?" she asked carefully.

"In the mall, by school."

She grabbed both of her son's arms, squeezed. "I told you never to go near the mall."

"It's all closed up. You can't even get in."

"It doesn't matter. It's dangerous. The building's unsafe, and gangs hang out there."

"I didn't see anybody but Daddy."

"What was he doing there?"

Glen shrugged. "I don't know. I just saw him through the door. I peeked through the door to see if I could see inside there, but it was all dark. Then I saw Daddy standing in the middle of the mall. I waved to him, but he didn't see me. Then he went downstairs and he didn't come back."

Marylynn finished fastening Glen's vest, pulling his t-shirt on over it. "Why would your father be inside the mall? How would he get in there? That's just stupid." She gave him a small slap on the bottom. "Now go and brush your teeth before school. And I don't want you going anywhere near the mall, you understand me?"

"Mom…"

"Don't 'mom' me. You go straight to school and come straight back. You hear?"

"Yeah." Glen reluctantly walked into the bathroom to brush his teeth.

Marylynn frowned. Now he was seeing his daddy in abandoned buildings. She shook her head. It was her fault. It was all her fault. She shouldn't have babied him this long. She should have been honest with him. She should have told him the truth long ago.

She should have told him that she'd killed his daddy.

There was another drive-by shooting, a third-grader was taken down, and once again school was let out early. Glen considered calling his mom and telling her, maybe asking her to give him a ride home, but he decided to walk instead.

He waited in the library until he was sure that the bad kids were gone and the campus was empty, then walked past the closed classroom doors, through the parking lot, and down the cracked and broken sidewalk toward home.

He slowed his pace as he passed the mall. The gigantic building, which had once housed hundreds of shops, was now abandoned and covered with graffiti. From this angle, near the weedy asphalt field that had been the upper parking lot, it looked like some great beast hunkered down and ready to pounce, the upward slope of the empty Nordstrom's resembling haunches, the jutting square of the Sears a head.

Glen stopped walking. The mall scared him, had always scared him, and he was not sure why he had disobeyed his mom's orders yesterday and snuck through one of the holes in the chain-link fence that surrounded the block to trek across the lot and peek into the mall. It had been a stupid thing to do. He had known it was stupid even while doing it, had been aware of the dangers, but something had compelled him to continue on, and before he knew it, he had found himself standing in front of one of the old doors and peeking through the smoked glass.

Where he had seen Daddy.

Daddy.

Even the word was magic, and just saying it to himself made Glen feel better, made him feel more secure, less afraid.

He said it aloud: "Daddy."

Whispered it again: "Daddy."

And once more he found himself sneaking through the fence, walking through the waist-high weeds of the parking lot, leaping the ruts and potholes, until he was standing before the entrance of the mall.

He felt good, happy. It seemed to him almost like his birthday or Christmas, the excited expectancy was so strong within him.

Daddy.

It was a different door than the one he'd peeked through yesterday, and it was covered with a layer of tough dirt that would not wipe off no matter how much spit he used or how hard he rubbed it with his palm. Unable to clear a spot on the glass, he simply pressed his face against the outside of the door and used his hands to block out the side glare of the sun. Through the filth he could make out vague shapes in the darkness, boxes and triangles and the skeletons of indoor trees.

And Daddy.

He was standing in front of a square black hole that led into one of the old department stores. He wasn't doing anything, just standing there. He was closer than he had been yesterday, and Glen could see him more clearly. He looked different than he used to, Glen thought. His skin was all white and his clothes looked torn and raggedy.

If he was living this close, Glen wondered, how come he never came by? Mom had said that he'd moved away, that he'd gotten a job in another state.

Maybe this raggedy man wasn't Daddy.

But then the man waved, smiled, and Glen knew that it was Daddy.

"Glen!"

He turned around at the sound of the voice and saw his mom standing outside the fence across the parking lot.

"Get away from there! Right now!"

Glen hazarded one last look through the door before leaving. He saw that the mall was empty, his daddy gone, and then he was running back across the empty parking lot toward his mom.

She was furious, her face red, but he thought he saw fear there as well as anger.

"What the hell do you think you're doing?" she demanded. She grabbed him by the arm, gave him a swift hard swat on the seat of the pants and pushed him into the car. "I told you to stay away from here!"

A lowrider drove by, filled with dark faces. "Hey, mama!" someone called out. "Sit on my face!"

His mom ignored the taunt and, tight-lipped, got behind the wheel. She glared at Glen. "We're going to have a serious talk, young man."

He nodded, saying nothing.

They drove home in silence.

◆

Marylynn sat in the living room, staring at the face of the television. A program was on, a sitcom, but she wasn't watching it and couldn't have said what it was. Glen was in the bathroom, taking a bath. She could hear the sound of the water running. He'd been in there for nearly a half hour now, and she knew that he was taking his time, stretching out his bath, trying to avoid her.

She didn't blame him. In a way, she was kind of glad. She still hadn't decided what to tell him and what not to tell him, still hadn't worked out the approach to take. For some reason, she felt uncomfortable, almost frightened. She wasn't really afraid that Glen was in physical danger. He'd lived in the city all his life and knew how to take care of himself. She was more afraid of the psychological damage he might suffer. It might not be good for him to know that his father was dead, but it couldn't be any healthier for

{ THE MALL }

him to think his father was alive when he wasn't. Glen had thought he'd seen his daddy before: in the crowd of a televised baseball game, once turning a corner down a busy street at Christmastime. If this continued, he would soon be seeing his daddy everywhere.

But it wasn't just the idea of Glen thinking he'd seen his father that bothered her. She was embarrassed to admit it even to herself, but it was the fact that he had seen his father in the mall that tinged her worry with fear.

The mall.

The mall had scared her even in the old days, even when it had been open. It had been dying back then, of course. Nordstrom's was already gone and Macy's was leaving, but most of the smaller stores had still been there, and she and her friends had often spent their Saturdays browsing through the clothes boutiques, looking for bargains. She had gone there alone, as well, and she'd been attacked once, in the long hallway that led to the ladies' room—a spiky-haired white boy who grabbed her through her pants and squeezed while he yanked the purse from her shoulder.

It was not the attack that had frightened her, though, not the increasingly rough makeup of the patrons that had made her nervous. No, it had been something about the mall itself, something about the high narrow design of the structure and the angled arrangement of the shops. She had never said anything to anyone about her feelings, but she thought she'd heard agreement with her position in the veiled comments of other shoppers, thought she'd seen understanding in the faces of occasional customers.

She and her friends had stopped going to the mall long before it finally closed for good.

Glen emerged from the bathroom wearing pajamas, his hair wet and wild.

"Go dry your hair," she told him. "And then we're going to talk."

"I won't go back there again," he promised. "I learned my lesson."

"Dry your hair. And then we'll talk."

WALKING ALONE Bentley Little

His mom picked him up from school on Thursday, Friday and Monday, but on Tuesday she had to work late and Glen found himself once again wandering slowly past the chain-link fence that enclosed the abandoned mall. He had dreamed about the mall last night, dreamed about Daddy. Daddy had been trapped inside the hulking structure, and Glen had had to smash one of the glass doors to let him out and save him. Daddy had emerged tall and strong and happy, with a big grin on his face, and he had hoisted Glen on top of his shoulders, piggy-back, the way he used to, and the two of them had run home, where Mom had made a special cake as a reward.

Glen stopped walking, hooked his fingers between the wires, and stared through the fence. He had not forgotten the bad times. He remembered when Daddy had beaten Mom up and broken her arm, how Daddy had told him afterward that from now on he was supposed to call his mom "Slut" instead of "Mommy," and how it had made his mom cry when he'd said that word. He remembered the times Daddy had beaten him for no reason, and how he'd once said that he'd kill him if he didn't stop crying, and how he'd known that Daddy meant it.

But somehow the good times seemed more important than the bad times now. And there seemed to be a lot more of them. He remembered the bedtime stories, the trips to movies—they never went to movies anymore—the basketball games at the old church.

He missed his daddy.

And then he was through the fence and walking across the weedy parking lot toward the mall. He walked up to the same door he'd peeked through the last time he'd come here and pressed his face against the dark glass. From underneath a stairway that led down to the lower level of the mall, he saw a pulsing whitish glow that grew progressively stronger. The inside of the mall, Glen noticed, no longer looked as dirty as it had before, no longer looked as rundown. His eyes scanned the vast interior and there, standing next to a planter of budding flowers, stood Daddy.

"Glen."

"Daddy!" Glen waved to his father.

{ THE MALL }

"Glen."

Daddy's voice was the same, yet different. There seemed to be an echo behind it, even though he was whispering. "I'm glad you came back to see me. I've been waiting for you."

"Me too."

"I want you to come and live with me."

Glen stared, surprised. "Really?"

"Really." Daddy laughed.

"Where? In the mall?"

Daddy nodded. "In the mall."

"What about Mom?"

"Your mom's a bitch," Daddy said in that soft resonant tone, and Glen's eyes widened as he heard the bad word. "She's a whore of a bitch and she deserves to die."

Glen moved away from the glass door, frightened. Daddy was still smiling, his voice still soft, but there was something about his eyes that didn't look right and that made him feel suddenly very cold.

"Glen!" Daddy called, and now his voice was not so soft. "I'm not through talking to you!"

Afraid, Glen once again pressed his face to the glass. He stood there, listening, as his daddy talked, explained things, and the coldness within him grew.

He pulled away only when Daddy said goodbye and the light in the mall began to fade.

She deserves to die.

He closed his eyes, heard Daddy's echoing voice.

Deserves to die.

He ran all the way across the parking lot and ripped the pocket of his jacket as he climbed quickly through the hole in the fence.

He did not stop running until he was a block away from home.

# WALKING ALONE … Bentley Little

Glen brought it up himself this time, at dinner. Marylynn had known that something was bothering him, but she thought that after the discussion they'd had the other night, at least this subject had been straightened out.

So, she was surprised when Glen took a drink of milk and blurted out: "I saw Daddy at the mall again!"

She swallowed the bite of casserole in her mouth, stared at him. He looked away, squirming. He seemed unusually uncomfortable, almost afraid, and she found herself wondering if something more than that might have happened.

"Glen," she said. "You didn't really see Daddy, did you?"

"I did!" he insisted.

She put down her fork, faced him. It was her fault. Again, it was her fault. She should have told him everything last time; she shouldn't have tried to spare him at all. Her heart was pounding, and for some reason as she looked at Glen, squirming uncomfortably in his seat, she felt afraid. "Glen," she said slowly, straightforwardly. He looked up at her. "You didn't see Daddy."

"I did!"

"You couldn't've seen him. I killed him."

He stared back at her dumbly.

"Daddy lied to us. He didn't get out. He was still in the gang. And he wanted to sell you back."

Glen blinked. He looked blankly at her, as though he hadn't heard what she'd said.

She walked around the table, put an arm on her son's shoulder. "I killed him and then I turned him in. I didn't tell you because…well, because I wanted you to grow up thinking you had a good Daddy. I didn't want you to be like the other children whose fathers were killed. And I wanted to make sure you didn't get involved in a gang." She held his shoulders, looked into his face. "That's why you have to stay away from the mall. Do you understand? I don't know who's talking to you, but he's not your father, and I don't want you going anywhere near him. He's probably just a child molester, but…but the mall's a bad place, Glen. A bad place. A dangerous place. Do you understand me?"

{ THE MALL }

He looked at her, saying nothing. She had expected him to cry when she told him, but his eyes weren't even wet. She had expected denial, but there was nothing.

"I killed Daddy. He's never coming back."

"I'm not hungry anymore. I'm going to bed." Glen pushed his chair away from the table and ran out of the kitchen, down the hallway. She heard his door slam.

Marylynn moved back to her side of the table, slumped in her seat. She'd finally told him. And finally, he had reacted normally. She felt tired, drained, as though she had been exercising all day. It would take a while, but Glen would get used to the idea, and he would realize that, in the long run, she had done right.

Or maybe not. Maybe he would end up hating her his whole life.

Either way, she had the feeling that at least he wouldn't be seeing his Daddy at the mall anymore.

Glen stared up at the ceiling of his room. *Dead. Killed.* That was exactly what Daddy had told him she'd say. "She wants you to think I'm dead, Glen," he'd said. "But I'm not. She's always been a jealous bitch, and that's why she tells those lies about me. She knows I love you more than she does. She knows that I can give you a better life and a happier home, but she doesn't want that. She doesn't love you, but she puts up with you just to get back at me. I love you, though. I love you."

Glen thought about those words, and even in his memory they sounded good: *I love you.*

He tried to concentrate on those words, tried to say them over and over again to himself, but other words kept intruding.

Bitch.

Whore.

Deserves to die.

He lay there thinking, not falling asleep.

WALKING ALONE — Bentley Little

Later, after his mom turned off the television, after he heard her get into bed and turn out the lights, he went down to the kitchen—where his mom kept the knives.

◆

Glen stood on the cracked cement outside the mall entrance and peered through the glass door.

"I offed her," he said, and Daddy smiled and the light in the mall became stronger. Where before had been dimness, Glen could now see stores, wonderful stores, filled with merchandise. A music store with racks of CDs, walls covered with posters, cool tunes blaring from hidden speakers. A food store filled with candy and Cokes. A toy store stocked with every game, action figure and model imaginable. Daddy's smile broadened. He held his hands out toward Glen, and the dirty glass door separating them slowly opened. Glen felt cool air, smelled spice and food.

"Then come with me."

Glen walked into the mall. He smiled at his daddy, but the smile was not entirely real. That echoing sound in Daddy's voice was back, and this close it sounded a little bit…scary.

"We have friends here," Daddy said. "Lots of friends."

In the recesses of the mall, almost visible in the bright light, Glen could see dark figures walking in and out of the stores carrying packages, shopping. He squinted, peering more closely, and thought he recognized some of the figures. Carlos Mondragon's father. Leroy Washington's brother. John Jefferson and David Hernandez.

Dead gang members.

Glen looked back over his shoulder. The door to the mall was still open, and through the entrance he could see his mom running across the parking lot toward him. Frightened, he faced forward again.

Daddy's eyes flashed. "You lied to me."

"I couldn't, Daddy! I couldn't!" He stepped backward.

Then Daddy was smiling again. "It's okay, Glen. It's okay." His smile

THE MALL

grew broader. "But even though you didn't kill her, you still don't want to live with her, do you? In that little teeny tiny apartment?" He gestured expansively. "Wouldn't you rather live here, with me?"

Glen's lips suddenly felt dry. Inside, he felt the same coldness he'd felt yesterday when Daddy had told him what he must do. Behind him, he heard his mom's voice screaming his name. Her voice was angry, scared, cracked, crying, and to him it sounded absolutely wonderful.

He took a step backward.

Daddy looked sad. "Glen?" He crouched down, reached in his pocket, pulled out a candy bar. "I love you, son."

Glen turned around. The door to the mall closed just as she reached it, cutting off her cries. He looked toward his daddy, smiling, clean, wearing a new suit, bending down on one knee, holding out a candy bar, then back toward his mom, dirty, sobbing, hair matted and tangled, face red from screaming, wearing her stained and ripped bathrobe. She looked plain and old and alone against the backdrop of the empty parking lot.

"Glen," Daddy said warningly.

He didn't think. He just ran back toward his mom, away from the pulsing lighted heart of the mall, and he pulled open the mall door and dashed outside into her arms.

"Glen," she sobbed. "Glen." She held him tight, almost hurting him with her hug, but he didn't mind, and then he was crying too.

He looked back into the mall. The illuminated stores were already fading, the tropical plants dying, the merchandise disappearing. The lights in the music store winked out of existence. What had been the toy shop became once again a large empty room dissected by two fallen roof beams.

Glen wiped his eyes and glanced over his mom's shoulder. Daddy stood, pocketed the candy bar and walked away without even waving goodbye. For a brief second before he turned, Glen thought he saw a terrifying expression of rage and hate on that once familiar face. Then the last of the store lights dimmed, and only a weak shadow remained where Daddy had been, and then even the shadow was gone.

Glen hugged his mom.

"It really was your daddy," she said wonderingly.

Glen shook his head against her breast. "I don't think so."

"I think it was."

He lifted his head, looked into her face and decided not to argue.

And with the mall at their backs, the two of them walked across the parking lot toward the car.

HUNTING

(1994)

More than anything else, I think, it was the special quality of the air that I loved, those attributes that seemed to exist only when I was out hunting with my father. In town, we breathed the same air everyone else breathed, but in the wilderness it was only the trees, the plants, the insects, the animals and us, and the air seemed somehow cleaner, clearer, fresher, with an identifiable texture unlike anything I'd experienced before or have experienced since. Sound was remixed, important noises magnified, unimportant noises decreased in volume, so that the wind through the trees sounded like the rushing of a raging river and the words of our infrequent talk were muffled and flattened into nothing.

My father worked for the U. S. Forest Service, so he was always careful to make sure that we hunted in season and obtained the proper permits, but he also knew the land better and more intimately than most of the other hunters in town, and he had an inside track each season on the good hunting spots. No matter how often we went out, though, no matter how long we spent, we never seemed to do much shooting. I can count the number of times we actually bagged a buck on the fingers of one hand. Not that it mattered. Hunting was just an excuse, a pretext. What really mattered was being out there, my father and me, alone in the wilderness. It was the ritual of hunting that was important—the hiking, the making of camp, the cleaning of the rifles, the stalking of the prey—not the actual act of killing itself.

{ WALKING ALONE } Bentley Little

More often than not, despite our grand plans and stated goals, we'd end up flushing grouse and, on the last afternoon of our last day, shooting enough to justify the time we'd spent hunting—packing the birds in our by-now-empty ice chest and lugging it back to the truck. My mother always exclaimed over our haul, and I was never sure if she was legitimately impressed with what we'd brought back or if she was just playing along with us. Either way, she'd pluck and cook the game birds, and we'd end up eating them.

I was eleven I guess, eleven or twelve, when my father invited Gary Knox to hunt with us. The Knoxes were friends of my parents, the only friends my parents had, really, and they used to come over about once a month for dinner and bridge, and sometimes the four of them would go out somewhere, getting all dressed up, leaving me with a babysitter. I think I resented my father a little for inviting Gary Knox into what had been, until now, our own private world, but I said nothing.

The difference was obvious almost immediately. We never talked much on our trips, my father and I. We never talked much anyway. We didn't have to. It wasn't until later, when I was older, when I read about it in books and saw it in movies and on TV, that I learned that we were supposed to talk, that we were supposed to act like friends. Back then, he was the father and I was the son and we went hunting and didn't talk much and both of us thought that we were having a good time and that this was the way things were supposed to be.

But Gary Knox was a talker. He talked on the drive up the Forest Service trail, he talked while we unpacked the truck and divided up the gear, he talked while we hiked up and over the hills. I don't know what all he talked about, but it seemed boring and pointless and entirely inappropriate to me, and I found myself hanging back from the two of them as we hiked along the path that would lead us to our campsite.

We walked for over two and a half hours, Gary Knox talking all the while about work or something he'd read in the newspaper or some other subject that interested him. He seemed to pay no attention whatsoever to the land around us. We moved from scrub oak to ponderosa, the trail transforming from dirt to rock as we climbed Cook's Mountain and skirted the canyon

HUNTING

on its west side. We passed dripping black stains on the side of the cliff, plant rot that had been transformed into distinctive geologic markings, and we looked out at low clouds that made the mountains into mesas, capping the canyon with a ceiling of grayish white.

And Gary Knox talked office talk.

I tried to tune him out, tried not to listen, but though I could not hear the specifics of his conversation, I got the gist of it from his tone of voice and it depressed me. He was bringing the real world into our sanctuary. The apartness of the wilderness, everything that I loved most about it, that made it special to me, was to him merely background, white noise, meaningless, nothing. The trip had barely started and it was already ruined for me, and I wished more than anything that Gary Knox had not come with us. I looked at the back of my father's head as we walked, and though he said nothing, I somehow knew that he wished he had not come along either, and that made me feel better.

We made camp in a grove of poplars just over a hill from the river. The two of them set up the tent while I scavenged for dry wood we could use for our fire that night. They worked quickly, and the tent was up before I'd collected my second armload of kindling. Gary Knox offered to collect the rest of the wood, saying he wanted to scout around anyway, and while he went hiking off into the woods my father dug a hole for the campfire and I rolled the rocks to line it. We did not speak as we worked, and with Gary Knox gone it seemed almost like one of our regular hunting trips.

When he returned, he announced that he was going to go fishing. "The river's full of 'em," he told us. "I could see 'em jumping up, just itching to be caught."

My father loved fishing more than hunting, and even though we hadn't brought our poles, I expected that we'd tag along. Especially if the fish were jumping. But to my surprise, my father looked at me and said, "You catch us enough for supper, then, Gary. We're going to do a little tracking before the big day tomorrow."

Gary Knox grinned as he rummaged through his equipment for his fly hat. "I'll catch us enough for supper, breakfast and dinner."

WALKING ALONE — Bentley Little

I stared at my father, grateful, and he smiled at me and winked.

We spent the rest of the afternoon following two trails that wound along the base of the hill and around a ridge. We saw spoor but no game, but it didn't really matter. We were out here, alone, and the air was the way it was supposed to be and I could hear the thunder of the river and couldn't hear Gary Knox's talking, and everything was perfect.

The second trail ended just this side of a sloping meadow, and after the trail petered out we crossed the last line of trees into the grass. Clover was mixed with ferns here, stretching away from us in a natural bowl shape, and the ground smelled as though it had just rained, although it hadn't rained for several weeks.

We saw a doe in the trees across the meadow, standing stock still and staring at us through the low branches. I spotted the animal first, and I was proud of myself because it was the first time I'd sighted anything before my father. He clapped me on the back, and we watched as the doe bolted away from us through the trees.

When we returned, Gary Knox was frying up the fish he'd caught, cooking it on a flat skillet he'd laid over the top of the campfire. He breathed deeply, looked over at my father and grinned. "Smells like a woman, don't it? Ain't nothing like the smell of a woman, is there, Steve?"

My father shook his head. It was clear that he felt uncomfortable, and he changed the subject and started talking about that doe we'd seen.

I took a deep breath, sniffing the air, and looked at Gary Knox, puzzled. I didn't smell anything but fish. I didn't smell perfume or bath oil or any of the other scents I associated with women, and I thought that the reason my father had wanted to change the subject was because he was embarrassed that his friend had said something so ignorant. I knew what that was like. I was friends with Marty Dailey at school and Marty wasn't real quick, and I was always a little embarrassed to talk to him around other people. It was fine if we were by ourselves, but I was kind of uncomfortable being with Marty around normal kids. Maybe my father felt the same way. I myself had never thought that Gary Knox was especially bright.

Or maybe his wife really did smell like fish.

{ HUNTING }

The thought of that made me laugh, and though both of them looked at me quizzically and asked what was so funny, I just shook my head and kept laughing.

We hunted the next day, although none of us got anything. We saw the doe again around midday and Gary Knox shot at it, but he missed and scared the animal off. I was glad. My father and I shot only at bucks, and though my father didn't say anything about it, only pretended to be sorry about the shot, I thought it was wrong to try for a doe.

By the end of the third day we still hadn't gotten anything, hadn't even seen anything besides skunks and birds and rabbits, and on the morning of the fourth we went back to a marshy pond we'd found, flushed some grouse and packed the birds up along with our gear the way we usually did.

Gary Knox talked all the way back to the truck, the way he'd talked all the way over to the campsite, the way he'd talked all the time we'd been hunting. My father talked with him, joked with him, and when we all piled into the vehicle and started back toward town, they both told each other what a great time they'd had and how they should do this again.

The funny thing was that Gary Knox did not really seem to like my father. He pretended to, but I could tell that he didn't. The entire trip, he'd kept getting in little digs when he could, making fun of my father's clothes or his gun or his camping gear, but my father either didn't notice or decided to ignore it, and he said nothing. On the way home, after we'd dropped him off at his house, I asked my father if he liked Gary Knox, but he wouldn't answer me directly. He would only say, "Yes, your mother and I like the Knoxes." I told him that I didn't think Gary Knox liked us all that much, and I asked him why someone would go on a trip with people if he didn't like them. My father looked at me, shook his head and sighed. "Adults have to do a lot of things they don't want to do," he said. I didn't know what he meant, but I pretended that I did and nodded.

I got sick from that trip, sick with the flu, and my mother kept me home from school for two days, feeding me toast and tea, chicken soup and crackers, letting me watch game shows on TV. I was in heaven, and though I couldn't go out and play in the afternoon like I usually did, missing school more than made up for it, and my friends came over with comic books and the homework they'd picked up for me, and I thought that it was almost like having servants.

On the second day, after lunch, after "Andy Griffith" had ended and the afternoon's endless spate of boring soap operas had begun, I was sitting up in bed next to the window, pretending to look at the math homework I was supposed to be doing, when I saw Gary Knox coming up the walk to the house. His car wasn't in the driveway or on the street, and I wondered how he'd gotten here. I watched him, humming to himself and smiling, and I suddenly felt strange. Uncomfortable, and for some reason a little bit scared. I ducked behind the curtains. I'd seen him but he hadn't seen me, and for some reason I didn't *want* him to see me. I wondered why he was coming over. Didn't he know that my father was at work?

There was a cheerful shave-and-a-haircut knock on the doorframe, and I heard the screen open. "Elaine?" he called. "Elaine?"

He was coming into the house by himself! He had never done that before. No one had ever done that before except Grandma and Grandpa.

"Elaine!"

Where was my mother?

"Wait!" I heard her call from the bathroom.

The toilet flushed, and then I heard her running quickly down the hall to the kitchen, her bare feet slapping against the hardwood floor. I held my breath as she passed the closed door of my bedroom, not wanting her to hear me, thinking childishly that if she could not hear me she would not know that I could hear her.

The south wall of my room was the north wall of the kitchen, and I pushed aside my books and scrambled to the foot of the bed, pressing my ear against the wall. I heard the two of them talking in low voices, and a moment later I heard Gary Knox say in a too-loud voice, "I'll come back when Steve's here then."

I moved back to my position by the window at the head of the bed, hiding behind the drapes, peeking out at Gary Knox, who glanced toward my window as he walked back down the driveway. I heard my mother's footsteps

{ HUNTING }

in the hall, and I quickly laid down, closed my eyes and pretended to be asleep. I had a hunch that she was going to check in on me, and I didn't want her to know that I was awake.

She did check on me, and I heard the door to my room open, heard her whisper my name, then heard my door close. I heard her walk back down the hall to the bathroom.

When my father came home that evening, she did not tell him that Gary Knox had stopped by. I had not expected her to, and somehow that made me feel even worse. I kept wanting her to tell my father, to just mention that Gary Knox had been over so that I would know that everything was fine, everything was normal, but she said nothing.

It frightened me that she kept his visit a secret.

Gary Knox did not return like he said he would. Not that night nor any night that week. He did not even call to talk to my father, and though he might have called the ranger station during the day, somehow I did not think he had done so.

The next weekend, the Knoxes came over for bridge. My father and Gary Knox got drunk, and both my mother and Mrs. Knox ended up getting mad at them. I was supposed to stay in my room, but I snuck into the kitchen a couple times to get a drink of water, and I heard my dad and Gary Knox laughing, heard my mother and Mrs. Knox lecturing them.

I fell asleep listening to them argue.

When I awoke it was late, after midnight. I did not have a clock in my room, but the house felt different to me—quieter, colder, darker—and I knew that I was awake later than I had ever been before. Usually, I fell asleep while my parents were still awake, watching TV in the living room, and I slept until morning. But all the water I'd drunk had filled my bladder and awakened me with the need to pee.

I got out of bed and walked across the dark room, opening the door and walking down the hallway toward the bathroom. I'd thought my parents were asleep, the house seemed so quiet, but in the hall I heard the monotonic sound of private conversation. I walked slowly across the carpet, trying not to make any noise. Their bedroom door was open, and I could hear them talking inside. My father said something low and inaudible. "No," my mom said in response, and there was disgust in her voice.

I wasn't sure exactly what they were talking about, but I thought I had a pretty good idea. I wasn't supposed to be hearing this, and I didn't want to hear it, and I plugged my ears and hurried down the hall to the bathroom. I was afraid to flush the toilet after I was through, afraid they'd hear me and know that I'd heard them talking, so I just snuck out of the bathroom and padded quickly back to my bedroom.

I heard my father say, "Do I have to do it myself again?" Then I closed my door and hopped back into bed and covered my ears with the edges of the blanket and willed myself to go back to sleep.

In the morning, everything was fine, everything was normal. Or at least they pretended it was.

I pretended it was, too.

I was sick again a few weeks later, this time with an ear infection. My mother took me to the doctor, then left me at home in bed while she went to the drug store to get my prescription. I was restless, antsy, and did not feel like lying in bed, so as soon as my mother's car pulled out of the driveway, I got up to wander around the house.

I found myself drawn to my parents' bedroom. I had spent a lot of time in their room when I was little—sleeping in their bed when I had nightmares, talking to my father as he dressed for work—but over the past few years there had been between us the unspoken understanding that the room was off-limits to me.

Now, as I entered the bedroom, it was as if I were trespassing on private property, treading on sacred ground, and the guilt and exhilaration I felt as I walked over to the once-familiar bed was that of breaking a long-observed taboo. I sat down on the bed, looked around the room. It seemed different to me somehow, its character changed though the physical objects within it had not.

I stood, walked over to the nightstand next to my mother's side of the bed and began looking through it. Almost immediately, I found a book. I picked up the volume, opened it. It was a book of pictures. Pictures of naked people. Only they weren't just naked, they were…doing things. I turned the

{ HUNTING }

pages slowly. This was sex, I knew, and although I was aroused by the photographs and would have loved to look at them if they had been shown to me by Terence or Billy or one of my other friends, the fact that the book was my mother's bothered me. I saw a woman, smiling, squatting down, holding a hand between her legs. I saw a man standing there with his…thing sticking out. Another of a woman kneeling before a man, kissing him there.

I quickly put the book away, not wanting to see anymore. My hands were shaking. I felt ashamed and sickened and excited at the same time, and it was a disturbing, unsettling feeling. I thought of my mother buying the book and looking at the pictures.

I forced myself to think of something else.

I was back in bed by the time my mother returned with my medicine. I sat up in bed as she spooned it into my mouth, and I wondered if that was what she did during the day when I was at school and my father was at work—look at the sex pictures. I stared at her, and she suddenly looked different to me than she had before. She no longer looked to me like a mother. She looked like a woman pretending to be my mother. I let her feel my forehead, take my temperature, ask me how I felt, but I was grateful when she finally left.

I ate lunch in bed, took a nap, and when I woke up, she was on the phone in the kitchen, talking low. She stayed on the phone for a long time, and though part of me wanted to sneak into the hall and hear what she was talking about, part of me didn't.

She came into my bedroom after she got off the phone, to give me my medicine again, and she sat on the edge of the bed and looked at me for a while. There was something strange about the way she looked at me, and I couldn't tell if she was sad or angry. I wondered if she knew that I had seen her book of pictures, if that was what was making her seem so strange, and I grimaced and held my ear and pretended to be sicker than I really was so she wouldn't get mad at me.

"Are you happy?" she asked finally.

I looked up at her, thrown off by the question, not really understanding what she was getting at. "Yeah. I guess."

She stared into my eyes. "Do you think we're happy? Your father and I?"

I felt uncomfortable. I didn't want to have this conversation. "I don't know," I mumbled.

"Do you think we're a happy family?"

I wanted her to go away, and I scrunched up my face and lay back down on the pillow. "My ear hurts," I said.

She nodded, smoothed back my hair, gave me a kiss on the forehead. "I know."

I noticed, that night at supper, that my parents didn't talk much to each other. They talked to me—or, rather, they talked *at* me, telling me to eat my salad, to eat my peas, to clean my plate—but they didn't seem to talk directly to each other.

Had they ever?

I couldn't remember, and that bothered me. This was my home, these were my parents, we ate together like this every day. Yet I couldn't recall if they usually talked to each other or if they had never done so. It was as though my mind had been washed clean, my supper memories beginning with today's meal.

I pretended that my ear had flared up again and excused myself early from the table and went into my bedroom and went to bed.

We went out again one more time that season, my father and I, this time just the two of us, and it was the best hunting trip we ever had. We didn't shoot anything, didn't even shoot *at* anything, but simply tracked and walked and watched and listened. It was as if we were not intruders in the wilderness but were part of the wilderness, and it felt good, it felt right. We did not see another person for nearly a week, and by the end of that time, our camp felt more like home to me than our real home did, and I did not want to go back.

We did go back, though, arriving home in the early afternoon, and I unpacked my gear in my bedroom while my father washed the car in the driveway. I was putting away my unused underwear when I heard my mother call my name. It sounded as though she was in her bedroom, and I walked down the hall, but the bedroom was empty. The wastebasket next to the door

HUNTING

was not empty, however. It was filled with wadded up Kleenex, so much so that it overflowed onto the floor, and I stared at it. Was it from my mother? Had she been crying? Had she missed us that much? I felt better all of a sudden. I looked down at the Kleenex and, between two wadded tissue balls, protruding from the chaos of white, I saw what looked like a deflated yellowish balloon. I bent down to pick it up, but it was sticky to my touch and I dropped it instantly.

"So now you know."

I turned around and my mother was standing in the doorway behind me. She looked angry for some reason. "Happy?" she said.

I wasn't happy, and though I didn't know what she thought I knew, I wished I'd never looked into the wastebasket. I wanted to tell her that, wanted to tell her I was sorry, but I hadn't been accused of anything and I didn't really know what I was being sorry for.

"Get out of here," she said.

I maneuvered around her and hurried back to my bedroom. I didn't know why she'd called me to begin with, but she didn't call me back or come looking for me, and I stayed away from her for the rest of the afternoon. I saw her again at supper, and I pretended like nothing had happened, but I felt uncomfortable around her even with my father there. I realized that I no longer felt like her son. I felt like a boarder, someone who happened to live in the same house as her.

And I was afraid of her.

The fear did not go away the next day. Or the next. Or the next.

Whatever had happened between us, it had put us on opposite sides, pitting us against each other, and I did not know enough to be able to bring things back to the way they were.

I felt sorry for my father somehow. I didn't know why, but there seemed something sad about him, something that hadn't been there before our trip, and I wondered if it had to do with those secret Kleenexes in my mother's wastebasket. He and my mother hardly talked at all now, were seldom even in the same room together, and I tried to be with my dad as much as possible, to help him in the garage, to sit next to him on the couch, to show him that I was on his side and supported him, but he either didn't notice or didn't care.

I was on my way home from school a week or so later, when I saw Gary Knox's car parked a few houses down from ours.

I knew instantly that he was with my mother.

I stood for the longest time on the sidewalk at the foot of the driveway, not wanting to have my suspicions confirmed but needing to know the truth. I thought of running back to school, of going to one of my friends' houses, of going to the park, but instead I walked up the driveway and, as carefully and quietly as possible, opened the front door.

I stepped inside.

They were not where I'd hoped they'd be—sitting on the couch, drinking coffee and talking. They were not in the dining room or the kitchen. I took off my shoes and walked down the hall toward the closed door of my parents' bedroom. I stood there for a moment, leaning against the wall, feeling as though I'd been punched in the stomach. I could not see them but I could hear them perfectly. "Mmmmmmm," Gary Knox said. "You smell so good."

Ain't nothing like the smell of a woman.

My mother laughed. Then she made a noise like a gasp and a cry at the same time, and though it sounded like she was in pain, I knew she was not. I could not hear Gary Knox at all anymore, but my mother started to moan in a strange rhythmic way I'd never heard before. I knew what was happening, and I felt sick. My head was pounding. I thought of that book in my mother's drawer, that book of naked pictures, and suddenly I hated my mother. I wished she were dead. I wished she'd never been born.

Her moaning grew louder, more animalistic, more disgusting, and I inched away from the closed door and walked slowly down the hall to my bedroom. I thought for a moment, then slammed my bedroom door as hard as I could.

The noises were silenced.

A few minutes later, Gary Knox hurried down the hallway and out of the house. I watched him through the drapes.

{ HUNTING }

My mother did not come to see me.

I did not leave my room.

I waited for my father to come home.

I didn't tell my father anything. But he must have found out somehow because the next time he went on a hunting trip, the last time, he didn't invite me along, and when I asked him if I could go, he stared at me for a long time, and then shook his head and said quietly, "No."

It was not until the next day that I realized hunting season had ended the week before.

THE PIANO PLAYER HAS NO FINGERS

(1996)

It started with a double-cross.

The way it usually starts in Arizona.

Ed Hernandez had paid all of the legitimate fees and the illegitimate bribes, and he'd been promised by Jim Fredericks, the planning commissioner in one of our newer suburb cities, that the project was a go, that he would be the one to get the development. But then the Sunworks Corporation, the conglomerate responsible for most of the lookalike peach and pink condos now littering the desert west of Phoenix, had put in its bid, and Ed's done deal was history. Fees were returned, bribes were kept, and Fredericks and Sunworks were in business.

So, Ed walked into city hall with a twelve-gauge and blew Fredericks away.

That's the way it usually *ends* in Arizona.

Only Ed's a pal of mine, and I didn't quite buy it. Ed had a shotgun, yeah, but he wasn't the type to use it on someone, no matter how much he hated him. And a bureaucratic double-cross sure didn't deserve the death penalty. Slashed tires, maybe. A wife-fuck, perhaps. Petty vandalism and sleazy revenge.

Not murder.

WALKING ALONE — Bentley Little

It was a sweeps week, though, and the local news programs needed ratings, so they made old Ed look like a crazed and dangerous killer, a ticking time bomb that had just been waiting to go off.

I couldn't help thinking how royally the media could screw up the picture of me if I ever stepped in it.

So, I went down to County for a visit. Ed hadn't called me, probably hadn't even thought of me since he'd been arrested, but I knew I could do him some good, and I called in a favor one of the deputy DAs owed me, getting myself an audience.

We met in an interrogation room: me, Ed and his lawyer.

Ed looked bad. It had only been a few days, but he obviously hadn't slept and he appeared to have lost weight. There were bags under his eyes, and his lips were the same pale color as his skin. He walked in with a defeated shuffle, and when he and his lawyer sat at the table opposite me, he wouldn't meet my gaze.

"They rough you up?" I asked.

He nodded silently.

"Inmates?"

A shake of the head.

"Pigs?"

A nod.

"Why didn't you tell me?" the lawyer demanded. "I could've—"

"Can it," I told him. "You couldn't've done shit. Ed's a crazed killer and a Mexican besides. You think anyone in the system's going to have pity for him?"

"We could sue the county," the lawyer said.

I looked at him admiringly. "That might work."

Ed met my eyes for the first time. His face and arms were clear, and I knew they'd purposely left bruises only in places that could not be seen by TV news cameras.

Fredericks had friends with pull.

"Did you do it?" I asked.

"Don't answer that," the lawyer commanded. He faced me across the table. "I don't know who you think you are, but if you expect my client to—"

❦ THE PIANO PLAYER HAS NO FINGERS ❦

"I did and I didn't," Ed said.

"I told you!" the lawyer shouted.

We both ignored him.

"What happened?" I prodded.

The lawyer's face was red. "If you're—"

"Shut up!" Ed shouted at him.

The lawyer lapsed into silence.

"Me and Fredericks had a deal on the subdivision. He screwed me. I was ticked off, so I went out and got drunk, tried to think up some way to throw a monkey wrench into the project and maybe get it back for myself, and the next thing I know, I'm going home, taking out my shotgun, loading it and driving over to city hall. I knew what I was doing, and I'm thinking those thoughts, but...it's not me. Something's *forcing* me to do all this, and..." He shook his head. "You wouldn't believe it."

"Try me."

"It seemed like...Mart. Some of the words I was saying to myself, the way I was thinking, it was like Mart."

"You think it was her?"

"I think she forced me to do it."

"I'm not following this," the lawyer said. "Run that by me again."

Ed looked at me, frustrated by the lawyer's incomprehension.

"He thinks his ex-wife did it," I said.

"Isn't she dead?"

"She is," I replied.

The lawyer's ears pricked up. "Insanity plea?"

"I don't think he's insane."

There was a long, irritated exhalation of breath. "You're *both* insane."

"What if I can prove it?" I asked him.

"This isn't goddamn *Miracle on 34th Street*. You're not going to convince the court that a ghost possessed him and made him kill someone."

"Not a ghost," Ed said. "A demon."

Even I perked up at that one.

"Mart's a demon," he told me. "And I'm not so sure she's dead."

"Hold on there," I said. "I was at her funeral, remember? It was an open casket. She was in there. She was dead and then she was buried."

"But she might've got out. I never told anybody she was a demon. Didn't want anyone to know. And when she died, I was so broke up over it that I didn't..." He took a deep breath. "She told me what to do if she died. There were words I was supposed to say, things I was supposed to do to her head. I didn't do any of 'em."

"But how could she possess you? And why would she?"

He shook his head miserably. "I don't know."

"I'll find out what's what," I said, standing.

The lawyer snorted. "The piano player has no fingers."

"Huh?"

"That dog won't hunt."

"What?"

"It's a dead end. It won't fucking work."

I looked at Ed. "Tell that asshole to shut up," I said.

He turned to his lawyer. "Shut up, asshole."

"I'll find out," I promised.

"Go see Sutton," Ed suggested.

"Why? You think he knows something?"

"Maybe, maybe not. But he was hinting around to me about Mart last time I saw him. I ignored him because I didn't want to talk about it."

"It's a place to start," I said.

"Good luck."

◆

Gil Sutton was working on Van Buren, managing one of those hooker hotels. Probably managing more than that. He'd been legit when I first met him, a buyer for Checker Auto, but even then he'd been borderline, always on the lookout for some scam. He'd been fired from that job for faking invoice receipts and substituting copycat parts for the real thing. The last

THE PIANO PLAYER HAS NO FINGERS

time I'd had any contact with him, a year or so back, he'd been working part-time as a trainer at the dog track, running numbers by night.

I drove east, following the flow of traffic. At the far end of the Valley, the Superstitions were visible for the first time this week, a jagged bluish mass, individual features flattened out and obscured by smog. Time was when the mountains could be clearly viewed any day of the year from any point in the Phoenix area. But that was before all the people and the polluters, before the general public had been conned into believing that the price of individual freedom was allowing power companies to pump toxic shit into our air. Now it was a point of pride. This was the west and we were westerners, and no bureaucrat in Washington was going to regulate what *our* companies did in *our* state. So, we gulped down hot smog and pretended like we enjoyed it because we were too fucking stupid to look out for our own best interests.

I came to an intersection, stopped at the light. There'd been a convenience store on the southwest corner at one time, but it had been torn down in preparation for a new business that had never arrived, and desert had retaken the land. I took advantage of the open space and looked past the empty lot down the row of competing signs until I saw what I was looking for: The Shady Palm Motel.

The light changed. I eased into the right lane and pulled up in front of the motel, parking on the street next to the red curb. A dented green Torino with gray primer patches on its side blocked the motel driveway, and a drunken piece of white trash was sitting on the small square of dead lawn in front of the office, passing a brown-bagged bottle to a shirtless Mexican man. An overweight black woman in shocking pink hot pants and a spangled halter top walked up and down the sidewalk, smiling at traffic.

Looked like Sutton's kind of place.

I walked around the Torino, ignoring the jeers of the drunks and the taunts of the whore, and stepped into the office. The shades were down and a fan was on, but the office windows still faced the sun, and nothing short of an honest-to-God air-conditioner could hope to cut the heat on a day like today.

WALKING ALONE   Bentley Little

A skinny teenage girl with too-white skin and a Squeaky Fromm face stared belligerently at me from behind the scuffed counter. In the small dark room behind her, a black-and-white television was tuned to a soap opera. "Whatcha want?" she said.

"I'm looking for Sutton," I told her.

"He ain't here."

"Can you tell me where he is?"

"He ain't here," she repeated.

"Where *is* he?"

"You wanna room or not?"

I walked around the counter and poked my head into the dark space behind her.

"Hey!" she exclaimed.

I saw the television, an ice chest, a sagging couch, a pile of dirty laundry and an empty bag of potato chips on the floor.

"I'm callin' the police!" she said.

"Go ahead. Ask for Lieutenant Armstrong. He's a good friend of mine."

She'd picked up the phone receiver and was already pretending to dial. She put it back in its cradle. "You a cop?"

"No. I'm just looking for Sutton."

She stared stupidly, and I could almost see the thoughts slowly processing in her head. Finally, she sighed. "Come on."

I followed her through the back room, through another doorway and into a hall. She stopped before a closet covered by a tie-dyed curtain. "Here," she said disgustedly. She pulled the curtain aside.

Gil Sutton was crouched in the closet, clutching a rosary, his eyes closed, mumbling a prayer.

"Didn't know you were Catholic," I said.

Sutton's eyes opened, and for a brief second, an expression of hope crossed his face. Then he shook his head, shut his eyes and went back to his prayer.

"He's been like that since Monday."

Monday.

That's when Ed had shot Fredericks.

{ THE PIANO PLAYER HAS NO FINGERS }

I crouched down so that I was on Sutton's level. "Ed said you might know where Mart is," I said.

He continued to mumble and finger his rosary, but he shook his head rapidly back and forth.

"Sutton?"

More emphatic head shaking.

"You know where she is?"

"No!" he shouted.

I slapped him. Hard. "Where's Mart?"

"She's not dead!" He began laughing hysterically. "She's not dead!"

I slapped him again, and he returned to his rosary and his prayers.

He wasn't going to be any help at all. I stood. Before me, on the back of the closet wall above a small empty shelf, I saw a red diagram. A lightning bolt in a circle. I turned to the girl. "What's that?"

She shrugged. "I don't know."

I pulled Mart's picture from the pocket of my shirt, showing it to her. "You ever seen this woman?"

She let the curtain fall, moved away from the closet. "Oh yeah." She nodded. "I seen her."

"Know where I can find her?"

The girl shook her head. "She was workin' out front for a couple months. I heard she broke off some guy's dick." Her voice lowered. "When he was *inside* her. I ain't seen her since."

"Her name's Mart. Martina Hernandez. She's the woman I'm looking for. You know anyone who might be able to tell me where she is?"

The girl shrugged.

"Okay." I started back toward the front office.

"Wait a minute." The girl hurried up beside me. "Robin might know."

"Robin?"

"That black bitch works out front? She might know."

"Thanks."

"Arn'tcha gonna give me a couple bucks? Ain't that what you guys're suppose to do when someone tips you off?"

"No."

I walked out to the front of the motel, but the hooker was gone. I went over to my car, got in and sat there for a while listening to the radio, waiting for her to come back. About ten minutes later, she was dropped off by some middle-aged white guy in a Subaru, and I got out of the car and walked over. I showed her the photo. "Know where she is?"

The hooker didn't even look at the picture. "No."

"I'm not a cop."

"Yeah, right." She moved away from me.

"She won a big prize. A lot of money. I'm trying to track her down for the company."

"Those stings don't work no more."

"All right. Her ex-husband's in jail for murder and she's the only one who can clear him." I pulled out another photo. Ed and Mart together. She still wouldn't look, so I shoved the picture in front of her face.

She squinted. "Hey, I saw that dude on TV. He's the one who killed that planning commissioner."

A hooker who paid attention to current events.

"Yeah, and he's Mart's husband, and she's the only one who can get him out of it."

The hooker thought for a moment.

"It's important."

"I *might* know where she is."

I took out my wallet, peeled off a ten.

"She was here when it happened, though. I'll testify to that."

"This isn't a court. Was she *really* here?"

"I'll testify to it."

"Fine. Just tell me where she is."

"End of the road."

"End of the road?"

"Where the freeway ends. One of them abandoned homes there. Least that's where I dropped her off."

"Thanks."

{ THE PIANO PLAYER HAS NO FINGERS }

"Hey!" the teenager screamed at me from the office door. "How come she got money and I didn't?"

Ignoring her, I got in my car and took off.

It was hot as hell, and my throat was parched. I could've used a real drink, but I was supposed to be on the wagon, so I stopped off at a 7-Eleven and bought a Big Gulp. There was a pay phone next to the entrance, and I still had some change from my drink, so I called my buddy Cal in the DA's office and asked about the status of the case, trying to figure out if anything new had come up.

He said that Fredericks' body had been stolen from the morgue.

I didn't like that. Even though I was sweating from the heat, I shivered. Something was wrong. I could feel it.

I'd been here before.

"How'd it happen?"

"No one knows. It was there, then it was gone. No one saw anybody come or go, no record of any visitors."

"Security camera?"

"Broken."

"So, is this good news or bad?"

"For your guy? Neither. Word in the corridors is that the coconut's going down come hell or high water." He cleared his throat. "And I heard, third-hand, that Armstrong's running around putting *his* two-cent's worth in to whoever'll listen."

"Let me guess. I should be restrained and prohibited from investigating this because of my affinity for taking on Hispanic clients."

"Well, because you're a 'bean-eating chihuahua lover' is how I heard it put, but I guess the sentiment's the same."

"Thanks Cal," I said. "I owe you."

"You're damn right you do."

He hung up on me, and I stood for a moment in front of the 7-Eleven, thinking. I didn't like the fact that the body had been stolen. And the fact that it had been done so cleanly worried me even more.

A homeless guy, a Gabby Hayes lookalike, walked up and asked for some change, but I shook my head and walked back to the car.

WALKING ALONE — Bentley Little

I drove to the end of the road.

There was only one house left, a condemned pink tract home in the direct path of the new freeway extension. Roadwork progressed slowly in Arizona, so a person could probably squat there for half a year or more before having to find new digs. It was a smart idea if you were homeless, but I couldn't see why a woman like Mart would stoop so low.

Mart's a demon.

I'd been sort of ignoring that part up to now, but it was time to face the situation head on. I wasn't sure I believed what Ed had said, not totally, but I believed enough of it to think that she was no longer dead, that she'd come back and somehow, for some reason, forced her husband to kill the planning commissioner.

It was hot as I got out of the air-conditioned car, but there were goosebumps on my skin. The ground in front of the pink house was graded sand, flat and white, scarred with the big-tread tracks of earthmoving equipment. Behind the structure were twin concrete posts for the raised future freeway.

Mart's a demon.

Was Mart really a demon? If so, had Ed known what she was before he married her? Had he found out afterward? *How* had he found out? There were so many questions I wanted answered, but most of them were peripheral questions, human interest questions.

What kind of powers did a demon have?

That was a real question. I'd asked Ed that before I left, but he hadn't been able to tell me. He knew very little about that side of his wife, and I got the impression that after he'd discovered what she was, he'd done everything possible to forget it. He knew what he was supposed to do after she died, the ritual he was supposed to perform at her burial, but other than that, his knowledge appeared to be almost nonexistent.

Mart had looked human when I'd known her, completely and perfectly female, and I found myself wondering if there were other demons living among us, if I encountered them every day, disguised as regular people.

I guess I *did* believe she was a demon.

⊦ THE PIANO PLAYER HAS NO FINGERS ⊣

I walked up to the front door of the house. Like the windows, it was covered with unpainted plywood, a "Do Not Enter" warning spray-stenciled at eye level.

"Mart?" I called out.

No answer.

I pulled off the plywood, kicked open the door.

The interior walls of the house had been removed and the inside was one huge open room.

Covered with bloody symbols.

I stood in the doorway, staring. Figures and pictographic characters had been painted with blood on the ceiling and the four sheetrock walls. The unnatural and profane renderings, only partially illuminated by the diffused light that filtered around me from outside, were truly frightening, and made me want to instinctively turn tail and run. But I stepped inside, moving to the right in order to let more light in from the doorway. In the center of the room, on a raised tier of dirt, I saw Fredericks' body, laid out in an awkward pose that looked vaguely ritualistic. He was nude, and the shotgun hole in his chest was clean and bloodless. There were twin pools of shadow where his eyes should have been.

At his feet crouched Mart.

The breath caught in my throat.

Mart.

It was Ed's dead wife all right, but I could hardly recognize her. She'd been one hell of a beautiful woman, tall and thin, gorgeous face, *Playboy* body, but she appeared to have shrunk about three feet and was now squat, toadlike and thoroughly repulsive. Enough of her basic facial structure remained for me to discern who it was, but the specifics had been hideously distorted. She looked like a cross between a woman, a reptile and a baboon, and the end result was something simultaneously less and more than human.

Next to her, on the dirt, was a pile of white skin that she had shed.

I tried to remain calm, though I was anything but. "Mart," I said.

She cackled. "I didn't expect to see you here." Her voice was a shrill screech.

"What's going on?"

"I'm going to eat his soul."

"Did you kill him?"

She looked at me slyly. "Who wants to know?"

I met her eyes. "Ed."

The change that came over her was instantaneous. Her smile disappeared, and the expression on her face collapsed into what looked like grief. Her voice, while still rough, lost some of its high-registered screechiness. "Ed?" she said.

I didn't answer. The inside of the house smelled, not just of rot and decay and the chemicals of death from Fredericks' body, but of something far worse. I looked at Mart. "You're dead, aren't you?"

She nodded.

"Why did you kill yourself?"

"He was fucking that bim."

"Cheree?"

"Don't even say her name!" The screeching was back.

"He never cared about her."

"I caught them!"

"He loved you. Still does."

"Bullshit!"

"Then why didn't he cut off your head and do all those other things to make sure you didn't come back?"

"Stupidity."

"Love." I looked at her. "That bitch was a one-off. She threw herself at him, he was weak, and he caved. But he never saw her again. You were his real love, his true love."

"And look at me now."

My eyes moved from her snout to her slimy elongated fingers. "That's why you're punishing him?"

"Punishing him?" She stood to her full height. "I've been watching out for him. I've been helping him. How do you think he got that deal in the first place?" She kicked Fredericks' corpse. "And when our buddy here sold him out, who do you think made sure he got what was coming to him?"

⦃ THE PIANO PLAYER HAS NO FINGERS ⦄

My fear was gone. I walked forward, into the center of the house. It all seemed so…petty. Demons were supposed to have cosmic goals, incomprehensible intentions beyond the ken of us mere mortals. But she'd done all this because Fredericks had fucked up her ex-husband's business plans.

She really had loved him, still did, perhaps, and I appealed to that. "You didn't help him. He's taking the fall."

Her emotions downshifted again. "I didn't know it would be him. The spells aren't that specific. They focus on the end, not the means. That's left up to the discretion of the intermediary."

"Who was the intermediary?"

"I don't know."

"Isn't there a way to find out?"

She shook her head.

"Ed's in jail," I said softly, "and he'll probably get the death penalty."

"I'll kill them all! I'll explode their heads! I'll—"

I sighed. "Just get him out of it."

"I can't."

"Why not?"

"That's not the way it works."

"Not the way *what* works?"

"Magic."

I shut up. I was out of my depth here, and I knew it. I watched her face as she thought things through. I'd laid out the scenario, and she knew what was going down. She also knew what could and couldn't be done. If either of us was going to figure a way to get Ed out of this, it would have to be her.

A black tear rolled down her discolored cheek. Angrily, she kicked Fredericks' body. "It's all your fault!" she screamed. "I'll eat your soul and shit it into hell!"

I looked down at the corpse. On Fredericks' chest was carved a lightning bolt in a circle.

The same symbol I'd seen in Sutton's closet.

"Could it be Sutton?" I asked.

She looked up sharply, eyes narrowing. "What?"

"Gil Sutton. Could he be the intermediary?"

She shook her head.

I pointed down at the symbol. "I saw that in his closet, on the wall. He was hiding in there, praying, scared out of his wits. Girl said he'd been in there since Monday, the day of the shooting."

"That son of a bitch." Mart was suddenly all business. She motioned toward the open door. "Shut that thing. I need darkness."

"Why?"

"For what I'm going to do."

"What *are* you going to do?"

She looked at me, and in those beady eyes I saw traces of the old Mart, the human Mart, but her voice when she spoke was flat and cold and even more monstrous than it had been before. A chill surfed down my spine. "You don't want to know."

She was right. I *didn't* want to know.

But I had to know.

"What?" I said.

"He did it on purpose," Mart mumbled, talking more to herself than me. "He put me into Ed on purpose. I knew he dabbled, but I didn't think he could be an intermediary…" She trailed off.

"Tell me what happened."

"I went out with Gil. A long time ago. Back in Tucson. He even asked me to marry him. This was way before I met Ed. I never told Gil what I was, but he knew anyway, somehow, and I think that's why he wanted me." She sighed, a gruff inhuman sound. "I *think*. Maybe not. Who knows? He said he loved me and maybe he did. He followed me to Phoenix. He kept in contact. I think he might've been behind the obscene phone calls I used to get."

"Did Ed know?"

Mart shook her nightmarish head. "I didn't want to hurt him. I let him think he and Gil met by accident. I never let on that I knew Gil from before."

"Sutton introduced Ed to Cheree," I said quietly.

Mart's eyes widened.

{ THE PIANO PLAYER HAS NO FINGERS }

I nodded.

"Now I understand." There was rage in her voice, and she busied herself picking up a handful of dirt from the floor and sprinkling it into the holes that had been Fredericks' eyes. She mumbled something I couldn't make out.

"Why is Sutton hiding in that closet? Why's he so...scared? Because he knew what you'd do if you found out?"

"Because he's an amateur," Mart said scornfully. "He couldn't handle what came with being an intermediary."

"What are you going to do?"

She used one long fingernail to draw blood from her misshapen chest. "I'm going to set things right." The fingernail drew a pattern on Fredericks' feet.

"What's that mean?"

"I'm going to get Ed out of this. And I'm not going to use an intermediary."

"So..."

"I won't survive," she said flatly. "Neither will Gil."

I didn't know how to respond. She was going to do what she was going to do, no matter what I said, but I'd been conditioned by movies and books and family and society to think it was my obligation to try and talk her out of it, to tell her that she shouldn't go through with her plans.

Instead, I said, "You'd do that for Ed?"

"I love him," she said simply.

"Do it," I told her.

She was moving her hands in the air, making strange motions that seemed nonsensical but nevertheless spoke to me and chilled me to the bone. Fredericks' corpse was shaking slightly, as though going into convulsions, and I could feel the vibrations in my gut. I backed toward the door. "I'll tell him," I said. "I'll tell him what you did."

Mart looked at me. "Don't."

It was the last human word she spoke, and I hurried out of the house and across the sand to my car. Outside, it was light, but the influence of Mart's lair stretched even to here, and the air felt strange, thick, heavy.

I got in the car and sped away.

Demons, spells and a love quadrangle.

WALKING ALONE — Bentley Little

They'll fuck things up every time.

The Shady Palm wasn't really on my way back downtown, but I went by anyway. Even before I turned onto Van Buren, I saw the smoke. Sure enough, the motel was in flames, Squeaky Fromm screaming out front, the hooker trying to pull her away from the blaze. In the distance, I heard the sound of sirens.

I didn't even slow down as I passed the site. I just kept driving.

By the time I reached the County complex, it had all been taken care of. The paperwork, everything. I marveled at the extent of it. The cops who let Ed out were apologetic and deferential. The reporters who two days ago had been calling for Ed's execution were now bullying County officials, asking how a miscarriage of justice like this could occur. Even that racist asshole Armstrong was being conciliatory. The entire world had reconformed to Mart's dictates, and the history of the past several days had been scratched and rewritten. This magic was some damn powerful stuff, and I wondered how much of this went on without me knowing about it, how many times a week the reality around me was reconfigured without my knowledge.

As near as I could gather, Sutton was now believed to have committed the murder. He'd burned down the motel and killed himself out of remorse when he found that the planning commissioner's death was being blamed on his old friend Ed Hernandez.

On the development front, the Sunworks Corporation was out and Ed was back in business. Only Ed had never been out of business. In this brave new world, he had gotten the contract fair and square, and Sunworks had never even bid on the project.

I thought of Mart, debating whether or not to tell Ed what had happened. He deserved to know, I thought, and I decided to give him a bare bones outline but spare him the hurtful details. There was no need to describe what Mart had become after death, what she looked like in demon form, and I thought it was best to let him live with his old image of her.

I met him inside, while he was collecting his belongings, and we stood for a few minutes in the vestibule, away from the reporters and the lawyers and the administrators and the cops. I told him that Mart *had* been alive, that she had used him to kill Fredericks, but that she had done so in order to

{ THE PIANO PLAYER HAS NO FINGERS }

avenge the wrong the planning commissioner had perpetrated on him. She hadn't known he would be involved, though, and she had sacrificed herself to free Ed once she found out.

I made no mention of Sutton.

Ed nodded, said nothing. I knew he still had questions, but he didn't really want to know the answers and I sure as hell didn't want to tell him.

"Thanks," he told me. "Thanks for everything."

"What are friends for?" We walked outside, down the steps to the sidewalk. "I guess the piano player *does* have fingers," I said.

He looked up at the hot blue sky, looked at me and smiled sadly. "Yeah," he said. "I guess he does."

THE MAN WHO WATCHED CARTOONS

(1999)

The Smurfs were on. Watering the lawn, Marilyn could hear the bastardization of classical music which served as the soundtrack to the blue creatures' lives, the tunes coming from both her own house and from the open window of Mr. Gault's next door. She hated the Smurfs, had hated them while she was growing up and hated them even more now that reruns had been recycled on cable for her daughter's consumption. *Bugs Bunny* was fine, as were *The Jetsons*, *The Flintstones* and *Tom and Jerry*. Even some of the newer ones were okay.

But *The Smurfs* grated on her. She hated the monotony of the voices, the monotony of the animation, the monotony of the stories. Jenny loved the cartoon, however, and Marilyn reluctantly allowed her daughter to watch it.

She wasn't sure why Mr. Gault tuned in the cartoon. Movies were being broadcast on other channels, sports were on…there were other things he could have been watching.

But he, too, liked *The Smurfs*. He liked cartoons in general, she noticed. After his stroke last year, he had become partially paralyzed, and it was difficult for him to move around. When he did come outside, it was at his wife's side and in his wheelchair. More and more, however, he stayed inside, watching TV, watching cartoons.

WALKING ALONE — Bentley Little

Watching the damn *Smurfs*.

A commercial came on, and Jenny stuck her head out the side window of the living room.

"Hi!" she called out to Mr. Gault.

The old man responded with a throaty chuckle. "Hi there, sprout!"

A second later, the screen door banged open, and Jenny came racing out the front of the house. "Can I go to Mr. Gault's?" she asked breathlessly. "He's watching cartoons, too, and he has a bigger TV."

Marilyn laughed. "All right," she said. "But you come back when *The Smurfs* are over. Don't tire out Mr. Gault. He needs his rest."

Jenny was off and running after "All right," and Marilyn called after her, "Slow down! You'll trip!"

The girl did not slow down, however, but rushed next door so she'd be seated in front of the television before the commercial ended. Marilyn waited a moment, and as she heard no scream or cry or panicked outburst, she assumed Jenny had made it safely to the Gaults' couch.

Marilyn moved over to water the tulips that marked the border of the two yards. Warm weather had caused the bulbs to bloom early this year, and though tulip season was just starting, hers were in full blossom. She switched hands, moving the hose from her left to her right, and checked her watch. Ten o'clock. Stepping forward, she heard Jenny's high thin laugh and Mr. Gault's low rough voice below the noise of the cartoon. She smiled, moving closer, pulling the hose with her until she was between the two houses and almost under the window.

"Damn," Jenny said.

Marilyn stopped.

"Bitch."

Her mind went blank, and it felt as though someone had punched her in the stomach. Her first thought was that she had not heard correctly, that her mind or her ears had transformed perfectly innocent words into profanity, but when she heard her daughter's high voice say, "Damn the bitch to hell," that rationalization went out the window.

⦃ THE MAN WHO WATCHED CARTOONS ⦄

She looked up at the Gaults' house. She and David never swore in front of their daughter, and they did not take Jenny to movies in which profanity was used. Even her television viewing was closely monitored.

Mr. Gault said something she could not quite catch.

"My ass," Jenny said.

Mr. Gault laughed.

Marilyn dropped the hose and hurried as quickly as she could over the tulip barrier and up the porch steps of her neighbors' house. She stormed inside without knocking, saw her daughter and the old man seated side-by-side on the couch in front of the television. "What are you teaching my daughter?" she demanded.

The old man looked up at her innocently. "What do you mean, Marilyn?"

"I heard what she was saying!" She motioned to Jenny. "Get over here! Now!"

"Damn," Jenny said, scooting off the couch.

Marilyn's eyes widened, and she was afraid her voice would crack. "What did you say?"

"That's what a beaver builds," Mr. Gault offered.

Jenny grinned. "Beaver!"

The old man chuckled. "That's right. Now what do we call a boy chicken, a rooster?"

"A cock!" the girl said, laughing.

"A cat?"

"Pussy! Pussy, pussy, pussy!"

"We're going," Marilyn said, grabbing her daughter's hand. She was shaking, with fear as well as anger, and she wanted to get out of this house as quickly as possible so she could think, so she could decide how to deal with this. Jenny's little hand seemed warm in hers, and as they walked out on the porch and onto the lawn, she realized that she was mad at her daughter. She was afraid for Jenny, but she was angry with her as well, and the second they stepped onto their own lawn, she stopped walking and looked down at the girl. "What were you doing in there?" she demanded.

"Watching cartoons."

"I heard what you were saying."

Jenny shrugged.

"Did Mr. Gault teach you those words?"

"What words?"

Marilyn could feel her anger rise. "Don't play games with me, young lady. You know very well what words."

"Pussy?"

"That's a bad word. I don't want to ever hear you say that again."

"What's bad about it?"

"Did Mr. Gault teach you that word?"

Jenny looked up at her innocently. "Are all pussies hairy?"

"That's it." Marilyn grabbed her arm. "We're going to talk to your father."

"Why?"

"You know why."

"Why?"

Marilyn did not bother to answer. She was angry with her daughter, but she realized that a lot of that was probably displaced. It was toward Mr. Gault that her feelings were really directed. She wanted to kill the old man. Underneath his guise of kindly neighborhood invalid, he was a pervert, probably a pedophile. God knew how long this had been going on or how many other neighborhood children had been corrupted. She didn't know if she had legal recourse, if she could have him arrested, but she was damn sure going to talk to David and make sure they did *something* to punish the sicko.

They walked up the porch. Jenny was starting to get worried. "Are you really going to tell Daddy?"

"Yes."

"Tell him what?"

"I'm going to tell your father what you said."

"What did I say?"

"You know."

"Pee?" she said. "Cock? Pussy?"

Marilyn's mouth grew tight. They stepped into the family room, where David was watching a game on TV. "Shut that off," she told him.

{ THE MAN WHO WATCHED CARTOONS }

He must have sensed the seriousness in her tone, because he used the remote to turn off the set without question. He stood. "What is it?"

She told him, explaining how she'd been watering and had allowed Jenny to go next door to watch cartoons with Mr. Gault and how she'd overheard their daughter spouting obscenities. David seemed incredulous, particularly when she described the almost gleeful way in which the old man had goaded Jenny into saying even more nasty words in front of her.

Still, the two of them had always presented a united front in dealings with their daughter, and David looked stern. "Is this true, Jenny?"

"I don't know what Mommy's talking about." The girl's eyes brimmed with tears. "I was watching *The Smurfs* with Mr. Gault and Mommy started screaming at me and dragged me out."

"She knows exactly what I'm talking about, and I don't know why she's covering for that old pervert, but that just proves how much influence he has over her. It scares the hell out of me, David, and if you were there and heard what I heard, you'd be scared, too."

"I didn't do anything," Jenny cried. She stamped her foot in frustration.

Marilyn whirled to face her. "One more lie like that, young lady, and you won't be leaving your room for a month!"

"Marilyn..." David said. It was clear that he did not believe her, that he wanted to discuss this in private, away from Jenny, but Marilyn could not allow the girl to see this as any kind of victory, could not allow her daughter to think that she could do something wrong and get away with it by lying.

Marilyn leaned forward. "Do you know what she said right before we walked into this room?" She whispered in David's ear: "Pee. Cock. Pussy."

Jenny obviously overheard, and she looked innocently up at her father, wiping the tears from her eyes. "Peacock," she said. "It's a bird. A bird with a pretty tail."

"What about the other word?" Marilyn demanded.

"Pussy? What's wrong with that? What's so bad about a pussycat?"

David smiled at Jenny. "You go and play, sweetie. Mommy and Daddy need to talk."

The girl turned away, and David lowered his voice. "You should be ashamed of yourself." He glared at Marilyn. "You have a dirty mind." His jaw was set; she could see the pulsing of agitated muscles on the side of his face as he gritted his teeth.

"I know what I heard."

He strode out of the room, saying nothing more, and Marilyn quickly hurried after him.

"Eat me," Jenny said softly behind her. "Eat my beaver."

Marilyn grabbed David's shoulder. "You didn't hear what she just said?"

He shook his head.

"She said, 'Eat my beaver.'"

"What if she did? She's a child, for God's sake. It's probably part of some nursery rhyme or Dr. Seuss story. She's talking about the animals who build dams, furry guys with buck teeth. Jesus, how can you be so sick? She's only a little girl. Stop trying to push her into—"

"Push her?" Marilyn yelled. "I'm trying to protect her from the pervert next door, and you're not doing a damn thing to help me!"

"Damn," Jenny repeated behind them.

"*That's* where she gets it from," David said, pointing.

"Oh, now it's my fault, is it? Jesus, I can't believe this!"

"Then stop putting a sick spin on everything everyone says. You've always been overprotective, and now you're acting just plain crazy. Our next-door neighbor, an old man confined to a wheelchair, is teaching our daughter obscene words while they watch cartoons together? Does that make any sense?" He shook his head. "You're overreacting to things that aren't even there."

"I'm not overreacting!"

He met her eyes. "Yes. You are."

They glared at each other for a moment, then David turned away. She stood there, watching him walk down the hall to the bathroom, before turning around and looking back into the family room.

Jenny smiled.

⊱ THE MAN WHO WATCHED CARTOONS ⊰

That afternoon, after feeding David and Jenny lunch, after seeing them off on a trip to the grocery store, Marilyn walked over to the Gaults' and knocked determinedly on the door. Mrs. Gault answered, and she seemed surprised at Marilyn's tone when she told the old woman that she had to speak to her, alone, about her husband. Mr. Gault, as usual, was watching television in the living room, and the two of them repaired to the kitchen.

She had no idea where to start or how to begin, so Marilyn simply explained what happened, describing how she'd been watering the side yard between the houses and overheard Jenny and Mr. Gault.

"Your husband was talking to her," Marilyn said, eyeing the open doorway to the living room. "About sex."

The other woman's mouth tightened. "That's not funny."

"I'm not joking. I'm dead serious. And I thought you should know."

"You're a liar."

"I'm not lying. That's the truth. I don't know what I'm going to do about it, but my daughter is never coming over here again, and if I ever see your husband trying to talk to her, I will call the police and have him arrested."

"Get out of this house!" Mrs. Gault yelled. "Get out of this house and never come back! You are not welcome here, and I never want to see you again!"

Marilyn was surprised by the vehemence of the old woman's reaction. She'd expected doubt, defensiveness, disbelief, but she was not prepared for this wholesale rejection of everything she'd said.

"Your husband's sick."

"Get out!" Mrs. Gault screamed.

She left, exiting the house the way she'd come in. Passing by the living room on her way out, she heard Mr. Gault chuckling. "Bitch," he said.

That night, she let David read Jenny a story before going to bed.

WALKING ALONE   Bentley Little

The next week was tense. She and David stayed out of each other's way, speaking only when necessary. She knew what had really gone on, however, and she refused to give in, refused to back down, and she could tell that the conflicting signals Jenny was getting from her parents made their daughter uneasy. It was as if she'd expected to have gained the upper hand in the constant power struggle with her mother and had counted on her father as an ally, but was now discomfited because though Marilyn and David didn't speak with a single voice, their mixed messages carried equal weight.

By the following weekend, things had settled down some, though. At breakfast on Saturday, David actually made an effort to talk to her in a normal manner, as though nothing had happened and they were one big happy family, and she met him halfway by going along with it. As she rinsed the dishes before putting them in the dishwasher, he walked past and touched her shoulder, giving her a small squeeze, and she knew that the hostilities were over.

David went into the family room to read the morning paper while Jenny watched cartoons, and after putting away the dishes, Marilyn walked outside to feed and water her plants. David was supposed to mow the lawn this weekend, but procrastinator that he was, she had no idea when he'd actually get around to doing so, and she couldn't postpone her watering just because he didn't like to use the mower on wet grass. Her flowers needed food.

She was disconnecting the sprinkler when the front door slammed, and she looked up, expecting to see David, but instead Jenny was skipping across the lawn.

The girl stopped, looked up at her. "I'm going to play over at Mr. Gault's. Daddy said I could."

Her tone of voice wasn't *nah-nah-nanah-naah*, and she didn't stick her tongue out in defiance, but the result was the same, and Marilyn watched, furious, as her daughter ran next door and raced up the Gaults' porch steps. She was torn between going after Jenny and confronting David, and it took her only a minute to decide that it would be more effective to get David and

⊦ THE MAN WHO WATCHED CARTOONS ⊧

have him hear what was going on in that house. Mrs. Gault was home—Marilyn had heard the old woman's voice—and she was fairly certain the old man wouldn't do anything *really* bad with his wife nearby.

She strode back indoors. "David!"

He was out of his chair before she'd even entered the family room, obviously alerted by the anger and edge in her voice, and the expression on his face was one of quizzical surprise.

She did not even allow him to get out a word. "You told Jenny she could play at Mr. Gault's?"

David frowned. "What are you talking about?"

"You told her she could go next door and play?"

"I didn't tell her anything! I don't know what you're talking about!"

Fear slipped into her heart through a crack in the anger. "Jenny just went next door and told me you said she could go over there."

"She never even asked me. She said her cartoon was over and I could watch what I wanted, so I put on the ball game. I thought she was in her room."

Marilyn turned and hurried out of the house, across the front yard. David followed hastily.

From the Gaults' open window came the sound of that damn *Smurfs* music. And voices.

"Dick," Mr. Gault said.

Jenny laughed. "Big dick!"

Marilyn stopped, turned toward David. "What do you make of that?"

"It's probably the name of someone on the show they're watching."

"How much you want to bet that when we go in there, there's not one character named 'Dick'?"

"Jenny!" David called out.

She rushed to the front window, looked down at them. "Hi!"

"You get out here. Right now."

She frowned. "But Daddy, we're—"

"*Now*," he told her.

She moved reluctantly back from the window, and they heard her saying goodbye.

"We've known Gault for nine years," David said. "That's two years longer than we've had Jenny."

"But what do we really know about him? We say 'hi' and 'bye,' comment on the weather, and that's about it. He could be burying bodies in the back yard for all we know."

"Marilyn!"

"Well. Interviews with the neighbors of child molesters and mass murderers always say they were nice pleasant people, and everyone's always shocked and surprised when they find out the truth."

"I still think Gault is probably okay."

She looked at him evenly. "Are you willing to take that chance?"

David shook his head slowly. "No," he admitted.

"Let's just make sure Jenny stays away from him."

They looked toward the Gaults' porch as their daughter came bounding out. She smiled, running toward them, not a trace of guilt in her face, no indication that she had done anything wrong.

"Jenny," David said sternly. "You lied to your mother."

"You're in big trouble," Marilyn said.

Jenny looked up at her, frowning. "Bitch." She turned sweetly to her father. "That's what they call a female dog. It's not nasty."

Marilyn and David shared a glance.

Without waiting for another word, Jenny ran into the house.

Marilyn wanted to resist, but she couldn't help it. "I told you so."

David nodded wearily.

Inside, the volume of the television suddenly increased, and there was the roar of a crowd, the hyperactive patter of a sportscaster.

"Tits!" Jenny announced, her voice carrying through the open window. "Big giant titties!"

◆

They stayed away from the Gaults after that. It was difficult, living next door to each other and not having any contact, especially since they'd once

⟨ THE MAN WHO WATCHED CARTOONS ⟩

been so friendly, but the anger did not abate, and every time Marilyn looked over at that house, she felt like burning it down. They'd discussed going to the police or putting up neighborhood flyers, but David convinced her that Mr. Gault had not actually done anything illegal, and they suffered in silence. She took to keeping the drapes closed on that side of the house, so they wouldn't have to look at the Gaults', and they both made sure that Jenny was closely watched and supervised every time she played outside. For her part, the forced estrangement from Mr. Gault seemed to do Jenny a world of good.

The bad words disappeared from her vocabulary, and the defiant yet secretive attitude Marilyn had sensed in her seemed to fade as well.

But a month or so later, Jenny was playing with her friend Jasmine in the front yard while Marilyn watched them through the window. She saw Mr. Gault roll his wheelchair out to the sidewalk and Jenny run over to him. It looked like he had an envelope in his hand, a letter of some sort, and that he wanted to give it to her. Marilyn dashed out of the house, called out "Jenny!" in her sternest voice and strode over to the sidewalk, grabbing her daughter's arm. "Get inside!"

"But—"

"Get in the house!"

Jenny ran inside, practically in tears, a confused Jasmine following her, and Marilyn turned to face the old man on the sidewalk. "You are not to speak to my daughter again, do you understand? If you so much as look in her direction, I'll have you in jail so fast your head will be spinning."

He swiveled his chair and wheeled away from her. She thought she heard a muttered "Cunt," but he was already moving quickly up the walk the way he'd come, and she turned, heading back across her own yard and inside.

She sent Jasmine home, and she and David had a talk with Jenny about how she knew she was not to see Mr. Gault anymore and how important it was that she follow that rule. Jenny seemed to understand, but Marilyn could not help thinking about how enthusiastically the girl had run over to Mr. Gault, how she had seemed ready to take the envelope from the old man.

That afternoon, David took Jenny to the park. On an impulse, Marilyn went into the girl's room and started searching through her desk and toybox and bookcase and belongings. She doubted that this was the first time the old pervert had tried to contact their daughter, and while she didn't know exactly what she was looking for, she had no doubt that she would find some type of evidence that Mr. Gault had secretly communicated with Jenny.

There was nothing in the toybox, nothing in the bookcase. She sorted through the top drawer of the dresser, the second drawer, the third.

She found it in the bottom drawer.

Proof.

It had not been her imagination, she had not been overreacting. He *was* after her.

Marilyn took out of her daughter's drawer a small garter belt and baby black lace bra. The pounding of her heart overrode all other sounds, the heat of hatred flushed her skin. It felt as though her insides had been scooped out. She felt empty, hollow, and in terrible pain, and without thinking, without even realizing what she was doing or what she was *planning* to do, she grasped the child-sized lingerie and stormed out of the house, walking up the Gaults' porch and into their house.

As always, the door was unlocked. She had no idea where Mrs. Gault was, didn't even care, but Mr. Gault was right where she'd known he'd be, in front of the television, watching cartoons, and she pushed him with all of her strength, knocking him out of his wheelchair and onto the floor. She was still gripping the garter belt and bra in her right hand, and with her left she instinctively grabbed a throw pillow off the couch and dropped to her knees, straddling the old man's chest.

She placed the pillow over the bastard's face and pressed down on both sides of his thin head. He seemed stunned, didn't appear to know for a second what was happening, didn't move, but then he was wildly thrashing, kicking out with his bony old legs, punching with his ancient arms, jerking his entire body in a futile effort to escape death. She could feel his screams more than hear them, desperately unbridled cries that came from deep within his diaphragm but were effectively muffled by the pillow.

He died. It took longer than she thought, and almost all of her strength was drained by the time he finally kicked his last, but eventually she extinguished the life of the sicko who had corrupted her daughter.

┥ THE MAN WHO WATCHED CARTOONS ┝

She was still not thinking right, still not thinking straight. She knew that, was aware of it on some sublevel, but the knowledge seemed filtered, disassociated, and it did not really connect with her. She had just killed her next-door neighbor, and if she was behaving rationally she would have thought of a way to make it look like an accident or self-defense or try in some way to deflect blame from herself, but she did not even bother to check if his wife was in another room. She simply stood, left the pillow, garter belt and bra in place and, in a kind of daze, wandered out of the house.

Back home, back in Jenny's room, behaving as if nothing out of the ordinary had happened, as though she had merely taken a short bathroom break, Marilyn continued searching through the bottom drawer of her daughter's dresser. There was nothing out of the ordinary here, but when she started rummaging through the contents of the girl's desk, she found, underneath a stack of *Hello Kitty* stationary, a full-color Frederick's of Hollywood catalog.

Marilyn picked up the glossy bulletin. What fell out was a lingerie order form.

Filled out in Jenny's sloppy childish hand.

She started tearing up the room, going through everything, searching for other hidden evidence that Mr. Gault had been corrupting her daughter, exploiting the little girl's innocence for his own perverted ends.

She was not prepared for what she found.

Underneath Jenny's mattress, next to a foil-wrapped condom, was a crumpled list, on which she'd written the names of several men on the block. Mr. Gault's and Mr. Kreski's names had red stars next to them, and Marilyn recalled with a sudden twist in her guts that before she'd had a falling out with the Kreski twins, Jenny used to sleep over at their house quite often, and that she'd spoken enthusiastically about how nice their father was.

Maybe it hadn't been Mr. Gault after all.

She hated herself for having such a thought, but once there it would not go away, and a cold chill gripped Marilyn's heart.

The front door opened. "We're back!" David announced.

⊦ WALKING ALONE ⊣   Bentley Little

Stunned, Marilyn shuffled out of her daughter's bedroom. David did not even seem to see her as he moved past her in the hallway and flipped the light on in the bathroom, shutting the door behind him.

Marilyn went into the living room, moving past the sofa, past the coffee table. Glancing out the open window, she saw her daughter talking to Mr. Miller, the retired computer programmer from up the street.

Mr. Miller, Marilyn recalled, was another name on the list.

She stepped back from the window, not wanting to be seen, suddenly conscious of the fact that she was *afraid* of letting Jenny see her. She grabbed the curtain, peeked around the edge.

Outside, Jenny looked around to make sure that no one was about. Satisfied that she was unobserved, she smiled slyly up at the old man.

"I'll show you my pussy," she said, "if you show me your cock."

APT PUNISHMENT

(2016)

"**I'd rather saw** off Mommy's legs than eat another ranch biscuit," I proclaimed.

So that's exactly what Father made me do.

BLACK FRIDAY

(2016)

"What's the total?"
"One dead, six injured."
"That's it?"
"Apparently."
"There were no—"
"No."
The police chief exhaled in relief. "Thank God," he said.
"A good year."
"Yes."

Donald and Cat arrived without warning.

The plan had been to have a quiet Thanksgiving by themselves, and they'd almost pulled it off. Zac's parents were going to spend the holiday with his brother's family in Michigan this year, and Aviva's mom and dad had for some reason decided to take a Caribbean cruise for the week. So, traditions were out the window, and their plan was to order take-out Chinese food and stay in all day watching the *Twilight Zone* marathon. "I can't think of a more American way to spend Thanksgiving," Zac said.

{ WALKING ALONE }   Bentley Little

Then Donald and Cat stopped by.

It was the day before the holiday, so technically they could have gotten away with sticking to the plan, but Aviva made the mistake of inviting the other couple to stay ("You've driven so far!"), and their friends were only too happy to take them up on the offer.

In their younger days, in the 1980s, when all four of them had lived in Milwaukee, they'd been inseparable, but after Zac and Aviva had moved to California, they'd gradually grown apart. While they still communicated through Facebook, actual visits were down to once a year, phone calls not much more than that.

This stopover was not only completely unexpected but completely out of character. Donald was probably the least spontaneous person Zac had ever met, and he didn't do anything without planning for it extensively. His claim to have woken up the other day deciding to drive aimlessly west did not ring true—or if it *was* true, it indicated that there were far deeper problems in their lives than they were willing to admit.

Indeed, Donald and Cat's marriage did not seem to be going well. In the year since he'd seen them, their banter had become sour. What had been playful little digs were now pointed criticisms, meant to hurt, and he found it uncomfortable to be around them.

"It's only a few days," Aviva told him when he followed her into the kitchen, leaving Donald and Cat alone. "They're leaving on Sunday."

That was true, but three days was a long time to spend with people he didn't really know anymore and wasn't sure he liked. Aviva was better at the social stuff than he was, thank God, because he ran out of things to talk about almost immediately. Even with her skills, however, the mood was awkward and often tense, particularly between Donald and Cat, who seemed to take turns sulking and being silent. Initially, Zac hoped that they would offer to leave on their own, but he soon got the impression that he and Aviva were being used as buffers, that their friends didn't *want* to be alone with each other.

Which meant it was going to be a long, long weekend.

Thanksgiving was taken care of. They were all *Twilight Zone* fans, so the plan was still to order Chinese and watch the marathon. But after that...?

BLACK FRIDAY

At dinner Wednesday night, Cat drank too much wine and, in the middle of recounting their trip to the Grand Canyon, said that she'd wanted to take the Bright Angel Trail but that Donald hadn't been "enough of a man" to go on the hike. "Not enough of a man," she repeated, taking another sip of wine.

Aviva tried to defuse the situation. "We actually have dessert—"

"In more ways than one," Cat said insinuatingly.

"Your hole's as *big* as the Grand Canyon," Donald retorted.

"Well, it sure didn't get stretched out from *you*," she shot back.

Zac stood, hastily following his wife into the kitchen. "I'll help you with the dessert," he said, grateful to get away.

"Oh God," Aviva whispered. "Oh God. Why'd they even come? And why didn't they call us first? I mean, it's common courtesy…"

You're the one who invited them to stay, Zac was tempted to tell her, but of course he didn't.

"What are we going to do with them after tomorrow? We can't just sit around while they attack each other. We need to find some way to keep them busy."

"Something touristy?"

"Something."

In bed that night, Zac brought up the two days that stretched before them. "Any ideas yet?" he asked Aviva.

"Maybe. I was thinking about Downtown Disney? Cat did mention that she wanted to buy some presents for her family back home."

He turned to her. "There are a lot of good bargains the day after Thanksgiving."

She paled. "You're not thinking…"

"I'm just saying—"

"You're talking about Black Friday."

He nodded.

"They're supposed to be our *friends*," Aviva said.

"But are they? Really?"

They were both silent.

"I didn't mean that," he conceded. "Of course they're our friends. And we wouldn't let them get too close to the front."

"No," she said. "It's too dangerous."

"They'll stay back. They'll be safe." He paused. "But they'll *be* there."

She looked at him, and he saw the fear in her eyes.

"And maybe they'll see her."

Aviva shook her head vehemently. "No."

"Wouldn't you like to find out?"

"There's nothing *to* find out." She shut off the bed stand light, grabbed her side of the blanket, rolled over and faced away from him.

He knew better than to press her, and he lay there, staring upward, listening to her breathing as she gradually fell asleep.

Zac had suggested to Aviva that they make Thanksgiving as awkward as possible so their friends would get the hint and leave early, but Donald and Cat kept things far more awkward than he or Aviva ever could, and the couple showed no indication that they were even *thinking* about leaving before Sunday. They all liked the food, however, and got through the meal itself with minimal unpleasantness. And the morning they devoted to watching TV was spent in silence, which meant no sniping or fighting. So, under the circumstances, it was probably the best that could be hoped for.

There was a lull in the afternoon, however, when the *Twilight Zone* marathon switched from the classic half-hour shows to the more boring hour-long episodes, and the atmosphere in the house began to grow increasingly uncomfortable. Aviva had advocated for an alcohol-free holiday, but Zac knew he wouldn't be able to survive without a little lubrication, and wine had been served with the meal. Cat had drunk more than her share, and afterward had discovered the liquor cabinet, where she'd liberated an unopened bottle of scotch that they'd received as a housewarming present years ago. She was getting downright belligerent toward Donald, though the rest of them were either ignoring her or trying to change the subject.

{ BLACK FRIDAY }

A commercial came on for Black Friday savings at Wal-Mart. Zac glanced over at Aviva, meeting her eyes. She shook her head no.

He remembered seeing on the news last year that there'd been a near riot at a Wal-Mart store over a limited number of price-slashed flat screen televisions. Several people had been taken to the hospital, and although that had been in some midwestern state, there'd been similar incidents right here in Southern California.

He had worked at J.C. Penney as a college student. He had been in the trenches. He knew what Black Friday was like.

But that was the old days. Before things had gotten so crazy. Before…

He pushed the image from his mind. He didn't want to think about it.

Cat was the one who broached the subject. "Have you heard from Leslie?"

"Cat!" Donald warned her.

She was too tipsy to be dissuaded. "It's the elephant in the room. We're all thinking it."

"No," Zac said in an attempt to cut her off.

Aviva was looking down at the floor.

"I don't know how you guys bear it. The not knowing? I mean, if my daughter ran off—"

"That's enough!" Donald told her, and apparently his tone was sharp enough that it cut through the haze of alcohol. She stopped talking, blinked, then sank back into her chair.

"I'm sorry," Donald apologized.

Zac waved him away.

He glanced over at Aviva, still staring at the floor. That was the story they'd settled on, the one they'd told to friends and family: Leslie had run away from home. It had been unbelievable: Leslie was such a nice girl, so responsible, such a good student, and the three of them were so close. But it was believably unbelievable: yes, she was a good kid, but that was the kind of thing that happened sometimes, and maybe she'd fallen in with a bad group of friends or maybe she'd cracked from the pressure of college.

The truth…

WALKING ALONE — Bentley Little

He could hardly bear to face the truth—and Aviva refused to face it at all. It never left him, though, and those images were always in his mind, permanently etched onto his cerebral cortex.

Another commercial came on, this one for Black Friday bargains at The Store. There was a new generation Samsung tablet on sale for fifty dollars, even though it was supposed to retail at three ninety-nine, and a plasma TV being offered for a hundred bucks.

"You know," Zac commented. "Those are some damn good deals." From the corner of his eye, he saw Aviva's head snap up, but he refused to look at her.

Donald shrugged. "I'm not sure it's worth it to fight those crowds."

"Oh, it's worth it. Friend of mine saved himself over a thousand dollars last Christmas," Zac lied. "Just from one Black Friday sale." He knew Donald and Cat were strapped for cash and he was trying to hit them where they lived. "The Store's just a mile or so away. If you're looking for gifts to bring back to the family, you should check it out. Doors open at five. You'd be in and out before breakfast."

"It might not be a bad idea at that," Donald acknowledged. He glanced at Cat, who shrugged noncommittally. "I'd actually like to get one of those tablets for myself."

"You should," Zac encouraged him.

"Are you guys going?" Donald asked.

"No," Aviva said quickly.

Zac looked at her, then took a deep breath and turned to face Donald. "Yes."

"No!"

"They're good deals," he said lamely.

"It's Black Friday!" Aviva was practically shouting.

Cat snorted. "Bitch out why don't you?"

Aviva turned on her. "Stay out of this! You don't know what the hell you're talking about!"

Cat raised her hands in passive surrender.

"Sorry," Zac offered. He tried to smile. "But, like I said, we'll be back before breakfast."

BLACK FRIDAY

"Fuck you!" Aviva stormed off, and seconds later they heard the bedroom door slam shut.

Now it was their friends' turn to feel uncomfortable, and for Zac that almost made everything worthwhile. He knew he would have to face his wife later, however, and as Cat got increasingly more drunk, and he and Donald silently watched the marathon, Zac began planning what he would say, how he would justify his actions.

The truth was, he'd felt a little tingle at the second he'd agreed to go with Donald and Cat to The Store, a *frisson* of excited anticipation. He'd wanted to do this for the past three years, though that was not a desire he'd admitted even to himself. He had not been there when Leslie had...turned. He had no reason to doubt Aviva's account; in fact, he believed every word of it. But knowing each detail, even from his wife's exhaustive description, was not the same as experiencing it, and there was some part of him that needed to endure Black Friday himself.

Besides, he wanted to see Leslie again.

When all was said and done, it came down to that. He missed his daughter, and he wanted reassurance that she was still alive. He knew she was not the same person she had been, knew from Aviva's description that she had gone over, that she was one of *them*, but she was still his little girl, and he longed to see her face, even from afar. Not a day went by that he didn't curse himself for waiting in the car instead of going with them into the department store. He'd never liked shopping, and it was what he had done a hundred times before, but he couldn't help thinking that if he had been there, he could have saved her, could have protected her, could have held on to her until the wave had passed.

Did that mean that he blamed Aviva for what had happened? Maybe he did, a little. And maybe she blamed him, too. Seeing Leslie again would not ameliorate any of that, but he thought, at the very least, it might grant him a little peace.

Of course, there was no reason to think that Leslie would even be at The Store tomorrow. Or here in Brea. When she'd turned, it had been at a Macy's in Newport Beach. If she were to show up anywhere, it would probably be at the location where she'd gone over. But who could tell? Maybe she'd made her way back.

And maybe he could capture her.

Bring her home.

That was the real reason he wanted to go. It was a ludicrous idea, but that didn't mean it was impossible, and he would not be able to live with himself if he didn't at least make the effort.

That's what he told Aviva when he gathered up the courage to go into the bedroom and face her. She didn't understand. She hit him, she screamed at him, but she couldn't stop him, and in the end her terrified anger turned to frightened grief at the thought that she might lose him, too.

"I'm immune," he promised her. "You know me. I *hate* shopping."

She had to admit that was true, and it eased her fears slightly, but when he asked her to come with him, she instantly shot the idea down. She was *not* immune. She *loved* shopping. And she did not want to be taken.

Dinner was as pleasant as possible under the circumstances, and they all went to bed early. The Store was opening at five, so he set his alarm for four. Before rolling over and going to sleep, Aviva touched his cheek and looked into his eyes. "Be careful," she said.

"I will," he promised.

"Stay back. Don't get too close."

"I won't."

Aviva took a deep breath. "And if you see her…"

"What?" he prodded.

"I don't know."

◆

Zac drove them to The Store in his car. He'd been feeling pretty brave, but his heart started pounding and his palms began to sweat when he pulled into the parking lot and saw the line. The sun was not yet up, the sky dark save for a slight brightening on the horizon, and security lights illuminated a column of people snaking out from the store's glass front, around the corner of the building, into the side parking lot.

It looked exactly the way Aviva had described the scene at Macy's.

There were extra security guards patrolling the property, alert for any signs of trouble, and it appeared that there were enough of them that if something...*happened*, they'd probably be able to handle it. That sort of rational analysis didn't make him feel any better, however, because his gut told him that no amount of uniformed men would have been able to stop what had befallen Leslie.

He pulled the Toyota into an open space, and the three of them got out, walking around the side of the building to the end of the line. In front of them, a middle-aged man and his teenage son were mapping out a strategy to get first dibs on both a new phone and a new X-Box. Zac imagined Aviva and Leslie having a similar conversation about clothes and shoes outside Macy's.

"Why do people from New York say that you stand *on* line instead of *in* line?" Cat wondered. "Especially these days when 'on line' means 'online,' like the computer."

"I was always curious about that, too," Donald admitted. "I mean, we're not standing *on* a line here. We *are* the line. We're *in* the line."

The conversation was inane, but Zac was grateful for it. Talking kept his mind off what was coming next.

Moments later, the line began moving. His pulse quickened. Had they opened the doors early? No. He saw as they rounded the corner that the orderly queue in front of the store had disintegrated into an amorphous mob pushing toward the still-closed entrance, growing as it absorbed the line of people feeding into it from behind. His heart was pounding, but he moved in lockstep with the man and boy before him until the line broke apart, all of them spreading out to join the group fanning around the front of the store. Pressure from behind pushed his body into the rear end of a shapely young woman, who glared at him over her shoulder. He glanced around to see who was pressing against him, expecting to see Donald and Cat, but they were nowhere to be found, and the two people behind him were a pair of elderly fat twins whose eyes seemed to be hypnotized by The Store sign lit up on the side of the building.

This was not starting out well.

With a sense of growing panic, he searched the faces of the crowd for Donald and Cat. There was no sign of either, and he sidled his way between pressed bodies, calling out their names. "Cat! Donald! Cat!"

Suddenly, *they* were there.

As Aviva had described, he felt a difference in the air, an increase in temperature, as though a gigantic space heater had been turned on. He knew what was happening immediately, and he saw them first from the corner of his eye, purposeful movement cutting through the swelling crowd. One passed by him, elbowing people aside, a tall white-skinned man in a long dark coat, and Zac followed in the man's wake, slipping between couples, families and individuals until he found himself at the head of the throng, facing the lighted doors of the store.

Something was shifting in the mood of the crowd. Excitement had turned to aggression, anticipation to something much darker, much more primal. There was no conversation among the people around him, only grunts and wordless exclamations. A fist punched him in the back. He kicked out behind him, gratified to feel his foot connect with another's leg, thinking: *Serves you right, asshole!*

The mob was pushing forward—and then it wasn't. Then it was. And then it wasn't. It was as though he were at the forefront of a living, pulsing being, a single creature breathing in and out, preparing to rush forward at the instant the store's doors were opened.

A line of green uniformed employees within the lighted store approached the entrance, unlocked the doors and opened them.

The screams that greeted this act were deafening, and, as one, the crowd surged, dozens, perhaps hundreds, of people all competing to be first through the doors. An old woman was knocked over and abandoned by the wayside. A stroller carrying a crying infant rolled off to the right as the bargain hunters swarmed past it, heedless. Zac himself was swept along by the wave and pushed into the store. Someone yelled at him to "Get out of the way!" and another person pushed him into a washer/dryer that had two men on top of it, fighting to determine who would lay claim to the half-off appliance.

His eyes scanned the mass of frantically scrambling shoppers.

And there she was.

Leslie.

She had changed, and although he'd been prepared for that, the extent of it shocked him. Rather than the tight jeans, hip t-shirts and sneakers she'd favored since junior high, she was decked out in a designer dress and high heels that he recognized as being Black Friday bargains from last year. Never one to wear jewelry previously, she now had on bracelets, earrings, necklaces, brooches. Her face was almost unrecognizable. Haggard and pale, lined and scarred, it was almost skull-like, and the dullness suggested by her slack open mouth was belied by the hyped-up fanaticism in her too-sharp eyes.

He called out her name. Yelled it. Even amidst the noise of the rush, it should have been loud enough for her to hear, but she remained completely oblivious, not even glancing in his direction as she sprinted past him toward women's clothing. He hurried after her. "Leslie!" he called. "Leslie!"

Did she even remember her name? That was the thought that occurred to him because she actually glanced for half a second in his direction, her attention diverted by his shouting, and there was a complete lack of recognition in her eyes.

Others like her were sprinting past the ordinary shoppers, standing out from the crowd with their pale skin and expensive costumes, with their speed and single-minded focus. What were they? Zac wondered. What had they become?

Someone screamed near the rear of the store. He heard shouting behind him as shoppers got into a fight.

He followed Leslie, who was pushing her way through groups of women battling over sweaters and swimsuits, taking the path of least resistance between shelves and circular racks until she found what she was looking for: a bin of purses that were eighty percent off. She was the first one there, and when another woman came up behind her to sort through the choices as well, Leslie used her elbow to hit the woman in the throat, causing her to fall to the floor, gasping for breath.

Zac reached his daughter, grabbed for her, but she'd already picked out the two purses she wanted and was speeding away from him toward the jewelry counter. He saw where she was headed and also saw an opportunity to cut her off before she got there. Dashing into the main aisle, he was almost run down by a group of men and women screeching incoherently. Donald and Cat were running with the pack, their arms filled with bargains they had grabbed. In their eyes was the same acquisitive fanaticism he'd seen in Leslie. He even imagined that the color had left their skin, although he was not sure that was actually the case.

He ran down the aisle, cut through the lingerie section and reached the jewelry counter before Leslie, throwing himself in front of her, as he tried to block her way. Waving his hands in semaphore style in an effort to get her attention, he shouted, "Stop! Leslie! It's me! Dad!"

She ran over him in her single-minded pursuit of jewelry bargains, knocking him to the floor, her foot slamming into his chest, breaking multiple ribs as her high heel stomped on his sternum.

The pain was excruciating. It was suddenly impossible to breathe; there was no air in his lungs, and when he tried to draw in a breath, it felt as though he were being stabbed with a serrated knife. He tried to get up, but the pain was too great, and then another woman kicked his side. He would have yelled if he'd had the breath, but he let out only a small ineffectual croak.

People were all around him now, pushing and shoving in their efforts to reach the jewelry counter. A fat woman was tripped or pushed and fell down on top of him, followed almost immediately by a small elderly Asian man.

It was over, he realized. He was down, and he wasn't getting back up. He was going to die here.

What's more, he had lost Leslie. He couldn't see her and didn't know where she was. He felt the weight of the crowd press down on him, and realized that Aviva would never know that he had found their daughter. He wished he had called her immediately, wished he could reach his phone now, but people were piling on top of him, squishing him, smothering him, and he could do nothing but wait for the end.

Would this be on the news? he wondered. Would there be security footage of the rush into the store? Would PR people and police refer to it as a riot, the way they always did the day after?

Maybe Aviva would get to look at the security tape. Maybe she would spot Leslie.

The three things he remembered at the end: his daughter at six, telling him that she wanted to be an astronaut when she grew up; Aviva when he'd proposed to her, the way she'd cried, even though she'd known it was coming because he'd accidentally let the cat out of the bag the day before; the way the Sears store always smelled like popcorn when he was a child.

Why didn't Sears smell like popcorn anymore? he wondered.

Popcorn, he thought, just before his windpipe was crushed.

Popcorn.

"Totals?"

"Two deaths, eighteen injuries…" There was a pause.

Too long a pause.

"And?" the police chief prodded.

"Five recruitments."

"Damn it!"

"Want me to put together a press release?"

"Yeah. But leave out the…"

"I always do."

"We don't want people to freak out about—"

"I know."

"Okay, then." The chief looked out the window, sighed. "Five, huh?"

"Yeah. But at least it's over."

"For this year," the chief said. "For this year."

MoNA RETROSPECTIVE, LOS ANGELES

(2016)

The stereotype is that California is a vast cultural wasteland, the tired Woody Allen canard adopted by pseudointellectuals everywhere after they saw *Annie Hall*. But it's not true, it never has been true, and this weekend's program at the Museum of Nu Art proves it. For MoNA is offering a retrospective of some of the best installations and performance art pieces of the '80s and '90s, including several of those famously defunded by the NEA.

DAY 1

It's odd to realize that what was once new and cutting edge is now old and safe, with formerly "dangerous" artists now comfortably middle-aged and taking the work from their glory days on a greatest hits tour to contemporary audiences in direct violation of the philosophies they once espoused. Several of the artists, however, will be premiering new pieces, including Mark Lunch, the artist I'm most looking forward to seeing.

I initially discovered Lunch's work in college. Gay, black and proud, Lunch created pieces that were often violent and sexually explicit. This did not sit well with the university's donors during the Reagan era, and his sole

WALKING ALONE — Bentley Little

local exhibit was actually not on campus but in a rented space nearby. I had never seen any of Lunch's work at that point, had in fact never heard of him, but an article in the university newspaper detailing how his installations had been banned by the administration was enough to get my First Amendment dander up, and I accompanied a group of like-minded friends to the empty warehouse where his show was being presented.

I was blown away.

The most impressive piece consisted of playground equipment constructed from the bones of Ku Klux Klansmen that had been dug up by African American children under Lunch's supervision. The ropes on the swing set were made from nooses that had lynched black men in the 1960s.

The most outrageous piece, innocently titled "Reversal," involved a jar of white men's toes that Lunch had amputated and pickled. As patrons strolled in and out of a small room, he sat on a black toilet and, one by one, ate the toes. "Reversal" ended eight hours later when the toes had been digested and defecated.

Controversy had followed Lunch throughout that period, and he had thrived on it, creating one groundbreaking installation after another between 1985 and 1995. Reportedly suffering a nervous breakdown after the disastrous reception of a piece that consisted of a séance conducted at the Metropolitan Museum of Art in 1997, Lunch had lain low in the intervening years, and rumors swirled about his whereabouts. Occasional accounts surfaced that had him studying with Sufi mystics, moving to Haiti, or living with a Native American shaman, but it was never clear whether those stories were true, false or fell somewhere in between.

This MoNA retrospective is supposed to be his re-entry into the North American art world, and for it he has prepared a new work. I am beyond excited, and I actually arrive an hour early, taking a chair near the front of the gallery, facing what appears to be an upright coffin "decorated," if it can be called that, with racist invectives. I am not the only one seated this early, and within the next fifteen minutes all of the seats are taken, the room filling with pale-skinned young women in horn-rimmed glasses and thin young men dressed in form-fitting black. The usual suspects.

{ MoNA RETROSPECTIVE, LOS ANGELES }

Eventually, Mark Lunch himself comes out to a rock star ovation. He's wearing dirty work jeans and an Isaac Hayes chain vest. He holds up a leather-bound book titled *Quotes From the Senate Floor* and with no preamble begins reading outrageous statements of racism and homophobia as, on the white wall behind both him and the coffin, photographs of the senators who spoke those words are projected.

Two stooped and elderly black men emerge from behind us and walk slowly up the center aisle toward the front of the gallery, a figure in a Ku Klux Klan robe sandwiched between them. When they reach the coffin, they remove the Klansman's robe and there is no one beneath it. A magician's trick. They spread the white sheet over the coffin, and on it is projected the face of an angry white man. Beneath the man's face are the words, "Jesse Helms, Senator (R-NC)."

For the next five minutes, Lunch continues to read hateful words that were presumably spoken by Senator Helms. He drops the book on the floor, then stands there as the two old men, singing "Dixie," take the sheet off the coffin, carefully fold it, drop it on the floor and stomp on it. Lunch walks over and slowly opens the coffin. There is a figure inside.

It's Jesse Helms.

He comes out buck-dancing as the two old men continue to sing "Dixie."

"I thought he was dead!" someone in the rear calls out jokingly.

"He's died many times," the artist replies, and there's a ripple of hip chuckles.

But I'm not laughing. Because it *is* Jesse Helms. It's not an impersonator, someone made up to look like him for the purpose of the piece; it's the racist old fuck himself, and he's not dead but very much alive. *How is that possible?* I wonder.

As a senator, Helms was at the forefront of those trying to defund the NEA in the 1980s, and he got a lot of mileage out of demonizing Robert Mapplethorpe and the NEA 7. But it was for Mark Lunch that he honed his sharpest knives, and now the artist is having his revenge.

Literally.

For Lunch has withdrawn a large knife from somewhere—another magician's trick—and he uses it to stab the senator. The blade slices through

Helms' abdomen as he screams in agony, blood like a waterfall cascading down the front of his crotch and legs. Lunch makes a vertical incision, pulls apart the skin and muscle, and withdraws something from the opening. It is not entrails as we expect but a gelatinous mass that already possesses the semblance of a human form and resembles a miniature embryonic version of the dead senator.

I don't know how this is possible. I catch Lunch's eye, and he knows that I know. This piece will be performed often in the future, and each time, Jesse Helms will die anew, suffering at the hands of Mark Lunch.

The two old men wrap the gutted bloody body in the KKK sheet and carry it away. Lunch shoves the nascent Helms into the coffin and closes it. Before the lights go down and a single spotlight shines on that most abhorrent of racial epithets, Lunch and I share a smile, and all is right with the world.

A masterpiece.

DAY 2

I arrive late, though I am on time. The Reynold Salton show has started early, and I should have prepared for this because it is part of Salton's shtick. I recognize the faces of several fellow reviewers and bloggers in the crowd.

Why Salton is part of this exhibition is a mystery. Trendy in the early 1990s, his work has not aged well. "Skeleton Boy," in which the skeleton of a boy was placed in such a position as to make it look as though it were fellating a department store mannequin, had lost more than half of its peak value by the time it was last sold at auction. It is one of the pieces here today, as is "Chink," a trivial work in which the viewer is invited to peer through a crack in the breastplate of a suit of armor to see a three-dimensional collage of Asian-American faces.

But Salton is performing a new piece, and against my will, I find myself drawn in. The cognoscenti are blasé at first, too cool to become involved with the proceedings, which at the moment seem to involve only the projection of an amorphous black shape on the white wall behind the spot where Salton is standing. The shape moves in a manner that seems organic, however, and

{ MoNA RETROSPECTIVE, LOS ANGELES }

there is something about it that speaks to me. *I should know what it is,* I think, but I don't.

The shape is replaced by text. It appears first as a page torn from a book, then the words are enlarged and turn out to be a list of names.

Our names are displayed. Those of the people attending the performance.

One name—"Agafia Cornell," a name I do not recognize—emerges from the list and grows to the size of the entire wall. At the same time, the woman next to me is grabbed from behind by a masked hooded figure and shoved before Salton. The artist reads a quote, "The piece is a kick in the head to anyone with refined sensibilities." He then kicks the woman in the head. She screams, and he kicks her again. He continues to kick her until she has passed out.

Another name fills the wall: Annenberg Johanssen.

A fellow blogger, he is ripped from the crowd and brought before Salton, who intones, "The lack of subtlety was like being beaten with a large stick," as the hooded figure beats Johanssen with a large stick.

This goes on. Salton is settling old scores, and I don't know how he has gotten the names of all of the people attending the MoNA event, but he has.

Who will be next?

It is of legitimate concern, because it appears that Salton has nothing to lose. *Have I said anything against him publicly?* I wonder. *Have I given him any negative reviews or mentioned him derogatorily in the review of another?* I don't think so, but he is much more likely to know the answer to those questions than I am, and I tense up, waiting to be attacked, waiting for my words to show up and mock me.

Bodies are piling up at his feet. They are not dead but they are injured, and the ones that are moving are moaning.

Several people have left quickly, obviously afraid of what might come their way, but others have arrived to take their place, and one of them, an older woman, is plucked from the crowd, stripped and thrashed on the buttocks with, of all things, a horse's leg, which coincides with the decidedly odd criticism she had apparently made regarding "Chink."

Salton bows, the list of names disappears, and the original projection returns.

… **WALKING ALONE** … Bentley Little

We all recognize it now.
It is the shape of fear.
Sometimes even lesser talents can surprise.
Bravo!

DAY 3

Linda Gash is so popular that advance tickets are required for her performance. Gash creates what she still calls BitchArt, though the word "bitch" has been bastardized into meaninglessness over the past few decades. What once described an angry hostile woman is now used in the popular vernacular to describe what used to be called a "crybaby," a man who behaves like a weak little girl, the exact opposite of its original intent, although how and why such a shift occurred remains a mystery. Linda Gash, however, proudly owns the word in its original form. She is a strong woman, she is angry, and she is not here to be nice to anyone, particularly men.

Gash has been allotted the largest space for her new work, and at first it appears to be a maze. We walk one-by-one through a twisting narrow passage whose walls are made from white-sheeted mattresses. Halfway through, we hear a terrible cacophonous noise.

The sound of women being butchered.

Of course, this is Linda Gash, and when we reach the end of the maze and enter an abattoir decorated like a locker room, it turns out that it is not women being butchered but men. College athletes, in fact, all of whom have been publicly accused of sexual assault. They are naked and lashed to lockers lined up on the left wall, label-maker tape with their names on it affixed to the metal doors, while women in sports uniforms stab them with knives. The men are screaming like women, and that is Gash's point, that we are all "women" when we are murdered, all of us weak and submissive, none of us in charge of our own fates—all of the attributes a patriarchal society traditionally imparts to females.

Against a row of lockers along the right wall, a group of anonymous men in underwear and jockstraps have been tied. Linda Gash herself is

{ MoNA RETROSPECTIVE, LOS ANGELES }

using a straight razor to slice the eyebrows and eyelashes off a crying athlete. Attendees are invited to choose from a variety of tools and weapons spread across a locker room bench, and join in the butchery.

Men and women pick up hammers and screwdrivers, knives and razors, hatpins and tweezers. They begin attacking the bound subjects, creating an uproar of agonized cries.

I am here as a reviewer, but Gash invites me to participate, taking the notepad from my hand and trading it for a pair of shears. "Cut something," she recommends helpfully. I see her looking at the shriveled gonads of the jock in front of me, but that's a little hardcore for my taste, so I settle for snipping off a finger. It is still unnerving—the tactile pressure, the spurting blood, the screaming—but there is something strangely satisfying about it as well, particularly knowing that this man is a sexual predator.

There are ten dead bodies on the floor of the gallery at the conclusion of the evening, and Gash exhorts the women who participated in the event to take a souvenir. Her face is bruised and battered, but I recognize Agafia Cornell from the Salton performance, and I watch as she picks up a football player's amputated nipples. She places them in a plastic bag Gash provides her.

Unique and harrowing, the experience is vintage Linda Gash.

◆

All in all, the MoNA retrospective is a satisfying collection of classic installations and new performances by some of the most recognizable names in the nu-art world.

It runs each weekend through the end of the month.

JORGENSENS' FENCE

(2016)

"**I really like** that new fence the Jorgensens are putting in." Rich glanced over at the house across the street as he pulled out of the driveway. "We oughtta do something like that."

"We don't need a fence," Phyllis told him.

"No one *needs* a fence. But it looks sharp. Especially that kind of white picket deal. It looks like a magazine cover."

"No one else on the street has a fenced-in front yard," she pointed out. "It seems snobby, like they're trying to keep the rest of us out, like they're afraid one of us'll walk on their precious lawn."

He was getting frustrated. "That's not the point."

"What *is* the point?"

"I'm just saying that the fence looks nice. It gives the neighborhood a little class. It might even boost property values, unlike that dirty weed patch the Caldwells have." He turned onto First Street. "I was walking Sprinkles the other day—"

Sprinkles.

Why in the hell had she named the puppy **Sprinkles**?

"—and I saw those fence boards up close. Smooth. Perfect. I don't know what they're made out of—some kind of recycled material, maybe—but I've never seen anything like it."

"We're not putting up a fence in the front yard," Phyllis said.

"Jesus Christ!"

"Don't take the Lord's name in vain."

"As usual, you're missing the damn point. I didn't say anything about putting up a fence in *our* yard. I was just pointing out that it looks nice in *their* yard. That's it. Period."

But, of course, he *had* been talking about fencing in their front lawn. He was tired of every mangy animal on the street crapping all over his grass, tired of seeing those snot-nosed Caldwell kids and their white-trash friends using his sycamore tree as third base when they played baseball in the street. A little privacy would definitely be appreciated.

But he could kiss that hope goodbye. Phyllis had obviously taken a stand against front-yard fences, and only Jesus himself could make her change her mind once she'd staked out a position.

He wondered, not for the first time, what his life would be like if he'd married Joanie Murdoch instead of Phyllis. Joanie had been his first girlfriend, and if she hadn't moved away after senior year, who knows what might have happened?

But she *had* moved away.

And he'd ended up with Phyllis.

They were silent the rest of the way to The Store, and, once inside, split off in separate directions, he to Hardware, she to Health and Beauty.

———◆———

Rich was walking Sprinkles that evening, and he chose to head west instead of east so he could go past the Jorgensens'. As Sprinkles did his business against a skinny tree on the narrow strip between the sidewalk and the street, Rich ran his hands along the boards of the fence. Whether they actually *were* boards was open to debate. The material, smooth and cool to his touch, was definitely not wood; it felt more like plastic, and there was something about its perfectly even texture that appealed to him.

"Hey, Rich."

{ JORGENSEN'S FENCE }

He jumped, startled, and quickly pulled his hand away from the fence.
Ted Jorgensen laughed. "I didn't mean to frighten you."
"You didn't. I was just..." He couldn't think of a way to finish the sentence.
"Admiring my fence?"
"Yeah," Rich admitted. "It's pretty damn sharp."
"Thank you. I made it myself."

Rich was surprised. Jorgensen didn't look like a particularly handy guy, and he'd automatically assumed that his neighbor had hired someone to put up the fence. He looked to his left, toward the gate. *When* did the fence go up? He realized that not only hadn't he seen anyone working on it, but he couldn't recall exactly when he'd first noticed that it was there. No doubt it had gone up in the middle of a weekday when he'd been at work, but for some reason, the image in his mind was of Jorgensen installing it in the middle of the night.

He didn't like that image.

"Where did you get the boards?" he wondered.
"Like I said. Made them myself."
"The *boards*?" Rich said, incredulous.

Jorgensen chuckled. "Oh, yeah. It's a Swedish system. I have a cousin lives in Lund, and he got me this machine that forms the boards out of raw material and cuts them to length. Want to see it?"

He did...and he didn't. Something here seemed off; there was something about his neighbor that didn't feel quite right. But Rich acquiesced when Jorgensen opened the gate and motioned him into the yard, and the two of them walked up the short driveway to the garage. He tied Sprinkles' leash to a faucet on the side of the house, then followed Jorgensen to a small door at the back of the garage. The other man took out a key, unlocked the door, then walked inside, flipping a light on as he did so.

"There she is."

It was an interesting contraption and unlike anything he'd ever seen. Seven feet tall, it took up the entire center of the garage, a smooth boxy metallic device with lighted buttons lined up above two joystick levers, one red, one green. To the right of these controls was a square opening roughly the size of a front-loading washing machine's door. Differently sized glass tubes protruded from the top of the device.

How had Jorgensen's cousin gotten it here? Rich wondered. It was much too big to be sent through the mail. Maybe it had come in pieces and Jorgensen had put it together. Apparently, he was far more skilled than Rich could have guessed.

"How does it work?"

"Simple. You put the body in here…"

He heard nothing after that. *The body?* He'd felt uneasy ever since his neighbor had surprised him from the other side of the fence, had been wary walking onto the man's property, but now there was a real reason for the uneasiness. *The body?*

"The *body*?" he said.

Jorgensen chuckled. "I know. Sounds crazy, doesn't it? But it works, by God. Want me to show you? Here…" He led Rich around to the other side of the machine, and there on the floor, atop a black plastic tarp, was the dead body of a homeless man. Rich recognized him instantly. He was the crazy person who sat on the steps of the post office and called everyone "Steve."

He felt as though he'd been punched in the gut. What had he walked into here?

"Now watch this." Proudly, Jorgensen opened a door in the board maker, taking out a looped chain that he pulled over the homeless man's head and arms. He hurried back to the other side of the machine, and with surprising quiet, the chain and body were drawn inside.

"Come here!"

Rich walked hesitantly around to where his neighbor stood pressing buttons. From deep within the machine came an efficient whirring.

Seconds later, a bundle of boards pushed halfway out of the opening.

Jorgensen pulled down on the red lever. "Done!"

"That was a *man*," Rich said finally.

His neighbor nodded. "Yes," he acknowledged.

"You killed him."

"I did him a favor. He's much more useful this way."

{ JORGENSEN'S FENCE }

"But you *killed* him."

"I didn't come up with it. It's a Swedish system."

"But they can't..."

"Can't what?"

"I mean, in Sweden. They don't *kill* people to make *boards*."

"Of course they do. Why do you think those Scandinavian countries are so clean? They don't have a homeless problem because they've found a way to make use of the most useless members of society. These people are contributing to the betterment of their country. Death gives them purpose."

It wasn't possible. It *couldn't* be possible. But when Rich tried to recall if he'd ever seen a photo of a Scandinavian homeless person, or a street where people were sleeping on the sidewalk, he couldn't. A few years ago, he remembered, in Denmark or Norway, there'd been protests by nationalists over Muslim refugees seeking asylum. He'd never heard the outcome of that, but the problem was no longer in the news. What had happened to those refugees?

Had they been made into building materials?

That was crazy.

Only it wasn't. The proof was right in front of him.

He couldn't help reaching out and running his hands over the boards. They were smooth and pleasing to the touch, satisfyingly warm.

"Lucite flash-sealed," Jorgensen said proudly.

Rich pulled his hands quickly away. "I'd better go," he said.

"You don't have to."

"Yes, I do."

Jorgensen frowned. "You're not thinking of...?"

Calling the police? That's exactly what he was thinking of doing. But there was an implicit threat in his neighbor's trailing sentence that made Rich try to read the man's face.

He could be made into boards, he realized.

And no one would know.

No one would *believe* it.

"I'm supposed to be walking the dog." Rich played the you're-a-man-you-know-how-it-is card. "My wife'll be on my ass if I'm gone too long."

WALKING ALONE — Bentley Little

The unstated implication was that if he didn't return soon, he would have to explain to Phyllis *why* he was late.

The approach seemed to work. His neighbor smiled. "Well, don't be a stranger."

Rich nodded, starting for the door. "Thanks," he said, "for—" He glanced furtively toward the boards. "—everything."

He was not able to breathe freely until he and Sprinkles were back on the sidewalk. He hadn't exactly been holding his breath the entire time he'd been in the garage, but there'd definitely been tension, and he didn't realize until he was out of there how nervous he had been.

How could he *not* be nervous?

Ted Jorgensen had made his fence out of dead bodies.

Just like the people in Sweden.

It was almost impossible to wrap his head around. He felt overwhelmed, and he hurried back home, where he locked the front door before going from room to room, quickly closing all of the windows. He met up with Phyllis in the bedroom.

"What are you doing?" she asked.

"Making sure all the windows are closed and locked."

"But it's hot tonight—"

He turned on her. "All the doors and windows need to be locked!"

She was taken aback, clearly surprised by the vehemence of his reaction, and she stood back as he frantically checked the last of the rooms.

"What's going on?" she said.

"Nothing!"

"Something."

"Let's just go to bed," he told her.

"It's only eight o'clock!"

"Well, I'm going to bed. I'm tired."

She went back out to the living room, but, true to his word, he took off his clothes and got under the covers. Ten minutes later, he was dead asleep.

In his dream, he was on a narrow street in war-torn Rwanda. To his left were nicely maintained homes with perfect fences. To his right were piles of

JORGENSEN'S FENCE

slaughtered African children. In the center of the street stood a smiling Ted Jorgensen, his machine working at full capacity, taking in bodies, churning out boards.

◆

"The Jorgensens invited us over for a barbecue this Saturday," Phyllis said.

Just home from work, his mind focused on going into the kitchen and getting himself a beer, Rich didn't register what she'd said at first. "Huh?"

"The Jorgensens have invited us over for a barbecue."

He heard her this time. "No," he told her.

"I already said yes."

"You didn't even ask me!"

"I knew you'd say no."

"So, you said yes."

"It'll be a chance for you to admire their precious fence up close."

Don't even joke about that! he wanted to yell at her. But he kept his calm. "I'm not going." He opened up the refrigerator, pulling out a Heineken, and headed back out to the living room, where he plopped down on the couch.

"Oh, yes you are," Phyllis told him.

"Oh, no I'm not."

"Well, I am."

"I thought you said they were snobby..."

"Well, I want to see for myself. And I'll be sure to tell them how you want to put up a fence like theirs—"

"Stop it with the fence!"

She stared at him, taken aback by the vehemence of his response. "What is *with* you? What's going *on*?"

"Nothing." He gulped down a huge swig of beer.

The doorbell rang at that moment, and rather than escalate the argument, Phyllis went to answer it. Rich turned on the TV, tuning in to the local news. Behind him, he could hear one of the Caldwell kids asking if he could get the baseball his brother had accidentally hit into the back yard. "Go ahead," Phyllis told him. "The gate's open."

"I'm going to lock that gate," Rich said after she'd closed the door. "I don't want those little bastards back there."

"Why don't you build a new *fence* to keep them out?"

"Enough with the fence!" he shouted.

"Jesus! What's up with you?" Phyllis stormed off into the kitchen, and seconds later he heard the slamming of cupboards, the banging of pots on the stove.

He considered telling her about the fence, about the Swedish machine, about the homeless guy—

Hi Steve!

—but Phyllis was not someone who could keep a secret. She would blab to everyone she knew, and if she did that, Rich was not sure what Jorgensen's response would be. Maybe she'd end up as part of his patio. Maybe they both would.

On the other hand, Phyllis might go directly to the police, and they would find out what was going on, and Jorgensen would be arrested.

It was impossible to say what would happen. Which was why his plan was to completely avoid the man, and hope that Jorgensen and his wife moved far, far away.

◆

They both ended up going to the barbecue.

Rich couldn't find a way to get out of it.

It had been his hope that it was a *neighborhood* barbecue, that there would be others there and he could spend as little time as possible with Ted Jorgensen, but that was not the case. They were the only couple invited, and of course the wives paired off, leaving him stuck.

His strategy was to avoid any subject that might relate back to the machine, to keep the conversation on safe superficial topics, then to eat quickly and leave for home as early as possible. But it was Jorgensen who, after placing four steaks on the grill, walked over to the garage, opened the small side door and motioned for Rich to follow him.

He hesitated only briefly before accompanying his neighbor inside.

To his relief, nothing seemed to have changed. The boards that had been made earlier in the week were piled in the same spot, and nothing new had been added. The machine sat there dormant, and as they walked around it, Rich was glad to see no black tarps on the floor.

"Work's been kind of slow," Jorgensen joked. "I've been thinking about actually going to Lowes or Home Depot to *buy* boards."

The words were music to his ears, but he found himself asking, "What about animals? Can you make boards out of animals?"

"You can, but, surprisingly, they're not as good. People just have all the right elements the machine needs. Unless something turns up soon, though, I'm going to have to pause on my plans for back yard renovation."

Unless something turns up soon.

The man was a serial killer. That was the truth of it, although the thought had not really occurred to him, at least not so clearly and bluntly, until now. Jorgensen continued to talk reasonably, again bringing up the Scandinavian countries where this was supposedly common practice, but the only thing Rich could think about was the fact that this garage was where his neighbor brought the dead bodies of the people he killed.

How was he going to extricate himself from this? The two of them lived on the same street. And now they were socializing! Were he and Phyllis going to have to move in order to break free?

From outside, the scent of cooking steaks met his nostrils, and though it smelled good, the idea of eating meat this man had grilled made him gag. Who knew *what* kind of steaks those were?

"Time to turn 'em over," Jorgensen said, grinning. "Let's head back out."

They got through the rest of the evening without incident. No one mentioned the fence, the machine or Sweden, and conversation remained on the superficial level of gossip. Rich ate too little and drank too much, but they'd walked here, so he didn't have to worry about driving home. Back at the house, Phyllis wanted sex, but he didn't, and she angrily stormed into the bathroom, slamming the door behind her, as he went around the house making sure all of the doors and windows were locked.

He had never been anything other than a social drinker, but during the week following the barbecue, Rich found himself stopping off at a bar near his work before going home each day and downing a few just to "take the edge off." It was the biggest cliché in the book, the rationalization of an emerging alcoholic. He knew this, but he didn't care. Driving home sober, passing the Jorgensens' house, seeing that perfect white fence, made his stomach knot up and his muscles tense. It was a weight too heavy to carry, and he considered going to the police but realized how crazy his story would sound. There was proof—they could test the DNA of the boards—but he knew that no judge would ever approve such a request.

So, he drank.

Should he have told Phyllis? Maybe. But he wanted to keep her out of it, didn't want to burden her conscience.

And a small petty part of him didn't want to admit to her that he'd been wrong about the fence.

On Friday, with the prospect of the weekend looming before him, he stayed at the bar one scotch longer than usual. Unlike drinking establishments depicted in movies and on TV, there were no friendly barflies here, no affable group of regulars, only solitary individuals lost in their own thoughts—which suited him fine. He wasn't here to make friends; he just wanted to dull his senses and stay away from his neighborhood for as long as possible.

Since his encounter with Ted Jorgensen, he'd been walking Sprinkles down the sidewalk in the opposite direction each evening. And he knew that he could spend both Saturday and Sunday having no contact with either Ted or his wife. But each time he had to drive to the store, he would have to pass their house, and even if he locked himself inside all weekend, he would still *know* that their house was there.

JORGENSEN'S FENCE

With its fence made out of people.

And the machine in the garage.

He actually felt a little unsteady as he left the bar, but it was a good feeling, and as he got into the car, he thought it would be nice to feel this way all the time.

No.

He couldn't go down that road. He had to keep it together. He couldn't let Jorgensen's fence completely derail his life.

He drove extra carefully, hyper-aware that his perceptions were altered, that his reaction time was compromised. He drove slowly around the corner, onto his street—

—and crashed into a kid who ran out from a driveway, chasing a dog.

He slammed on the brakes. The impact had been hard, solid, and he knew even before he got out of the vehicle that there was very little chance the kid was alive. Rich was shaking, and he bent down next to the crumpled bloody body lying just in front of his bumper to see if the boy was dead. He heard no sound, saw no sign of movement. It was one of those bratty Caldwell kids, though he didn't know which one, and he glanced up to see if any of the brothers were around or if anyone else had witnessed the accident.

He saw Ted Jorgensen walking over.

This nightmare was never going to end. That serial killer was going to live happily ever after in his Swedish-clean suburban paradise, while Rich would spend the rest of his life in jail because of one stupid accident—

Jorgensen picked up the Caldwell boy's body. "Open it," he said, kicking the car's passenger door.

Too stunned to disobey, Rich did as he was told. Jorgensen threw in the body and closed the door. "Park in my driveway," he ordered. "I'll meet you there."

He started walking down the street back to his house.

Filled with panic, knowing this was the wrong thing to do but not thinking clearly enough to do the right thing, he put the car into gear, drove to the Jorgensens' house and pulled into the driveway. Ted arrived just at that moment, opened the passenger door, took out the Caldwell kid as though he were unpacking groceries, and carried the boy to the garage.

Now Rich knew what was going on.

There wasn't even time to sort out how he felt about it. Part of him was absolutely horrified—

Was the Caldwell boy even dead?

—but part of him was thinking that if this worked, he would be in the clear and wouldn't have to face jail or *any* consequences.

The machine was on.

The body went in.

Boards emerged white and smooth and pleasantly warm.

The machine was shut off, and the two of them looked at each other across the garage. Rich didn't know what to say.

It was Jorgensen who spoke first. "Two more and you'll have enough to make a new dog house for Sprinkles."

That sobered him up. "*Two more*? It's not like I'm going to be—"

Jorgensen looked at him flatly. "Two more."

Rich's mouth was suddenly dry.

"I'll keep these boards here until you have enough. Then they're all yours."

It was a threat, but he still wasn't thinking clearly enough to be able to determine how or why it was a threat. The other man seemed to sense this. "Go home," he said. "We'll talk about it later. And hose off your bumper," he added. "There's probably blood on it."

Two more.

A half hour later, after a surreptitious car wash in the dark, he tried to sneak into the house.

Two more.

Phyllis was waiting for him. "You're actually drunk this time, aren't you? *Aren't* you?"

He blinked, said nothing.

"I've had about enough of this crap! You come home late every day, won't tell me where you've been—"

"I'm not..."

⊦ JORGENSEN'S FENCE ⊣

"Shut up! You're going to listen for once! I don't know what's going on with you, but for the past week..."

Tuning out her voice, Rich looked at his wife.

Two more.

Was he still drunk?

Maybe.

But he thought about the way she was always nagging him, and the weight she'd gained over the past year, and decided that sometime this week, maybe tomorrow morning, the two of them would take a little trip over to the Jorgensens' garage.

THE SILENCE OF TREES

(2016)

I'd left Phoenix over a decade and a half ago, after the Y2K disaster didn't happen, burned out on my job, my life, the state of the goddamn world. I hadn't been back since. I'd been living in Pinetop in a rented cabin with an old-school satellite dish, working for the big casino at nearby Hon-Dah on the Fort Apache reservation. My official title was "casino detective," but basically all I did was walk around, make my presence known, and try to put the fear of God into employees and customers who were even *thinking* about doing what they shouldn't. It wasn't much of a job, but I didn't hate it.

I existed.

Change came in the form of a woman. Doesn't it always? She was tall and dark, thin and gorgeous, and there in the north country she stood out like a polished ruby among rough chunks of broken cement. Hon-Dah's customers were primarily local yokels and rich residents from down south who had summer homes in the pines, and while there was a consistent flow of women through our doors, they were usually older and accompanied by their husbands. The few lookers who came this far out were invariably with the band performing in the showroom or the arm candy of wealthy businessmen up for a short weekend.

This one was different, though. She was alone and it was mid-morning, mid-week. She was obviously looking for someone, and when her eyes found me, chatting with the pit boss by the central station, she made her way straight past the tables and slots to the spot where we stood. She looked familiar, I thought as she drew closer, and when she smiled at me and said my name, I knew I knew her, though I still couldn't place the face.

Then it came to me. Frieda Balderama, Carlos' little girl, only all grown up. She'd been a cute twelve-year-old the last time I'd seen her, but that had been a long time ago, and now she was a stunning young woman. Carlos was one of the good guys, one of the few people I missed, and while I hadn't seen or talked to him since leaving the Valley, our bond was solid enough that I knew we'd be able to pick it up no matter how much time had passed.

Frieda asked if we could talk. Alone. The pit boss wandered away, and I offered Frieda a drink. "Coffee, tea, soda, water?" She shook her head, said she was fine. There was sadness behind her smile, and all of a sudden, I knew that she'd come here to deliver bad news. I braced myself.

"My dad's dead."

I'd been expecting the words, but it was still a shock to hear them. Carlos was dead? He was only a few years older than I was. "What happened?" I asked. *Cancer*, I was thinking. *Heart attack*.

She met my gaze and I saw the pain in her eyes. "He was murdered."

The news hit me hard. Carlos might have known some sketchy people in his younger days, but no one serious. And ever since his daughter was born, he'd been walking the straight and narrow. I found it hard to imagine a scenario where he'd have been in real danger.

Maybe it had been random.

Maybe. But I didn't think his little girl would be up here looking for me if that were the case.

However it had gone down, I hoped it was quick. I'd been around, I'd seen things, and I knew that a killing was the worst way to go, worse even than disease. Disease might be agonizing, but in its way it was natural. A murder? If it was drawn out, there was nothing more evil, because facing certain death, a death that shouldn't be, a death that didn't have to happen, was beyond tortuous.

I cleared my throat. "Did they catch—"

"Would I be here if they did?"

I took a deep breath. "Tell me."

She opened her mouth, and I could see that she wanted to spill, but she just couldn't. Not yet. "Maybe I will take that water," Frieda said.

A few minutes later, seated at a table, her whistle wet, she gave it another shot. "Two months ago, my dad was driving up the Beeline to Payson to see his friend Hilly. You know Hilly?"

I shook my head.

"It doesn't matter. The point is, he never got there. Hilly called me up several hours later, asking where he was, and I tried his cell phone but there was no answer. There could have been many reasons why he hadn't made it to Hilly's yet, and I thought about waiting until he showed up, but I sensed something was wrong. So did Hilly, and we decided to trace the route *Papi* would have taken, from opposite ends. I started up from Phoenix; he started down from Payson.

"He was the one who found my dad's truck. And my dad."

She had to stop for a moment. I didn't push, just waited. Frieda wiped her eyes, finished her water, and I signaled for another glass.

"He'd driven off the side of the road, and the truck had hit a boulder. They said at first that he'd been drunk, but I told them that he didn't drink. You knew that, right?"

I nodded.

"So that's what I told them. They thought he might have had a heart attack or a seizure, but when they did an autopsy, they couldn't find anything like that. Finally, they put it down to some type of accident. They said maybe he'd swerved to avoid a deer or a coyote or something, and he'd bumped his head in the crash and that had killed him."

"You don't believe that, though?"

"No."

"What do you think happened?" I asked.

She looked at me. "I think Lieutenant Armstrong killed him."

That wasn't possible. Armstrong had been dead for five years, killed by a motorist he'd stopped on the Beeline. It had been big news, all over the papers and TV. The racist fuck had lost his job after a bad arrest that had cost the department over a million dollars in settlement fees, but he'd somehow landed a position with the highway patrol, and there on Beeline Highway, he'd been ticketing people for speeding and illegal lane changes, targeting, I'm sure, drivers with brown faces. He'd finally pulled over the wrong man and had ended up shot in the face and left for dead by the side of the road. I didn't know many people who mourned Armstrong's passing, but the brutality of the crime had been good for ratings, remaining the top story on the news for over a week, and the highway patrol, seeking to capitalize on the free publicity, had renamed a short stretch of the Beeline in his honor, calling it the "Donald R. Armstrong Memorial Highway."

I knew Frieda was hurting, and I tried to let her down easy. "Armstrong's dead," I said. "It couldn't have been him."

"It was him," she insisted. "Remember how he used to do that stupid movie thing where he'd leave a Frito on the forehead of any Latino whose death he had to investigate? So everyone would know it was his case? And that it probably wouldn't be solved? Well, there was a Frito on my dad's forehead. Hilly saw it, too.

"Besides..." She paused. "Dad died in exactly the same spot Lieutenant Armstrong did."

That lent it all a little more credence.

I felt myself being drawn in.

"I need help. And Dad always told me that you were the guy who handled these kinds of things."

That was true. But not because I wanted to. Things had just worked out that way. I'd been tiptoeing around superstitions for years, but after my experience in Bumblebee, it was like the floodgates opened. Word spread somehow, and I gained kind of a reputation for investigating matters that regular law enforcement would not even acknowledge existed. It was lucrative, I'll admit that. But it took a toll, and the truth was that it was one of the reasons I'd pulled a Houdini and headed north after the turn of the millennium.

This was Frieda, though, Carlos' little girl, and I owed it to her, to him, to look into this.

{ THE SILENCE OF TREES }

"I can pay you," she offered.

I looked at her, offended. "No. You can't."

She dropped the subject, nodding her understanding, smiling her gratitude.

"Take me there," I told her. "Let me see where it happened myself."

"Okay."

"I'll follow you. Meet me in the parking lot. I just have to clear a few things with management first."

She took my phone from me, programmed her number into it so we could communicate on the way, then went out the way she came in. I told the pit boss that I was taking a day or two: my first vacation since I'd been hired. I got the go-ahead, as long as I was back by Friday night, and I walked out to the employees' parking lot behind the casino, where there was a crappy Pontiac with a faded bumper sticker touting a long gone local DJ from the 1990s.

Mine.

I pulled out to the front, where Frieda was waiting in a considerably nicer vehicle: a new blue Lexus. She was obviously doing well for herself, and I was glad. Carlos had been a good guy, and Frieda was her daddy's girl.

We headed west, through Show Low and Heber, turning south at Payson. Two hours later, Frieda pulled over at the spot where Armstrong had been killed, and I parked on the shoulder behind her. There was a plaque by the side of the road, donated by the PBA, as well as several bunches of bleached plastic flowers. Another car, an empty beat-up Chevy, was parked on the other side of the plaque.

The highway here sloped down into a wash, and at the bottom, where Armstrong had been gunned down, was a small grove of cottonwood trees. She showed me the boulder that her father's truck had hit, explaining in a choked voice where everything had been when they'd found him.

I took it all in, then wandered down to where Armstrong had gotten it. Immediately, I sensed that something was off, something was wrong, though it took me a moment to figure out what it was that I found so disturbing.

It was the silence of the trees.

I'd been living up in the pines for a long time, and one thing I'd noticed was the *aliveness* of the outdoors. Not that I'm a nature guy. I don't hunt, fish, hike, bike or do any of that crap. Never have. But even a city boy like me can't help noticing something when it stares him in the face every day. And these trees were utterly still, completely unmoving. *Silent*. Even though a slight breeze was ruffling my hair and sending the dead crackling leaves from a nearby sycamore skittering across the dry rocks of the wash. I felt the back of my neck prickle. It was as if the trees existed in a vacuum, a bubble from which no sound could escape.

I looked around, trying to figure out what the cause might be.

And saw a body in the wash.

I slid down the slight incline, causing an avalanche of small rocks. It was an older Mexican man, wearing what appeared to be a janitorial uniform. The Chevy must have been his. Why he was out here in the first place was a mystery, but the cause of his death wasn't.

There was a Frito on his forehead.

Frieda was right. It was Armstrong. The spirit of that racist fuck was trapped here along this stretch of roadway, and like a spider waiting in its web for flies to land, Armstrong remained in place, saving his strength until one of his enemies traveled through his territory.

"Do you recognize him?" I asked Frieda, nodding down at the body.

She was hanging back, afraid to come closer, and she shook her head emphatically, though I knew she was too far away to see his face.

That didn't matter. What mattered was that it was Armstrong, and I tried to think of what could be keeping him here and what I could do about it.

"It *is* Lieutenant Armstrong, isn't it?" Frieda asked me when I walked back up the incline.

I nodded.

"How do we stop him?"

"I don't know. But I'll find out," I promised.

"What are you going to do?"

That was a good question. "Talk to some people," I said vaguely.

"I'm going with you." Her gaze was defiant.

"No, you're not. We're dealing with dangerous stuff here, and your dad wouldn't want me to drag you into this."

⟨ THE SILENCE OF TREES ⟩

"I dragged *you* into this!"

"You know what I mean." I put my hands gently on her shoulders, and she wasn't a beautiful young woman to me but Carlos' little girl, frightened and full of questions and worried about her father. "This is what I do. It's my job. I'll keep you informed, tell you what's happening every step of the way, but I work alone."

"I'm—"

"I work alone, or I don't work at all."

I hated to pull that on her, but I could see the stubbornness in her eyes and knew that she wouldn't back off unless she was forced to.

"You call 911," I told her. "Report this. Let the cops investigate it in their way. I'll see what I can do about Armstrong." I pulled out my phone, moved away toward the pile of plastic flowers. "I'm going to make a few calls myself."

Bark Herrington's was one of the only phone numbers I still knew by heart. Bark knew more about what he called "the uncanny" than any man I could think of. I'd met him on a case in the mid-nineties, a guy who'd claimed his house had been built on top of an Apache burial ground and spirits or demons were stealing his wife's jewelry. Turned out the wife had a coke habit and was hocking her own jewelry to pay for the snow, but I wouldn't've figured that out as quickly as I did if Bark hadn't helped me rule out all of the supernatural possibilities. The man knew his stuff. Which was why I'd used him as a resource on probably a dozen other cases.

Bark lived out past Superior, though, and it wasn't worth the three-hour round trip just to ask him a couple of questions. He was skittish about the phone, and it was hit or miss whether he'd even answer, but I gave it a shot, and he picked up on the nineteenth ring, obviously figuring that if someone was that persistent, the call must be important.

As usual, there was no preamble.

"Herrington here."

"It's me," I said.

If he noticed that I hadn't been in touch for over a decade, it didn't register. "Hey," he said. "What's up?"

I gave him the rundown.

"*How* was the cop killed?" he asked.

"Shot."

"*Who* killed him, then?"

"Why?"

"If it's not the how, it's the who. One of those two things is the reason he's dead and kicking."

"Regular con, so far as I know."

"I'd talk to him if I were you, check up on that. Something's out of whack in this equation, and my money's on the shooter."

"Thanks," I said.

"Don't be such a stranger," Bark told me. He immediately hung up.

I smiled. That was about as emotional as Bark ever got, and for him that was a big admission. He'd missed me. I missed him, too, I realized, and for the first time, I admitted to myself that I missed *this*. I missed The Job.

They'd pinned Armstrong's murder on a Papago gun runner who I was pretty sure was serving time in Florence. I couldn't remember his name, so I called Phoenix to see if any of my old contacts were still working. Santucci was long gone, but his flunky Nakamura was still on the state payroll, and while the two of us had never been bosom buddies, there was no bad blood between us, either. A little sweet talking, and he was at his computer, typing away.

The Papago's name was Cameron Wood, and he wasn't at Florence but was being housed at the prison in Winslow, that dying town's only real source of employment. If I headed back up the Beeline, I could probably make it there in two.

"Got a lead," I told Frieda. She was still on the phone with a 911 operator. "I'm going. I'll call you if I find anything out."

She was stuck in her conversation and thankfully couldn't talk back, and I waved to her as I got in my car.

I headed out.

◆

{ THE SILENCE OF TREES }

Winslow.

Drunk or wasted men sat ass-flat on the dirty sidewalk, their backs against the shuttered storefronts. By the McDonald's, a thuggish group of teens eyed my car suspiciously. Two bratty little kids were throwing rocks at the Standing-on-the-Corner statue, a misguided piece of public art that was supposed to lure tourists because The Eagles had once referenced this shithole in a song.

I had no authority to see anyone in the prison, but I hauled out my Hon-Dah ID and told the halfwit acting as gatekeeper that an accomplice of Wood's was suspected of ripping off the casino, and I was here to interview him about it.

The two of us met over phones, across glass.

Wood frowned at me. "Who the hell are you?"

"A guy. I have some questions about the Armstrong murder."

"Didn't do it." He hung up the phone and got up to leave.

I tapped on the glass, which earned me a warning from the guard at the other end of the room. Wood thought for a moment, then picked up the phone again, probably remembering that he didn't have anything better to do.

"What?" he said.

"I'm not the law," I told him. "I'm private. On a case. I don't know if you did it or not, but I want to talk to you about it."

That seemed to soothe his ego. He nodded. "Okay, shoot."

"You say you didn't kill Armstrong—"

"I didn't." The convict shrugged. "Not that I *wouldn't've*. I just didn't get the chance because someone else got there first. Some*thing*," he corrected himself. "Some*thing* took out that asshole. I was just in the wrong place at the right time."

"What do you mean some*thing*?"

He shook his head. "I gotta go."

"You don't gotta do shit and we both know it."

"The pig was dead when I got there."

"What do you mean some*thing*?"

He leaned forward. "That's bad land," he said. "It's always been bad land."

I thought of the silence there, that heavy oppressiveness I'd encountered.

He must have read the expression on my face. "You know it, don't you? You've been there."

I nodded.

"It's not just a Papago thing. Any tribe could've told you about that spot. But does anyone ask us about it? No. They just build their highway right through it and then wonder why things go wrong."

"What's bad about that land?"

"What lives there."

"What *does* live there?"

He stood. "Nice talking to you."

The phone was still in his hand, so I knew he wanted something in exchange for the information. "What can I do?" I asked.

"A favor."

"If I can."

"Check up on my wife. I think she might be spreading for a guy named Joe David. I don't expect her to wait forever, and I'm cool with that, but Joe's supposed to be my bro, and I don't want him bangin' my old lady. It ain't right."

"Then you'll tell me about that spot?"

He nodded.

"What's her name and where can I find her?"

◆

Tiffany Wood worked part-time at a Holbrook fish farm and lived in a trailer just outside of town. I'd put more miles on the Pontiac in one day than I had in the past fifteen, and the sun was low behind me when I pulled off I-40.

Sitting on blocks in the middle of a yard that was mostly dirt, the run-down metal rectangle looked more like a meth lab than a home. Tiffany answered the door wearing a Toby Keith t-shirt and what looked like pajama bottoms. Her belly was hanging out, and a cigarette dangled from her lips in that gravity-defying way usually seen only in movies. She narrowed her eyes at me. "Who're you?"

"I'm looking into a murder. I talked to Cameron, and he sent me your way."

"You don't look like a cop."

"I'm not. Just a concerned citizen."

"So, this is about his case?"

"Not exactly. But it's connected. He said he didn't kill Armstrong."

She laughed, a harsh rasp that shifted into a cough. "That's what he told you?"

I nodded.

She leaned in closer. "Bullshit. All bullshit. He did kill that cop. And that cop deserved it. But Cameron was *hired* to do it. Some guy named…" She frowned, thinking. "Balderama, I think. He wanted the pig taken out. Paid Cam big bucks for it, too."

I tried not to let the surprise show on my face. "Balderama? Was that… *Carlos* Balderama?"

She nodded. "Yeah, that's it. Carlos. Skinny dude. Dressed straight. Looked like an accountant."

That was him all right.

I was thrown. Why would Carlos put out a hit on Armstrong? To my knowledge, the two had barely had any contact with each other. Had Carlos gotten involved with things he shouldn't have since I'd left town?

Honesty wasn't always the best policy, but sometimes it was, and I told her about Carlos getting killed in the same spot as Armstrong, and about what Cameron had said about something *else* killing the cop, something he was reluctant to talk about.

She snorted. "He doesn't know shit about any of that. He was just playing you." She took a long drag on her cigarette, then grew thoughtful. "Although…" She paused for a moment, thinking. "He was worried about driving because of a…situation he had, so I think he actually might've gone there with his friend Lewis instead of just by himself. Lewis might've actually driven. He's not a rat, he wouldn't roll over, so even if Lewis had been there, Cam wouldn't say nothing about it, but I'm pretty sure he was."

"Lewis is into *all* that stuff. I've never been able to tell if it's a scam or not, part of some long con, but the past year or so, he's been calling himself a *shaman* and getting some extra gigs casting spells or making curses or whatever the fuck. You might want to talk to him about that." She took another drag on her cigarette. "I don't believe any of that crap, but sometimes I think Cam does. His whole family's kind of superstitious. Dumb and superstitious. So, you might talk to Lewis."

"Where's this Lewis when he's at home?"

"Hold on a sec." She disappeared inside the trailer, then emerged a moment later with an address on a scrap of paper. "Here."

"You have a pen?" I asked. "So I can copy this?"

"Take it," she told me. "Cam's gone, and I sure as shit don't need that numb nuts' address."

"Thanks." I put the paper in my pocket. "Oh, by the way. Cameron said he wants you to stay away from Joe David. He thinks you two are..." I left the rest unsaid.

"*Joe?*" She laughed so hard she had a coughing fit. "I wouldn't touch Joe if he won the lottery."

"Good to know," I said. "Tell Cameron that."

I got back in my car. Lewis lived in Seligman, a couple hundred miles west. There was no way I'd be able to get there before nightfall, so I splurged and got a room at the Route 66 Inn in Flagstaff. Before heading out for my Taco Bell Value Menu dinner, I called Frieda and gave her the scoop on what I'd found. Sort of. I left out the part about her dad ordering the hit. That still made no sense to me, and I hoped that when everything came out in the wash, I'd have a perfectly innocent explanation that both of us could live with.

In the morning, I drove west to Seligman.

Lewis, to my surprise, lived in a neighborhood near the center of town in a tract home surrounded by identical tract homes. To my greater surprise, he was white. He had the scummy appearance of a low-level loser, and with his bandana headband, tribal tattoos and motorcycle boots, he definitely looked like a companion of Wood's.

"Yeah?" he said, opening the door after I'd knocked.

"Tiffany Wood sent me. I have a few questions about Cameron and why he's in prison."

"You the law?" he asked suspiciously.

"No," I said, holding out a twenty. "Just helping out a friend."

"What friend?"

"Doesn't matter."

He looked at me for a moment, then pocketed the money. "So, what is it you want to know?"

"Armstrong. The cop Balderama paid to be hit. I need to know what happened. Tiffany said Wood did it, but Cameron said there was something *else* there."

Lewis nodded. "He's telling you true. I drove Cameron out to the Beeline on account of he'd lost his license and couldn't afford to get busted again, at least not on that road. I didn't know anything about him planning to—"

"Yeah, yeah," I said. "I believe you. You were just an innocent bystander. Get to the point. Wood went out there to do the job and…"

"And we waited. He'd already picked out a spot. We put the hood up, pretended the car had broken down, and waited for the pig to show up. But… there was something there, man. Something in that wash. I didn't see it, but I felt it, and Cameron did, too. I told him maybe we should move the car somewhere else, and I think he was about to agree, when the cop car pulled up."

"So, you—I mean, so *Wood* really *did* kill him."

"No."

"Then what happened?"

"The pig got out, came over, instead of offering to help us said it was illegal to park here and he was going to have to give us a ticket."

That sounded like Armstrong.

"The plan was to take him off the highway and take him out, away from any cars that might drive by and see. It was actually a pretty crowded day. We didn't even have to force him off the road or lure him away, because right after he said he was going to give us a ticket, there was a noise down in the wash. A… weird noise. Like a yell, kind of, but… *squishy*. He took out his gun and told us to wait there, then he walked down to the wash to check it out. Cameron didn't want to have a shootout with him—cops are trained for that shit—so the plan was to either wait until he holstered the gun again or just shine the whole thing on, but…" Lewis took a deep breath. "He didn't come back.

"We waited and waited, but when the wait had gone on way too long, we went down to check it out, and he was dead."

"Shot?"

"Oh, no. That's what the cops told the news, but that ain't what happened. He was *gutted*. Face up over a rock and *opened*. We saw that and ran like hell. We took off and went back, went our separate ways, and a day later, they picked Cam up. Someone must have seen the car and taken down the plates, I guess." He looked me in the eye. "He kept me out of it."

"You're still out of it," I assured him. "I'm just trying to find out what happened."

"That's what happened."

"So, what was it? What killed Armstrong?"

"I've been trying to figure that out." Lewis drew himself up higher. "I'm a shaman, you know."

"So I heard."

He missed the sarcasm. "Whatever it is, it's not a spirit, it's a…" He seemed to be at a loss for words. "It's a *thing*. I talked to a guy, and he said that when there's bad land, it's because a creature's living there."

"A *creature*?"

"Yeah. Like, an actual beast, one that's left over from the old times. That's why the land's bad."

Bad land again.

"Like I said, we didn't see it, but we *felt* it. And we saw what it did."

"Is there any way to get rid of it?"

"I've been thinking about that, too. I talked to a guy—not the same guy, a different guy—and he said he saw something himself once, up by Sycamore Creek, which is a bad place, too. He said the thing was small, the size of a ferret or something, more like an animal than anything else. It had just killed a group of campers, gutted 'em and eaten their heads, and it was looking for someone new. Thing is, he said it *acted* like the campers. I don't know how that's possible, it being a rat and all, but somehow it made him think it was one of the campers."

"What'd he do?"

"Killed it."

"So, they can be killed." That was good news.

"Apparently so."

"Is there some kind of ritual you have to—"

"No, he just shot it."

"Shot it."

"Yeah." Lewis shrugged. "Blew it away with a twenty-two. End of story."

"That land there," I asked. "Is it still bad?"

"You got me. But the thing's dead."

Lewis had definitely earned his twenty. I took the back way to the Beeline, through Flagstaff, past the two Lake Marys and what was left of Mormon Lake. I had a lot of time to think.

So, the killer of Carlos hadn't been Armstrong after all. It was…something else, something much older than Armstrong, something that had absorbed the cop's essence, taken on his personality and his prejudices and used them to satisfy its own bloody needs.

But it was something that could be killed.

I'm not a gun guy. Never have been. But there was a loaded Glock in the glove compartment that I kept on hand just for emergencies. This was an emergency, and when I reached the PBA plaque that marked the spot on the highway where Armstrong had been taken down, I parked and took it out. It felt unfamiliar in my hand, and I hoped I'd be able to hit the creature when I saw it. It had been a long time since I'd practiced shooting.

I got out of the car and walked away from the highway, into the silence.

It felt just like before—wrong. There were no new bodies here, but I sensed that there could be, and I proceeded slowly, glad to have the gun in my hand. Once more, nature was still, as though it had been frozen, but only in the trees. My instinct was to head toward the wash, where the bodies had been found, but it seemed more logical to assume that whatever the monster was, it lived in the trees. I stopped just inside the copse of cottonwoods and sycamores, looking around, absorbing the silence. I glanced up, half-expecting to see something swinging overhead, ready to pounce on me, but the branches above were empty.

All of a sudden, I felt the presence of Armstrong. I didn't see him, sure as hell didn't hear him, but somehow I was overtaken by the certainty that he was nearby. I hadn't seen that fat fuck since I'd left Phoenix, but I hadn't forgotten what it felt like to be confronted by him, and that's what I was experiencing now. I swiveled around, half-expecting to find him getting ready to choke me out.

Instead, I saw movement low on the ground next to a giant cottonwood, a ratlike thing made of mud and leaves that was scuttling toward me and that, inexplicably, made me think of Armstrong.

And then…

It was Carlos.

Had it taken over and trapped Carlos' soul when it killed him? Had it merely made a copy of the man? I had no idea what the thing was or what it did, but I sensed my old friend, felt his presence, and I was glad his daughter wasn't here right now because I didn't think she'd allow me to do what I needed to do.

I started shooting.

It didn't seem right that it should be this simple, but it was. The creature scurried toward me, and I emptied the gun into its body. It might have been short, but it was wide, and it made for a surprisingly easy target. Ten feet away from me, it collapsed and stopped moving, bleeding out into the sand, and it was if my ears had suddenly become unclogged. The trees were alive again, there was noise, and whatever pall had been hanging over this spot had been lifted.

I walked over to the body, looked down at it. What had happened to Armstrong? To Carlos? Were they both gone? Were they both still here? Who the hell knew?

Just to make sure, I picked up a big rock and smashed the creature's head. I picked up another and another, dropping them onto the body until it was bloody and flattened and buried.

┥ THE SILENCE OF TREES ┝

Back up by my car on the edge of the highway, I called Frieda. She answered on the first ring. I didn't want to go into detail with her, didn't think the truth would satisfy her anyway, so I told her she was right, it had been Armstrong, but I'd taken care of things.

"Like an exorcism or something?" she asked.

"Or something," I responded, but I wasn't in the mood to explain. "It's over," I told her.

"Is he in hell?"

I heard something then in her voice, a hardness I wouldn't have associated with her. It took me aback, and I was reminded of the big bucks Carlos had paid the Papago to take out Armstrong, and the new blue Lexus Frieda drove, and I thought that maybe she wasn't as sweet and innocent as I'd been thinking she was. Maybe she and her dad had *both* been involved in something I didn't want to know about.

"It's done," I said tiredly, and clicked off the phone.

I stood there a few minutes, hearing wind rustle the leaves in the trees. I felt good and bad at the same time, satisfied and disappointed, the way I'd always felt after closing a case, the way I hadn't felt in a long time.

I felt alive.

I got in the car, turned on the ignition, and sat there in the idling Pontiac, thinking.

I thought about turning left, heading north, going back to my cabin and my job at the casino—and I almost did—but instead I decided to turn right, south, toward Phoenix.

I pulled onto the highway. There was a semi on the road ahead, and I gunned the car so I could speed by on the incline before the passenger lane ended. I topped the hill, seeing Weaver's Needle and the Superstitions across the desert in front of me. Pushing the first preset on my radio, I picked up a station. It played Mexican music now rather than country, but it came in clear and it was from the city. It made me feel good, and I smiled to myself as I saw the Valley ahead, its buildings obscured by a familiar haze.

I pressed down on the gas, gunning it up to eighty.

I was back.

STICKY NOTE

(2016)

He saw it in the gutter while on his morning walk: the familiar square of yellow paper. It sat atop a small heap of brown leaves that had been pushed against the curb by the street sweeper but somehow not picked up. Definitely the worse for wear, the Post-It was dirty, faded, crinkled, smudged and lying face down, and Gary didn't know why he reached down to grab it, but he did.

From the paper's soiled appearance, he'd automatically assumed that the adhesive strip at the top had lost its stickiness, but it practically leapt onto his finger, adhering instantly to his skin, and he brought it up to eye-level, turning it over to see if anything had been written on it.

Kill her

The message, scribbled lightly in pencil by a very shaky hand, was shocking in its bluntness, and he pulled the sticky note off his finger and dropped it back in the gutter. It was probably a joke, or part of a game, but the words left him feeling uneasy, and despite his attempt to rationalize the existence of the scrawled command, he could think of no plausible reason why anyone would write it.

Maybe it was part of someone's to-do list.

That was ridiculous.

Only...what if it wasn't?

WALKING ALONE — Bentley Little

Gary looked around. Despite minor differences in house color and landscaping, each home was typical of the neighborhood, all of them upper middle-class residences similar to his own. Not the sort of place where one would expect to find a person who'd write that type of note.

Kill her

Could it be an order from a gang leader to one of his followers?

No. Gang leaders gave verbal orders. They didn't put anything in writing. Besides, who would they be targeting in this neighborhood?

A command from a father to his son?

He didn't want to even think about that. Besides, the idea was completely ridiculous.

Gary continued his walk around the block, heading home, feeling more disturbed than he should have.

He had only a half-hour left to shower, change and make it in to the office. Maggie was already dressed and ready to leave for work, and he caught her in the hall, wanting to tell her what he'd found, but knowing that, in the few moments available to them, he'd be unable to impart to her the *feeling* he'd gotten from the sticky note, the odd sense of disquiet the simple message had engendered within him.

He'd tell her tonight, he decided, and tried to give her a quick kiss on her way out. She deflected him, as she did too often these days, and they ended up saying curt goodbyes to each other, both put out for no real reason.

At the office, he found himself staring at the small pad of Post-Its on his desk. He seldom used the notes, but everyone else's desks were awash with the little yellow squares, which were stuck to folders and piles of paperclipped pages, as well as to desk drawers, computer terminals and phones. Nearly all of the notes were reminders from people to themselves, which made him think that the one he'd found in the gutter this morning—

Kill her

—was also a prompt to someone about something he was supposed to do.

Had it already been done?

Gary didn't know, and he went online to see if he could find information about any murders or assaults that might have occurred in his neighborhood.

{ STICKY NOTE }

There were none, but that did not set his mind at rest, and he spent the rest of the day wondering if some friendless old lady's body was rotting undiscovered in one of the houses.

When he got home, Maggie wasn't there, but she'd left a Post-It on the middle of the TV screen where she knew he'd see it, telling him that she'd gone out for dinner with her friend Cindy and would be back later in the evening. Another note below that contained a P.S. telling him there were leftover crab cakes in the refrigerator that he could heat up if he wanted.

He found himself looking at her handwriting, mentally comparing it to that on the sticky note he'd found in the gutter. *Why? Did he think she'd written it?* Definitely not, but there was still something reassuring about seeing her firm bold lettering, written in pen and so different from that faint shaky pencil.

Kill her

He ate the crab cakes while watching the national news. By the time the program was over, it was dark outside, and he went to the front window, looking out at the street for a sign of Maggie's car. He realized that she had not given him a specific time when she'd be back, but had only said "later," which was not at all like her. There was a slight breeze out, and when he saw a scrap of white paper blow onto his lawn and catch on one of Maggie's rosebushes, it made him think of the sticky note in the gutter. Was it still there? It probably was, but what difference did that make? Why was he even thinking about it?

He didn't know, but he was half-tempted to walk down the street and around the block to the spot where he'd found the yellow square.

That was just craziness.

Headlights shone in his eyes as Maggie pulled into the driveway, and he moved away from the window, happy to be distracted from his thoughts.

In the morning, he retraced his same route from the day before. He usually varied his exercise routine, and he told himself that he wasn't walking this way on purpose, that it was just a coincidence and meant nothing, but that wasn't true, because he slowed down when he reached the spot, looking into the gutter.

WALKING ALONE — Bentley Little

There it was.

He didn't pick it up. He had enough self-control that he continued on, but he *knew* it was there, and its presence haunted him. For the rest of the morning, his mind kept coming back to that dirty rumpled Post-It and its simple terrible message.

Kill her

He went out for lunch with Steve from Accounting, who spent most of the meal texting on his phone. They were seated at a sidewalk table outside the Southwest Grille, where they often ate, and at one point, he glanced up and thought he saw Maggie pass by in the passenger seat of a red convertible. Maggie? In a red convertible? That was impossible because she was at an all-day conference in Anaheim.

Or was she?

He didn't dare try to call or text her with Steve around—nothing spread faster through the office than personal gossip—but as soon as he was back in his office, Gary dialed her cell number. It went immediately to voice mail.

Who had been driving that car? Was it a man? He hadn't noticed.

He pushed the thought from his mind. That was ridiculous. Forcing himself to get back to work, he spent the rest of the afternoon concentrating on a project that he had due at the end of the week.

Still, he looked carefully at Maggie's hair when he got home. It did appear slightly messier than it had in the morning, slightly more *windblown*. He wished he'd been able to see what the woman in the car had been wearing.

"I went to lunch with Steve today," he said casually. "The Southwest Grille."

She didn't even bother to glance in his direction. "Oh?"

"I thought I saw you passing by. In a red car."

"A red car? Whose red car?"

"That's what I was wondering."

"I was in Anaheim."

She went into the kitchen, and he followed her.

"I called you."

Taking a package of frozen shrimp out of the freezer, she frowned. "I didn't get any messages."

{ STICKY NOTE }

"I didn't leave any. You didn't answer, so I just hung up."

She faced him. "Do you have a point? I don't understand what you're on about."

"Nothing," he said, walking back into the living room. "Nothing."

Lying awake that night, unable to sleep, it occurred to Gary that perhaps the message had been meant for him, that *he* was its intended reader.

Kill her

No, that was lunacy. He hadn't known himself that he was going to take that route until he did so. It could not have been deliberately left for him to find. When he walked, he followed no set pattern. In fact, that was one of the advantages of walking in the neighborhood rather than using the treadmill or the exercise bike: he could vary the view, go where he felt like going, see new things every time.

But maybe that's why the Post-It was in such bad shape: it had been sitting there for several days, *waiting* for him to come by.

That was crazy thinking. He could have just as easily been focused on the houses or the sky or the sidewalk in front of him or a car that was passing by or a jogger or a biker. It was pure happenstance that he had glanced down in that direction at that moment, seen the little yellow square and picked it up.

Only what if it wasn't?

His head hurt from indulging in such pointless speculation, and Gary tried to think about something else.

Maggie.

Why hadn't she answered her phone when he called? And that woman in the convertible had looked a *lot* like her.

He fell asleep. Eventually.

He decided not to exercise in the morning—or at least not to walk. Maybe he'd take an extra half hour at lunch and drop in at the company's gym in the basement, make it up.

He did call Maggie's phone several times throughout the day. She answered each call, and by the third time, she'd figured out that his prepared topics of conversation were bogus and he was just checking up on her. She let him have it on the fourth call, but he didn't need to keep tabs on her after that, because by then it was mid-afternoon, and she wouldn't have had time to do anything outside her office anyway.

The atmosphere at home was chilly, but Gary decided to pretend that it wasn't. He knew this emotional frost was mostly his fault, but it wasn't entirely his fault, and he couldn't shake the idea that Maggie was hiding something. So, he acted as though it were a normal evening, ignoring her stony silence, heating up some leftovers in the microwave and watching the nightly news on TV. Halfway through the news, she got a call on her cell, and she left to take it in the other room. He thought of following her, spying on her, but decided to be big about it and watched a heartwarming end-of-the-news story about a blind veteran and his seeing-eye dog.

He went to bed early, well before she did, telling her that he was tired and not waiting to see if she answered him.

The night was windy and moonless, exactly the type of night that would have terrified him as a child. Outside, it sounded as though a banshee were howling somewhere far away, and closer in, tree branches struck the side of the house at odd irregular intervals. He found it hard to sleep, despite being so tired, and his last thought before he finally drifted off was that maybe the reason Maggie hadn't come to bed the same time he had was because she was trying to be faithful to her lover.

In the morning, the wind was gone, and after pulling on a pair of pants, Gary went out to pick up his copy of the newspaper in the driveway. Bending down to pick up the paper, he saw, out of the corner of his eye, a small yellow square sitting atop a mound of leaves that had been blown by the wind onto the sidewalk.

A sticky note.

Heart pounding, he walked slowly over and picked it up.

Kill her

He recognized the shaky hand, the light pencil. It was the same Post-It, a little worse for wear. How was that possible? The odds that a windstorm could pick up a piece of yellow note paper from a gutter three blocks over and deposit it on top of a pile of leaves on his sidewalk had to be astronomical.

Maybe someone was trying to tell him something.

{ STICKY NOTE }

Who? God? A spirit? Some type of supernatural presence? The idea was ridiculous. Still, it had entered his mind, and as much as he wanted to, he could not entirely dismiss it.

Perhaps the note *had* been meant for him.

He pocketed the Post-It and took the paper inside. Maggie was still asleep, and though he would ordinarily wake her up, he wasn't sure of their status at the moment, so he left her alone and went into the kitchen to put on some coffee. It was Saturday. Usually he would make himself pancakes or French toast, but he wasn't very hungry, so he just popped a couple of pieces of bread into the toaster.

He had just finished eating when, from down the hall, he heard Maggie go into the bathroom, locking the door behind her. On impulse, he hurried back to the bedroom, where he picked up her phone off the dresser and turned it on to check it.

Thirteen messages over the past three days to a number he did not recognize.

The name next to the number was Adrian.

Adrian

It was one of those unisex names that could be either a man or a woman. He tried to tell himself it was just a client from work, someone with whom she needed to get in touch as part of a project, but his mind refused to buy it. Whether Adrian was a man or a woman, Gary was pretty sure that he or she drove a red convertible and that Maggie's interest had nothing to do with work.

Kill her

The message on the note came back to him. His hand felt for the paper in his pocket. As beaten up as it was, its edges felt crisp and sharp.

This was wrong. He shouldn't be doing this, shouldn't be thinking this. He turned off the phone, put it back on the dresser, then hurried back down the hall to the kitchen, where he took the Post-It note out of his pocket, tore it up and dropped the pieces into the sink, turning on the water and washing them down the drain.

It was done.

Or was it?

WALKING ALONE — Bentley Little

What if he saw it again while walking through the neighborhood? What if it showed up on the doorstep of his office or on the windshield of his car? What would he do then?

He didn't know.

Maggie touched his shoulder, and he jumped, unaware that she'd come up behind him. She smiled. Her voice betrayed none of the animosity of the night before. "Why so jumpy? Are you all right?"

He looked into her eyes, thought of the sticky note.

"Yeah," he said and tried to smile.

"Are you sure?"

Kill her

He nodded, and for some reason felt unusually calm. "I'm fine," he told her. "Everything's fine."

THE SMELL OF OVERRIPE LOQUATS

(2016)

Johnny didn't like staying overnight at his grandmother's house.

She still lived in East L.A., where his mom had grown up, but over the years the neighborhood had deteriorated around her. Fences and garage doors were spray-painted with gang tags, and low-riding cars cruising the streets were driven by tough-looking men with shaved tattooed heads. His other grandparents, his dad's mom and dad, his *American* grandma and grandpa, lived in Boston, and he *loved* visiting them. For one thing, they lived far away, so the visits were vacations, family affairs where they got to fly on a plane, stay for a week, see aunts and uncles and cousins, and do fun touristy things. His grandparents' house was filled with old toys and games he could play with, and they always bought him a new present each time he came.

But his grandmother here in California, his *Mexican* grandma, *Abuela*, didn't plan anything special on the nights he stayed over. She was just babysitting him so his parents could have a night to themselves, and while she might bake him something nice for dessert, that was pretty much the extent of it.

There wasn't a whole lot to do at her house either. It was an old lady house. There were no toys or games, no computer or wi-fi. She didn't even have cable, only regular TV.

⊢ WALKING ALONE ⊣   Bentley Little

The worst part of it was that she was always trying to get him to play with the kids next door, the Orozcos, whose mom had been one of *his* mom's best friends when they were in grade school. He didn't like those kids much, and they didn't like him, but at his *Abuela*'s insistence, he would go over to their house for a while, hanging out with their mom in the kitchen or occupying himself alone in their back yard for a polite period of time before retreating back to his grandmother's.

The only time he and the neighbor kids were stuck with each other for any length of time was when he stayed overnight on a Saturday. His *Abuela*, who could not leave the house without a walker and so went to church midweek to avoid the crowds, insisted that he attend mass on Sunday morning. So, she invariably asked his mom's friend to take him to church with her family.

Which was why he preferred staying overnight on Friday.

Once again, though, his parents dropped him off after lunch on Saturday, his mom telling him brightly that they'd pick him up Sunday afternoon.

"I don't want to go to mass," he told her privately, whispering so his grandmother couldn't hear. "*Abuela* always makes me go to church."

His mom laughed lightly. "You'll be fine," she said. "I even packed your tie."

"But—"

"No 'buts,'" his dad said sternly.

So, the next morning, he had to go to church with the Orozcos.

St. Mary's was a little more than a block away and within walking distance. Ordinarily, all six of them would walk up the street in their dress clothes until they reached the steps of St. Mary's, but Mr. and Mrs. Orozco were both sick, so they put Roberto, their oldest son, in charge, and told him to make sure that his brother and sister and Johnny got safely to the church and back. They entrusted him with money for the collection plate, instructing him to give each of the others a dollar bill to contribute.

The four kids headed up the sidewalk toward St. Mary's, Roberto and Miguel in front, talking together in low tones, Johnny stuck next to Angelina behind them, the two of them silent, ignoring each other. They reached the corner, but instead of crossing the street and continuing on to the church, Roberto and Miguel turned left.

{ THE SMELL OF OVERRIPE LOQUATS }

Johnny stopped. "Hey, where are you going?"

Neither boy answered. Angelina pushed past him, following her brothers.

Johnny hurried to catch up. "This isn't the way to church," he said.

"We're not going there," Roberto informed him.

He felt a flicker of fear but did his best not to show it. "Where are we going, then?"

"You'll see."

They continued walking, crossing several streets, until they were in a neighborhood where the houses were even less nice. Several of them had been condemned, and others had been razed, leaving vacant lots filled with debris. Ahead, Johnny saw another boy and girl approaching from the opposite direction, both of them dressed in their Sunday best. The six of them met on the cracked sidewalk in front of a dilapidated stucco house with smashed windows and no front door. It was a bright morning, but the interior of the house was dark. Nothing could be seen inside.

They stood before the empty house, voices hushed. "He lives there," Roberto said.

"Who?" Johnny asked.

"God."

"*God?*"

"Our god."

A bolt of fear shot through him. *Our* god? What did that mean?

Whatever it meant was wrong, because there was only one god—God—and the thought that these kids worshipped some other deity, one who lived in their neighborhood, was beyond blasphemous.

They had to be messing with him. But when he looked into their faces, he saw nothing but complete sincerity. Even the new kids were looking at him with a calm serenity.

Did their parents know about this? They couldn't. He tried to think of how *Abuela* or even his mom or dad would react if they knew he was here, and he almost turned and ran away. But the other kids already thought he was a nerd, and he didn't want to give them any more ammunition against him. He tried to keep his voice normal and calm, as though this were the type of conversation he had every day. "I don't understand," he said. "There's a god in that house?"

"*Our* god," Roberto repeated.

Johnny peered at one of the broken windows, trying to see something within the blackness. "What does that mean?"

"We didn't like our parents' god. I mean, do *you* like that god?"

"That's *God*," Johnny said. "Everyone loves God. He loves us."

"Does he?"

"He doesn't like kids," Miguel piped up. "That's why we made our own god."

Johnny couldn't believe what he was hearing. "Made your *own*—"

"He doesn't like kids," Roberto agreed. "He wanted that one guy to kill his own son. And in that Ten Commandments story? He kills all of the Egyptian children. *All* of them! Why? What did *they* do? That pharaoh guy had all those first-born Jewish boys killed, which was wrong. God knew it was wrong. Everyone knows it was wrong. But did God kill that pharaoh? Did he kill the adults who helped the pharaoh, who actually did the killing? No. He killed the children. Innocent children who didn't know about any of this political stuff going on. He did the exact same thing he was punishing the Egyptians for." Roberto shook his head. "He's ruthless, that god. He doesn't care about kids. Never has, never will.

"That's why we had to make our own god. A god for *us*."

"But you can't *make* a god," Johnny protested.

Roberto pointed. "We did. And he's in there."

Johnny wanted to leave. This whole thing was freaking him out. He didn't believe a word of it, but it was clear that the Orozcos and their two friends did, and that was frightening. This was a bad neighborhood, however, and he was afraid to walk either to the church or back to *Abuela*'s by himself. The thought occurred to him that if he returned early, he would have to explain why, and he wasn't sure he wanted to turn in the Orozcos to their parents.

Three more kids came walking up the sidewalk toward them, dressed in church clothes.

Why couldn't he have stayed overnight on Friday?

{ THE SMELL OF OVERRIPE LOQUATS }

There was no way to avoid this, and when Roberto led his brother, sister and the other kids into the house, Johnny accompanied them.

The first thing he noticed when he walked through the open doorway into the darkened front room was the smell. It was obnoxious and nearly overpowering, sickening and sweet at the same time. His *Abuela* had fruit trees in her back yard—most of the houses in the neighborhood did—and he recognized the scent as that of overripe loquats. He knew that sometimes losers in his grandmother's neighborhood hopped over her back fence to steal fruit from her trees (her *guayabas* were always in particularly high demand), and he thought that maybe someone was doing that around here and storing the stolen fruit in the empty house in hopes of selling it later on a street corner or a freeway offramp.

They walked into the next room. Johnny expected to see boxes of rotting fruit, but that was not the sight that greeted him. Instead, a small figure stood alone in the center of a black burnt floor. Outside light from a halfway boarded-up window showed it to be a crude humanoid form made from squashed loquats, molded together. A basic round head sat atop a rudimentary body where slight indentations marked the location of primitive arms and legs. The entire thing was no more than two feet high.

Johnny had seen that shape before, though he could not remember where, and it jogged an emotional sense memory. Something about the figure frightened him, and suddenly he wished he *had* gone back to *Abuela's*—bad neighborhood or not—and *had* turned in the Orozco kids to their parents.

"Let us sit," Roberto said.

Angelina had gone into one of the corners of the room and brought out a stack of newspapers. She began spreading them out in a circle around the loquat figure, on the burnt floor, and one-by-one the other kids sat down cross-legged on the paper. When Miguel, next to him, did the same, Johnny followed suit.

"Who is coming today?" Roberto asked, once they were all seated. His speech had taken on a more formal, churchy tone.

One of the new kids, a chubby boy whose pantlegs were too short, said, "My sister. She should be here anytime."

They waited in silence.

WALKING ALONE Bentley Little

Outside, Johnny could hear the sounds of the neighborhood: cars going by, an angry man screaming in Spanish, dogs barking. Inside, there was nothing but their own breathing.

"Arturo?" a girl's voice called from the front of the house. "Are you in there?"

"Back here!" the chubby kid shouted.

A teenage girl wearing a peach dress and too much makeup stepped hesitantly into the room. "Arturo?"

"Over here," the boy said.

As her eyes adjusted, she saw the circle of kids sitting around the loquat figure. Roberto stood, formally took her hand as she approached, and led her into the center of the circle. "So, what am I supposed to do?" she asked, addressing her brother.

It was Roberto who answered. "When I sit back down, stand over it."

"That little orange guy?"

"Our god," Roberto told her.

The girl shrugged. "Okay."

Roberto took his seat again. He nodded, and the teenager stood over the small form. A swarm of gnats suddenly rose up from the molded fruit, flying up her dress, which billowed out as though pumped full of air. The girl began to laugh joyously. The room seemed brighter than it had, though there'd been no appreciable increase in light.

Everything was now clearer. Johnny could see everything. Gnats continued to fly upward from the loquat form between the teenage girl's legs and under her billowing dress. Her laughter did not abate, and to Johnny it no longer sounded happy—it sounded crazy. He looked around at the faces of the other kids, staring raptly at the spectacle. He wanted nothing more than to be as far away from here as possible.

He felt an elbow prod his side and turned to Miguel, sitting next to him. "Ask for something," Miguel suggested. "Our god will give it to you."

He was completely at a loss. "Like what?" Johnny asked.

"Here. Watch." Miguel stood, facing Arturo's sister. "God, please give me an A in math."

{ THE SMELL OF OVERRIPE LOQUATS }

The girl continued laughing, but underneath the laughter, or *out* of the laughter, came a deeper, more inhuman voice, a voice that shaped and twisted the random sounds of her hilarity into syllables, into words.

"It is done."

A shadow passed over the room. The thing made out of loquats *shifted*. For a brief second, the gnats flew down, out of the girl's dress, touching base with the small figure before swarming upward again.

"See?" Miguel said, sitting down.

Johnny wasn't sure he liked this. No, he *was* sure. He *didn't* like it. But, one by one, the Orozcos and the other kids who'd come in here with them stood and addressed their god, requesting victory in ball games, comeuppance against bullies, a new bike, parents who got along better. Each time, a shadow passed over the room, the girl's laughter transformed into words—

"It is done."

—and the gnats flew down from between her legs, touching base with the loquat figure before swarming upward again.

Finally, everyone had gone except Johnny.

All eyes turned to him.

His mouth was dry, and he had never been so frightened in his life. There was power here, he could feel it, but he could not shake the certainty that it was *evil* power. This was a god that had been created *against* God. It was wrong by its definition, its very existence an offense against the real God, who would probably damn all of these kids to hell. He couldn't participate. He had to leave, to run out of this room and this house and get as far away from here as fast as possible.

He stood.

Feeling the pressure of all those eyes on him, he went over a list in his mind, trying to find the smallest, most trivial thing that he truly wanted. "Please give *Abuela* cable TV," Johnny said.

He'd refused to call it "God" but that didn't seem to matter. There was the same shadow, the same words swirling out of the laughter—

"It is done."

—the same migration of the gnats. He was suddenly filled with a euphoric sensation, the feeling that all of his problems had been solved, that the future was bright and clean and perfect, and that nothing bad would ever happen to him again. The feeling faded after a few moments, but it did not go away entirely, and he was still feeling good when Roberto stood, thanked their god and took Arturo's sister's hand, pulling her out of the circle. She stopped laughing, her dress fell and flattened, and all of the gnats returned to the surface of squished loquats.

They broke up after that. Arturo left with his sister, and Roberto stood by the door of the room like a priest after mass, thanking everyone for coming.

None of them spoke on the walk back.

Johnny saw his parents' car in his grandmother's driveway when he returned. They'd come early to pick him up, and for that he was grateful.

"We're late because we stayed after mass," Roberto told them as they neared the houses. "Remember."

"Late?" Johnny said, frowning. He'd been wondering how they were going to explain returning so *early*. They'd only been gone for fifteen minutes or so.

"It's been about two hours," Roberto said, as if reading his thoughts. "Our god doesn't pay attention to our time."

They split up without saying goodbye, Johnny walking past his parents' car up his *Abuela's* driveway, the Orozcos continuing on to their house next door.

Inside, his parents were waiting for him on the living room couch with big smiles on their faces. "We got *Abuela* a present," his mom said. "Look."

A cable box sat atop the TV set.

"Please give Abuela cable TV."

Maybe it *was* a god.

He took the remote control his dad handed to him and flipped through channels, seeing movies, cartoons and television shows flash by.

He smiled.

◆

❧ THE SMELL OF OVERRIPE LOQUATS ❧

Johnny actually started *asking* if he could stay overnight at *Abuela's*. His parents thought it was because she now had cable—and that was definitely part of the reason, since she had a better package than they did. But what he really wanted was to see the neighborhood kids' god again. And ask it for things.

Over the next two months, he stayed overnight at his grandmother's house three times. Once, the Orozcos' parents were busy or incapacitated or something—Johnny never did get the story straight, although he was pretty sure Roberto and Miguel had something to do with it—and they met the other local kids in the abandoned house for their own ceremony. But the other two Sundays, he went with the entire Orozco family to mass. Afterward, he and the Orozco kids changed into play clothes and pretended that they were going to play basketball on the school playground. Instead, they gathered on the burnt floor around the loquat figure. There were other kids here with them this time, and Johnny wondered if different shifts of children came in and out all day.

The god gave him a Sonic the Hedgehog videogame, straight As on his report card and his own TV and VCR for his bedroom.

It was another month before he could go back again, and this time, the decaying figure was covered with fuzzy gray mold and had lost most of its shape. It looked like a mound of rotting garbage. The overpowering stench was more putrid than sweet now.

"His season's almost done," Roberto said sadly as they entered the dark room.

Johnny was confused. "So…your god's dead?"

"He'll be back next year," Miguel promised. "When the loquats are ripe."

It was true. They made their last requests of this season's god, with a girl named Maria's youngish aunt standing over the moldy form wearing a billowy skirt. The gnats swarmed up between her legs, she started laughing, and their wishes were granted. Next year, there was another loquat figure in place. Johnny had no idea who made it—and he never bothered to ask—but one Sunday morning, the Orozcos' parents were sick again, and Roberto led them all to the house.

WALKING ALONE — Bentley Little

There, in the center of the burnt floor, was the god.

It was different this year. The shadow passing over the room was darker and brought with it the chill of winter. There was a manic edge to the laughter of the older girls who stood above the god and translated its words, a hint of desperation rather than joy in the sound. The granting of wishes no longer brought with it a sense of euphoria, but instead inspired a dull feeling of dread that the bill was going to come due for these acts of generosity and that its cost was going to be personal.

Still, he continued to sit in the circle on the burnt floor, continued to ask the god for favors and presents. It was not that he *wanted* to—in fact there was a part of him that definitely did *not* want to—but visits to the god were what he did now, part of his life, and he saw no way of getting out of it.

The god gave him a new bicycle, a trip to Disneyland.

◆

They moved away when he was in eighth grade.

He thought of asking the god to let him stay, to not make his family move to Phoenix, but he was afraid to do so. There were glitches now in the way things worked, side-effects, and he was afraid that if he made that wish, the god would have his dad killed or something, that they would stay in Southern California but it would be because they *had* to stay, because some tragedy had befallen their family.

Besides, even though he'd miss his school and his friends, part of him wanted to leave. It would give him a reason for getting away from the god, an excuse that was not his fault.

So, he would not be punished.

He was not sure when he had developed the certainty that the god would punish him for not attending its services when he stayed overnight at his grandmother's, but it had been growing for some time, and Johnny had even hoped that there would be a blight on the loquat trees so the fruit would not grow this year, so the god could not be made.

{ THE SMELL OF OVERRIPE LOQUATS }

There'd been plenty of loquats, however, and even though he still had no idea who actually crafted the figure, the small form was in its usual place in the center of the burnt floor.

There was no final encounter. He and his parents visited *Abuela* many times before they moved, but always together, and he did not stay overnight.

When the movers had finally packed up and driven away with all of their furniture, and they were following in the car with the last and most personal of their belongings, heading across the desert to Arizona, Johnny actually experienced a sense of relief. Crossing the California border, he could almost feel the hold the god had over him waning. It was a small god after all, a local god, and its powers did not extend this far. Stopping for lunch at a hamburger joint, he smiled as he sat at the table eating with his parents, feeling free.

He thought about it often, though, throughout high school, throughout college. *Abuela* died two years after they moved, and the trip back for her funeral was the one and only time he returned to East L.A. The Orozcos attended the funeral—they were her neighbors and her friends—but Johnny stuck close to his parents and other than a polite acceptance of condolences from Mr. and Mrs. Orozco, he avoided any contact with the family. Roberto, Miguel and Angelina all looked unhappy, he thought, and while most of that could probably be put down to the fact that they were attending their neighbor's funeral, they also seemed thin and unhealthy, their faces drawn.

He was glad his family had moved away.

But he never stopped thinking of that small fruit figure in the abandoned house. Its bland blank form would occur to him at odd times, and he would remember the strange euphoria he'd initially felt upon having his wishes granted, and the way that feeling had gradually shifted to uneasy dread.

The Bible was wrong, Johnny decided. It had it all backward. God hadn't created people. People created God. Or gods. They came up with the ones they needed, and their need and belief gave those gods life. And power. It was the children of *Abuela*'s neighborhood, the ones offended by the Christian God's cruelty to kids, who had come up with this alternative, this small handmade deity who granted their wishes. But something had happened somewhere along the line, and rather than just *giving* them what they wanted, it had begun *taking* from them. He had gotten out early and escaped, but he wondered what the ultimate effect had been on those kids who had continued to visit the burned room in that abandoned house.

He did not do as well in college as he thought he would, and after graduation he ended up in a cubicle position rather than the job he really wanted. The ambitious girl he'd been dating dumped him, moving to Oregon to open a small business with a friend of hers. His parents were killed shortly after, faulty brakes on their car leading to a single-vehicle accident in the rain.

It was a tough couple of years, but things eventually evened out. He didn't love his job, but he got used to it, and he began going out with Susan, a data entry operator in his department. She was nice and kind, pleasant-tempered even if she wasn't a great beauty, and they lived together for a few years before getting married. For the honeymoon, Susan wanted to go to California, to stay in a hotel by the beach and go to Disneyland and Universal Studios. They had coordinated their vacations so they could both have a week off, and he booked five nights at a hotel in Laguna Beach overlooking the ocean.

In addition to doing touristy things, she wanted to see his childhood home, the place where he'd grown up, and he drove her down his old street in Orange, where new owners had let the lawn go and painted the house a hideous green.

He stayed as far away as possible from East L.A.

The honeymoon was fine, the marriage was fine. They bought a two-bedroom house in Mesa, and a few years later, they had a daughter. Susan wanted to name her Angelina. The name brought back bad memories for him—

Angelina Orozco laying out a circle of newspapers on the burnt floor for them to sit upon

—and he fought against it, but Angelina had been the name of Susan's grandmother, and she felt so strongly about it that eventually he gave in.

Angelina was a wonderful child. Smarter than both of them, more attractive than both of them, she was an enhanced combination of each of their very best qualities, and both Johnny and Susan loved her deeply and unconditionally.

{ THE SMELL OF OVERRIPE LOQUATS }

Which was why it was such a blow when they discovered that, at nine years old, she had somehow contracted a rare form of brain cancer.

They had good health insurance, and there was a Mayo Clinic in Scottsdale that Angelina's doctor referred them to, but the cancer she had was not one that responded easily to either chemo-therapy or radiation, and it was uncommon enough that there was no set course of treatment. The treatment she did undergo was aggressive and debilitating, and for two months after the diagnosis, she lived in the hospital. Sitting with her at night, after work, he would sometimes see stories on the news about sick children who raised money for the awareness of their disease by walking across country or opening a lemonade stand or collecting gifts for other sick children, and the stories always made him angry. Those feel-good puff pieces bore no relation to the reality of Angelina or the other kids on her ward, all of whom lay in bed day after day, suffering, while their parents tried to hold things together and go to work and keep their jobs and pay for the necessary treatment.

Susan showed a heretofore unexpressed interest in religion, her sudden belief no doubt fostered by their circumstances. She started attending mass, not just on Sunday but *every* day, and she convinced Johnny to join her. He prayed with her, wished with all his heart that a cure would be found, that some miracle would reverse what was happening, but he had no faith that God would answer their pleas.

This God.

One night in the hospital chapel, looking up at a crucified Christ, a mother came in to pray, kneeling in the pew behind them. The perfume she wore was strong and somehow fruity, and it brought to mind the smell of another fruit, the scent of overripe loquats. He suddenly saw in his mind the small figure in the empty room, remembering the times it had granted his wishes, recalling the sense of power that had gone through him, gone through the room, accompanied by that elusive shadow. He heard the laughter of the teenage girls as they stood over the small god and gnats swarmed up their skirts.

Johnny suddenly stood. "I have to go," he told Susan.

"What?" She stumbled as she got up from her kneeling position, and he took her arm. "Go where? What are you talking about?"

He couldn't explain it, and she wouldn't believe him even if he did.

"I'll be gone for a day or so—" he said.

Now she grabbed *his* arm, pulling him out of the chapel. "What? You'll be *gone*? With Angelina *here*?"

"I'm doing this for Angelina."

"Doing *what*?"

"Just trust me."

"Trust you? Johnny…"

The non-conversation continued out of the hospital and all the way out to the parking lot, where he took both of her arms in his and looked into her face before getting into his car. "I can't explain," he said. "And it would sound crazy if I did. But I might know a way to help Angelina."

"You're not making any sense!"

"I know," he said. "Watch her while I'm gone."

"Johnny!"

Then he was in the car and driving.

The Orozcos were long gone. He learned from neighbors that the family had not had an easy time of it, that the girl—

Angelina

—had died, and that one of the boys was in jail for drugs. The parents had lost their house paying for his defense. No one seemed to know what had happened to the other boy.

He had returned to East L.A. to see if the neighborhood god could cure his daughter, but after hearing about the Orozcos, the thought occurred to him that it was *because* of his experiences with the god that Angelina had been stricken. He didn't know about those other kids from other streets, but the lives of the people he knew seemed to have been ruined. It was as if they had all been punished for believing in the god. Maybe the Christian God,

THE SMELL OF OVERRIPE LOQUATS

the one they were *supposed* to have been worshipping at mass, had been angry at their defection and had penalized them for it.

Or maybe it was a psychic tradeoff. Maybe the small god had extracted what was good from their lives, providing them with the gifts they asked for, the wishes they requested, while leaving behind darkness and emptiness. If the first halves of their lives had been weighted toward happiness, the back ends were made up of misery. Angelina's cancer could be the payment for that trip to Disneyland and that new bike and the good grades.

There was no way to know, but whatever the truth, he was not afraid of repercussions. At this point, if Angelina could be cured, he would do whatever it took, no matter what the consequences.

Leaving his car parked on the street in front of what had been his grandmother's house, he walked the old familiar route. It was loquat season, and *Abuela*'s old neighborhood, even the blocks succumbing to gentrification, smelled of the fruit. The abandoned house was long gone, replaced by a taqueria, but he had no doubt that the god was here somewhere. He could *feel* its presence, a sense of hopefulness in the air as he passed a group of children playing on a swing set in a new small park, a tangible counterforce to the blankness he felt when he walked by St. Mary's.

Some of the kids who'd joined the Orozcos in the abandoned house must still live around here as grownups, must have inherited their parents' homes, and Johnny walked slowly in the direction from which those other kids had come, looking for faces that might be older yet familiar. He examined the faces of men mowing lawns, women tending flowers, couples manning garage sales. He walked into beauty salons and ethnic markets, but after a while he'd seen so many people that he wasn't sure he would be able to recognize anyone.

Then he saw an overweight woman with a noticeable birthmark above her right eyebrow.

She looked like an adult version of a chubby girl with a birthmark who had always wished for her parents to stay together, though Johnny remembered Roberto saying once that there was no indication her parents had any plans to split up.

WALKING ALONE — Bentley Little

He stopped in front of the woman. "Hello," he said.

She looked at him suspiciously. "Yeah?"

"I'm Johnny. My *Abuela* used to live next to the Orozcos."

The woman tried to have no expression, but the flicker in her eyes told him that she knew exactly who he was.

"Do you remember that house we used to go to on Sundays instead of going to mass?"

She shook her head, attempted to step past him.

He blocked her way. "I need to find it," he said, lowering his voice. "I need to find *him*."

"I don't know what you're talking about."

He was getting frustrated. "My daughter has cancer. She's going to die. I need her to be cured."

"My daughter *is* dead!" she spat back at him. "And so is my husband!" She pushed past him. "I don't want to talk to you!"

Johnny watched her go. He understood her pain—it was his pain, too—but he refused to give up. Time was wasting, and rather than pausing to formulate a coherent plan, he immediately started walking up and down neighborhood streets, knocking on doors, hoping to run into someone else he remembered or who remembered him. The search was fruitless. No one looked even remotely familiar, and after several hours, he took a break and bought himself a Coke at a convenience store. Standing outside with his drink, he was trying desperately to think of what he could do next, when he realized that tomorrow was Sunday.

Sunday.

He felt a small surge of hope. If the loquat god—or *any* god—was still around, Sunday was the day it would be visited. All he had to do was look for a group of kids who were dressed for church but *not* going to church—and follow them to their destination. But he would have to be careful, discreet. It was a god of children, and he was no longer a child. They would not let him in. He had no doubt that if he could *get* in, he would be able to petition the god for a cure, but he remembered how carefully he and the Orozcos had been to keep their visits secret and shield all knowledge of the god from any adult.

{ THE SMELL OF OVERRIPE LOQUATS }

He spent the night in a cheap and rather frightening motel, calling Susan from his cell to make sure that there was no news about Angelina. Everything back home was status quo, which was the best he could hope for under the circumstances, and in the morning, he awoke early, filled up the tank of his car with gas, and cruised slowly up and down the streets of *Abuela*'s old neighborhood. The few people he saw on the sidewalks were either homeless or turned out to be on their way to St. Mary's or a Korean church around the corner. Still, he refused to give up, and eventually found what he was looking for—a well-dressed boy and girl, brother and sister most likely, walking toward St. Mary's.

And then past it.

He parked the car halfway down the next block and got out, remaining far behind but following the brother and sister down the sidewalk, trying to appear casual and not draw attention to himself, aware of how this would look to an outsider. In his mind, he kept going over various scenarios and possible approaches, ways that he could get in to see the current incarnation of the god without the kids calling for help and having him arrested as a stalker and a pedophile.

Unfortunately, it turned out that the brother and sister were just on their way home, maybe from another local church, maybe from a relative's house. They went into the front unit of a duplex, speaking excited Spanish to a careworn woman who greeted them in the doorway.

Some sixth sense caused her to look up at him as he passed by, her eyes narrowing suspiciously, and he strode past purposefully, as though he had a specific destination and was late for a meeting.

Afraid to pass the apartment again, he walked all the way around the block and dejectedly back to the car. The morning was a bust, and he began to wonder if belief in the god had just died out over the years.

So what if it had?

That didn't mean it couldn't be resurrected.

The thought instantly galvanized him. Maybe the neighborhood kids were no longer sneaking off to worship their own homemade deity, but maybe he didn't really need them. He had belief and desire and need enough to power up a panoply of gods. On an impulse, he drove a mile or so east to where gentrification had not yet encroached. The homes were rundown, their windows protected by wrought iron, the brick walls shielding their back yards tagged with spray-painted graffiti. *This* was the East L.A. he remembered, and he cruised around for a while, up and down side streets, looking for something that would suit his purposes.

He found it finally on a block where several homes had been torn down and the rest were marked for demolition: an empty house that had been gutted by fire. In the back yard, next to the doorless garage at the end of the driveway, he could see a loquat tree full of fruit.

Johnny pulled next to the curb and got out of the car, walking straight into the back yard of the abandoned house, not caring if anyone saw him, thinking only of Angelina in her bed in the hospital. Most of the loquats were high on the tree, but the branches were thin, and he leapt upon the lowest ones, breaking them off and leaping aside as entire sections fell onto the dead brown grass. Loquats grew in clumps, and there were literally hundreds of the small yellow-orange fruits attached to the branches. Squatting down, he began picking off the clumps, throwing them into a pile on his right. When he had pulled down two more long branches and it seemed that he had what he needed, he began carrying armloads of the clumped fruit into the burned house, settling on a room with only one window that faced the side of the lot.

Once all of the loquats had been brought inside, he knelt down and started squishing them between his fingers, letting the sticky mash fall in front of him.

He molded the mashed fruit into a vaguely humanoid form.

Though it looked only glancingly like the god he remembered, he gazed upon the figure and believed in it.

He just needed a girl now, and here it was going to get tricky. He thought of trying to pick one up through a dating app or even calling for a young female Uber driver and then paying her extra to do what he needed, but those results could be iffy and would leave a traceable trail. He remembered Arturo's sister, the first girl he'd seen act as handmaiden to the god, and he decided to find a similarly slutty-looking teenager if he could. Sunday

THE SMELL OF OVERRIPE LOQUATS

probably wasn't the greatest day for it, but he went up to Whittier Boulevard, where stores and fast food restaurants were, then to various parks, searching for a girl who would fit the bill.

There were actually quite a few teenagers who might suffice, but nearly all of them were wearing pants. He finally found one wearing a babydoll dress standing outside a liquor store and smoking. She couldn't have been older than sixteen. "Hey," she said when she saw him walking up. "Do you think you could buy me a beer?"

"No," he told her. "But I could use a little help with something, if you'd be willing. I'll make it worth your while."

"You want me to suck it?" she asked in a voice that tried to be seductive but missed by a mile.

"No," he said. "I need you to do something else."

"I won't do—"

"It's not sex stuff," he promised her.

She dropped her cigarette and frowned, starting to get suspicious. "What do you want, then?"

"I just need you to go with me to a house. Literally, you will just stand there for a few minutes, then I'll drive you back here. I'll pay you…" He took out his wallet, looked to see how much money he had. "Forty dollars."

"Just for standing there."

"Right."

She seemed confused. "Are you going to take pictures, or…"

Johnny was starting to get frustrated. *How much time did Angelina have left?* "If you don't want to do it, I'll find someone else." He turned, starting back toward the car.

"I'll do it," the girl said, hurrying after him.

He kept walking. "Good. Get in."

She talked nervously as he drove back to the house, her breath smelling of cigarette smoke, but he ignored her, not listening, filled with a hope he had not had since hearing his daughter's diagnosis.

"Almost there," he said, turning onto the nearly empty street.

"You live *here?*"

"Oh, this isn't my house."

The girl was suddenly silent.

He pulled into the driveway. "We're going in there," he told her.

She looked frantically around at the bulldozed lots and condemned houses, the color draining out of her face. "Oh my God! You're going to kill me!" She already had her phone out and was desperately tapping on the screen.

He took the phone from her hand, throwing it in the backseat. "I'm not going to kill you."

"I knew there was something wrong with you! I should've trusted my instincts!"

"All you have to do is stand there. Like I said."

"That app I hit calls the cops! They know where I am! They're coming for me!"

"Then we'd better do this fast," he said. He didn't believe her, but in the state she was in, it was going to be hard to get her to cooperate, and the quicker they got this over the better. It occurred to him that he should just take her back and find someone else, someone more willing.

But he was so close.

And he wanted to get this done.

"Let's go," he said, getting out.

He half-expected her to run away, but she got out of the passenger side and walked in front of him, cowed. He led her through the open side door, through what had once been the kitchen, to the room where the god awaited. From outside, far away but getting closer, he could hear the sound of sirens.

She'd been telling the truth.

The girl was crying. "What do you want me to do? Please don't kill me. Please!"

"I told you, I'm not going to hurt you."

The sirens were louder now.

"See that…thing?" he said, pointing to the figure he had made. "I want you to stand over it."

"And do what?"

"Just stand there for a minute. Then it'll all be over."

{ THE SMELL OF OVERRIPE LOQUATS }

"It'll all be *over*? I'll be dead?" She started screaming. "Help!" she cried. "Help!"

He slapped her. "Stop it!"

The sirens were nearly here.

"Stand over it!" he ordered.

The girl was still crying, but she did as she was told.

Maybe it wouldn't work. Maybe the figure needed to set awhile. The loquats definitely hadn't been there long enough to attract gnats. Did it *need* the gnats?

Cars pulled up outside, at least two of them, sirens cutting off at the peak of their volume. Flashing red and blue lights entered through assorted broken windows, reflecting off the charred walls.

Was the girl still crying? Or was she laughing? He couldn't tell.

Police were shouting incomprehensible orders, though whether *to* each other or *at* him, Johnny wasn't sure.

The girl's skirt suddenly billowed upward.

Laughing. She was definitely laughing.

He heard footsteps in the front room, accompanied by loud voices.

It was now or never.

He sat down hard on the burnt floor, took a deep breath and addressed the figure.

"God—" he began.

THE MAID

(2016)

"I think the maid forgot to give us conditioner," Shauna announced, picking up the little plastic bottles from the bathroom sink counter and reading the labels. "There's shampoo and bath gel and lotion, but I don't see any conditioner."

"Damn it," Chapman said. "You pay top price to stay at a resort, you'd think they'd get these things right."

"We're not paying top price," Shauna pointed out. "It's their summer deal."

"That's not the point. You even get conditioner at Motel 6, for Christ's sake." He picked up the phone, dialed 0. "Listen," he said. "This is Chapman Davis in Room 312. The maid didn't leave us any hair conditioner. Could you send someone over to bring us some?" He didn't wait for an answer. "Thanks."

"It's not that big a deal," Shauna said.

"Then why did you mention it?"

"It was just something I noticed. I didn't know you were going to start making phone calls and throwing your weight around."

"It's the principal of the thing. We're staying here for three nights, damn it. We should get what we pay for." He turned away from her to make sure everything else in the room was satisfactory. The view, of course, was amazing. They'd asked for the room Jack Donaldson had told them about, and it overlooked both the lower pool and one of the gardens. Beyond that, the city of Tucson stretched out below them, and on a clear day like today, from this vantage point on the hillside, they could see almost all the way to Mexico. The room itself was spacious and elegantly furnished, with a flat screen TV in the sitting area and another on the wall in front of the bed. He opened the refrigerator: well-stocked. He tested the televisions: both worked. He checked for wi-fi: instantaneous. There was even a tray with a welcome note and two complimentary bottles of Perrier on top of the dresser.

All they had to do was wait for the conditioner to be delivered and they'd be set.

He leaned back on the bed and switched the channel to CNN, while Shauna continued unpacking the bathroom stuff. He half-hoped that she'd see him lying down, notice that he was aroused and…take care of things, but when she didn't, when she sat down in the sitting area, picked up a glossy lifestyle magazine off the table and started to read, he decided it was just as well. He'd be able to save his energy for tonight.

After three sets of commercials and three false promises of "breaking news after the break," Chapman sat up, annoyed. "Where's our conditioner?" he said.

Shauna did not even look up from her magazine. "Let it drop."

"I'm not going to let it drop. I called, and they were supposed to bring it to us. I'm going up to that front desk and give them hell."

"Chapman…"

"Stay here. I'll be back." He grabbed one of the key cards from the table in front of her and went out, closing the door behind him. Down the walkway that led to the lower parking lot, he spotted a maid pushing a cleaning cart away from their building.

"You!" he called out.

The woman turned to face him. Young, slim and Hispanic, she was prettier than he was expecting. Her nametag said *Rosa*.

The fact that she was attractive didn't give her a free pass. "Where's my hair conditioner?" Chapman demanded. "I called the office a half hour ago, and they were supposed to send someone over to deliver it to our room."

THE MAID

He had reached her by this point and saw, next to a clipboard on the cart, a tray of toiletries in plastic bottles. "Give me four of those," he said, pointing. "Hair conditioner."

"Yes, sir," the maid replied, looking at him boldly. He didn't like the expression on her face. What should have been a subservient smile was closer to a smirk. And was that "sir" sarcastic? He couldn't be sure, but it sounded that way to him. Bitch was probably illegal. He thought of threatening to call the INS if she didn't shape up, putting the fear of God in her, but this had already taken too much time and he wanted to hit the pool, so he took the bottles she chose for him and left. He'd complain to the management later. For a place with such a great reputation, the service here was so far disappointing.

They'd hear about it when he filled out the customer satisfaction card he'd seen on the desk in their room.

"Got 'em!" he announced when he returned.

Shauna was already getting into her bathing suit. She'd shaved since yesterday, he noticed. "Good for you," she replied. "I'm going to take a dip."

"Me, too," he told her. "Hold on a sec. Let me change."

Moments later, they were on their way down to the lower pool, she carrying several magazines, he with a hefty political biography he'd been meaning to read for the past year but had never gotten around to. They chose two lounge chairs near the deep end, slipping off their sandals as they put their reading material on the small glass-topped table between them. "Can you get us some towels?" Shauna asked, nodding toward a cabana near the shallow end of the pool.

"Be back in a minute." Passing other couples laying out, trying to avoid the splashing of a family playing Marco Polo in the water, Chapman made his way across the hot cement to the cabana. Inside, he saw the same maid he'd encountered earlier, talking to a young man holding a tray of drinks. She glanced in Chapman's direction, whispered something in the young man's ear and smiled. There was a sly look on her face that he didn't like.

This had to be nipped in the bud.

Chapman strode up to the cabana's counter. "Give me two towels," he ordered the maid.

She grabbed two from the shelf behind her as the kid with the drinks exited through a rear door. "Here, sir." But when he brought the white towels back to where Shauna was waiting and unfolded them, he saw that both had large yellow urine stains in the center of the terrycloth material.

"Jesus!" Grimacing, he dropped the towels on the ground at the foot of his chair and strode purposefully back to the cabana. "What's going on here?" he demanded.

The maid was gone, and behind the counter was a teenaged girl in a red one-piece bathing suit. His outburst startled her. "Sir?"

Chapman pointed across the pool to the small pile of white cloth at the foot of his lounge chair. "I just picked up two towels, and they had piss stains on them!"

The girl seemed flustered. "I'm…I'm sorry, sir. I don't know how that could have happened. Our towels are fresh laundered each day, and—"

He was distracted by movement off to his right. Someone waving. Glancing over, he saw the maid standing behind the Jacuzzi, her left arm wrapped around a pile of towels, her right arm moving back and forth in the air. Snickering, she turned away and disappeared behind a suite of rooms.

What the hell…?

He was almost tempted to follow her, but the girl in the cabana was shaking out some new towels to show him they were clean. "I'm sorry for what happened," she said again. "But these are nice and clean. And if you need any others—"

He took the towels and returned to their chairs. Someone had already come and taken the piss-stained towels away.

"It's that maid," he told Shauna. "The same one I got the conditioner from. Insolent bitch."

"Calm down," Shauna said. "We're here to enjoy ourselves. Get in the water and relax."

He got in the water, but he couldn't relax. Swimming laps to work off his frustration, he traversed the length of the pool, back and forth, back and forth, until his arms grew tired and he started to develop a cramp in his side. Shauna was already out and sunning herself, and he pulled himself out of the pool, toweled off and picked up the receiver from a nearby resort phone. "I'm going to order drinks," he told Shauna. "You want something?"

"A margarita would be nice."

He requested two when the phone was answered, charging the order to their room. Moments later, a runner brought the margaritas, setting the glasses down on the small table between them. Chapman tipped the kid a dollar, then picked up his glass. Something black caught his eye as he was about to lift the drink to his lips.

There was a dead beetle floating in his glass.

Caught off guard, he spilled half of the margarita on his stomach and bathing suit before putting the glass back on the tabletop. He could still see the black bug floating in what was left of the drink. His eyes searched the pool area for the employee who'd delivered their order.

Was the runner the same kid who'd been talking to the maid?

Now he was just being paranoid. Two coincidences did not make a conspiracy. The maid was not plotting against him. She hadn't purposely peed on their towels, and she hadn't told anyone to put a beetle in his drink.

But...

But she *had* been talking to a kid carrying a tray of drinks. And she *had* been the one to give him the towels. And she *did* seem to have an attitude.

He thought of the mocking way she'd waved at him before leaving the pool area.

Chapman stood. "I'm not putting up with this," he said.

"That bug probably just flew in there. I'm sure they'll give you another one—"

"It's not just that."

"Where are you going?" Shauna asked as he started away.

"To solve this."

Barefoot and wearing only his wet bathing suit, Chapman walked around the pool and up the path that led to the resort's lobby. A group of well-dressed Asian tourists were at the front desk, either checking in or checking out, and he waited, dripping on the carpet, until another clerk emerged from the back office. "May I help you, sir?"

"I'd like to see the manager," he told her.

"May I ask what this is about?"

"Inappropriate conduct by one of your employees. I'd like to see the manager."

"Just a minute," she said solicitously. "Let me get him."

Moments later, she returned, followed by a trim man in a blue suit who introduced himself as "Ralph Covey, general manager," and who formally shook his hand, a sight that must have looked ridiculous to anyone watching. "What seems to be the problem?" Covey asked.

"It's one of your maids. She was supposed to deliver hair conditioner to our room, didn't do it, then when I tracked her down, she was rude to me."

"I'm sorry. We try to—"

"*Then*," Chapman continued icily, "she gave me and my wife two towels for the pool that were supposed to be clean but instead had urine stains on them. Again, she behaved in a very disrespectful manner. Finally, I saw her conspiring with one of your waiters by the pool who gave me a drink with a very large beetle in it."

"I promise, I will get to the bottom of this," the manager said. "You wouldn't happen to know this maid's name?"

"I think her name's Rosa?"

"I'll look into this, and I assure you that it will not happen again. Our resort has the finest reputation—"

"It's why we're staying here," Chapman told him.

"—and we do everything we can to maintain that reputation." He motioned to the clerk at his side. "We'll be providing you with comped drinks for your entire stay and will do everything we can to make sure that the rest of your time here is as perfect as we can make it."

The clerk had gone around the side of the front desk and returned with an embossed envelope that she handed Chapman. He opened it to see a stack of tickets inside. "These are for your free drinks," she explained.

"If you need more, please let me know," Covey told him. He shook Chapman's hand again. "And I promise you, I will get this problem taken care of."

⟨ THE MAID ⟩

"Thank you," Chapman said. "I appreciate it." He walked out of the lobby the way he'd come and returned to the pool, where he and Shauna ordered new margaritas and spent the rest of the afternoon alternately swimming and lounging in the sun.

They had a nice dinner that evening at the resort's restaurant and ate on the patio so they could have a view of the city lights. There were several paths that wound around the grounds, and, afterward, they went for a long stroll, before ending up at their room, where they made love, watched TV and fell asleep.

Shauna was still asleep and the room was dark when he awoke around five. He had always been an early riser, even on vacations, though she preferred to sleep in. Getting up quietly, he walked slowly through the darkness toward the bathroom, using the bathroom light they'd left on all night to navigate. Once inside, he carefully closed the door, then peeled off his underwear and turned on the shower, letting the water heat up before he stepped in.

It felt good, the state-of-the-art shower head delivering a warm pulsing spray, and he let it hit his skin for a few moments, luxuriating in the sensation, before picking up the soap and starting to wash. He had opened up the little bottle and was about to shampoo his hair when the bathroom door opened. The shower curtain was pulled aside—

And the maid stood there, facing him.

It was the same maid as before, the impudent, attractive one—*Rosa*—and she met his eyes, pointed at his penis and laughed.

He grabbed the shower curtain from her and used the bottom portion to cover the lower half of his body. "What are you doing here?" he demanded.

She was still smiling. "I knock and there no answer. So, I come in to clean."

"It's six o'clock in the morning!"

"I thought you check out. I thought this room empty."

She was lying. She couldn't have knocked or she would have awoken Shauna. Which meant that she'd used her pass key and quietly sneaked in.

Not to mention the fact that, even before opening the bathroom door, she had to have heard the shower.

This was purposeful.

"Get out of here now," Chapman said through gritted teeth.

She nodded, smirking, and bowed an apology.

"You're fired," he said. "I'll make sure of it."

"Sorry, *sir*."

She left, not bothering to close the bathroom door.

Foregoing the shampoo, Chapman shut off the shower, reached out to pull the door shut and quickly toweled off. Shauna was awake, and she came into the bathroom, frowning. "Was the maid just in here? I woke up and thought I saw—"

"Yes!" Chapman said, furious. "She snuck into the bathroom while I was taking my shower."

"Didn't you hang the privacy sign on the doorknob?"

"Of course! But she purposely ignored it."

"They're not supposed to do that."

"No shit!" He got out of the shower and started drying himself. "I'm going straight up to the lobby. This is outrageous."

Five minutes later, he was dressed and storming up to the front desk, where a timid young woman backed away at his approach. "I want to see the manager!" he barked at her. "Now!"

She pressed a button on the phone console in front of her. "The night manager's here right now—"

"Get him!"

She pressed the button again. "*Yes?*" said a male voice through a tinny speaker.

"There's a guest out here who needs to talk to you," the clerk explained.

"Now!" Chapman bellowed.

"*I'll be right out.*"

Seconds later, a portly man in a blue suit emerged from the back office. "How may I help you?" he asked.

"You can fire one of your maids."

"What seems to be the problem, sir?"

"She walked in on me just now while I was taking a shower! Not only that, but she pulled open the shower curtain in order to see me naked, then

THE MAID

claimed it was an accident, that she thought we'd already checked out, even though my wife was asleep in the bed when she walked in, and when she came into the bathroom, the light was on, the shower was on, and she damn well knew I was there!"

The manager was contrite. "I'm *very* sorry, sir. That *definitely* should not have happened. I apologize—"

"I want her fired," Chapman demanded.

"I completely understand—"

"I. Want. Her. Fired." He fixed the night manager with his hardest stare, and the other man looked away.

"We do everything we can to make sure our guests are completely satisfied."

It was a vague answer and promised nothing, but Chapman knew enough not to press any harder on that particular point, so he subtly shifted his strategy, picking up a pen from the front desk and asking for a piece of paper, which the young woman behind the desk provided him. "Now what's your name and official title?" Chapman asked the night manager.

The man stiffened slightly. "John Marks. Sonoran Resort Off-Hours Manager."

Chapman put down the pen, folded the paper and put it in his shirt pocket. "Thank you," he said. "I expect you to take care of this."

He left the lobby without looking back.

They went out for breakfast—not to the resort's restaurant; he wasn't about to give them more money after what had happened—and returned to find that their beds were already made and the room had been tidied up. He saw two new bottles of Perrier on the dresser top as well as a complimentary tin of Danish cookies.

This was more like it.

Chapman turned on the television to the *Today* show. He'd had both coffee and orange juice with his breakfast, and needed to take a leak, so he walked past Shauna into the bathroom, pulled up the closed toilet lid—

—and promptly dropped it shut, gagging.

Someone had taken a shit in the bowl and not flushed it.

WALKING ALONE   Bentley Little

The maid.

He knew it was her, and he imagined that devious little bitch laughing to herself as she hiked up her uniform, sat down, took a dump and left. Trying not to throw up, he flushed the toilet. He no longer had to go to the bathroom, and he washed his hands in the sink, scrubbing them hard, before furiously marching up to the lobby.

The night manager was gone, and Ralph Covey, the original manager he'd spoken to, was back on duty.

There was no preamble this time. "She took a shit in my toilet!" Chapman shouted as he strode through the lobby. "She didn't even flush it!"

The young desk clerk looked panicked at his approach, but Covey was already out of his office helping a customer and immediately switched places with the desk clerk, greeting Chapman in a low calm voice clearly meant to placate him.

Chapman was having none of it. "I was in here less than an hour ago because she walked in on me taking a shower! Now she's taken a shit in my room!" He had reached the front desk.

"If you'll just keep your voice down…"

"I'll do no such thing! Bring her here! Now!"

"That's something we need to talk about, Mr. Davis."

"I'm done talking! If she isn't fired—"

"You mean Rosa."

"Of course I mean Rosa!"

"We've looked into that, sir, and there is no Rosa working at the resort."

Chapman stopped short. He frowned. Maybe he'd gotten the name wrong. Maybe…

No.

He specifically remembered seeing the name *Rosa* on her nametag.

"Then check which maid is assigned to our room," he demanded, "and call her in here. I want to speak to her in person."

The other customer was gone, the lobby now empty, and Covey told him to wait while he retrieved that information. The manager disappeared into his office, and Chapman and the desk clerk stood there uncomfortably, not

THE MAID

looking at each other. Moments later, Covey returned and announced that the maid was on her way.

The uniformed woman who entered through a side door was older, white and considerably overweight.

It wasn't her.

"This is Doris," the manager said. "She's assigned to your block of rooms."

The feeling he experienced was unfamiliar: a mixture of confusion and low-level fear. Who *was* the woman who'd been pretending to be a maid, then? Who *was* the person who'd been harassing him?

"It's not her," he said, stating the obvious.

"This is the woman—"

"It's not her! I know what she looks like. She's slim, Spanish, and her name's Rosa."

"I'm sorry. we have no Rosa—"

"She was talking to that kid by the pool," Chapman remembered. "The one delivering drinks. Ask *him* who she is!" He sounded desperate even to himself, and he was aware by the way the other three were looking at him that he was acting unhinged.

Was this part of her plan?

What plan? Did he actually think some wannabe maid was setting him up, playing out some elaborate scam in order to…what? Humiliate him? Make him think he was going crazy? Make *other* people think he was going crazy?

There was no acceptable way to extricate himself from this situation, so without saying anything else, he turned and left, going out the way he came in, knowing that the maid, the clerk and the manager would start talking behind his back the second the door closed.

He was still angry, but his anger had been tempered by bewilderment. He had no idea what was going on or why, and it had left him feeling decidedly uneasy. This was their last day in Tucson, however, so there wasn't much else that could go wrong. His goal at this point was to get through it, get out of here, then write a scathing email to the president of the company that owned the resort, letting him know exactly what type of shenanigans were happening on his watch.

Maybe their stay would be comped.

Or maybe they'd be offered a free stay next time—hopefully at another resort.

He and Shauna spent the day exploring Tucson, staying as far away from The Sonoran as possible. They returned in the evening after a nice dinner at a historic Mexican restaurant. The plan was to leave early in the morning so they could get back to San Diego by lunchtime.

It was their final night, and he expected Shauna to come in and share the shower with him, but she didn't, so he made a special point of not washing his crotch. Let her suck it dirty. Lightly toweling himself dry, he walked out of the spacious bathroom naked, ready to—

The bed was covered with blood.

No.

Heart pounding, he croaked out her name, though there was clearly no one else in the room. "Shauna?"

He moved forward on wobbly legs, checking to see if she—

her body

—was lying between the bed and the wall, but that narrow space was empty. Up close, the blood looked far too red, and there was much too much of it. A large spreading stain covered both the center of the fitted sheet and a significant portion of the turned-back covers. Splashes of blood had spattered on the pillows.

His eye was caught by something incongruously shiny in the center of all the gore.

A nametag.

Rosa.

Realization dawned on him.

She was trying to frame him for murder.

But how could all of this have happened in the ten minutes he'd been in the shower? And where was Shauna? Chapman rushed back into the bathroom and clumsily put on the clothes he'd taken off and left in a pile on the floor. His hands were shaking. He picked up his cell phone and tried to call 911, but a message on his screen said: *No Reception.* How was

{ THE MAID }

that possible? He immediately picked up the room phone, but there was no dial tone.

What was going on?

Feeling panicked, Chapman opened the door to the room, intending to rush over to the lobby and order someone to call the police. On the concrete path, heading toward him, dimly lit by lamps that lined the walkway, he saw a grim-faced Ralph Covey, the manager, flanked by two angry-looking security guards.

"Sir?" the security guard on the left said as Chapman approached. "Stay right where you are. I'm going to have to ask you to wait here until the police arrive."

"My wife…" Chapman managed to get out. "I can't find her." He gestured behind him, into the room. "There's…"

"We know all about it," Covey said coldly. "The police are on their way."

How did they know? Who could have told them?

"It was all within the last ten minutes! She either killed Shauna or kidnapped her, which means she can't be far!" He looked down at the ground, saw no trail of blood. Hope rose within him. Maybe it was all part of some elaborate hoax.

Covey frowned. "Who are you talking about?"

"The maid!"

In the darkness, Chapman saw movement over the men's shoulders. His eyes grew wide.

"There she is!"

The maid, pushing a towel cart, had moved into the illumination of one of the lamps lining the path.

The manager turned to look, then swiveled back, fixing him with a cold stare. "I just hired that woman. She's new. She started her first shift less than fifteen minutes ago."

"And that's when it happened! Fifteen minutes ago! She's the one who told you about it, right? And her name's Rosa?"

"Her name is not Rosa, but that's none of your business. We're just going to wait right here for the police to come and sort everything out."

"But it's her!" he insisted.

The maid had reached them by this time, and she left her cart, moved around the manager and walked up to Chapman. In her extended hands were four small bottles of hair conditioner. "Here you go, sir," she said.

Numbly, he took the plastic containers from her as, smiling, she turned away.

SCHOOLGIRLS

(2016)

When Cherie killed her parents, she didn't give it much thought. All the kids in the neighborhood were doing it. But when she awoke the next morning and there was no one to make her breakfast, it occurred to her that maybe she'd made a mistake.

There were still some Eggo waffles left in the freezer, and she popped two of them in the toaster before getting orange juice out of the refrigerator and pouring herself a glass. The bodies were already starting to smell, and she knew she was going to have to do something with them. Jan, next door, had dragged her mom into the alley and left her by the garbage cans so she could be picked up on Thursday when the truck came. Winston, across the street, dug a hole in the back yard and buried his parents in it.

Cherie pressed her nose into the orange juice glass to cover the stench. She was going to have to do *something*, but she was younger than most of the kids in the neighborhood, and her parents were fatter, so she was probably going to need some help.

At school, the kids on the playground still made fun of her. She thought they might start to be nicer since she'd killed her mom and dad, and they were, a little bit, before school, but at recess, things were back to normal. She had one of those no-plan, pay-as-you-go phones, and Shelley McComber laughed when Cherie pulled it out and tried to call her cousin Ray. Her parents had always told her to ignore those sorts of taunts, explaining that girls who made fun of things like what type of phone she had were just insecure, but her parents were dead, and they'd never really understood how important phones were for kids her age anyway.

Not only was her phone embarrassing, but she'd worn mismatched socks today, too. She'd noticed it in class and had made an effort when she stood to pull her pants lower so the pantlegs would cover her mistake, but it was impossible to hide something like that on the playground, and it was Shelley McComber's friend Dina who pointed and laughed and called her out.

It was par for the course. She never did anything right. Back in September, she'd been the last girl in her grade to kidnap an old person's pet, even though she *had* been the first one to eat it, and that had set the tone for the whole year. She always seemed to be behind the curve, and even when she wasn't, no one noticed.

It was only a matter of time before Dina and Shelley saw that she was wearing a baby brand of jeans, and that the stitching was coming undone beneath the left armpit of her shirt.

Maybe she could go back inside the classroom, Cherie thought. She could tell Miss Kaycey that her head hurt and that she needed to rest at her desk for a few minutes.

The teacher didn't open the door at recess anymore, though. Not after the principal had beaten her almost beyond recognition, walking into their classroom unannounced and, with no warning, punching her in the face. Miss Kaycey had cried out but made no effort to protect herself, and the principal had cuffed one side of her head and then the other before socking her right in the mouth and walking out.

The kids had all laughed at the way the teacher tried to talk through her swelling lips ("Retard!" Shelley McComber shouted at her, throwing a wadded piece of paper that bounced off her left boob, making the class laugh even harder). But Cherie knew what it felt like to be beaten, and she actually felt a little sorry for the teacher. She wasn't about to let anyone else know that, of course, and she kept her feelings to herself, but when she saw Miss

⊱ SCHOOLGIRLS ⊰

Kaycey crying after school that day, she made her a card covered with hearts and burned it and dropped the ashes into Miss Kaycey's purse when no one was looking. She'd felt closer to her teacher after that, had felt ever since as though they were kindred spirits. Maybe Miss Kaycey realized it, too, and maybe she *would* let her back into class.

Even if she didn't, though, Cherie could still stand in the hallway outside the classroom and wait until recess was over and the door opened. At least she'd get away from Shelley and Dina and their friends.

To her surprise, the classroom door was already open, though the teacher did not appear to be inside. "Miss Kaycey?" Cherie said, walking in slowly. She looked around to make sure the teacher wasn't lying on the floor or hadn't been strung up by the principal.

The room was empty, and, emboldened, Cherie walked over to the window, looking out at the playground. The other kids were playing on the swings, the slides, the monkey bars. Some of the girls from her class, the snobby ones who were always picking on her, had pulled down a younger boy's pants and were taking turns pulling on his little wiener, seeing who could make him scream the loudest.

She thought of what it would be like to set their hair on fire, and she laughed thinking about how the girls would look, running around and screaming, hitting their own heads in an effort to put out the flames.

"What are *you* laughing about?"

Cherie jumped, startled, and turned around.

It was Dina again. She'd come into the classroom, probably *looking* for her, and Cherie's heart started pounding. "Nothing," she said.

"No one laughs at nothing," the other girl said, advancing. "Not unless they're crazy. Are you crazy?"

"No," Cherie said defensively. She'd been retreating as Dina approached and had backed herself into the corner by the bookcase.

"I think you are. I think you're crazy. Do you know what happens to girls who are crazy?"

Miss Kaycey walked through the open doorway. She glanced from Cherie to Dina as she strode toward them. "What seems to be the problem here?"

Dina snickered. "What's the problem? Look at her socks! They're two different colors. And those pants—"

Miss Kaycey punched her hard in the stomach.

The other girl fell backward, gasping for air. Her head hit the floor, and the teacher kicked it as though it were a soccer ball. Cherie heard a satisfying thud as Miss Kaycey's shoe connected hard with the space behind Dina's ear. "Twat's that? I cunt hear you."

Dina was sobbing, and though she still hadn't completely caught her breath, she was able to croak out a weak "I'm telling—" before Miss Kaycey stomped on her midsection. A spurt of blood erupted from the girl's mouth, and then she was still.

Turning away, Miss Kaycey walked up to Cherie, smiling. "Feel better?"

She nodded, smiling back.

"And what was she talking about? What's wrong with your pants? I like your pants." She pointed to her own. "I'm wearing the same kind."

She was!

Cherie looked into her eyes. "Don't the other teachers—?"

"What? Make fun of my clothes?" She laughed easily, and Cherie thought she had never heard such a wonderful laugh in her life. "Adults don't do those kinds of things," she said. "Only schoolgirls pick on people who are different like that. Once you're a grownup, you get to be yourself and no one can tell you how to dress or how to talk or how to act or anything. It's all up to you."

That sounded wonderful, and she glanced over at Dina's bloody face, wondering why she had ever let girls like her and Shelley intimidate her.

Miss Kaycey must have guessed what she was thinking. "It gets easier when you get older," the teacher said kindly. "Didn't your parents ever tell you that?"

Cherie nodded slowly. "Yes, they did," she said, and began to cry. "Yes, they did."

UNDER MIDWEST SKIES

(2016)

The rental car did not have a satellite radio, and when the Wichita station finally faded completely into static, Louis pressed the Seek button, looking for something—anything—that would keep him awake along this endless stretch of straight flat highway. He was a New Yorker born and bred, and ordinarily everything he wanted or needed was within the twenty-two square miles of Manhattan. He was not used to driving for *hours* to get from one town to another.

But this new job required him to actually visit the local governments to whom they were trying to sell GIS systems instead of just emailing or talking over the phone. Lee was framing it as an exciting opportunity, but he and everyone else in his department knew that it was a demotion. This was grunt work, and it should have been handled by the newest newbie, the lowest man on the totem pole, not someone in his position. He should have remained in the office *monitoring* this trip, not taking it, but Lee had been out to get him ever since Louis had upstaged him at the September presentations, and it seemed as though the manager had finally found a way to insert the knife.

Although, if Louis *could* pull this off, Lee might soon find their roles reversed.

The radio stopped on a voice—98.7 on the dial—and he was grateful to hear the sound of another person. He only hoped it wasn't some hillbilly preacher giving a sermon about how the godless denizens of America's coasts were dragging the rest of the U.S. toward the pit of hell. He'd heard enough of that crap on this trip, and after two days, he was beginning to understand how paranoid conspiracy theories were able to take hold among the widely spaced residents of the vast rural Midwest.

This man on the radio didn't sound like a preacher, though, and it took Louis several seconds to realize that he was listening to some type of news bulletin or emergency announcement.

"*Repeat*," the broadcaster said. "*A tornado warning has been issued for Harris County. All residents are advised to take refuge in the nearest shelter. Travelers on Highway 55 are urged to pull off the road and follow proper procedures.*"

Highway 55?

He was on Highway 55!

Was he in Harris County? He didn't know. Louis experienced a rush of panic. What were "proper procedures?" Where was the "nearest shelter?" He was totally out of his element here. He'd seen the movie *Twister* as a kid, but that was the extent of his tornado knowledge. He knew nothing about what to do in the event of a tornado.

"*Repeat. A tornado warning has been issued for Harris County…*"

He peered through the windshield, looked out the side windows. There were clouds in the sky, but they didn't look like storm clouds. And he could see no sign of any tornado. Hell, there didn't even seem to be much of a breeze.

But his knowledge of tornados was on a par with his knowledge of Edwardian dress design. He knew jack shit about either. There was urgency in the voice of that repeated warning, and the smartest thing to do would be to find a town or a building, someplace with people who knew what to do.

"*Travelers on Highway 55 are urged to pull off the road and follow proper procedures…*"

There was a green sign ahead, and he sped up to reach it, then slowed so he could read the words. According to the sign, the town of Barclay was eighty miles in front of him. The town of Whitesville was a hundred miles beyond that. But a smaller second sign was posted below the first, and on it an arrow pointed to the left where the town of Hayfield was only six miles away. Indeed, there was a two-lane road intersecting the highway just past the sign, and Louis quickly turned on to the road, going well over the posted 25 miles per hour speed limit.

If he was going to find refuge from this tornado, it would be in Hayfield.

The asphalt ended, the paved road turning into a bumpy dirt lane. He continued on, speeding down a wash, up a small hill, not slowing until he saw a cluster of trees and buildings on the horizon ahead. What had happened to the tornado? Had it disappeared? Petered out? The radio station was now playing country music, and the warning he'd heard was no longer being repeated. Maybe he *wasn't* in Harris County. Maybe that was farther back on the highway. Or farther ahead.

The car suddenly started shuddering and shaking, and he gripped the steering wheel tighter as he braked to a halt. He recognized that shudder. It was a flat tire. Sure enough, when he got out to inspect the car, the right rear tire was little more than a ragged ribbon of black rubber surrounding the metal rim.

Taking out his cell phone, he tried to call AAA, but he had zero bars, no connection, and even a 911 call wouldn't go through. It could be due to the tornado—wherever that was—but, more likely, there were no cell towers out here and the locals relied on land lines.

He opened the trunk, looking for a jack and a spare, but saw neither. A lot of cars had them underneath the vehicle, but he wasn't about to go crawling around under there. He looked toward the buildings up ahead. Hayfield? Probably. And it couldn't be more than a fifteen-minute walk. His best bet would probably be to find a phone to call AAA, or have some local gas station mechanic either locate and put on the spare, or get him a new tire.

Louis glanced up at the sky. Still no sign of any tornado.

He locked the car, took out his laptop case—didn't want to leave *that* in there—and started up the road.

The town was farther away than it looked. It was six miles from the highway, and he wished he'd checked the odometer to see how far he'd come before breaking down. As it was, it took him nearly forty-five minutes to reach the first building, a real estate office. He was hot and sweaty, but at least the tornado had never shown up.

The dirt road had turned back into pavement, and he looked ahead as he walked, searching for a gas station or garage. Something about the town seemed wrong, and it took him a moment to figure out what it was.

Where were the cars?

Where were the *people*?

That was the real question, because while the town did not look abandoned—streets were nicely kept up, stores and businesses appeared to be open—he saw no sign of human habitation.

Only sheep.

That was the other weird thing. There seemed to be sheep everywhere, as though the fence of a nearby ranch had been breached and all of the animals had escaped. There was one standing on the sidewalk, two walking down the middle of the road, one actually lying on the front stoop of a closed hardware store.

Hayfield was small. Two main streets and four side roads were pretty much all there was. The buildings were in good shape, he noticed as he turned down the largest cross street, but the two cars he encountered both seemed to have fallen into disrepair. Tires were flat, windows covered with dust, and neither model was newer than ten years old.

Whatever was going on here, he didn't like it, and he cursed Lee for sending him out on this road trip.

Louis walked slowly up the block, looking around. Hayfield gave every appearance of being a ghost town.

The paranoia from those radio rants he'd heard on the road must have seeped into his brain because he started wondering if the people in town had just disappeared, like characters in some *Twilight Zone* episode.

He tried his phone again.

Nothing.

Maybe *everyone* was gone. Maybe he was the last person in the world and once he fixed his flat tire, he would be doomed to wander from empty city to empty city, searching for another survivor.

His flat tire.

That's what he needed to focus on. There had to be a garage here or an auto parts store. If he could just find the right-sized tire, or even a wrong-sized tire, anything that would fit on his car, he could get the hell out of here and be on the road again. He was becoming increasingly uncomfortable with Hayfield, and the sooner he could put this creepy town in his rearview mirror, the better it would be.

He walked up to the next street, turned left, and at the end of the block saw what appeared to be an open garage. A sign identified the building as Cook's Auto Repair.

Thank God.

He was hot, the laptop bag in his hand was getting heavy, and he desperately needed a drink of water. Picking up the pace, Louis strode up the street. He crossed the asphalt lot in front of the building and poked his head into the open garage door. "Hello?"

He didn't see anyone, but a Dodge pickup was parked in the bay to his left, while directly in front of him, some sort of 1960s muscle car was up on a lift.

"Anyone here?" he asked.

No one answered, but he heard a sound from the darkened rear of the garage, behind the pickup, and made his way back. "Excuse me," he said. A shadow separated itself from the inky space between the wall and the truck.

A mechanic?

A sheep.

Louis let out a small cry, startled.

The animal looked at him. It should have been startled, too, but somehow it wasn't, and Louis slowly backed away. He was not comfortable around animals. He didn't even like dogs, and being so close to a big wild animal like this (*wild* animal? Okay, *farm* animal), made him extremely nervous.

The sheep continued to look at him in a way that made him think it *knew* something. That was ridiculous, of course, but he could not shake the feeling that there was awareness in those black eyes, that what should have been a blank animal countenance possessed a sly cognizance.

{ WALKING ALONE } Bentley Little

He emerged from the garage back into the sunlight, wondering where he should go next, what he should do.

"Hello!" he yelled as loudly as he could. In a movie, his voice would have echoed through the empty town, but it died instantly here, reaching no farther than the other side of the road.

First things first. He needed to find something to drink. He had never been so thirsty in his entire life. Before he'd turned down this street, he'd seen a small grocery store on the main road in the direction he'd been heading. Even if this *were* a ghost town, even if he had to break a window to get in, he should be able to find something there.

He walked back the way he'd come, turning left at the corner. Even before the grocery store, there was a brick library on the right side of the street, and the door to the building was pulled open as if in invitation. Public buildings always had bathrooms and drinking fountains. As long as the facilities were working, he should be able to get some water, although with the way his luck had been going today, it seemed far more likely that he would encounter nothing but dry drinking fountains, dusty sinks and empty toilets.

Stepping through the doorway, it occurred to him that this might be a trap, that lawbreaking hillbillies might be lying in wait, having taken over the empty town for criminal purposes. But at this point he was too thirsty to care, and he advanced through the half-lit room past the circulation desk to an alcove containing not one drinking fountain but two! Reaching out, he twisted the silver metal knob, and water bubbled up, arcing into the air and hitting the grated drain.

It *was* working!

The water was cool, fresh and delicious. His grateful drinking, a series of slurps and swallows, was startlingly loud in the empty library, but he was so thirsty he hardly noticed.

He drank until he felt full, then straightened up and wiped his mouth. Ghost town or not, someone had to have paid the water bill, he thought, and he looked around, wondering what the hell was going on here. To his left, movement caught his eye, and he turned. Behind the same circulation desk that moments before had appeared empty and abandoned, a large sheep was standing on its hind legs, front hooves resting on top of the counter.

The animal stared at him and loudly tapped its right hoof three times on the wood.

A chill raced down Louis' spine. This was not only impossible, it was wrong. Sheep couldn't *stand*. Keeping his eye on the animal, he sidled slowly toward the doorway through which he'd entered. The sheep watched him, remaining upright, woolly head turning to follow his progress. He was almost past the front counter when the animal let out a low bleat. It seemed somehow threatening, and was accompanied by another three taps on the wood.

Was the sheep smiling? Maybe, maybe not, but from this angle, the corners of its black-lipped mouth appeared to be turned up in a malicious grin.

He was almost to the doorway and was quickening his pace in an effort to get out of the library when the sheep screamed at him. Louis jumped at the sudden sharp shriek, stopping in his tracks to look over at the circulation desk. The ear-piercing cry devolved into a series of bleats that seemed to vary in rhythm, duration and emphasis.

Almost like a language.

He needed to get the hell out of Hayfield. Even if it took him a day to get back to the highway and another day to reach a real city, he was not about to spend another second in this bizarro town.

He walked quickly out of the library—

—and was confronted by a gigantic herd of sheep that had massed in front of the building. Between fifty and a hundred animals stood before him on the street, with more coming in from both directions, all of them no doubt responding to the cries from within the library.

Every animal was staring at him.

Louis didn't know what to do. Try to run through them? Around them? Go behind the building and see if he could escape that way?

"Shoo!" he shouted, waving his arms. "Get out of here! Shoo!"

The sheep, staring, did not budge. He continued shouting and waving, but the tactic was completely ineffectual, and he quickly gave it up.

How was he going to get out of here?

WALKING ALONE — Bentley Little

As if in answer to his thought, a passage opened up in the middle of the horde, directly in front of him, sheep backing off to create a clear path through which he could walk. Louis didn't even pause to think about it. He sprinted forward, hoping to be able to make it through the opening to the other side, so he could keep on going and run right out of Hayfield. *(Could a person outrun sheep? They were slow animals, weren't they?)* But less than a yard in, he saw the space in front of him closing, heard the bleating of the sheep as they spoke to each other, felt the softness of wool brushing against the backs of his hands.

And then he was trapped.

He tried squeezing between the animals, but they pressed themselves closer together to keep him from getting through. One nipped at his fingers, drawing blood. He cried out, dropping his laptop case and lifting his arms high in the air.

For a moment, everything remained static, then the herd was moving, pushing him along with it. He was nudged to the left, shoved to the right, and it was all he could do to remain on his feet. He had no idea where they were headed or if they were headed anywhere, although he was acutely aware of the fact that he was probably one loud noise away from being trampled in a stampede.

As they progressed up the street, the open space around him grew, the sheep giving him more room to walk, although his route was still being determined by the movement of the herd. Eventually, it became clear that the animals were *driving* him toward an open field behind the town's small elementary school. He was marched across the parking lot, around the side of the rectangular one-story building, through a small blacktop playground. Ahead was the field, which, at first, he thought, local residents had been using as a makeshift dump since there appeared to be garbage scattered over the grass.

But those weren't pieces of garbage, he saw as he drew closer.

They were body parts.

Instinct took over. The sheep were taking him out to the field to kill him, the way they had the people of Hayfield. He didn't know how, why or when it had happened, and at this point, he didn't care. All he wanted to do was get the hell out of here, and as he was shepherded past a jungle gym, he jumped up, grabbed one of the bars and clambered up to the top. He was not remotely athletic and probably hadn't moved that quickly since he'd been in elementary school, but this was his *life*, and an instinct for self-preservation supplied him with a strength and coordination he had not known he had.

Sheep could not climb, even if they *could* stand on their hind legs, so he knew they would not be able to reach him up here, but there were scores of them and they could definitely wait him out. His sudden departure from their midst seemed to have thrown them, however, and without a leader to tell them how to respond, they milled about, confused.

This was why unthinking followers were called "sheep."

Taking advantage of the temporary disorder, he jumped off the jungle gym, over the heads of the animals, and grasped the long bar at the top of the swing set. The sheep were too tightly packed to be able to maneuver rapidly, and only a slow wavelike motion of the gathering offered any indication that there was even an attempt to react to his defection. The animals immediately around him had started bleating, but the combined volume of their cries blocked out any hope of hearing a response from any leader, and before that could change, he pulled himself hand-over-hand the length of the swing set until he reached the opposite end. A crossbar in the center of the triangular support frame gave him a place on which to stand, and Louis quickly noted that he was nearing the edge of the herd. The sheep were not packed quite as tightly here, and he took a chance and jumped to the ground, landing on his feet and zigzagging between animals until he had cleared the crowd.

There was a fence on his right, the school building behind him, and the sheep massed on the playground to his left. The only way out was through the field ahead, so he started running, hoping his theory that sheep were slow would hold true. He didn't look back—it had always seemed stupid to him when characters in movies wasted time and effort doing that—but plowed forward, feet pumping as fast as they could go. On the grass were rotting pieces of men, women and children. He ran past a half-eaten leg, stepped on a severed hand, almost tripped over a little girl's head.

WALKING ALONE   Bentley Little

At the far end of the field was a continuation of the same fence that had prevented him from escaping through the side of the school, only here it was working to his advantage. In the center of the chain-link was a single open gate that led to what was apparently a park behind the school. He would be able to run right through that narrow opening, but the sheep would have to file through one at a time, which, hopefully, would give him ample time to get away.

The bleating had stopped but the air was filled with an ominous lowing, a noise so substantial and pervasive that it seemed to be coming from all directions. *Was it?* Could whichever animal had coordinated the animals' actions have directed some of them to backtrack, swarm around the school and try to head him off?

Despite his previous reluctance to turn around, Louis hazarded a look back. Was the horde smaller?

Maybe they *were* planning to flank him.

His leg muscles were starting to hurt, but the necessity of getting out in front of this gave him a renewed burst of energy, and he sped across the field, through the gateway and into the park. He looked around, saw trees, grass, a sandlot. What direction was he facing? He wasn't sure. Being driven through Hayfield in the center of that multitudinous gathering had left him unable to get his bearings, and he had no idea which way he needed to go to get out of town.

He opted for the trees. At least they offered him some cover.

From the corner of his left eye, he saw movement—*white* movement—and when he glanced to his right, he saw more movement: individual sheep entering the park.

He was right.

They were trying to head him off.

Louis wasn't sure how good the animals' eyesight was, but they were still somewhat far away, and he crouched low, keeping close to bushes and trees, moving forward, until he reached the end of the park and a narrow lane. There were no sheep here, but it was only a matter of time, and he chose the direction that seemed to head away from the school. Staying on the edge of the road, close enough to jump into the brush and foliage on the side if it became necessary, he hurried past an empty Baptist church, and two houses that seemed unusually close together for having such big front yards.

Were the houses' occupants lying out there in the school's field?

He didn't want to think about that.

Having misjudged the direction in which he'd been heading, he quickly found himself back in the center of town as the lane emerged between a burnt-out building and an abandoned feed and grain store. Poking his head around the corner of the feed and grain, he could see the full length of the main street and its intersections with several side roads.

There were sheep everywhere.

Where was that tornado when he needed it?

The animals were not moving in one big herd or even in packs but seemed to be searching for him individually, and though he knew one bleat would send the others running, at least he had a sporting chance. The shadows were getting long, the light in the sky a yellowish orange. It was late afternoon, and it occurred to him that if he waited until nightfall, he might be able to sneak out of town unseen.

In the ruins of the burnt building to his left, he spotted a blackened alcove in an extant section of wall with a skinny charred door resting next to it: what must have once been a closet. Not thinking, again acting purely on instinct, he stumbled over the rubble, grabbed the sides of the sooty door and leaned it in front of him as he hid in the alcove. He ducked down, silent, and moments later heard one of the sheep bleating close by. Another answered from somewhere near.

Did sheep have a good sense of smell? Louis wasn't sure, but he didn't think so. He hoped not. Although, even if they did, the powerful smoke residue should definitely be able to hide his own scent.

He waited.

Thankfully, neither animal detected his presence. They wandered off, continuing their search. Over the next few hours, as the sky darkened, other sheep occasionally passed by, but none of them stopped or gave any indication that they suspected he was here.

WALKING ALONE — Bentley Little

Eventually, it seemed, they gave up, and while he couldn't be positive that was the case, the fact that he hadn't seen or heard anything in quite some time emboldened him to step out.

Hayfield seemed deserted. There was a full moon and no clouds, so he was able to see the buildings and the streets, but he perceived no other presences besides himself. They were here, he knew—*somewhere*—and that made him leery of passing through the town to get back to his car. He was much closer to the opposite side of the community, and he thought that if the main road continued on, past the town limits, he could follow it and see if it led to another city.

Of course, that would be even further away from the highway.

Maybe he could strike out across country, walk over to the land parallel to the highway and eventually work his way back.

He'd have to play it by ear. Moving stealthily, Louis slunk through the shadows away from the center of town. The buildings, already sparse and far apart, were replaced by open space. There was still no sign of any sheep, and he paused for a moment to get his bearings, hoping to see headlights off in the distance that would let him know where the highway was.

He saw no headlight beams, but there was radiance in the darkness off to his right. A cluster of stationary lights.

Another town.

Thank God! Louis felt like weeping. Never before in his life had he been so thankful for something so simple, so mundane, and the prospect of seeing other people again made him feel almost overwhelmed. Heedless of any possible danger, he began running down the center of the road toward the far-off town.

Nothing chased him, nothing tried to stop him, and other than a squirrel who ran crazily from one side of the asphalt to the other and then back again, he saw no animals.

As soon as he got out of this, he was hightailing it back to New York and never leaving the city again. Fuck Lee. Even if the manager fired him and Louis had to get a job as a janitor, he would be grateful. He had survived the inconceivable hell of Hayfield, and anything after that was gravy.

Of course...

If he could somehow steer Lee out here, convince him that Hayfield was an untapped potential market in desperate need of his particular knowledge and special touch with customers...

Louis smiled to himself.

He had no real conception of time, but it had to be well over an hour before he reached the other town. He didn't mind, though. Alone and unpursued, with his goal directly in front of him, always visible and getting larger by the minute, the time flew by. Amazingly, the first building he came to was a sheriff's office. Grateful that he'd be able to tell someone in authority about his ordeal, thinking of how a posse would go back there in the morning and blow the hell out of those beasts, shooting every last one of them, he bounded up the steps, pushed open the glass double doors and walked inside.

The sheriff's office was empty.

He stood in front of the desk, looking around to make sure he wasn't imagining it. "Hello?" he called tentatively.

No answer.

Feeling cold, he walked down the hallway to his left, looking for someone, anyone, but the building was deserted.

He hurried outside.

The town was empty, he saw now. The lights were on but no one was home.

He let out a crazy laugh that sounded far too loud in the stillness. "Hello!" he screamed at the top of his lungs. There was no response, and the only movement he saw was a lone chicken walking down the middle of the street.

His heart skipped a beat.

No.

The chicken saw him.

Stopped.

Slowly looked him over.

And walked purposefully toward him, clucking madly, as roosters and hens began streaming onto the road.

PICTURES OF HUXLEY

(2016)

It wasn't possible.

Just home from work, Jillian stared at the framed photo of Huxley on the breakfront, the one from picture day at preschool, where he'd been holding Tina Valdez's Paddington Bear. Parents were supposed to have brought their child's favorite stuffed animal to school that day, but it had been a hectic morning, and she'd forgotten, so he'd been forced to hold Tina's bear for the picture. The photo was still cute, but Jillian had always regretted the fact that he hadn't been holding his own Thumper, the stuffed bunny he'd slept with each night.

Now he *was* holding Thumper.

It couldn't be. But it was. She picked up the frame, examining it closely. There was dust on the glass, and on the wood of the frame itself. It hadn't been touched in who knew how long. So, it was clear no one had tampered with the picture.

Could she have remembered it wrong?

No. She had seen that photo a million times, and she recalled exactly what had happened that day.

Then how could he be holding Thumper?

Jillian looked carefully at the other photos on the breakfront to see if any of them had changed. Here was Huxley at Disneyland, sitting on Mickey

WALKING ALONE — Bentley Little

Mouse's lap and crying. There was Huxley at the beach, red plastic shovel in hand, intently focused on digging a hole in the sand. She went through each and every picture, and they were all as she remembered.

Except the one from preschool.

Her gaze fell upon a family photograph, one her mother had taken when they'd visited one Christmas. It was of Gene, Huxley and herself, and the three of them looked heartbreakingly happy. They were standing in front of her parents' Christmas tree in the corner of the living room, and Huxley was so small that Gene was holding him. How old had Huxley been then? One? Two? He was laughing, and she remembered his laugh at that age, a high-pitched infectious giggle that rolled out in waves without stopping for breath. She herself was smiling broadly, wearing a gaudy sweater she'd bought on sale at Dress Barn that at the time had seemed stylish. Gene was his normal disheveled self, and even in such a small photo, she could see the kindness in his eyes, the warmth and easiness of his smile.

Gene.

Where was Gene now? Jillian wondered. It was something she wondered often. They'd had a no-fault divorce with no alimony involved, so there was no reason for them to keep in touch after the marriage ended, and they hadn't. He'd been manager of the Borders Books in Brea, so at first she'd sometimes seen him there—she'd sometimes stopped by *just* to see him—but after the store closed, she'd lost track of his whereabouts. She wasn't even sure if he was still in Orange County. Or Southern California. Or the western part of the United States.

A feeling of sadness settled over her, and she moved into the living room, turning on the television so as to hear another human voice. In the kitchen, she thought about making lasagna—she'd bought all the ingredients over the weekend—but cooking for one took too much effort, and she ended up heating a Lean Cuisine casserole in the microwave.

She'd had a long day at work, completing Frank Becker's assignments as well as her own, since he had quit his job with no notice and left behind a mountain of paperwork to be processed. She'd barely had time for lunch. Maybe the stress of it all had affected her perception, had made her think

{ PICTURES OF HUXLEY }

she was seeing things that she wasn't. But that was a scary concept. Was she really so rattled by having to do some extra work that she could actually hallucinate an alternate photo of Huxley or misremember a photo of him that she had seen every day for the past decade and a half? Because those were the only two choices here, and to her, both of them seemed perilously close to mental illness.

Just to confirm that she'd seen what she thought she'd seen, she went back to the breakfront and looked at the preschool picture. Neither time nor a full stomach had changed anything. Her son was still holding Thumper.

Actually, she still had Thumper, along with all of Huxley's other baby toys, in the garage in a series of marked boxes. She was tempted to go in there right now and look through the boxes for his stuffed animal—she *had* sorted through the boxes before, more often than was healthy, probably—but Jillian knew it would make her sad, and instead she went into the living room, sat on the couch and watched an hour or two of mindless comedies on TV before deciding to go to bed early.

Crawling under the covers, she lay there staring up at the ceiling, aware for the first time in a long while of how big the bed was and how empty. Her left hand reached out to the spot where Gene had once lain, and the sheet was cold, the mattress firm and unyielding.

In her dream, they were at Disneyland, a place she and Gene had always wanted to take Huxley but never had. Gene took the boy on the Matterhorn and Space Mountain, because she didn't like thrill rides, but she took him on Dumbo and the other Fantasyland rides, laughing with him as he squealed with delight. All three of them went on Pirates of the Caribbean and the Haunted Mansion, but somehow Huxley got lost in the Haunted Mansion's stretching room, and she and Gene split up, trying to look for him, and then she lost Gene, and she spent the rest of the day in the park pushing through hordes of people, searching for her missing family.

The day dawned clear and bright, and for that she was grateful. She wasn't sure she'd be able to handle an overcast sky this morning.

Before heading off to work, on her way out the door, she glanced at the photos on the breakfront, her eye caught by a stray ray of sunshine that

WALKING ALONE — Bentley Little

glinted blindingly off the silver frame of a picture she'd taken of Huxley on the backyard swing. He'd smiled for the photo, but there'd been a Band-Aid on his nose because an hour before the picture had been taken, he'd fallen off that very same swing and landed face-first on a small rock. It was Christmas morning, the first day he had gotten the swing set, and after cleaning the small wound, putting Neosporin and a Band-Aid on it, it had taken them forty-five minutes to convince him to try the swing again. She had taken the picture so he could see how brave he was.

One step forward and the glare was gone.

Only in the photo Huxley had no Band-Aid on his nose, and his smile was much, much wider.

She halted, feeling a pressure behind her eyes that threatened to turn into a headache.

Not again.

She reached over, picked up the framed photo and examined it carefully, at the same time sorting through her memories. She'd not only taken the picture, she'd looked at it literally thousands of times and knew every centimeter of its composition.

There was no way around it.

The photo had changed.

Just like the one from preschool.

Things did change over time. She knew that. She recalled going to a concert a few years back, a punk rock concert by a band that had been very important to her as a teenager. The first time she'd seen them, when she was eighteen, she'd been blown away by the chaos of their performance. The drummer had broken a stick but hadn't cared and had kept on playing with his fist! A girl had handed the singer a bottle of something, and he'd dumped the contents on her head before smashing the bottle at his feet and stomping on the glass! It had been amazing!

But when she'd seen them again, the drummer was dead, replaced by his son, and the rest of the band seemed to be merely going through the motions. As he was singing, the singer had walked off the club's stage directly onto a table, stepping on and kicking over the patrons' food and drinks. It was supposed to be anarchic and punk, but it didn't seem real, seemed more like part of an act. People had paid for that food, and it was a stupid and immature thing to do; she knew it, and she knew that he knew it, too, and it made the whole thing feel kind of tired and sad.

So, things changed. It was an inevitability of life.

But the past didn't change.

The past couldn't change.

Yet it had.

Twice.

Jillian put the frame back in place and left the house, closing and locking the door behind her. She could not afford to be late for work, but all the way to the office her mind was on the altered photos. She wasn't quite sure how she felt about them. Was she scared? She probably should be, but that didn't really describe the feeling she'd gotten when she discovered that the pictures had been…revised. Because there was an odd hopefulness mixed in with the sense of distress and anxiety the photos engendered within her. She wasn't quite sure why, but it might have had something to do with the fact that she did not see the pictures as transformed so much as *corrected*, as though their previous incarnations had been wrong and this was the way they were supposed to have been all along.

At her desk for the rest of the day, her eyes kept looking toward the corner spot where she used to keep a picture of Huxley. She'd taken it down so people wouldn't ask questions, but she couldn't remember where she'd put it, and that memory lapse gnawed at her. She should have put it on the breakfront in the house with all her other photos, but she hadn't. It wasn't on her dresser in the bedroom, either, or on the fireplace mantle. Could she have put it in one of the boxes in the garage? That wouldn't have been right, and she could not imagine why she would do something so insensitive, but it seemed to be the only possibility that made any sense.

All the way home after work, she was gripped by a growing dread that the photos would have reverted back to their original versions by the time she arrived. She liked the new photos. This was the way they were supposed to be, and she found herself speeding up to get home early.

Two more were different this time.

One was his photo with the Santa from Sears. In the original, Huxley had been smiling, but nervously, because even though he loved the *idea* of Santa, the man's booming laugh frightened him a little. In the new shot, however, Huxley was grinning hugely, perfectly comfortable and at ease. In the other picture, her son looked the same as he had before, only his clothes were different, and she remembered that he had never liked that other shirt or those pants. He was now dressed in his favorite jeans and his beloved Scooby Doo sweater.

What was going on here?

Was time being rewritten?

*The past couldn't cha*nge, she thought again.

Unless...

Unless someone, somehow, was going back in time and altering what had occurred in order to create a new outcome.

That wasn't possible. Besides, even if it was, who would care about the minor details of her son's life? Who would make such an effort to alter specific Kodak moments in order to make them better?

Her.

That brought her up short.

Was it possible?

It couldn't be.

But what if it was? What if a future version of herself was going into the past to...to what?

Prevent Huxley from dying.

Jillian took a deep breath. That would be the goal, of course, but there was no way it could be done. Even if she lived to be a hundred, there would be no time travel within her lifetime. That was the stuff of movies and TV. It wasn't even close to becoming a reality. Besides, it couldn't be the case, because if she—or someone else—had gone into the past and changed something, the alteration would have become the fact. She wouldn't be able to recall the original timeline. She'd think that Huxley *had* brought Thumper to picture day; she wouldn't remember that he'd posed with Tina's Paddington. She'd believe that he'd never fallen off the swing, that he'd never been afraid of Santa, that he'd always worn his Scooby Doo sweater.

Her head hurt from thinking about the ripples and ramifications.

Maybe someone was just changing the pictures, substituting them with ones that had been Photoshopped.

But why? To torture her?

"Glen?" she said aloud.

No. The divorce had not been rancorous, and whatever his faults, Glen was not cruel. He would never torment her in this way.

Who, then?

She had no answer to that.

She inventoried the photos one more time before going into the kitchen and pouring herself a shot of Scotch from a bottle that Glen had bought years ago in case they ever had hard-drinking guests and that she had not touched since he left. Whatever was happening, she thought, the pace of it seemed to be speeding up. There'd been one altered photo yesterday, another one this morning, two during the day today.

Would all of them eventually be switched with pictures from an alternate reality?

She monitored things for the rest of the evening, checking periodically to see if anything had changed, hoping to catch it while it was happening, but there was nothing different in any of the photos by the time she went to bed at eleven.

The next day was Saturday, and Jillian awoke late, melancholy from the emotional residue of an unremembered dream. Sunlight was shining through the curtains, and the red digital numbers on the alarm clock next to her bed said that it was already 8:15. Slipping out of bed, she pulled on her robe and walked out of the bedroom to make herself a quick breakfast.

Framed photos lined the hallway.

She stopped outside her bedroom door, staring at the suddenly unfamiliar walls. She shook her head as if to clear it and blinked several times, but nothing changed. The framed photos were still there.

WALKING ALONE — Bentley Little

Reaching out with her fingers to reverently touch the glass, she examined the one closest to her bedroom door.

Huxley's high school graduation picture.

Jillian's breath caught in her throat.

Her son had been seven years old when the car hit him. He had never had a high school graduation. He had never even had an elementary school graduation. Yet now here he was, tall and handsome, looking a little like Gene, a little like her, but ultimately more attractive than either of them.

She walked slowly forward. There were other school photos of Huxley: on stage with the cast of a play, standing in the center, apparently the star; standing next to some sort of complicated science project, proudly holding up a blue ribbon in one hand and a certificate in the other; wearing a band uniform, holding a trombone.

Her eyes filled with tears. This is what should have been. This is the life Huxley deserved, the life he would have had if—

The door to Huxley's room was closed.

Jillian hadn't noticed it until now, but the band photo was hanging on the wall next to his old room, and the door was closed.

That door was never closed. It was always left open.

Within, she heard noise. The creak of bedsprings. Bare footsteps on the hardwood floor. The opening of a dresser drawer.

She wiped the tears from her suddenly dry eyes.

Heard a loud male yawn.

She took a deep breath. Heart pounding, she steeled herself, reached for the knob, opened the door.

"Huxley?" she said.

MY COLLEGE ADMISSION ESSAY

(2016)

Describe the obstacles you have had to overcome in your life that have molded you into the person you are today.

I have had to overcome numerous obstacles in my life, but I believe they have molded me into the person I am today and have made me into the kind of student who would excel in a college environment.

———◆———

My mother liked to tell me the story of when Ronald Reagan called her parents to console them about the loss of her brother, who had died in a training accident at Ft. Bragg. The president, she said, was drunk. At least it sounded that way to her. She was listening in on the extension phone, and he was slurring his words and saying things that made no sense. The one phrase she remembered him saying specifically was, "I'll eat a potato out of Mommy's ass," although she couldn't recall the context of the remark.

He had to be drunk, she said.

WALKING ALONE — Bentley Little

But I thought it might have been an early indication of Alzheimer's. My dad said he was just simple.

◆

My sister Suzie died when she was six months old.

◆

Throughout my school years, the smartest student in each of my classes was a girl. We all knew it, we all accepted it, but now, as adults, my friends act as though men are intellectually superior and women our not-quite-equal auxiliaries.

When did that mind-shift take place?

◆

I have always felt uncomfortable in the presence of clowns. Probably because, as a child, I was often beaten by my dad's clown friends. Especially Red Butt.

As a joke, Red Butt, who often stayed with us when he was in town, would purposely stick out one of his oversized shoes as I walked by, tripping me. He would laugh when I fell, and if I dared to complain or get mad or react in any way, he would leap out of his seat and cuff my head. At that point, it was on. I would try to get away, but his big-gloved clown hands would smite me with blows, and he would cackle uproariously as one of the knees within his polka-dotted pants would slam into my stomach, knocking the air out of me.

Sometimes the other clowns would join in, hitting me with their various props. One of them, Stinko, used to just stand in the background honking his horn, and while he didn't physically touch me, the sound of that horn was as bad as some of the blows, and I hated him as much or more than anyone except Red Butt himself.

{ MY COLLEGE ADMISSION ESSAY }

Eventually, my dad would chuckle and say, "Knock it off," and the clowns would retreat to the floor or the couch or the recliner, and, crying, I would go off to find my mother, who would clean my wounds, and put Bactine and Band-Aids on my cuts.

I don't know where Red Butt is now.

But I hope he's dead.

Stinko, too.

◆

It was my mother who found my sister's body that morning, smothered in her crib.

◆

What was Suzie like? It's hard to be like anything when you're only six months old, but I remember her as a noisy baby, always crying. My parents used to assure me when I asked that I was a very quiet baby. "You were easy," my mother would say, and she would pat my head. "You were a good boy."

◆

My mother was never quite right after Suzie's death.

There was nothing specific, nothing I could point to, but she was different, quieter, and sometimes she seemed forgetful, although I don't remember her actually forgetting anything.

Vague.

She seemed vague.

◆

People talking on handless devices always remind me of mental patients talking to themselves.

{ WALKING ALONE } Bentley Little

Mother used to talk to herself after Suzie died.

Or maybe she thought she was talking to Suzie.

We didn't have a house. We lived in an apartment. The apartment building was small, only four units, and located behind a much bigger house in a part of the city that had been nice at one time but was kind of rundown by the time we got to it. Looking back on it now, I think we might have lived in what were originally supposed to be servants' quarters.

The old man and old lady who lived in the apartment next door, the Ryersons, used to be really nice to me, giving me candy every time they saw me, but they stopped talking to me sometime after Suzie was born. I remember Mrs. Ryerson trying to tell my mother a way she knew to stop a "colicky" baby from crying and my mother slamming the door in her face. Mr. Ryerson tried to tell my dad that it was just that they were old and the crying kept them up at night. He said the walls were too thin. My dad told him to blow it out his ass.

I didn't like Suzie's crying, either.

My sister used to puke a lot. And she always smelled like shit.

From the time I was three until the time I was twelve, when I stopped trick-or-treating, my parents made me wear a clown costume. I NEVER wanted to

{ MY COLLEGE ADMISSION ESSAY }

be a clown. I wanted to be a pirate one year, and a monster the next. I always wanted to be Batman. But every Halloween my parents made me go out as a clown.

My dad would paint my face so I looked like Red Butt and then cuff my head.

For "good luck."

◆

It was because my sister wouldn't stop crying that I had to kill her.

I don't think she felt anything, though, because I put the pillow over her head while she was asleep. To her, it was just like never waking up after a long nap.

◆

My grades went down in elementary school after Suzie died, but I did pretty well in junior high, and by the time I got to high school, I was on the honor roll every semester.

◆

So, while I have had to overcome a lot in my life, I think that adversity has made me stronger. I am happy, healthy, well-adjusted and able to handle anything that is thrown at me.

This is why I firmly believe I would be a productive member of your academic community and a welcome addition to your college.

POOL, AIR CONDITIONING, FREE HBO

(2016)

"**Not exactly the** honeymoon I imagined," Heather said wryly.

He should have planned better, Todd thought. But who would have guessed that most of the small towns they'd be driving through would have no motels, and that the motels in the one decent-sized city they encountered would be completely booked. He should have looked things up, should have Googled their entire trip, but they'd wanted to be old school and analog, wanted to just pick a direction and drive, seeing what they could find, having unplanned adventures that would become great stories to tell their children and that they would remember for the rest of their lives.

Now they were stuck at this dump of a motor court outside the one-road town of Feldspar, New Mexico: a single-story, ten-room Bates Motel whose better days had been long before either of them were born.

They would definitely have a memorable story, but it was going to be one of those that was far better in the retelling than in the occurrence.

They'd reached the motor court late in the afternoon, and since the next town was an hour and a half away and there was no guarantee that it would have any place to stay at all, they made the decision to stop and check in for the night.

{ WALKING ALONE }   Bentley Little

Todd tried to make a joke of it. "At least it has free HBO," he said, pointing to the sign. But he felt guilty. Heather deserved more than this, and it was his fault for not planning out a more romantic honeymoon. He was always missing those sorts of social cues, and though he and Heather had always prided themselves on their unconventionality and had talked many times about a cross-country road trip, he should have figured out that the trip and the honeymoon were two different things and that, deep down, she wanted something more traditional.

They stepped out of the car. Behind windows so dusty that the glass appeared sepia-toned was the motor court's office, so designated by a metal sign mounted above the white wooden door. Todd pushed the door open, causing a buzzer to sound somewhere in the back. The office itself was small, a narrow space between the dusty windows and a shabby counter. Behind the counter, a doorway in the wall led to what appeared to be living quarters.

The buzzer had not caused anyone to come out to the front, and Todd was looking for a bell on the counter that he could hit in order to alert the manager to their presence, when he saw that there was already someone behind the counter.

A dwarf.

It was not the politically correct term, but the small man was wearing a red-and-white striped shirt that resembled something from a circus, and that was the first word that came to Todd's mind. Trying not to act as startled as he felt, he smiled as though everything were normal and took out his wallet. "We'd like a room, please."

"Cash only," the manager said in a high, whiny voice.

Cash?

That was weird.

But it was just as well. Todd was not sure he'd feel comfortable supplying his credit card number to a rundown motel on the edge of a middle-of-nowhere New Mexico town. It was an invitation to identity theft.

"That'll be fine," he said. "How much?"

"Fifty-nine forty-eight."

} POOL, AIR CONDIITONING, FREE HBO {

Todd took out his wallet, placing three twenties on the counter. He expected to have to fill out some sort of form with his address or phone number or, at the very least, license plate number—just in case he and Heather trashed the room—but the dwarf only took the money, put it somewhere beneath the counter, and said, "I'll get your change. Pennies okay?"

Pennies?

Todd nodded, and the little man withdrew into the back room, emerging with a mason jar filled with copper coins. He started doling out change. "Forty-eight," he began, then placed a penny on the counter. "Forty-nine." Another penny. "Fifty." Another penny. "Fifty-one..."

They stood there patiently until he reached a triumphant "Sixty dollars!"

Awkwardly, Todd scooped up the pennies. He placed a huge handful into his right front pocket, then attempted to grab the last six or seven, which lay flat on the counter and were practically impossible to pick up. It took him at least another minute, using his fingernails, to pry them loose and put them in his uncomfortably bulging pocket.

The manager waited, and when Todd had picked up all of his change, he turned around. "You can have..." There was a long pause as his short blunt fingers ran over a section of wall on which keys were hanging from individual nails. While it made absolutely no rational sense, there seemed something ominous in the pause, and Todd suddenly wished they had continued on to another town and taken their chances.

"Room six," the man said. He handed Todd a dull brass key attached to a ring anchored by a green plastic triangle on which the name of the motor court had been practically rubbed off by decades' worth of fingers. He pointed out the filthy window toward the middle of the longer wing of the L-shaped motel.

"Where's the pool?" Heather said suddenly. "Your sign says there's a pool."

"There used to be," the manager answered. "Not sure what happened to it."

Not sure what happened to it?

The feeling came again, a nagging sense that they should have passed this place by, slept in the car if it came to that.

WALKING ALONE — Bentley Little

Heather wasn't one to let such discrepancies pass by. "What do you mean you don't know what happened to it? Pools don't just disappear."

"It wasn't a real pool anyway. It was one of those blue above-ground things. You know, with the metal sides and the rubber lining? I think the owner just put it up so he could have that word 'pool' on the sign. Thought it would bring more people in. Mostly it was just a tub of leaves and algae. I think someone might have hit it with their car. Or maybe the water evaporated and it blew away in a dust storm."

Todd glanced over at Heather, shooting her a look telling her to let it drop so they could get out of here and into their room. He could tell from the expression on her face that she was as confused by the explanation as he was—how could the manager not remember whether the pool was hit by a car or blown away by wind? The two possibilities had nothing whatever in common—but she gave him a slight nod, and the two of them thanked the manager and walked outside.

Todd handed Heather the key. "It's only about twenty feet away. Why don't you walk there and I'll park the car?"

She nodded, took the key and marched down the intermittent walkway while he drove the car across the cracked asphalt and pulled into a marked space just in front of their room. She beat him there and, rather than waiting, used the key to open the door.

Looking around the motel room as Todd walked in behind her, Heather tried to hide her disappointment, although "disappointment" was a mild way of putting it. For the room was, without a doubt, the smallest, most depressing place she'd ever stayed. When she was a child, her family's vacations had always been tightly budgeted due to their permanently perilous finances, but the Super 8 Motels and Budget Inns at which they'd stayed had always been clean and well-maintained. This room looked as though it hadn't been cleaned in ages. The brown bedspread and orange shag carpet hid a multitude of sins, and every smooth surface boasted a thick layer of dust.

In addition to being stuffy, the room was hot, and Heather turned on the light switch, looking for the advertised air conditioning. The dull yellow glow of a single bedside lamp illuminated an ancient wall unit beneath the

{ POOL, AIR CONDIITONING, FREE HBO }

window, but when she went to turn it on, the appliance was dead. Todd pulled open the drapes, and they both checked to see if the window could be opened, but it was sealed shut.

"Well, this is romantic," Heather said.

Todd went back out to the car to get the suitcases, and she checked out the bathroom: small sink, rusty water in the open-lidded toilet, a shower/bath combo with a cracked fiberglass frame. On top of the toilet tank was an ice bucket and four wrapped plastic glasses. She was thirsty, Heather realized, and she washed out the bucket in the sink, then passed Todd, bringing in the snack bag from the car, telling him that she was going to get some ice.

The manager had not told them where the ice machine was, but she'd spotted a protruding "ICE" sign at the far end of the building, and she walked down there with the bucket. Most of the rooms she passed appeared to be empty, and only three had cars parked in front of them. All of the cars looked old and junky.

She reached the end of the building. The ice machine was around the corner, and though the sun had not yet gone down, the area was in shadow. It made her nervous to be out of sight of the rest of the motor court, and she quickly walked over to the machine, placed the bucket in the recess beneath the ice spout and pressed the red button.

Nothing.

No ice came out. There was not even that churning gravel sound ordinarily generated by empty ice machines. The device appeared to be dead.

She pulled the bucket out of its niche. On the ground to the right of the ice machine, she saw, was the desiccated corpse of some type of rodent, and it made her wonder how long it had been since anyone had been out here. She hurried back around the corner and down the length of the building to their room.

When she returned, Todd was just closing the door, planning to go to the bathroom, and she told him that she was going to go up to the office and tell the manager that the ice machine wasn't working.

"Go ahead," he said.

Closing the door behind her, she cut cattycorner across the lot to the manager's office, walking inside—

—where the dwarf stood on top of the counter, naked.

With a penis as long as his legs.

"Jesus!" She turned and ran back to the room, startled and frightened. She'd left the key inside, and she started pounding on the door, hoping Todd was out of the bathroom. "Todd!" she cried. "Open up!"

A woman from the room to the right came out, drawn by the sounds of tumult. She was thin, older and wearing a multi-colored muumuu. "Everything okay?" she asked.

Todd opened the door.

"It's fine," Heather told the woman, trying to move past Todd into the room.

"Are you two staying here?" the woman asked, coming over.

That was obvious, and Heather did not even bother to answer. She wanted to get safely inside the room. She glanced nervously over her shoulder at the motel office.

Todd, apparently, was in the mood to chat. "Yes, we are," he told the woman. He put an arm around Heather. "We're on our honeymoon."

The woman shook her head. "Shouldn't have done that."

"Gotten married?"

"No. Come here. You shouldn't have come here."

"Why?"

"Because he won't let you leave. The manager," she clarified.

Heather shivered as she thought of the small man and his huge appendage.

Todd frowned. "What do you mean he won't let us leave?"

She gestured toward the green T-Bird parked in front of her room. "He comes out at night and steals parts from your car. Then he says 'kids' did it. You call a mechanic to repair your car, and once it's fixed, it happens again. He steals some other part until finally you run out of money and you can't get it fixed anymore."

"Why would he do that?" Todd asked.

"I think he's crazy."

She was crazy, Heather thought, and she could tell from Todd's glance that he thought so, too.

⊦ POOL, AIR CONDIITONING, FREE HBO ⊣

"How long has this been going on?" Todd asked, patronizing her.

"Five years. I've been here for five years."

"We'll be careful," Heather said and ushered Todd into the room, closing the door behind her.

He laughed, though quietly, not wanting the woman to hear. "*She's* a character."

She was *something*, Heather had to admit. She looked over at her husband. She'd run back here to tell Todd what had happened in the motor court's office, but the encounter with their neighbor had thrown the timing off, and now the idea of bringing it up seemed weird and awkward. It seemed easier all of a sudden to just let it lie. They'd be gone in the morning, and that would be the end of it. She'd never have to think about this place again.

They drove back into town for dinner. The closest thing to a restaurant in Feldspar was a hamburger stand called Lucky's, and they sat on plastic stools and had greasy burgers, soggy fries and watered-down soft drinks.

It was fully night by the time they returned to the motor court, a much deeper night than she had ever experienced in Southern California. Others seemed to have checked in during their absence. There were more cars parked in front of the rooms than there had been before, although she wasn't sure where they had come from since the highway had been almost completely empty and they'd seen only one or two vehicles on their way into town.

The single bulb outside their room created a pyramid of radiance that illuminated the walkway and a section of the asphalt in front of the door, but the darkness and shadows were so close to the border of the light that they gave the impression they could engulf it anytime they chose. Not that darkness and shadows had sentience. Or did they? It was an odd thought, but one that seemed somehow appropriate in this place.

They got out of the car and went into the room, Todd still carrying his Coke cup. Like the land outside, the room was darker than it should have been, even after Heather turned on the bathroom light. There was nothing about this place she liked. Sitting on the edge of the bed, she turned on her phone, intending to call her mother, her sister, someone, anyone who could tether her to the real world, but the phone was dead.

How had that happened? There was a charger in her purse, and she took it out, plugging it into the wall socket in the bathroom.

Todd had turned on the television, but the only channel that came in was HBO, and the only thing on HBO was *Sesame Street*. Several minutes into the show, the picture froze on a shot of Big Bird. They left it on, hoping it would unfreeze, but the yellow smiling face of the oversized puppet remained onscreen, and after a while the permanent smile and blank plastic stare grew uncomfortable and then creepy. Todd picked up the remote and shut off the TV.

"Maybe we should just drive on," Heather suggested. "I'm not that tired. I could drive while you doze, and then when I start getting sleepy, we'll switch."

"Why?" Todd gestured around the room. "Granted, it's not deluxe accommodations, but we're here and we paid for it." He smiled, wiggling his eyebrows lasciviously. "We have a bed."

This was their honeymoon, and if there was any time she should be in the mood, it should be now. But she kept thinking of the small man with the gigantic penis. The thought was in no way sexual. It was, instead, unnerving, and it tainted the entire idea of sex for her. Looking around the dim room, she wondered if this was one of those creepy motels where the perverted owner had installed hidden cameras to spy on the guests. She imagined the dwarf watching them make love on a closed-circuit TV, using both hands to grasp his enormous—

"Hey, it's working again!" Todd had switched on the television. "Maybe all we needed to do was turn it off and on."

Ernie and Bert were staring out at her from the screen, their puppet mouths opening and closing out of time with what they were saying.

She turned away. Through the wall came the sound of muffled voices: the woman they'd talked to, and a man. The two were arguing, and although no words could be made out, the tone of the voices was angry.

Something hit the wall. It was followed by a woman's scream. And then silence.

Heather and Todd looked at each other.

Seconds later, there was a sharp knocking on their door.

{ POOL, AIR CONDIITONING, FREE HBO }

The pounding was loud and frantic, but it wasn't accompanied by a voice or any other sound and seemed to exist in a weird sort of vacuum. Todd got up to answer the door and see who it was, but Heather grabbed his arm. "Don't!"

He turned to her.

"We don't know who's out there!"

She expected disagreement, but he must have felt some of the same trepidation because instead of opening the door, he peeked through the peephole located above a yellowing sheet of paper outlining evacuation procedures that was framed and mounted in the center of the door. "It's her," he said. "That same woman."

"Don't—" *Don't open the door*, she'd been about to say, but Todd was already undoing the latch and turning the knob.

It was indeed the woman who had engaged them earlier, and to Heather's surprise, she looked neither hurt nor disheveled. She stood in the open doorway, an ice bucket in her hand. "I was wondering if I could trouble you for some water," she said in a calm and reasonable voice. "Our faucet isn't working."

Todd frowned. "We thought we heard…"

"Fighting," Heather finished for him. "It sounded like you were getting beat up." She held the woman's gaze.

The woman chuckled. "Oh, that wasn't us."

"It was from your room," Heather said evenly, pointing to the wall.

"Those are the others. The people in-between. You can hear them sometimes."

"In-between what?" Todd asked. "The wall?"

"No. In-between here and…" She shook her head. "I don't know. They're people that were here and now they're not. But they never left. They're… in-between."

This was getting too crazy. Heather took the ice bucket. "I'll fill that up," she said. She wanted that woman out of here. *She* wanted out of here. It occurred to her that the best thing she and Todd could do right now was leave. At the moment, parking by the side of the road and sleeping in the car seemed infinitely preferable to this.

281

The bucket was too big to fit under the sink faucet, so she used the one in the tub. When it was three-fourths filled, she turned off the water and brought it out, handing it to the woman.

"Could you fill up your bucket, too? And bring it over?"

No, Heather wanted to answer, but Todd was already agreeing to do so, and, shooting him an angry look, she grabbed their bucket from the dresser and stormed back into the bathroom.

"I just wanted to see her room," Todd said, appearing in the doorway. "And what type of person would marry her."

"She's mentally disturbed," Heather said, turning off the faucet and standing up. "We shouldn't have *any* contact with her."

"It'll just take a second."

"That's all it'll take to stab us."

He took the bucket from her hand. "I'll go in first," he promised.

"Scant comfort." But she followed him through their room and outside.

The woman's door was open, and when they stepped inside, she was pouring water from her ice bucket onto the bed, where what appeared to be a brown wrinkled watermelon lay in the center of the mattress.

"That's just my husband," she explained. "He'll be all right once we get him some more water. It's so dry here." She shook the last few drops onto the dead watermelon before tossing the bucket aside and reaching for the one in Todd's hands.

Heather's initial reaction was that the woman was even crazier than she originally thought. But when the water touched it, the dried-up object actually *moved*, and when water from the second bucket was poured onto the bed, it began to *stretch*, until it resembled a skinny miniature man. A squeaky voice issued from the open O mouth.

"Danny!" the woman said, dropping the second bucket on the floor. "You're back!"

Out of habit, Heather picked up their ice bucket, but then she and Todd were hightailing it out of the room, shutting the door behind them.

"What the hell?" Todd said outside.

She shook her head in disbelief.

{ POOL, AIR CONDIITONING, FREE HBO }

"I think it was alive."

The bucket was yanked out of Heather's hand, and she looked down to see an enormously fat man crawling backward, away from them, wearing the bucket on his head like a hat.

If she'd been thinking logically, she would have let him go and immediately locked herself in their room, but her instinctive reaction was to grab the bucket back from the person who'd taken it, and she lunged for the object. The fat man was quick, though, even crawling backward, and he not only eluded her clutching fingers but scurried into the room on the other side of theirs.

Heather dashed forward, Todd right behind, but the two of them stopped as they reached the open doorway.

The ice bucket had fallen off his head, but the man made no effort to retrieve it, instead crawling frantically back and forth between the doorway and the bathroom. An equally obese, equally grotesque woman had made the king-sized bed into a nest, with torn clothing and newspapers piled in a circle around her. She sat in the center of the mess, making clucking noises, moving her head from side to side in a herky-jerky manner.

This time, Heather and Todd did retreat to their room, locking the door the second they were inside. Both of them were breathing heavily. How were they supposed to process what they'd encountered? There were probably scenes such as those behind the doors of every occupied room, things that were *wrong*, and Heather looked over at Todd, who returned her gaze.

Todd's heart was pounding. He could hear the rapid pulse of blood in his ears, and when he looked at Heather, he saw in her eyes the same frightened panic he was feeling. They should not have stopped here, he thought. It had been a big mistake. What he'd hoped would be quirky and romantic had turned out to be a nightmare. He remembered seeing a car commercial a few years back in which a couple debated whether they should take the main highway or a small dirt road. A disastrous but interesting sojourn in which the couple encountered a skunk, a bear and some hillbillies was contrasted with a boring khaki clothing store. It was a piece of "the road less traveled" propaganda, and at the time Todd had bought into it. But right now, a khaki clothing store or a Days Inn sounded like heaven to him.

He wanted to get the hell off this less-traveled road and never look back.

They both voiced their thoughts at the same time: "Let's leave." "Let's get out of here."

With no need of further conversation, they closed their suitcases, grabbed their belongings, and hauled everything out to the car. Todd refilled his pocket with the fifty-two pennies he'd been given as change.

"Are you awake enough to drive?" she asked him as he closed the motel room door.

"I can drive all night," he assured her.

"Good."

They got in the car, and he backed up, swung around and pulled in front of the office. Dashing out, he ran inside, dropped their key on the counter and told the manager, "We're checking out!" He didn't wait for a response but ran back to the car, put the transmission in Drive and turned onto the highway.

Seconds later, the car started shaking, and they'd gone less than a quarter of a mile before it slowed…then stopped.

"Damn it!" Heather shouted, slamming her palm against the dash.

Todd could hear a hint of panic in her voice. He thought of what the weird woman in the room next to them had said about the manager.

He comes out at night and steals parts from your car.

Sure enough, when Todd got out and popped open the hood, it was clear that something was missing. He didn't know what it was—he wasn't really a car guy—but there was a circular zone within the tangle of hoses and intersecting parts that seemed empty and was considerably cleaner than the surrounding area. Whatever had been there, someone had taken it out.

He won't let you leave.

The fear in him was bone-deep. None of this made any sense. It was as if the logical world in which he'd spent his entire life had been yanked away and replaced by some irrational nightmare universe. He felt lost, adrift, with no idea what to do.

But he needed to stay cool for Heather's sake. This was supposed to be their honeymoon.

❴ POOL, AIR CONDIITONING, FREE HBO ❵

She got out and joined him, looking into the open engine space. Maybe, he thought, she knew something about cars and could figure out a solution. But she turned to him and said, "What do you think it is?"

"I don't know," he admitted.

"Then what are we going to do?"

"I think we have to go back," he said.

She shook her head emphatically. "No. We can't."

"We don't have a lot of choices here."

"We could sleep in the car!"

"What if someone came by and hit us? We're not even pulled all the way off the road."

"You're right," she admitted.

"Let's just do this." He closed the hood while she went back to the passenger side of the car and took out her purse before locking the doors.

Walking back along the side of the road, Todd thought that he had never seen a night so black. Not only was there no moon, there were no stars. All around them, the world was dark, the only exception the motor court and its sign.

In the front office, the manager was waiting for them, holding out the ring that held the key to their room. In the past five minutes, he had taken off his shirt and was now standing behind the counter bare-chested. Heather grabbed Todd's hand, squeezing it tightly enough to hurt, almost as though she were afraid of the dwarf. He flexed his fingers, trying to loosen her grip.

"Our car broke down," he said, nodding toward the highway.

"Really?" The manager's voice betrayed no surprise. He smiled at them. "The room's still yours. You can call a mechanic in the morning."

He won't let you leave.

Todd suppressed a shiver and took the proffered key.

Defeated, the two of them walked across the cracked asphalt. From within one of the rooms, he heard low growling. From another, high-pitched laughter.

They reached room six, and he used the key to open the door. The lights were still on. They must have forgotten to turn off the television because on

{ WALKING ALONE } Bentley Little

the screen was the frozen image of Grover from *Sesame Street*, the blue character's dead plastic eyes staring lifelessly out at them as they entered.

They paused for a moment, looked at each other in silence.

Todd closed the door behind them.

THE TRAIN

(2017)

Scott glanced over at his son as he drove. These were the days he looked forward to, and he realized how lucky he was to have a job that provided him with so much time off, and how lucky he was to be married to Violet, who did most of the parental grunt work, getting Vincent dressed, making his meals, reading him books, performing all of the boring foundational chores day in and day out that allowed him to be the fun parent.

Today, they were going on a field trip to McDougal Regional Park, a place Scott had heard about but never visited. It was Daddy Day at the preschool, and he and Vincent were supposed to meet the teacher, Miss Mike, as well as the other kids and their daddies, in the parking lot of the park at eleven. They would have a picnic lunch, participate in group games, go on a nature walk, then have free play until it was time to go.

He pulled up to the toll booth at the park's entrance. The surrounding hills were home to expensive gated developments, but the park itself, a sprawling 124 acres that had been set aside for protection, remained semi-wilderness. The huge parking lot was nearly deserted, and Scott pulled next to the handful of other vehicles that were near the picnic tables and playground, assuming they were from the pre-school.

They were. A few moms were here, too, and they were helping the teacher set up the picnic tables: pulling open tablecloths, setting out plates and cups, removing drinks from ice chests. If Scott had known that both parents were allowed on the field trip, Violet could have come, and he resented the fact that no one had told him that mommies were also welcome on Daddy Day.

Vincent ran off to the playground, immediately getting in line for the slide, while Scott took his place with the parents, asking the teacher if there was anything he could do. He'd brought hot dogs for barbecuing. Bob Greenleaf, whose son Nick was Vincent's best friend, had brought the charcoal, and the two of them were tasked with setting up the grill. There were rusted metal barbecues all around the picnic area, one per table, but it took a few minutes to find one that wasn't filled with broken beer bottles or scrunched up McDonald's bags. Neither he nor Bob had brought a brush to scrape the grill, so Bob walked back to his car to see if he could find something that would work while Scott dumped out the charcoal.

The day was colder than it should have been. Since they'd arrived, clouds had drifted over the sun, and a chill breeze had kicked up. He probably should have brought along a jacket. At least Violet had made Vincent bring a coat, and Scott motioned his son over and had him put it on.

Bob came back with two screwdrivers, and after they'd used the tools to scrape the grill as best they could, Bob put a match to the fast-light charcoal. They walked back to the table where the other parents were. Scott used the ladle to pour himself a glass of punch and grabbed a handful of ranch-flavored potato chips.

Gathering the children, all of whom had arrived by now, Miss Mike brought out a multi-colored parachute, and the parents stood in a circle, holding the edge of the parachute, raising it up and down, while the kids ran underneath, trying not to get trapped under the billowing material. The kids then played Hot Potato, ran a relay race and went on a scavenger hunt with their dads. Scott and Vincent came in second.

The teacher herded the children over to the playground. Scott got some more punch and took a few chocolate chip cookies. A couple of the dads were talking about a soccer league their older kids were involved with, a few of the others were talking or texting on their phones, Bob had gone to return the

{ THE TRAIN }

screwdrivers to his car, and the moms were either playing with their kids or taking pictures of them.

Scott walked over to where Miss Mike stood supervising the children. Next to the play area was a bulletin board on which was posted a map of the park. A red dot with a small arrow said, "You are here." Above that was the circular playground, and beyond that a line intersected by small crosses that wound through the wilderness area of the park and formed a closed loop. It looked like a train track. Glancing up, he saw, past the last slide on the far side of the playground, what appeared to be a playhouse-sized depot, and he walked through the sand to find a narrow-gauge track running along the ground in back of the depot and disappearing between two high dry hills.

"Hi, Daddy!" Vincent called, waving to him from the top of the slide.

Scott waved back. "Hi!"

He returned to where Miss Mike was now standing with several other dads, watching the kids on the playground. "What is that?" he asked the teacher, pointing toward the small building.

"Oh, they used to have a little train here. I don't think it's running anymore."

"Too bad," Scott said, and the other dads nodded. Most of the boys were at the age where they were heavily into trains. Vincent was even wearing a Thomas the Tank Engine shirt today, and Scott knew that he would have *loved* to take a train ride.

Bob had gone back to check the charcoal, and he came over to announce that the barbecue was ready. Scott went over to the ice chest where he'd put the oversized package of Costco hot dogs he'd brought. Jamal's dad picked up the package of meatless Smart Dogs he'd contributed, and all three of them headed toward the grill. Miss Mike and the moms gathered up the children and made them wash their hands.

Lunch was expectedly noisy and chaotic, with the spilling of punch and throwing of potato chips, and one little girl named Teena actually threw up because her friend whispered to her that there'd been a fly on her hot dog and she'd eaten it. Everyone was happy to be at the park and having a picnic, and though some of the parents tried to keep their kids from getting too hyped up, all of the students were loud, talkative and excited.

WALKING ALONE   Bentley Little

After lunch, they went on the nature hike, Miss Mike periodically consulting a wildflower guidebook in order to let the kids know which plants were poisonous. The wide dirt trail passed over hills and through gullies, past dried grass and cactus and native California trees. Most of the students were bored by the ten-minute mark, and when they reached a fork in the trail, one branch heading deeper into the wilderness, the other leading back to the parking lot, they opted for the latter.

The kids had been issued water bottles before the hike, and nearly all of them had drained their bottles dry, which meant there was a long line for the very primitive bathrooms when they returned. Scott heard a lot of giggling and a lot of jokes about how bad the bathrooms smelled. After checking to make sure each boy and girl had washed his or her hands, the teacher accompanied the children to the playground while the parents packed up the remaining food, drinks and supplies, taking any leftover items they'd brought back to their respective cars.

An hour later, as everyone was saying goodbye and getting ready to leave, there came a *click-clack...click-clack* from the area beyond the playground. Vincent recognized the sound instantly. "Train!" he shouted. "Daddy! It's a train!"

Sure enough, a small train, with four open cars and a diminutive engine on which an adult engineer sat scrunched at the controls, pulled up on the supposedly disused tracks in front of the little depot.

"Can we go on it, Daddy?" Vincent was practically jumping up and down with excitement. Most of the other boys were as well.

Miss Mike laughed as she headed off to her car. "You're on your own, daddies." She waved to the children. "See you tomorrow!" she called.

"Goodbye, Miss Mike!" they yelled, too loud, in unison.

All of the boys and most of the girls were holding their parents' hands and looking up into their faces, begging to ride the train, but when the dust settled, only Scott and Vincent, along with one other dad and his son opted to stay. The rest of the parents led their whining and disappointed kids to their cars.

"We'll see how much it costs," Scott told Vincent, making no promises.

⊰ THE TRAIN ⊱

"But if it's cheap, we'll go, right?"

Scott laughed. "If it's cheap, we'll go."

They hurried through the playground with the other boy and his dad, trying to reach the depot before the train left.

There were no prices posted anywhere on the depot or the train itself, so Scott walked up to the engineer, who was standing on the platform next to the narrow tracks, stretching his legs. "Excuse me," he said. "How much is it to ride the train?"

"Buck apiece." The engineer seemed bored and disengaged. He took the money perfunctorily when Scott paid and motioned indifferently toward the open cars behind him.

Vincent was bouncing excitedly. "I want to sit by the engine!"

"Sure," Scott said, and opened the gate of the first car, where the two of them sat next to each other on a hard, low bench. The other boy wanted to sit in the caboose, so he and his dad went to the opposite end of the train.

There were clearly no other riders, but the engineer stood there for another ten minutes, staring blandly out at the playground. Maybe he was due a break or maybe the train was supposed to leave at a specific time, but Scott had the feeling that the man was procrastinating on purpose, just to annoy the parents and frustrate the kids.

Scott *was* annoyed, but Vincent wasn't frustrated. He remained excited, and he chattered away about where the train might go, and about trains in general.

Eventually, the man wandered back, took his place in the cramped confines of the engine and started up the train. With a sad, tired whistle, the train began moving.

Click-clack...click-clack...click-clack...

The sound of the wheels on the rails grated on him for some reason, and Scott tried to shut out the noise as the train slowly pulled away from the little station. They gained a little speed but not much, and ended up traveling at walking speed between two small hills and into the backcountry of the wilderness park.

Scott had to admit that the scenery was impressive. Orange County was so overdeveloped these days that it was sometimes hard to remember that the region had once looked like this. They passed eroded boulders honeycombed with Swiss cheese-like holes, chugged through a grove of hardy oak trees, their leaves green even though the surrounding grasses were dead and brown. Moments after leaving the depot, there was no sign of civilization, and though he had never been here before, Scott was glad that this area had been protected. This was nice.

Click-clack…click-clack…click-clack…

Although the noise of the train itself was pretty irritating.

The engineer pulled a cord, and there was another anemic whistle as the train rounded a bend.

Vincent grinned up at him. "Isn't this great, Daddy?"

Scott put his arm around his son's shoulder and smiled. "It sure is."

They passed through a narrow gulch. Dry grasses the pale color of a file folder grew high on both sides. With a metallic screech of brakes, the train began to slow. He thought at first that there was something on the tracks ahead, something blocking the train, an animal perhaps, but as the engine decelerated, he saw that the engineer was slowing to allow them to look at a model town that had been built on a small section of man-made hills. It was an Old West mining town, with buildings the size of shoeboxes. In the center of one of the hills was the mine itself, a mini mining car piled high with gold ore sitting at the entrance to the tunnel, tracks winding down the hillside to an assaying office at the bottom. Along the main street of the town were several saloons, a blacksmith's shop, a hotel, a general store, some buildings of indeterminate function and, at the end of the street, a white-steepled church. Between, on the sides of and on top of the other hills were various ranch houses.

Someone had put a lot of work into making this little community. It was incredibly detailed, and he understood why the train stopped here.

But he didn't like the miniature town.

They had stopped in front of a tiny two-story bordello. The crudely painted sign above the veranda read: CAT HOUSE.

"What's a cat house?" Vincent asked. "Is that like a vet?"

Scott nodded. "Yeah," he lied.

{ THE TRAIN }

In the last car, the other dad was using his cell phone to take pictures. Scott was glad Vincent wasn't asking him to photograph the town because the last thing he wanted to do was preserve an image of this place so they could study it at their leisure. Something about it made him feel uneasy, and he wished the train would move on.

His eye was drawn to a series of rundown cottages and lean-tos on a dirt road behind the bordello.

Was that a face peering out from the front window of one of the miniature shacks?

It was gone before he was even sure that he'd seen it, but the impression lingered, and it was all he could do not to yell at the engineer to start the train and get out of here. He was not just uneasy now, he was frightened, and he quickly scanned the windows of the other buildings, looking for signs of movement. He saw nothing, but that didn't mean there was nothing to be seen.

Scott turned to see the reaction of the other dad in the rear car, but the man did not seem to have noticed anything out of the ordinary.

With a mechanical lurch, the train started up again.

Click-clack...click-clack...

The sound not only grated on him, but, more than that, was beginning to unnerve him. It made absolutely no sense, yet he felt it in his bones, a deep distaste that made him feel more than a little unsettled. He wished he had left the park when the other parents had and that he had not taken Vincent on the train.

They passed by a dead tree with a frayed noose hanging from one of its top branches.

"Daddy!" Vincent said excitedly. "Look! A tunnel!"

Sure enough, the tracks ahead disappeared into an arched black hole in the hillside before them.

Something like panic overtook him. He did *not* want to go into that tunnel. He was about to call out to the engineer and ask him to stop or back up, but then they were inside, engulfed in darkness.

Click-clack...click-clack...

❴ WALKING ALONE ❵   Bentley Little

The sound of metal wheels on track grew even louder in the lightless shaft, and the rhythm took on an offensive syncopation that put Scott in mind of the slaughterhouse machinery he'd encountered the one time he'd toured the processing plant where his father worked.

"It's long!" Vincent said. "You can't even see the end!"

The air was warm and stifling; Scott was finding it difficult to breathe. He was holding tightly to Vincent's hand, afraid that if he did not, he would lose his son. The fear was irrational but none the less real for that, and when he sensed a lightening of the tunnel ahead, he was grateful.

It was not the exit, however, and there was no sign of daylight. There was only a cheap diorama in the center of the tunnel, dusty yellowish lightbulbs illuminating a primitive scene in which three-foot high lumberjack mannequins were at a sort of party in the woods, the trees represented by branches that had been affixed to the floor. Once again, the train slowed, then stopped, so they could look. Examined more carefully, it looked like a scene out of *Seven Brides for Seven Brothers*, because there were women here as well.

Only...

Only something was wrong with the women. One had a freakishly thick leg, as though she were suffering from elephantiasis. Another, posed as if dancing with a bearded lumberjack, had shaved half of her head and wore an expression of unbridled insanity. Still another had two tiny doll arms and only one eye. All of the mannequins, the men and the women, were still, their positions fixed and unmoving.

Except one.

Scott shivered and held Vincent's hand even tighter as he saw a blond woman in a blue chiffon dress peeking out from behind one of the trees, smiling broadly at him, her eyebrows wiggling up and down.

With a jerk, the train started moving again. Behind the diorama, Scott noticed for the first time, was a mirrored wall. He supposed it was meant to make the forest look bigger, but the train was visible in the glass above the trees, and when he saw his own reflection, he was surprised at how frightened he looked.

{ THE TRAIN }

They exited the tunnel a moment later, and Scott turned to look behind him at the dad and his son in the other car. Both seemed somewhat subdued, although Vincent was still animated and enthusiastic, leaning his head out of the car to see where the track was headed, chattering away happily. He seemed unfazed by anything he had seen, unaware of how genuinely strange things seemed to have gotten, and for that Scott was glad.

There were so many bushes in this post-tunnel area that it was impossible to tell in which direction they were headed. He remembered the map of the park, and on it, the train loop hadn't looked that big. Unless the map had been drawn incorrectly, they had to be on the return leg of the trip by now.

"Look!" Vincent said, pointing.

ZOO, read a small hand-painted sign by the side of the tracks, and immediately after, they saw the first of a series of "animals," a wooden deer made from a sawhorse and some sanded pieces of lumber. That was followed by a metal pipe sculpture designed to look like a giraffe, and a chicken-wire-framed lion.

There were sixteen or seventeen "animals" altogether, but the last was the only one Scott found unsettling.

It was a dog made out of meat.

The dog was life-sized, and he wasn't sure how, but various cuts and types of meat had been molded together and attached to form a remarkable likeness of a German shepherd. A chicken breast snout with a cut rib-eye nose was connected to a face of sculpted hamburger. Lambchops and pork tenderloins were somehow meat-welded to hot dogs and steaks in order to form the astoundingly realistic body.

How had this been made? Scott wondered. And *when*? It had to have been today, maybe within the hour, because the meat looked fresh. If it had been out in the sun for any length of time, it would have started to turn. This close, they would have been able to smell the beginning of rot.

Who had made it?

That was the question that most concerned him. Because if there was a person roaming the back regions of the wilderness park making models of dogs out of meat, Scott did *not* want to meet him.

WALKING ALONE   Bentley Little

He decided to ask the engineer. The man kept stopping at various sites, so it was clear he was supposed to be some sort of tour guide. Maybe he would have some answers.

"Excuse me!" Scott said loudly.

The engineer did not turn around. He probably couldn't hear over the noise of the engine and the sound of the wheels on the tracks.

Click-clack…click-clack…

Scott tried again, shouting this time. "Excuse me! Sir?"

The man continued to face forward but shook his head in obvious response.

"I just want to—"

Another, firmer head shake.

"I don't think he's supposed to talk while he's driving," Vincent confided. "I think it's a train rule."

Scott patted his son's head and nodded, though he knew that wasn't the case. He had no alternate explanation, however, and those he could come up with were unsatisfactory.

Click-clack…click-clack…

He had come to dread that sound.

He looked back to see how the other passengers were holding up.

The other dad and his son were no longer in the last car.

His heart seemed to skip a beat. Where were they? They could not have gotten off because the train had not stopped since he'd last looked over at them. Were they lying on the floor? Had they, for some reason, jumped off the train? It wasn't going very fast, so that would probably be easy to do, though he'd neither seen nor heard any such thing.

His mind was searching for a logical reason for their disappearance, but deep down he was afraid that there *was* no such rational explanation.

Maybe they *were* on the floor of their car, he thought.

Maybe they were dead.

Why would he even think such a thing? He didn't know, but it did not seem out of the realm of possibility.

Scott took out his phone, switching it on. He actually wasn't sure who to call, but he wanted to hear another adult voice, a normal person, someone

{ THE TRAIN }

outside of the park. His impulse was to call 911, though he knew he had no concrete reason to do so.

As he'd feared, as he'd somehow *known*, there was no reception here. He was not able to dial out or call anyone, and a cold fear settled over him. He was suddenly gripped by the certainty that he would never see Violet again.

Why had he taken this damn train?

Because Vincent wanted to. And his son was *still* excited by the trip somehow, excitedly awaiting whatever was beyond the next turn, seemingly unaware of everything that Scott found so disturbing.

The train passed under a curved trellis supporting a tangle of green vines. Past the trellis, on a stick, was a sign:

BYE!

The engineer spoke for the first time, using a microphone in the engine to deliver a laconic announcement that was broadcast through a scratchy speaker located in the wall of the car: "We're coming up on the station, folks. Hope you all enjoyed your trip."

Scott was filled with an unaccountable feeling of dread. He didn't know why—he should have been happy the ride was over—but some sixth sense was telling him that it *wasn't* over.

They pulled in front of the depot. Stopped.

This was not where they had started.

"Again, Daddy!" Vincent said excitedly. "Again!"

"Again?" the engineer asked, walking over.

Scott looked into the man's bored, disinterested face and saw something there he didn't like and didn't quite understand. But when he looked toward where the parking lot was supposed to be and saw instead a pond, when his eyes finally found the parking lot in the location where the picnic tables should have been, and there were no cars in the lot, he nodded numbly and took two dollars out of his wallet, placing the bills in the engineer's rough hand.

"Again," he said.

A RANDOM THOUGHT FROM GOD'S DAY

(2017)

That stupid football player is kneeling down in front of everyone to thank ME because he made a touchdown? He actually thinks I care whether or not he caught a ball and ran over a chalk line on a patch of grass? That arrogant little pissant. When he dies, I'm sending him straight to hell.
    Straight.
    To.
    Hell.